Tendrils in the Dark

Eight Tales of Horror

By

Martin V. Parece II

Other Titles by Martin V. Parece II:
Blood and Steel (The Cor Chronicles, Vol. I)
Fire and Steel (The Cor Chronicles, Vol. II)
Darkness and Steel (The Cor Chronicles, Vol. III)
Gods and Steel (The Cor Chronicles, Vol. IV)
Blood Betrayal (The Cor Chronicles, Vol. V)
Blood Loss (The Chronicle of Rael)

Copyright 2020
Parece Publishing, Martin V. Parece II
ISBN 9798668540785

Cover Art by
Hana K. Parece
clya.artstation.com

Other artwork by Martin V. Parece II

All rights reserved.
No part of this book may be printed, scanned, reproduced, or distributed in any printed or electronic form without permission.

Tendrils in the Dark: Eight Tales of Horror

Table of Contents

Wewelsburg	6
A Devil in Gold	18
Hunted	78
The Lady in Yellow	106
Eyes of a Madman	258
Containment	266
Overslept	278
Calvin	286
A Little Bonus	333

WEWELSBURG

Captain John Hartman crept south through the forests of Paderborn. Cold air swept in swiftly when the calendar turned to October, and Hartman only kept from shivering through his own pure strength of will. He enjoyed the feel of the crisp, clean air in his lungs, but there was a deep cold to it, a foreshadowing of a hard winter. He liked to travel light, carrying merely a compass, knife, and canteen as well as a Luger pistol, all of German manufacture of course. While the Waffen SS uniform he wore seemed to be a bit more suited to the cold than his old Army uniform, he questioned the intelligence of not bringing a heavy coat.

That was irony. Hartman joined the Office of Strategic Services back in December of forty-two, when an O.S.S. officer found extensive use of the fluent French and German he'd learned from his mother and father respectively, to say nothing of his fighting ability. In nearly two years, he had been all over the world it seemed, fomenting rebellion in Axis controlled regions, training and equipping local armies and freedom fighters. But he also, and more importantly, gathered information. Intelligence was his business, and all his information led him here – skulking through a forest as he walked the seven miles between the villages of Thüle and Wewelsburg wishing, to some extent, that he was back with his fellow soldiers some four hundred miles away in France.

But Heinrich Himmler had been collecting silver SS rings from dead soldiers for years, and Hartman wanted to know why. That was why he had come here. The official answer was that it memorialized the fallen soldier's membership in the elite SS after his death, indeed forever in the new world order, but Hartman had a sick feeling in his stomach that Himmler had some other plan at work. The more he'd investigated the head of the SS, the more he realized that the man had been pulling strings in the Nazi regime for years, even decades.

What was Himmler's plan? The man was far too crafty to be left holding the check when the Americans won, and they were going to win. No one doubted that. There were over a hundred thousand troops swarming over France alone, to say nothing of the Brits, Canadians and even free French. Was he melting the rings down for the silver perhaps to buy his freedom when the bill came due? Many high-ranking Nazis have contacts in South America, Argentina especially. Maybe he planned on using the silver to buy his safe passage and retirement. Regardless, Hartman came to Germany to find out or, perhaps, even eliminate Himmler should the opportunity present itself.

When he joined up, John Hartman was the picture-perfect American soldier. At eighteen, he graduated high school in the top ten percent of his class with height to match at a hint over six-foot-two. Strong and athletic, he had a scholarship to Penn State, which of course got put on hold with the happenings of December seventh. Light brown hair, gray eyes and a solid jawline with cleft chin completed him as the perfect ideal of American strength, intelligence, and charm.

"Cold, Herr Hartman? There is a clearing up ahead with a shack," Kurt whispered to him in heavily accented English. "We can rest there for a few minutes."

"My German is far better than your English, if you'd prefer," Hartman replied with a smile. "There aren't many Americans who would understand what you just said."

"Then it is a good thing they sent you."

Hartman's smile disappeared as he said, "I sent myself. How far now?"

"About a kilometer to Wewelsburg, less than three to the castle."

Kurt Meyer was a good man, a German approaching fifty whom, despite being of excellent health and physical condition, was considered too old to serve. That was fine by him, as he had already fought in one apocalyptic war in his life, and he had no desire to serve a leadership that was an affront to common decency. Kurt waited and watched, and one day he made contact with an American who convinced him that he could help bring down Hitler and his Nazis. He had a square face with a thick brown beard and matching hair, both of which were kept to various lengths to make his appearance somewhat fluid.

Their heads snapped to the left as a sound broke the relative silence of the night – a brief rustle of some fallen leaves or something passing between some bushes. It was impossible to tell how far away it was; sounds in a dark wood tend to sound both at once far away from and right next to the listener. Both men froze in place as they listened to the night. After a minute, Hartman relaxed his tensed muscles, and the two shared a sigh just as a long howl pierced the air somewhere behind and to their right.

"*Wölfe*," hissed Kurt, "we better get to the shack. This is their forest."

They hurried on, and Kurt was true to his word. They had gone little more than fifteen feet further into the darkness before emerging into a roughly circular clearing, well illuminated by the moon and measuring about forty feet across. More noise erupted in the woods behind them, and they then broke into a run, crossing the open to the safety of a small, aged wooden building. A rusted metal latch held the door shut, and Kurt undid it and yanked the door open before shutting it behind them.

Once his eyes adjusted, Hartman saw that ancient lumber and hand tools filled the ten-foot square shack. Kurt held a single finger to pursed lips as he put an ear to a miniscule crack in a wall.

Another howl sounded in the night, thought Hartman had no sense of the distance. As the minutes passed, he grew anxious to act as he always did, his ingrained need to do *something*. A third howl came, and he had no doubt this one was just outside the shack in the clearing. He held his breath as he drew his pistol and knife, one in each hand. For a few seconds, something sniffed and snorted, not unlike a dog, its way around the base of the door. It ended abruptly, and one last howl was heard, lonesome and well in the distance.

"I think they've moved on," Kurt whispered. He smiled broadly and asked, "Were you planning to shoot them or stab them?"

"Both, if I had to," he replied, taking a deep breath, forcing himself to relax. Too much adrenaline caused a man to get the jitters, sometimes pull a trigger before he meant to, and he tended to shiver as he came down from that elevated place. He was cold enough as it was.

Kurt gently pushed the rickety door open and stuck his head out into the crisp air. After a moment of looking and listening, he nodded at Hartman and said, "All clear. Let's be quick."

Hartman put his weapons away as they stepped back into the clearing and continued south. They left the bright, bluish-white moon behind as the fir trees blocked out the light from overhead. They traveled slowly, working carefully through the wood. Hartman had no interest in a broken ankle; he didn't know if his forged papers would get him past any intense scrutiny, not to mention that having an injury like that when wolves were about was not an inviting prospect.

He calculated they were about halfway to the village outskirts when he reached out and placed a halting hand on Kurt's arm. The German looked at him with a furrowed brow and questioning eyes, and Hartman answered with a raised hand. The hair on the back of his neck had stood on end, and he felt the goose flesh on his arms under the wool uniform. Neither came from the cold, which was now completely forgotten. Either from a preternatural sense handed down from far thrown Neanderthal or Cro-Magnon ancestors or just the feeling of wrongness in the air, Hartman knew somehow that he was being hunted.

"There's something over there," Hartman whispered, motioning with a nod to a copse of ash trees some fifteen feet away.

"I do not see any -" Kurt stopped in mid-reply as something moved amidst the bushes and tall grass that adorned the base of the trees.

A pair of eyes appeared close to the ground, seemingly out of nowhere, red eyes that glared back at them intently. Hartman knew little about wolves, especially their eyes, but these seemed to have an intelligent malevolence about them that made him tense and uneasy. And that wasn't the worst part about that pair of eyes. It was not just that they seemed to reflect the feeble, constricted light of the moon overhead, but they glowed with an infernal light of their own. A second pair of eyes uncloaked just left of the first, followed by a third to the right.

Hartman's knife and pistol were out again. Back home in Pennsylvania, it was well known that he could bat just as well from the left side of the plate as the right and that he could throw and catch with either hand. On the ball field, his defensive and offensive options were many with this ambidexterity, and it translated well into his fighting abilities. He could shoot or throw grenades with either hand, and he even learned to fight with a knife in each hand in close quarters.

A low growl sounded to his right, and Hartman shot his eyes that direction. Yet another set of the hellish red eyes were there only five or six feet away, and he could see the entire creature in its proximity. A wolf, crouched low with bared teeth, stopped its approach to stare back at him unblinking. Patches and stripes of silver broke up the black fur that comprised the animal's natural nighttime camouflage.

"Can we make a run for it?" Hartman asked softly, his eyes fixed on the yellow-white teeth and flattened ears of the wolf.

"No, they'll chase us down. Back away slowly -" Kurt's words ended abruptly as his shout of surprise split the night. In the half second it took Hartman to turn towards the man, he no longer stood there. He screamed for help as something dragged him into the darkness, and his arms flailed as his hands attempted to gain purchase on anything for just a moment. Hartman's keen hearing made him aware of something else – he turned back to the wolf to find the animal in mid-air, having leapt from its place.

Hartman's reflexes and sharp eye served him well against the pitchers of other school's baseball teams. No one with any sense placed a pitch in the strike zone, even on the edge of it, without the expectation that the big kid wearing number four wouldn't make you pay for it. Even if your pitch broke to the strike zone at the last moment, quick hands often let him put wood on the ball enough to foul it away.

Hartman's knife impaled the wolf through the bottom of its jaws, the blade sliding into the roof of its mouth and into its brain. At the same time, he instinctively fired his Luger several times into its belly. Hot blood streamed over his hand, and the animal whimpered just a bit while its legs quivered spasmodically. Hartman yanked the knife away, and the wolf's corpse fell to the ground while he turned to face where Kurt Meyer had disappeared to.

His screams continued, but they sounded further away. The three sets of eyes still regarded him from the cluster of ash trees, and they struck him with an intelligent hatred impossible to mere animals. He took aim at them and squeezed the Luger's trigger over and over, but the wolves' eyes seemed to disappear into the darkness just before any of his bullets made contact. The gun ran out of rounds, his eight shots expended, and Hartman stood alone, in darkness and complete silence. Even Kurt's screams had ceased.

"*Schiesse*," he swore aloud. He'd always preferred the German epithet to the English, and there never existed a better time for it. He slowly, deliberately, stepped backward once, twice, three times while listening for any sign that the wolfpack still stalked him. He knew they were out there, and as terrible as he felt about poor Kurt, he hoped the man's death would provide him the precious time he needed to escape. With that last thought, John Hartman turned on his heel and broke into a full run back the way they had come.

He charged through brush and bushes, ducked branches and jumped logs, his natural sure-footedness somehow preventing him from falling or injury. His breath came and went quickly, further spurred nearly to hyperventilation at the sounds of barks and howls behind him. The pack followed, and their voices reminded him somehow of the whoops and hollers of a band of street thugs rather than a pack of wolves. Something crashed through the woods off to his right and then turned directly for him. At the last moment, it seemed to veer off behind him, and he swore he heard the snap of canine jaws just behind him. Within seconds, it happened again, but this time from his left.

My god, he thought, *they're enjoying this!*

At some point, he instinctively began to reload his pistol, the discarded magazine falling away along with the knife in his other hand. He needed that hand to find his spare mag and reload the weapon, which he accomplished without actually looking at either, something he had practiced many times all the way back to Basic.

He burst from the woods into the supposed safety of the clearing. A man walked across the open expanse, stopping just in front of the wooden shack, his face registering surprise at the onward charging Hartman. He wore a German uniform, no, a gray SS uniform, and a strange rifle was slung over his shoulder, very different from the standard Gewehr or MP40.

"Hide!" Hartman shouted as he nearly bowled the soldier over. With his momentum and the near collision, he somehow shot past the door to the shack. Hearing the wolves behind him in the woods, he muscled the shocked German around the far side of the rickety building, throwing the man and his own back up against the wall. It creaked and groaned in complaint.

"*Sir? What -*" the soldier began to ask in German.

"*Be quiet!*" Hartman replied in an urgent whisper. He listened to the night, which had again gone eerily silent. Nothing moved that he could see, and no sound at all reached his ears. The wolfpack seemed suddenly gone.

"*Excuse me, sir? What did you say before?*" the soldier asked. Hartman glanced at the man's collar to see the Oberschütze rank. He was young, maybe only eighteen or nineteen, judging from his smooth face. In his rush, Hartman told the kid to hide in English. His only chance was that his officer's rank of Hauptsturmführer would protect him. "*What is* hide*?*" the trooper continued in a rough approximation of the English word.

"*I said be quiet! That's an order. Wolves,*" Hartman answered with his best officer's voice, a sound all trained soldiers across Earth understood, and it seemed to work as the German's sense of duty took hold. "*Stay here.*"

Hartman moved to one corner and listened intently for a moment. Hearing nothing, he hazarded a glance around the rear corner of the shed, finding nothing but short grass and silvery moonlight. His Luger in hand, he cautiously, soundlessly advanced around the corner, leaving the SS trooper behind. He had no sense of where the pack had gone. There was nothing to see, nothing to hear.

Until fabric tearing and splitting, as if a medic tore a uniform to treat a wound, sounded from behind him. Hartman squinted slightly, his brow furrowed in confusion at such an out of place sound, and then his eyes widened in frightened realization as he straightened to his full height out of a hunched posture he hadn't realized he held. He turned about, his pistol at the ready, but nothing he'd seen in the war thus far prepared Hartman for what stood behind him as it growled and glowered at him.

A creature with the head and muzzle of a wolf towered over him by almost a foot. The body was shaped roughly like a man, though more well-muscled than even that of a carnival strongman. Long arms thick with corded sinews ended in manlike hands with razor sharp claws instead of fingers, and around one of these on the left hand was the silver ring of an SS soldier. The remnants of a tattered gray uniform meant for a much smaller body hung about its shoulders and upper arms. A belt still held up the remains of pants that had split around mid-thigh, unable to contain the thick legs of the thing. It still wore black boots, but clawed feet stuck out comically from the torn apart toes. Silver and gray patches occasionally broke up the black fur that covered every exposed part of the monster.

Hartman blinked and then shook his head from side to side. He couldn't believe what he saw, and yet there it was! Lon Chaney, Jr. and his on-screen transformation, which seemed so terrible to behold just a few years ago, paled in comparison to this thing Hartman confronted. It reared back its head and loosed a terrifying mix between a howl and a raging growl as it fixed its glowing, red eyes back on the American. Hartman stepped backward instinctively, tripping over his own heel and falling backward to the ground. It howled, this time an honest to God howl, perhaps reveling in the kill it was about to make.

Hartman lifted his pistol just as it moved in. Seeing this the creature lunged only to meet the explosive report of the German pistol. He fired into the thing four times before it fell on him and another two when the wolfman's full weight bore down on him. Realizing quickly that he was not dead, though the monster was not trying to gut him with its claws or rip his throat out with a mouthful of teeth, Hartman heaved the weight up off him to the side. It rolled onto its back and lay there unmoving as it struggled to breathe, a death rattle sounding in its chest with every breath. Hartman lowered the gun to the wolfman's head and popped off his last two rounds.

He took a moment to get his bearings, to check out his person and find that he was somehow whole and uninjured. He was out of ammunition for the Luger, so he holstered it and instead took up the rifle the soldier had apparently shrugged off during whatever transformation turned him into the monster Hartman just killed. He recognized it instantly – a Sturmgewehr 44. They had been mostly used against the Russians, so it was odd to find it this far west. Regardless, the Brits had been unimpressed by the early models they had captured, but O.S.S. knew them to be deadly assault rifles.

Hartman locked his jaw. Whatever these things were – wolves, werewolves, wolfmen, whatever – they may have stopped him from reaching Wewelsburg, but he would be back, next time with more appropriate firepower. For now, he decided to head back to Thüle, then Paderborn and then back out of Germany. If they wanted to stop him from leaving, and he hoped that they did, they would just have to face the fury of a pissed off American armed with a machine gun.

Before he turned to leave, he took one last look at the wolfman's corpse to find it replaced with a young German soldier, apparently dead from multiple bullet wounds to the chest and head. The body, partially draped in a shredded uniform, had already grown cold in the October night air. Hartman knelt and slipped the silver "Death's Head" ring off the man's left ring finger. He dropped it in his pocket and then started to hightail it out of the clearing, the sounds of wolves behind him.

A DEVIL IN GOLD

This is the first I've taken the time to commit to paper for posterity those events that took place some fifty years ago in 1883. It's important that the happenings are preserved on paper so that future generations know not to look too deeply into that mine or its adjoining cave system that made me so unalterably rich. I tried verbalizing it once to two men, one of the psychological profession and the other of law, in a late night moment of drunken weakness. When it was done, they applauded me for providing them such a wonderful and terrible tale to help keep them awake at night in glorious anticipation of such horror. Obviously, such was not my intention, so I've instead chosen to write it all down in as much detail as possible.

I have already amended my Last Will and Testament to include the instructions that the mine is never again to be unearthed and the land under which the caves lay will never be sold or disturbed ever in the future. Additionally, my sole son, whom is the beneficiary of all I own, is to include the same instructions in his Will as well. Every Landis generation from my death to time immemorial will have a guardian of these secrets, a gatekeeper to the unfathomable Hell that sleeps under Boulder Spring, New Mexico.

For the sake of brevity, allow me to simply say that, as a young man of only twenty, I had sold everything I owned in the city of Omaha and wagered it all in a game of poker, a twelve-hour endeavor that left me fairly wealthy, at least by my standards of the time. I had managed to win deeds to several hundred acres of land near Boulder Spring, terminating at the southwestern edge of the town limits, as well as a truly impressive sum of nearly twelve thousand dollars. I quickly purchased several expensive suits and disembarked the next day for my destiny.

The rails took me most of the distance, all the way to Santa Fe, in the most modern of luxuries. I had never been on a train before, and I found wonder at first just in watching the landscape roll by. It amazed me that I could cross such a distance, over eight hundred miles in little more than two days, all the while enjoying the comforts of first-class rail cars. I indulged in some minor banter with other travelers, but generally avoided detailed explanations of who I was and where I was going. My life as a gambler and general scoundrel in Omaha had taught me to divulge as few details as possible.

Santa Fe was a bustling southwestern town, every bit as picturesque and romantic as one back east would expect from the stories that no doubt had been told. I understand that the town had very little to attract newcomers until 1880; that's when the railroad named after the city finally reached the town. In the following three years, the city grew with rapidity, and I spent several days (and nights) enjoying its sights, saloons, and gambling halls. Although, I took great care to spend as little money as possible.

The next leg of my trip could only be undertaken by stagecoach, as Boulder Spring was almost a hundred miles away through rough and mountainous terrain. I booked passage as one of several passengers on two coaches. We left early in the morning and expected to arrive somewhere in the middle of the next day. I won't bore you with the details of this uncomfortable journey, except to detail a singular encounter.

On the morning of the second day, the day we expected to arrive in Boulder Spring, we had been on the move less than an hour before I heard the drivers call, "Whoa!" and pull the horses to a stop. I ignored the puzzled exclamations of the young couple with whom I rode, and instead decided to act. I opened the door to the coach and stuck my head into the warm, dry mountain air.

"Why are we stopping?" I asked the driver.

"Apaches," came the terse reply, followed by, "Stay inside."

Of course, I did no such thing. Those who know me understand that I have rebellious streak over a mile wide, and I generally do not take well to being told what to do, especially by a figure of authority. But this man was, in my view, under my employ, and that even further increased my disdain for his orders. I immediately dropped out of the coach to the dusty trail to take a look at these Indians, and that was probably my true motive for disobeying the driver's instructions. Growing up in Omaha, I certainly saw Indians, but never had I seen them in their native wilderness. My sense of romanticism was too much to bear, and the Colt Army 1860 that I picked up before leaving Santa Fe that hung heavy on my belt probably instilled a sense of invincibility within me as well.

The driver, a rough and ponderous man with a long, black beard barked at me, "I said stay inside!"

I locked eyes with him for a long moment before resting my gaze on the Winchester that stood propped against his bench less than a foot from his reach. However, I doubted that he could move so quickly as to drop his reins, take up the rifle and manage an aimed shot before these Apaches turned him into a pincushion.

Facing them, however, my sense of romance was both rewarded and dispelled at once. They certainly looked the part, from everything I had heard, and yet were so much more than expected. I had never before seen four men who looked so fierce and yet were completely calm. A solemn kindness seemed to fill their large eyes, but their faces were hard as stone, their true feelings inscrutable. I noted finally one other detail, that among the trappings I expected of native Apaches – animal skins, bows, arrows and the like – there were also boots, steel knives and guns.

I realized suddenly that hostility was probably ill advised. While I knew my way around a gun, I was no means a soldier or an expert in any way. And while these men were far from the whooping, hollering savages that I had been told to expect, I was certain that they were far more proficient with weapons than I. I made certain that my jacket kept my pistol out of view.

One stepped forward – a young man with slight creases at the corners of his mouth from laughing. I dare say he was beautiful, and I think he might have been about my age. Though even in my now advanced years, I have a difficult time judging the age of anyone not of Anglo descent. I would not begin to approximate the sounds of his language, but he held his open hand up, palm out in a non-threatening manner as he spoke.

"What did he say?" I asked with a look at my ruffian stagecoach driver.

"I don' rightly know," he replied gruffly. "Sumtin' 'bout some curse or land or sumtin'."

"We are going to Boulder Spring," I said loudly, as if my volume alone would somehow explain our intentions.

The Apache repeated his statement. At least, it sounded like the same series of sounds, but I found the strangeness of the words left my English mind before I could take a hold of them. I looked at the driver, and he merely shrugged unhelpfully.

"We," I said slowly, pointing at myself, then the stagecoaches and finished pointing off into the distance past the Indians, "are going to Boulder Spring."

The four Apaches simply stared back at me for what felt like an hour, and I had the strange feeling that it was in fact I who was the savage. They finally broke their staring silence by filing over to the edge of the trail, parting the brush and disappearing into the wilderness. The man who spoke, the last to leave the trail, stopped short to give me a long, almost sorrowful gaze. He said the words one more time, one more hopeful attempt to make his meaning plain, and seeing no reaction from me, he followed his brethren.

Boulder Spring did not impress me at first glance. It was certainly no growing town like Santa Fe, nor even a city like Omaha and certainly not a bustling metropolis like Chicago, which I had been to once some ten years prior. A wide avenue ran right through the center of the town, which contained all there was to see – a general store, barber's shop and assorted other buildings necessary to day-to-day life. Off to one side stood a building that I recognized immediately as a jailhouse, complete, I was sure, with the sheriff's quarters. The drivers stopped directly in front of the largest building in the town, a rather ambitious looking hotel that might have been more likely found elsewhere. It dwarfed everything else in the town, standing five stories, and it looked very modern, very metropolitan in stark contrast to the dusty, arid town around it.

"Welcome, newcomers!" called a man who approached as we unloaded our luggage. He was perhaps ten years my senior with an impressively bushy, dark brown mustache. He wore a wide brimmed hat to keep the sun off his head and an inexpensive but functional black suit with brown boots and spurs that *clinked* as he walked. The gun on his belt and the star on his chest made his profession clear.

"Good afternoon, Sherriff. Sherriff?" I responded warmly with an outstretched hand. I learned a long time ago that those who seemed to hide from lawmen were frequently suspected by lawmen.

"Sam Johnson," he replied affably with a deep and gravelly voice as he took my hand.

"John Landis, Sherriff Johnson," I replied as we shook, and his hand felt rough in mine and as strong as iron.

"Please, call me Sam. What brings you folk out to Boulder Spring?"

"Well, I can't say for my travelling companions," I replied cocking my head toward the young couple unloading their luggage, "but I'm here to claim my new property."

"Oh?" Sam asked, but his face shrugged off the puzzlement almost as soon as it arrived. "I wasn't aware of any more Federal land grants out this way."

"Nothin' Federal 'bout it, Sherriff," I replied, my speech adopting some of the sloppiness I had heard from most of the people out in this part of the country. I pushed back my jacket for a moment as I reached into an inner pocket for the deeds to my new land and produced them to show the Sherriff. "I acquired these back home in Omaha. Thought it'd be a chance to see somethin' and someplace new."

"I see. Now Mr. Landis, I don't expect a landowner such as yourself would plan on causing no trouble, would you?"

"Of course not, Sherriff. Why would you ask?" I asked, and I may have played up my surprise a little too much.

"That's quite a hog leg you've got on there."

"Oh?" I asked, looking down at the gun I must have exposed. "Honestly, I'm really not any good with it, but I'm told a man has to protect what's his."

"That's true, Mr. Landis, but we don't allow firearms in public here in Boulder Spring. You can own a gun, you can carry a gun, but you can't carry one in town except in your own home."

"I'm afraid I don't have a home."

"Not true. That land of yours out on the edge of town has a house on it, if you can call it that. I could ask you to turn in your pistol and return it to you at the limits, but how 'bout I just walk you over there."

"I'd be obliged, Sherriff."

"Call me Sam, Mr. Landis."

"Call me John, Sam," I said with a genuine smile, and I hefted the massive trunk that held my meager belongings up onto my back. He motioned the way, and he was kind enough to slow his pace to allow me to keep up. "So, tell me Sam, what else is on this land of mine?"

"Not much of nothin', I'm afraid. A stream passes through it, probably a tribitry of the river."

It took me a moment to decipher that he meant a tributary, and I hadn't seen a river anywhere. "What river?"

"It's underground. Comes out of the mountains and breaks through amidst some boulders some three hundred yards that way," he replied with a back handed motion off to the east. "That's why the town's called Boulder Spring, but back to your question – you got a mine, too."

"What kind of mine?"

"Well, Anthony La Vey had your land originally, a man of French descent, I think. He found some flecks of gold in his stream, so he started digging. Wasn't long before he had a full-fledged mine, was sure he had gold in his hills. He found a few nuggets, but never found anything big."

"What happened to him?"

The Sherriff shot me an appraising sidelong glance before answering, "I'd have thought you know, since you bought the deeds to his land."

"No, I got them from someone else."

"Hmmm. Well, one morning he just packed up and joined a wagon going to Santa Fe. We never saw him again. I figured he just ran out of money."

We walked almost to the edge of town, and a good look around told me that I truly was in the wilderness in Boulder Spring. There wasn't much of anything here, wasn't anything for a hundred miles in any direction, and I started to wonder if this had been a big mistake. On the other hand, I had only dipped into my excessive cash winnings by a mere few hundred dollars, so I had time to sort things out. A tiny, white-washed church with a steeple pointing straight to heaven marked the northwestern edge of the town.

"Can I ask you something?"

Sam stopped at my question, I suppose sensing something deeper in the sound of it. He turned toward me a bit and replied, "Of course."

"We were stopped just a few miles out of town in a most curious encounter."

"Apaches?" he asked, but I sensed that he already knew the answer. I nodded, and he matched the motion. "They do that. Don't many people come here, but they stop those that do."

I lowered the trunk to the ground, as it seemed we might be standing in this one spot for a moment. Quite suddenly, he seemed very solemn. It felt as if I had stumbled on some wonderful mystery, and Sherriff Sam Johnson knew something about it, if I was in fact any judge of character whatsoever. Back home as a child, I heard the stories about the Indians, stories about burial grounds and curses on white men who took certain pieces of land for their own, and I couldn't help but wonder if I had blundered into one of those terribly exciting tales.

"Is the land here important to them?"

"Well," Sam began, and then he paused with a cock of his head, as if he were unsure how to continue.

"They seemed more concerned than angry, like they were trying to tell us something," I prompted.

"A few of them speak English. They say something about a land ghost."

"A land ghost?" I repeated, genuinely confused.

"Blasphemy to be sure!" a clear, strong voice without accent almost shouted from right behind me, making me jump a foot high as I whirled to face it.

The man I beheld was young, perhaps about my age. He stood well over six feet in height and had a wide, powerful frame. Under clothing of all black, held tightly closed by a white collar at his throat, seemed to be the body of a man more suited to the pugilist's arena than the pulpit. His jawline was solid, angular, and distinctly German in nature, making me think that I might break the bones in my hand should I choose to strike him. He was fair haired, and his blue eyes stared back at me with a disquieting intensity.

Sam chuckled as he produced a cigar from somewhere. As he lit it, he said between puffs, "Now, that is no way to greet one of our newest property owners. Mr. John Landis, meet Reverend Michael Spratley. He runs the gospel mill every Sunday, starting at seven sharp."

"The church is open always, not just Sunday, Sherriff," replied Spratley, "and you should attend more often. We are all drenched in sin, and it is only the waters of Our Lord and Savior that can wash us clean. Without them, we are condemned to the Fires of Damnation."

"I'm pretty sure the Lord knows what's in my heart, and I think he'll be lookin' out for me when my time comes."

"He does indeed," Spratley agreed, at least to Sam's first statement, but then he rested his eyes on me. "And what about you, Mr. Landis? Are you saved?"

"I didn't know I was lost, Reverend," I answered, and Sam exploded behind me in raucous laughter.

I bent down to again heft my trunk, but Sam said, "Let me help you with that." Each carrying an end, we hobbled away from Reverend Spratley, carrying on like old friends as his lingering stare burned a brand into our backs like something out of Hawthorne. My property apparently started right at the end of town, and within a few more minutes' walk, a rotting and dilapidated hovel came into view.

"Welcome home," Sam said, nodding toward the tiny shack as we set the trunk down.

"Looks… wonderful."

"It's a shithole, but it's yours. One other thing you should know, John. That army pistol of yours can bring down a man easy enough, but you only got six shots. And it's no good at a distance. Pick yourself up a good rifle, maybe a Henry, and at least another pistol."

"Is there something else I should know?" I asked him, suddenly concerned.

"I don't think so, but like you said earlier – a man needs to defend his property."

Sherriff Sam Johnson was, unfortunately, spot on in his appraisal of my new home. The miniscule, one room shack barely gave me enough room to move around. I looked on with serious doubt at its spiderweb covered wood burning stove and the dusty, straw and insect filled mattress. Instead, I checked my pistol with Sam and rented a room at the hotel for the next couple of months, during which time I paid handsomely for several carpenters and a number of laborers to build me a modest, three-room home.

I also investigated my new mine, finding it to be little more than a hole in the ground. I should be clear that I had no knowledge of mining at all, so I had no use for the abandoned picks and miscellaneous tools, nor the steel girded, wooden car that ran on a set of rusted rails from inside the mine to just outside of its mouth. Finding no one in Boulder Spring had knowledge of mining either, I hired a man out of Santa Fe by the name of Thomas Rawlings for the exorbitant sum of five dollars per day. Within a week, Tom had hired a half dozen men to help him with the labor, and my mine became active, churning out hundreds of pounds of rock per day.

As it turned out, Sam owned the hotel, having bought it for pennies on the dollar from the family that built it. Apparently, they had expected Boulder Spring to become the next great gold rush town, but they had instead moved further west to California, nearly broken. Sam was thankful to me for the additional business, as the men working in my mine rented rooms by the week from him.

I ate breakfast with Sam almost every morning, even after the carpenters finished my house. He was a good man who actually enjoyed the quiet life of Boulder Spring. As he put it, those growing towns like Santa Fe had more trouble than their law could handle. Reverend Spratley joined us on occasion, but we often ran him off. We found the easiest way to do that was to begin discussing the latest published scientific theory. "An affront to God!" or "Blasphemy!" he would often exclaim and return to his church, Sam and I enjoying the indignant bluster to no end.

It was the morning of Thursday the fifth of July, and a hot one at that, when everything in my life changed forever. The summer started hot and dry, rain refusing to come which caused dust devils to blow and swirl down Boulder Spring's main avenue. The few farmers in town lamented greatly, and even I began to doubt the wisdom in coming here. I had just begun to bring up the subject to Sam over breakfast when Tom charged through the door to Boulder Spring's lone saloon, nearly colliding with a table and several chairs in his hurry.

"Mr. Landis, thank God. I need you at the mine!" he panted as he spoke, struggling to get words out in between breaths. Tom was a short man, little more than five feet, with a most unassuming and underwhelming appearance, but he was strong as a bull. He looked like everyone and no one all at once, which I might have found useful back home in Omaha during one of my less lawful endeavors.

"What's happened?" I asked, standing so quickly as to almost upend my chair. Picturesque scenes of a cave in filled my head, with men partially buried under thousands of pounds of rock, moaning as they waived limbs toward me begging for help.

"Come see," he replied, leaning on his knees. "Follow me."

With a glance at Sam, I followed Tom out into the dry, dusty air back toward my property. I had no idea what had him worked up so, but he refused to explain it to me. "Let me show you," was all he would say, and Sam just seemed content to follow us. We stopped for a moment just outside the mine where Tom's half dozen men milled about. I could sense the change in the air; something exciting had happened, as was obvious by the way the men stood and the glint in their eyes.

"What is it, Tom?" I asked again,

"We have to go in," he explained, lighting two oil wick lamps, one for each of us.

"All right, lead on," I said, and I turned to look at Sam. "You comin', Sam?"

"Uhhh, no. I ain't in no rush to get below ground," he replied. He then added with a lopsided grin, "I imagine I'll get there soon enough, but not today."

I chuckled as I followed Tom into my mine, my back hunched over to keep from hitting my head on the wooden beams above. Of course, I had been in the mine a few times before, but I was still surprised by the sudden downward slope of the entrance. Generally, I avoided the place. I found the air hard to breathe, and it felt like the walls and ceiling pressed in on me, trapping me in a claustrophobia from which there was no escape. Also, I couldn't dispel the sense of dread that at any moment, the whole thing would come crashing down upon itself, and I had no doubt the mine would wait for me to be inside it for that to happen.

"How much further?" I asked after what felt like hours of keeping down primeval panic.

"Not far, just to the end here."

"How far down are we now?" I asked, glancing back up the way we came. I was surprised to see warm daylight behind us, as I felt as if we had walked deep into the bowels of the Earth.

"Well, when we started, the mine went about three hundred feet, and we've added another two."

"We're five hundred feet down?" I asked incredulously, the sense that I needed to leave building steadily.

"No, no, Mr. Landis. The mine is about five hundred feet total, but we're only, I don't know…," Tom stopped for a moment looking up at something only he could see. "We're maybe eighty, ninety feet down."

"That seems impressive."

"Well, maybe, but back home in Pennsylvania, it wasn't nuthin' for a coal mine to go over a thousand feet down," Tom said, and he came to a stop. "We're here."

I had no idea what I was supposed to be seeing. Of course, the lamps provided only enough light to see just in front of us and not much further. Clearly, we were at the end of the mine, for we could make no further progress. I saw little other than some temporarily discarded tools, some loose rubble and walls of dirt and stone held at bay by lumber. Tom had extended the mining rail as he tunneled, I assumed to help him move debris out quickly by a cart, and that also stopped here.

"I don't see anything," I said, confused, but my words staggered out a bit as my eyes came to rest on a dark spot set into some bare stone, that only just barely contrasted with the gray around it. I moved closer to better illuminate it, as our lamps threw light for little more than a foot, and I realized that I looked into a hole of some kind set right into the rock about chest height. Small, it was little bigger than my hand.

"We just knocked it in," Tom said, as if his words explained clearly what I was seeing.

"What is it?" I asked, trying to see inside.

"It's a cave, Mr. Landis. Stand back a moment."

As I did so, Tom tore a sizeable piece of fabric from his shirt sleeve, causing me to wince slightly. He was a working man, so his clothes were often rough and well worn, and he obviously thought nothing of destroying this particular article of clothing. Even still, it would cost him money to replace it, and I made a mental note to handle that expense for him. He balled the fabric up a bit and set it to the wick of his lamp. It lit nicely, and Tom unceremoniously tossed it through the hole and into the cave beyond.

"Look now," Tom said, a huge grin breaking across his face.

As I put my eyes up to the portal, I gasped, and my heart seemed to stop in my chest as I held my breath. I couldn't see the burning piece of cotton somewhere below my eye level, and its light faded fast as it burned out. But before it did so, tiny blaze illuminated a portion of the cave beyond, the light reflecting off many surfaces with a warm golden glow. It filled my being as it assaulted my eyes, and all my worries of being crushed to death were forgotten in an instant.

"Sweet Jesus," I exhaled softly.

"Gold, Mr. Landis. It's a cave of gold!"

We sent the men home early with a sizeable cash bonus right out of my pocket – ten dollars to each of them with the expectation that they said nothing to anyone about what we found. I even gave them the rest of the week off with pay while Tom and I talked and planned. We talked late that first night, arose early the next few days and continued to talk well after dark, sometimes going into the mine ourselves to work. We widened the opening to the cave enough for a man to crawl through, so that Tom could get a good sense of what I had.

I still didn't know anything about mining, gold or otherwise (that was Tom's field of expertise), but I knew how hard it was to protect something of great value once someone else knew about it. I needed a man I could trust to help me run and keep an eye on things, and I figured Tom was that man. My first move was to make him my partner, and he jumped at what I considered to be a paltry twenty percent of the profits. I probably dealt him in for too much, but I needed to know I could trust him.

Tom and I planned to hire another twenty men from Santa Fe for labor, as well as a half dozen men who were good with guns to protect the mine. He assured me he could get the laborers for about forty dollars per month, though the gunslingers would cost about double that. We decided to bore a second mine into the ground, some hundred feet or more from the first, with the intention of connecting it to the "gold cave" as we had come to call it. He made a list of supplies as well, telling me it would take him several days at least to pull everything and everyone together.

Tom had only spent a few minutes in the cave, but from what he had seen, he was absolutely certain he could deliver as much as a hundred troy ounces of gold per day of work and maybe more once the second mine was up and running! My math skills have always been sharp, especially when calculating profit on a job, and I quickly realized I was looking at a profit of some forty thousand dollars per month. I had just made Thomas Rawlings one of the richest miners in all of New Mexico! I should have offered him ten percent.

Four days after discovering our destiny, Tom and I happened to be in town eating lunch with Sam at his hotel. Two stagecoaches and several large horse drawn wagons rolled into town and began to deposit no less than a dozen persons. They were mostly men of the working-class sort, but a few of them had brought wives and children.

"I guess I better go see about them," Sam said with a sigh, decidedly planting his hat on top of his head.

"We'll join you," I said, and we left our food behind.

We stayed a number of feet back while Sam did his introduction to the newcomers, confiscating several guns in the process. When he walked back to us, he wore the concerned guise of a man who knew his life was about to become very complex. He stood close to us and said in hushed tones, "They're here because they heard about gold. I suppose one of your men spilled the beans. It's made it back to Santa Fe. We're going to have a lot more than jus' them showin' up real soon."

I shrugged my eyebrows. I had a bad feeling those men would have loose lips, despite the extra cash I paid them. The only way you could keep a secret this big is if only two people knew about it, and one was dead.

I looked at Tom, "You better get on to Santa Fe, then. Get together everything we need."

"I'm sure one of them," Sam explained with a point at one of the coaches, "would be happy to take you. He's got another load of people waitin' on him. John?"

"Yeah?"

"I hope you bought those extra guns I told you about back when you first got here. You're goin' need 'em."

Despite Sam's warning, I had little trouble while I awaited Tom's return. My land was clearly marked all around, and I had several high points that allowed me to survey much of it. I spent most of my time standing guard outside the mine itself, even sleeping there at night. The worst I had to do was run off a couple of teenaged boys who had co-opted a pickaxe from somewhere or someone and started to dig a hole down in one of my gullies. A simple word about sending the Sherriff to their homes gave them cause to leave and not come back.

On the second night, I got tired of just sitting there waiting, listening to the sounds of town in the distance and the baying of coyotes. I realized I hadn't entered the cave like Tom had, which seemed to be a serious oversight by someone in my position. My old life started to itch the back of my brain for a moment, and I wondered if Tom knew about something in that cave that I didn't. I didn't know what could be more important than all that gold, but it seemed prudent to have a look. I took two of the oil wick lamps, as many candles as I could carry and a full box of matches.

I had quickly become at home in the mine (the promise of so much wealth will do that to a man) and within ten minutes I stood at the opening into the cave. I gingerly worked my upper body through the hole and lit one of the lamps. Such a device puts off very little light, but it gave me enough by which to work. I leaned into the cave, balancing my midsection across the entrance, and leaned down to place the lamp on the ground. I then placed both of my hands on the cold cave floor and dragged the rest of my body inside.

I sat cross-legged as I considered my surroundings. The cave floor was hard and dry, just solid, cold rock. I don't know why, but I expected it to be damp or moist, and to punctuate that thought, a dripping of water into a pool sounded regularly every few seconds somewhere off in the darkness. I felt a horrible presence, as if the darkness itself were pressing in upon me, and I frantically began lighting matches and candles until I had made a circle of light, a protective shield perhaps six feet across from the murkiness. I sat in a passageway of sorts that lead before and behind into darkness. The cave walls were riddled with yellowish tint of gold, and I assumed it to be the genuine article for Tom to have been so worked up about it.

"Much ado about nothing," I said to no one, and I cursed my sudden panic. I was no mere child to be frightened by the dark, and there was nothing to fear down here. I was far more likely to encounter a coyote or rattlesnake in the dark above ground than to find anything alive down in this cave.

I slowly stood up, taking care to neither brain myself on the close ceiling, nor to spill melting wax on my hand. I chose to go forward, counting my paces as I went. The cave seemed to naturally narrow and widen as I went, but consistently curved to the left in a long slow arc. At thirty-two paces, the passageway bent to the left at an almost right angle, and I nearly missed an opening in the cave wall to the right as it was located near my feet. Noting it, I continued in the main passage, following its leftward turn.

I stopped for just a moment after another twenty paces or so, as I realized I heard the dripping water again, this time clearly over the sound of my movement. I cautiously approached the sound until the cave came to another hard, left turn. To the right stood a shelf (for lack of a better word) made of solid rock that jutted from the cave wall about waist high. It had a lip around the edge, creating a pool of water into which fell a solitary drop of water every few seconds from somewhere above me in the dark. Points of light from the pool drew my attention, and as I peered more closely, I could clearly see small crystalline formations under the water, each no larger than an inch tall and each giving off a pinkish luminescence. Fascinated, I almost fell into the pool in my examination of them, but it did allow me to see that the pool disappeared underneath the cave wall itself, perhaps providing access to another part of the cave system, if I but had the fortitude to try and squeeze myself through.

"Another adventure for another day, I suppose," I said aloud. Even now, I find it fascinating that men feel the need to speak to themselves, so as to dispel the illusion of true solitude. Clearly, the Lord in His wisdom never intended man to be alone.

And it was at that moment that something in the cave answered me. A chill ran up my spine as a long, low moan echoed through the passageway. It sounded lonely, ancient, and mournful, and the similarity to a woman calling, "Hello?" caused every hair on my arms and neck to stand on end. Instinctively, I drew my pistol, dropping half of my light in the process.

"Damn," I swore, and as I bent down to retrieve some of the fallen candles, the voice called again through the caves. This time, I dropped the lamp in my left hand, causing it to break open on the cave floor. The precious oil inside lit quickly, giving me substantial light for a few brief moments as I turned round and round to face whatever ghostly presence awaited me.

As the fire went out, and my light with it, I calmed myself. Instinctual panic would do me no good here, and I needed to find my way back to the mine. Of course, the worst possible thing that could happen would mean me staying in this cave for the next day or so until Tom discovered me – not a delightful prospect, but I would be found. I began to shiver with the chillness of the air as I listened to the water drip into the pool.

I don't know how long I waited – minutes or hours – but finally I fumbled around in the dark for the candles at my feet. Finding several, I holstered my gun and relit them, holding the light like a brand in each hand. I had gotten turned around, so I took a moment to orient myself – with the pool of water to my right, the passage continued to the left. I certainly could have returned the way I had come, but I continued onward with a hunch. I nearly cried out with joy when I saw a fading circle of light ahead of me, when the passage came full circle to where I started.

I stood once again in the ring of candles, and I very nearly made good my escape. However, the sorrowful calling voice sounded again, though now it seemed less a disembodied spirit or a lost woman and something far more ordinary.

I went back through the cave toward the first left turn, and when I arrived, I knelt to inspect the opening just large enough for a man. My candles threw off little light, but the crawlspace seemed to extend for some distance. In the flickering gloom, I barely made out a shape in the crevasse; it was small, only about six inches in each dimension, and it almost looked like a parcel of some kind. I was about to reach for it, when the voice sounded once more, but this time, it incited no such horror as before. Clearly, it was caused by a current of air somewhere at the end of the crawlspace, making ghostly sounds in the way a man would play a flute.

I shuffled my ever-shortening candles to my left hand and reached deeply into tiny passage until my fingertips touched the rectangular object I saw within. Surprisingly, it gave slightly to my touch and felt like some sort of leather or animal skin. Curious, I pulled it out to give it a thorough examination, and just as I determined it was certainly some sort of satchel, a slight puff of wind came out of the crawlspace and extinguished the flames of my candles.

Having thoroughly had more than enough of this deep place, I immediately turned and went back the way I had come with all speed, using my sense of direction and touch to guide me back to my entry point. My other lamp still burned, but most of the candles consisted of puddles of wax. I wasted no time exiting into the mine and making my way to the surface.

I chose not to guard the mine that night. A terrible gale had sprung from the east, blowing chill air with frightening force across Boulder Spring. I braved it for only a few minutes before I retired to my modest home. Only three rooms total, it was a vast upgrade over the shack that had stood here before, and I had one room with the old wood stove that I had somehow fancied my study, despite the noticeable lack of books.

Once I had the stove warm and burning nicely, I settled into a high-backed chair to investigate the satchel that I had brought above with me. It clearly was of Indian manufacture, Apache or otherwise I did not know, being very similar to the skins I had seen them wear. It seemed to contain one object of bizarre shape, and I produced it from within after unlacing the flap that held the satchel closed.

My stomach turned immediately at the sight of the thing, and I instantly dropped it onto the satchel in my lap so that I would no longer have to touch it. The head of a rat – no, two rat heads! – had been attached, perhaps sown, to the body of a black bird, but where a feathered tail should have been was instead the rattle of a snake. The entire thing was dried and desiccated, mummified instead of rotted, and it made my skin crawl with the knowledge that I had touched whatever evil amulet it was.

With a snarl, I opened the wood burning stove and tossed the abomination, satchel, and all, into the fire.

It took little time to forget the macabre events of that night, and though at the time I was able to dismiss any misgivings through my own grounded rationality, I now understand that mankind has certain instincts for a reason. We have natural and sometimes visceral reactions to certain things, objects, and creatures, and while Darwin may have written off such reactions as the remains of our primordial, apish ancestors, it's not unintelligent or irrational to pay them some heed.

Regardless, Tom returned quickly with a small army of men, most of whose weapons would be the pickaxe, hammer, and chisel and perhaps a bucket. He quickly broke more fully into the cave, widening its entrance considerably, and it was only days before the mine car brought load after load of raw gold ore to the surface. Every miner and laborer submitted to a search at the end of their shift, for I would not tolerate theft of any amount. While the first mine produced amply, Tom focused on starting the second shaft to further increase production. We spent night after night for the first month celebrating in town and generally spreading the wealth.

Boulder Spring grew. In the latter half of the nineteenth century, any town rumored or, better yet, proven to have gold or silver veins saw massive immigration. Usually, the newcomers would move on quickly as the precious metals were exhausted, but my mines continued to produce copious amounts of gold. More and more people came, and they needed a place to stay. This filled Sam's hotel quickly, almost too quickly, and he had to hire help from some of the new residents. The town's saloon filled to capacity every night, and some enterprising soul began building another one with weeks. Reverend Spratley enjoyed the largest crowds he had ever seen for his particular brand of thrice weekly fire and brimstone, "we're all damned sinners going to Hell" invocations. The general store couldn't keep up with the demand of basic goods, and even "Pops" McGhee, the barber, hired a boy to help clean up after each customer so he could quickly move to the next.

However, all the sudden prosperity came with some difficulty. Prospectors tended to be a notoriously ornery and rowdy lot, and there were droves of them in Boulder Spring. Also, anywhere productive persons work hard to make an honest living came thieves and scoundrels – persons who would much rather lie, cheat or steal their living, a lifestyle that I was uncomfortably familiar with, though no one in Boulder Spring knew it. Sam couldn't keep up with the constant complaints and accusations, not to mention just meeting everyone, so he quickly began recruiting deputies from reputable local landowners, such as myself of course.

It's interesting that of all the people who benefited from my goldmine that I could've mentioned, Pops is the one that came to mind, for he is the focal point for where it all started. He was a good, fair-minded man who only wanted to talk to pass the time while you sat in his chair. Pops was old, somewhere in his sixties with white hair and a matching beard he kept neat. Narrow of frame, he stood maybe five and a half feet tall, making him extraordinarily unassuming and nonthreatening. The rumor was that Pops had served as a surgeon in the Army of Northern Virginia, but he never talked about it. I never asked out of respect.

One afternoon about four months after my mining operations were in full swing, Sam and I greeted some new arrivals – two families that had come to Boulder Spring by way of Santa Fe. They seemed to be the honest, hardworking sort with only a rifle between them, which I confiscated right away, explaining that it would be held for them at the jailhouse until they left town or moved into a home outside of the limits. It was a talk I'd had at least a dozen times already and this sort of folk never caused a ruckus over it.

A loud voice from across the street drew my attention. "Sam," I said to get his attention, followed by a nod over at Pops'.

We began to walk across, when Sam said, "That man's armed."

A balding man with a long, unkempt gray beard stood on the porch of the barber's storefront, two steps outside the door. He was short and wiry, and even his stance had a desperate appeal to it. I didn't recognize him as anyone who had come to town in the last few weeks, and I certainly would have recognized the Remington on his hip. Pops stood in the doorway, his ever-present white apron on over his shirt, necktie and trousers, and he clearly wasn't having anything the armed man offered.

"I said I'm good for it!" he shouted at Pops, and we picked up our pace, breaking into a jog across the dusty thoroughfare. He pulled his Remington revolver and pointed it right at Pops' chest, "Damn it, old man, I need the laudanum!"

I broke into a run. I was never much of a man of action before, but I had started to sprout a relatively new sense of responsibility since becoming embarrassingly wealthy. I thought perhaps I could just run him down or wrestle him to the ground and fight for the gun. After all, there were two of us; surely between both Sam and I we could handle this one poor soul.

Sam must have had other ideas, however, because as we closed the distance, he reached his hand to his mouth and loosed an ear-piercing whistle. He then shouted, "Hey there!", drawing the man's attention for just a moment.

We skidded and slid to a halt kicking up a small cloud of dust and dirt, and I now had a better look at the man as he edged away from us while keeping his pistol trained on Pops. He wore a once white, now filthy cotton shirt tucked into threadbare brown wool trousers held up by matching suspenders. His cavalry style boots had seen better days, perhaps worn through the sole. His grimace, either from pain, desperation or both showed a mouth full of blackened, broken teeth.

"Settle down there, now," Sam said soothingly, his palms open toward the assailant. "Let's just all settle down. What's the low down here, Pops?"

"I jus' needs some laudnums," the man preempted Pops. "My head hurts real bad."

"How 'bout it, Pops?"

"He still owes me for yesterday and the day before," Pops replied gruffly, but not abrasively.

"All right," Sam nodded, and he kept his voice low, calm. "I'll cover what he owes you. Why don't you go get him what he needs."

Pops grunted his assent, which sounded more like a man with tuberculosis clearing his throat. He turned in the doorway and disappeared into his shop. I had already, slowly, begun to circle around to the left so that I was standing almost directly behind the disgruntled addict. I had my hand on my pistol, but my thought was to bash the back of the man's head with the handle rather than shoot him with it. I hadn't shot at a man yet, and I wasn't sure I was too fond of the idea.

"All right, mister," Sam continued, "while Pops gets it for you, I need you to put that shooting iron down."

He looked at Sam uncertainly, his gun still pointed at the doorway of the barber shop. He asked, "My firearm?"

"That's right, I need you to put it on the ground."

"You ain't takin' my firearm."

"I don't wanna' keep it," Sam assured, "but I can't have you walkin' round town with it. You can have it back when yer ready to leave."

"You ain't takin my firearm," he repeated, his agitation rising again.

"Well, ya' see, it's a Boulder Spring ordnance – no firearms allowed in town. So, I need you to set it on the ground -"

"I said, you ain't takin' my damn firearm!" the man shouted back at Sam. Spittle and phlegm flew from his cracked lips, tangling in his beard and making impacts on the dusty ground, and Sam stepped back from the unexpected force of the outburst.

And I acted. I pulled my pistol from its holster, and before the poor wretch had any inkling that the blow was coming, I brought the butt of the handle right down on the back of his head. Perhaps I hadn't thought the attack through, but at the time, I did not see any other options for disarming the opiate addict. When my blow fell, he grunted and crumpled immediately, and perhaps out of reaction, he fired a round out of his Remington into Pops' shop with a breaking of glass.

"Got his gun," Sam said as he collected the weapon, and I rushed down to collect the vagrant. "Pops, we got him. You can come out now."

Then we heard a sound that I can still hear in my mind today – the sound of the first man I ever killed. A thud hit the porch of Pops' shop, but it was more than just a thud. It sounded as if someone dropped a great sack of potatoes onto the deck boards, and it landed with almost a shuffling slide. I stood quickly to see Pops' body lying in the doorway of his barber shop, a pool of blood growing beneath him. A bottle of laudanum fell off his midsection and rolled across the floor into his shop, producing a disconcerting hum until it came to a stop.

Pops had no family of which anyone in Boulder Spring was aware. Reverend Spratley allowed us to lay him out within the church while his burial was prepared. I helped dig the grave myself, some small penance despite assurances from Sam that I was not to blame for Pops' death. Regardless, it didn't stop me from getting ridiculously drunk that night, happily throwing myself into the blissful oblivion provided by as much whiskey as I could manage to consume. I managed to make it home that night, but I immediately renewed my intake of potent potables the next day. Sometime in the late afternoon, Sam and Tom woke me from a stupor and carried me to sleep it off back at the jailhouse.

I awoke in the morning to an hellacious clamor. For some reason, several men felt the need to have a conversation while screaming at the top of their lungs. They apparently had no regard for my current tender condition, and I opened my eyes groggily to behold lances of sunlight overpowering all other sights in the room. I rubbed at my eyes seemingly for hours before finally clearing them enough to make out Sam talking to Reverend Spratley and another of the townsfolk whose name I don't recall.

"Must you gentlemen make such a commotion?" I groaned, catching a long, disapproving stare from the good reverend. I stretched from my curled-up position on the floor, and every sinew and joint screamed at me as I did so. I nodded toward an empty cell and said, "We usually lock up the drunks, Sam."

"Oh, I didn't think it was really necessary."

"Is the Reverend here to pray for my soul after I killed poor ol' Pops?"

"No, John, he's -"

"Be mindful of your words, Mr. Landis," interrupted Spratley. "While you blaspheme, I pray for all of our souls every day, and you will most assuredly have your day of reckoning with the Lord over the death of Pops. But no, I am not here for that. Pops' body is gone!"

"Could you please lower your voice?" I asked with clinched eyes and a furrowed brow, and then his words finally pierced through the aftermath of too much consumption. "What did you say?"

"You heard me, Mr. Landis. Some demon has stolen Pops' body away from the church. And on the day of his burial as well!"

"I'm sure there's a reasonable explanation," Sam assured us both. "I am sure no demon is to blame."

"I meant it figuratively, Sherriff, for surely a man must be as a demon to take Pops' last shred of dignity."

"Let's look into it. John are you up to it?" Sam asked.

Before I could answer, a boy burst through the door into the jailhouse from outside. He panted heavily as he leaned on his knees trying to catch his breath, and I recognized him instantly. His name was Christopher Fields, and he was the boy that Pops had hired some months ago to help keep his shop clean with the sudden onslaught of customers.

"I... came... as...," he mustered. After a second, he started again, "Need... Sherriff... shop..."

"Settle down, son," Sam said in his somehow always calm, affable voice. "Just calm down and tell me why you ran all the way over here."

Christopher nodded and swallowed before making a studied attempt to slow his breathing. Finally, he said, "Sherriff, it's Pops. He's... he's back at the shop!"

"Someone brought his body to the shop?" Sam asked.

"No," the boy emphatically swung his head left to right and back, "Pops is at the shop. He's... working!"

"What?" was all anyone could manage, and I don't even know who whispered it.

I pushed my discomfort aside and climbed to my feet and took my gun belt and pistol from where someone had left it on one of the side tables. I belted it on and checked to make sure the gun was in fact still loaded before holstering it. "Boy, you stay here. Let's go," I said.

Sam, Reverend Spratley and I stood outside of Pops' shop a few minutes later, almost in the exact spot I had stood two days previously when I had gotten the kind old surgeon shot. I could still see the blood stains on the porch, leading into the shop itself whose door stood wide open for business as it had every day since I arrived in Boulder Spring, excluding Sundays of course. Inside, I heard Pops' voice raising to dizzying levels as he shouted or raged about something. As we approached the three steps leading to the wooden porch, we could hear him more clearly, and we stood as if Medusa herself had turned us to stone at the words we heard.

"Christopher! God damn it, boy! Where have you gone? I told you to clean up this mess! If I find you lazing around, boy I am going to fucking kill you!"

"Have you ever heard...?" I began to ask, but Sam's shaking head told me the answer I needed.

"Pops McGhee is one of the most God-fearing men I know."

I glance over at Spratley, who did not return the gaze. The man seemed truly petrified, but it was out of some sort of resolve rather than fear or trepidation. He would have made the most splendid of models for Michelangelo at that moment in time. A fire burned deeply in his cool blue eyes, a belief in something that I had never found the time or need to contemplate.

I was the first to start toward those steps, but Sam and Spratley fell in almost right beside me. The planks creaked as we took them, causing the cursing and raging voice of Pops to fall eerily quiet. On the porch, we stood almost shoulder to shoulder peering inside the shop, none of us ready to cross that accursed threshold where a beneficent old man named Pops had lost his life and on the other side of which he now seemed to live again.

"Well come on in, gentlemen," Pops' voice intoned quietly, and that voice contained something else, some sort of darkness or eldritch knowledge not common to gentile civilization or minds.

Pops appeared from somewhere out of view, perhaps only five feet inside the shop. He wore the same clothes he had worn when he was shot and killed, the same clothes he had been in when we laid him in the church. A wound, a bullet's wound showed in his chest, at the top of the white apron now stained reddish brown with old, dried blood. It gaped and led right to the heart, a heart that I refused to believe beat inside Pops' chest. His skin had a sickly sheen, and I saw a number of blisters on the skin of his hands and neck. His arms hung limply at his sides, and he held a long and wickedly sharp razor in his right hand.

"Can I interest you gentlemen in a shave?" Pops asked in a chilling tone. He brought the blade up to right side of his face and slid it slowly upward and against the grain of his beard, carving a layer of flesh as he did so. "It won't take any time at all."

"Angels and ministers of grace defend us," I quoted the Bard in a whisper, and Pops began to laugh, a deep laugh containing a wetness akin to phlegm moving about in one's chest.

Then Reverend Michael Spratley crossed the threshold, a man of pure purpose and vision, protected by his God and his faith. He stepped slowly, not out of fear or caution, but rather a quiet confidence. He held a leather-bound Bible before him, which I both never noticed him carrying and yet knew he always had. Pops leered as Spratley approached.

"The Lord God and His son, Jesus Christ, protect me. You cannot harm me, and I compel you to leave," he said, and his voice rose to a thundering volume as he advanced. "Leave this good man's body and return to the Pits of Hell. You cannot harm me! You have no place here, desecrating this place and this man's memory! The Lord God compels you to leave this place! The Lord God damns you back to Hell!"

Pops' visage seemed to adopt a calm aspect as Spratley approached him, the hand with the razor again dropping to his side. I thought that maybe it was time to be saved, that maybe Spratley could help me find God once we were past this unenviable moment. I thought that Spratley must truly have the protection of the divine to enter that room and confront whatever evil animated Pops' corpse.

And then Pops moved with the speed of a lightning bolt. The razor flew up and over once, blood flinging in a continuation of the blade's course, before reversing and coming back again. Spratley staggered backward a step or two. His Bible fell to the floor, and blood dropped onto its open pages. The Reverend's left hand went to his mouth, while the other to his throat, and he turned and fell out of the barber shop and into our arms.

We retreated down the steps in a sort of controlled fall, bringing Spratley down slowly to the ground. We spoke promises and platitudes, but Sam and I knew they were all useless, as Pops' razor had neatly sliced through over two inches of flesh at Spratley's neck. One of the strikes, I know not which, also bisected his cheeks, the blade having passed through his mouth as well. The Reverend made sounds I will never be rid of in my memory, gargling coughs as he choked on his own blood, and it ran like rivers through his and our fingers. His body grew still, and the fire left his eyes in mere moments.

I heard Pops' diseased laugh again, and I looked up to see the man, no, the thing that was once Pops, standing just inside the threshold.

"I suppose that shave was too close," Pops said with a shrug, and he resumed his incessant, infernal chuckling.

I stood, pulled my Colt Army pistol from its holster, and immediately fired. I fired four shots, all right into the chest of Pops, all from less than six feet away. I advanced slowly as my shots sent Pops backward a step at a time. I didn't stop to think about it, to realize that this was the first time I had ever actually fired my gun at a man, but even still, it would have given me no pause. Whatever stood in front of us was no man, for had he been a man, my four rounds would have easily been fatal. I stopped with two bullets left, and Pops stood staring at me, his fresh wounds barely bleeding.

"That tickled," Pops said with a shrug, and I fired my gun again right as he opened his mouth to say something else. Blood and gore shot out of the back of his head to paint the wall behind him like a macabre canvas.

"Do you want to know about this 'good man'?" Pops asked, despite the hole in the back of his head. "Do you know the things he has done? The surgeries? The amputations? The…"

I took aim one more time, a few inches higher than the last, and I fired my last round straight into the middle of Pops' forehead. I didn't know what manner of creature was he, but nothing Created by God could live without its brain. Bits of brain and skull showered behind Pops, as much of his head exploded outward with the bullet's exit, and yet he still stood facing me, looking almost confused at my reaction to his questions.

"That was rude, son," he chided. "Let's talk about it over a shave."

I quickly backpedaled out of shop of horrors and raced back to Sam. Pops' voice rang out after me, taunting, "Come back soon!" Throngs of people began to gather around on the street outside. Word seemed to have gotten around that something terrible was afoot. Either that, or they had simply heard my gunshots. They chattered and whispered, and one man even bent down to examine Spratley's corpse.

"Go on!" I shouted. "Go back to your homes and stay there! It's not safe! Go!"

Sam stood and added his authority to mine, and after a few minutes, the crowd had all but dispersed. Sam and I stood over the dead preacher, not daring to look back toward the barber shop's doorway.

"John, I..." Sam started, but he faltered and seemed to become distant. Finally, he mustered, "What in God's name do we do?"

"I don't know," I whispered, "but help me carry Reverend Spratley to the jailhouse."

We placed the good reverend in a cell, locked tight with Sam of course having the only key. Sam didn't warm to the idea at first; I suppose he considered it somehow disrespectful to such an ardent man of God, which was almost funny to me because he had never shown such feelings toward Spratley in the months I had been there. I knew he liked the preacher and enjoyed his company, but he mostly spent his time trying to raise Spratley's righteous indignance. To suddenly be concerned about how much respect he showed the man, or his god, now seemed out of character.

Regardless, I broke his fragile resolve with one simple question, "And what if he comes back like Pops?" I'd guess you can say that it had the desired effect.

We left the jailhouse, much to the screaming displeasure of the opium addict locked in the cell next to Spratley's body, and I returned to my mine while Sam went to keep an eye on Pops. By the time I arrived, a rough plan had formed in my mind. I pulled Tom aside and walked him back to town, all the while explaining everything that had happened. He smiled, nodded, and even almost laughed once as I talked, a reaction that I certainly had not expected from the man, considering the rather grim subject matter of the tale.

We came to a stop right in front of the barber shop, and Tom said, "Mr. Landis you may have a promising career as an author when you retire from mining."

Before I could respond, Pops voice called out from inside, "You're looking a little scruffy, Mr. Rawlings. Could I give you a cutting?"

Tom looked to the shop and was about to reply when he saw the terrible spectacle of Pops' walking, talking corpse, complete with mortal wounds to the chest, to say nothing of the extensive trauma to his head. Tom, always pragmatic, calm, and unflappable, turned as pale as our former preacher's sheets and instinctually took a step or two backward. This elicited one of Pops terrible, grating laughs.

"Holy God," Tom said as he crossed himself.

"I don't think God's got nuthin' to do with this," said Sam.

"I need you, Tom," I said, placing a firm hand on the man's shoulder. It pulled the man's attention back to the normal, the comprehensible as he nodded toward me.

"Pull some of our men off the mine to guard Pops, here. I want no one going near his shop. He hasn't shown any interest to leave, and I'm hoping that doesn't change. They're to report anything that happens to Sam at the jailhouse. Is that understood?"

"Yes, but I don't think they're gonna' want to stick around when they see this."

"Pay 'em. Pay 'em whatever it takes. We've got a hundred thousand dollars of gold waiting to go back to Sante Fe."

"What about the mine? Do we shut it down for now?"

"No," I immediately replied, but then I thought better of it. "Yes. Send everyone else home, and I mean home, away from Boulder Spring. Pay them a month's wages if need be. I don't want anyone in this town that doesn't need to be here. We'll rehire in Santa Fe once we get this all settled."

"Where are you gonna' be during all this?" Sam asked.

I paused a moment before answering, "I gotta' find some Apaches. I gotta' find out what they know about this place."

"They ain't gonna' let you find them unless they wanna' be found," Sam said.

"So, what do I do? Wander the wilderness until I stumble across 'em?"

"Just as likely to catch a bullet or an arrow that way," Sam nodded grimly.

"There's one that comes and goes in Santa Fe you can ask about," Tom offered, quickly silencing us. "His name's William Sharpnose."

"I didn't know Indians took English names," I pondered.

"Well, word is Sharpnose was raised by Christians, and I don't think that's even his real name.

He's a tracker. They say he can sniff out anyone or anything, he can follow a ghost across a lake in a thunderstorm."

"I've never heard that expression before," I said with a wide smile at Tom. "So, it's decided. I'm I goin' to Santa Fe."

I took the best horse I could find in Boulder Spring, paying no small sum to her owner even though Sam said I could simply take her as it was of the utmost importance to the town. I might have "borrowed" a horse for short term use at some point in my past, but now that I had so much of my own to protect, I suddenly understood the value of others' property. A trip that would take a stagecoach a day and a half, required merely five or six hours for one man and a good horse, so I took with me no food, only ample water for proof against the summer heat, my pistol and a Henry rifle.

About an hour out of town, I slowed the horse to an easy walk. Partially, I wanted to ease her efforts for a bit as the day grew hot, but the truth of it was that I estimated myself to be in the general area that Apaches tended to intercept people with their warnings. I hoped that they would make an appearance, and then maybe I could find a way to communicate, find a way to tell them about what had happened. I felt certain that they could somehow help, but we continued completely unmolested. Perhaps they made no appearance because they already knew what had happened those miles behind me, or perhaps they simply ignored those who left Boulder Spring. Regardless, none appeared, and after about an hour, I picked up the pace again. I made it to the edge of Santa Fe just as the sun had passed behind the mountains to the West, barely illumining the horizon in shades of red and dark orange.

I didn't locate William Sharpnose until the next morning, and, somehow, he wasn't what I expected, though I'm not sure what that expectation was. I came upon him as he readied a horse and mule, and from the look of his guns and supplies, he intended to be gone for some time. He had the reddish-brown skin and long, fine black hair of the other Apaches I had seen those months ago, but he dressed little different from any other cowboy. But unlike those others, lines crossed this man's face, lines of passing years and worry. Were he of my race, I'd have thought him in his fifties.

"Mr. William Sharpnose," I called, and he stopped long enough to look my way. His dark eyes were a sea of calm, his thoughts as he watched me approach completely inscrutable.

"I am," he replied distantly as he double checked some saddlebags, and his peaceful, serene voice carried above Santa Fe's noises, despite being somehow soft and low of register.

"Could I speak with you, please sir?"

"I do not have time. You can look for me when I return."

"I don't have time, sir. I just need a few minutes. I can pay you well."

"I do not need your money," Sharpnose said, turning to face me with his left hand stroking his horse's neck. "What is it? Your wife ran away, or perhaps someone stole one of your horses?"

"Nothing of the sort. My name is John Landis. I'm from -"

"I know who you are, Mr. Landis."

"You do?" I asked with raised eyebrows, genuinely surprised.

"There's been a lot of gold coming through here lately. Folk say it's yours."

"I suppose so," I said with a nod. Of course, my name was known around Santa Fe. Back home I always knew who the real players were, even if I had never met them.

"I do not understand white men. It is not enough for you to own the land, but you must plunder its heart as well. We have nothing to speak of."

Despite the lack of inflection, accent or emphasis on any words the man spoke, the statement had such a tone of finality to it that I was unsure of what to say back to him. He turned away from me, untied his horse from the hitching post and led the horse away a few feet. Sharpnose lifted himself into his saddle, turned towards me and said, "Goodbye, Mr. Landis." He began to ride away at a slow walk.

"Something has happened," I called after him, the words bringing him to a stop. "Something is wrong in Boulder Spring. The Apaches know what it is, don't they."

He straightened in his saddle for just a moment before letting out a long sigh. As the breath escaped him, his shoulders and back seemed to slump. He turned around in his saddle to regard me, and it felt as if he stared right into my very being, judging my soul by what he saw there.

"What is it?" I asked.

William Sharpnose dismounted and walked his horse back to the hitching post. After securing the animal, he removed a shotgun and a rifle from holsters attached to the saddle and turned toward me.

"Let us talk indoors," he said, motioning with his eyes toward a hotel on the other side of the street.

"Your town should not be there," Sharpnose said a few minutes later, after we had isolated ourselves to a quiet corner of the hotel's saloon. "There is something in the land there, something that should not be disturbed. You, and anyone else, should leave. My people are nomadic. We move, we settle, we move again, but we will not settle there."

"I found something down in my mine, well, in a cave we found."

"What did you find?" he asked, but I felt like he knew the answer.

"It's hard to explain. It was a... a chimera of sorts. Some vile thing sown together from bits of other animals – the body of a black bird, a rattlesnake's tail and two rat heads. It was old, dried out, brittle."

"You found it in a cave?"

"In a tunnel leading from the cave, perhaps large enough for a man to squeeze through. What was its purpose? Why would your people make such a thing?"

"My people did not make it," he replied. A less observant man wouldn't have noticed the subtle shift in his voice bespeaking anger, or perhaps indignance, but as someone who, up until very recently, made his living through gambling and other less honest means, I was self-taught in the ways of reading a person's true feelings. "It comes from a time before the Apaches."

"A time before...?"

"You white men are all the same. You do not understand the world. You think that because you came to this place called the New World that its history started when you came four hundred years ago. You think the peoples you found here have always lived the way you found them. The world, both New and Old, is far more ancient than any of us know, and the land holds vast secrets, both incredible and terrible to behold," Sharpnose explained, and his voice had returned to its previous even serenity.

"And what is under Boulder Spring is one of those secrets?" I asked, at once bewildered by and afraid of the answer I knew to come.

"It is – a spirit from ancient times, perhaps from even when the world was made. No one knows."

"How do you know?"

"Stories passed down by my people for generations," he explained shortly, and he changed the subject, apparently tired of this line of questioning, "You said something happened. What is it?"

"A man was killed, a barber, murdered. A couple of days later he was again in his shop, walking and talking, but it wasn't him," I explained, lowering my voice. Sharpnose only nodded, so I explained all the events with as much detail as I could recall.

"An act of evil begets evil," he replied softly. "Your preacher will be next, and the evil will spread throughout your town."

"How can we stop it?"

"You cannot. It can only be contained. Where is the guardian you found?"

"The guardian?" I asked, and then I realized he meant the wretched thing that I destroyed months ago. My face must have blanched, a poor admission for a poker player, for he looked at me even more intently. "I… I took it out of the mine with me to inspect it. When I saw what it was, I tossed it into a fire."

"Foolish, just like the rest of your kind – destroying that which you do not understand."

"Can't we just make another? Maybe your people can -"

"Even if the Apaches were willing, we do not know the medicine needed."

"So, what do I do?" I asked, suddenly feeling very desperate.

"The evil underneath Boulder Spring existed there long before your people or mine. It was there before the first men settled there. If it cannot be contained, it must be left alone."

"Are you saying, I need to make everyone leave Boulder Spring?" I asked incredulously.

"The man who died," Sharpnose started.

"Pops," I supplied.

"Pops. How long after he was killed did he stay dead? Two days? Do you think your preacher will not return, also? Do you believe that Pops, and whatever spirit infests him, will be content to stay in his barber shop?"

"What do I do?" I asked again, but then I thought better of the question. "What can I do?"

"Your town must be cleansed. I do not know what medicine is needed, but Boulder Spring must disappear from the land and never return."

"I'll buy the whole town if I have to. Buy the whole town and make everyone go back to Santa Fe." I looked down at the table in thought for a moment, my hands idly turning the half empty whiskey glass as my mind worked through the next bit. An idea struck me, and I raised my gaze back to his. "Then, I'll burn it to the ground, Pops and Michael included. Will you help me?"

"I cannot, will not go to that place. I am sorry, Mr. Landis," Sharpnose said as he stood from the table, the wooden legs of his chair scraping across the wood floor, "but there is nothing more I can do for you."

As he walked past me toward the door, my hand shot out and took his arm. Another man might have shown anger, perhaps even drawn a weapon or thrown a fist my way. William Sharpnose was ever the picture of silent serenity, and his eyes merely searched mine for an explanation.

"Will it end there? How do I know?" I asked him.

"I suppose you may never know," he replied. "Good luck, Mr. Landis."

I released his arm, and he silently went on his way, leaving me with my thoughts and just a little whiskey. I threw that back quickly, enjoying the burn as it slid down my throat. I stood up and left the empty glass and a dollar on the bar before heading back to my horse.

I wasted no time mounting up to start my return to Boulder Spring, taking one last glance at the Apache as he rode slowly out to the north. I went slowly. I figured that I could spend some time to carefully think out my next steps and still arrive at the town before nightfall, and as such, I paid little attention to anything around me as my horse trod what had grown in recent months from a dirt path to a well-traveled road.

It grew hot as the sun reached its zenith overhead, so I decided to stop briefly to rest and water my horse. I let him walk free to graze, though there was little for him to graze upon. I was about to continue on my way when I heard the sounds of horses, and I climbed atop my horse to give me some additional height to see further down the road. I saw a number of mounted men, but also several drawn wagons as well. As they continued toward me, I began to recognize some of the faces - some newcomers, some permanent residents, but all from Boulder Spring. The first two men on horseback rode past me silently, avoiding my questioning gaze as they were actually *my* men, men with guns I had contracted to protect my gold.

Many of the others were just people from town, including the white-haired Morgan Wyatt who ran the general store. I didn't know what would cause him to leave his place behind, but I pulled my horse to a stop as his wagon drew near. His widowed daughter and two grandsons rode on the bench with him. I held up my hand to wave, but also to make sure he stopped as well.

"What's going on here, Mr. Wyatt?" I asked when he pulled his horses to a stop just next to mine. "You left your store?"

"Anyone with any sense would leave, and many have. There's more coming behind us," he replied.

"What happened?"

"The sheriff's dead, and so are a lot of other good people."

"Sam's dead?" I gasped, and the world began to spin crazily around me, even though I was perfectly still. I took a firm hold on my saddle horn and asked again, "What happened?"

"This morning, your man watching Pops went to relieve himself. I saw Pops cross town and go into the jailhouse. He came out a few minutes later with the reverend."

"The reverend is dead," I said numbly.

"Dead and walking just the same as Pops," Wyatt nodded. "Pops started slashing with his razor at anyone he could catch. The reverend chased people, smashing their heads with his bible or choking them."

"For the love of God," I whispered.

"There's more. Everyone ran indoors, and the two of them broke into homes to get at people. I don't know how many... No one could fight them off. Pops is missing most of his head already. We packed everything we could carry and left."

"You did right," I said, and the world around me had started to settle down a bit. "How many more are coming?"

"I don't know," Wyatt mused, and he made a half-hearted attempt to turn and look behind his wagon. "Honestly, I ain't looked back."

"Can't say as I blame you," I said, gazing into the distance. I saw movement further down the road to Boulder Spring, more horses, a few wagons and maybe even some people walking on foot.

"Does anyone bring their dead with them?" a monotone, soothing voice came from behind me, breaking me from my thoughts. I turned in my saddle and smiled when I saw Sharpnose just behind me. He continued, "The dead must be burned to ash or they, too, will rise."

"How do you know?" I asked.

"Your town is not the first time men have settled on that land. My people did once. Long ago."

"What can we do? Burn the town?"

Sharpnose nodded, "Along with any who have been killed. We must seal your mine as well."

"That's easy. We have dynamite at the mine," I replied with raised eyebrows. I looked back to Morgan Wyatt and said, "Get your family to Santa Fe. I'll come when we finish this."

"God speed, Mr. Landis," Wyatt intoned, and he started his horses again with a light crack of the reins.

I turned back to Sharpnose and considered him for a moment before asking, "Why did you change your mind? Why did you come back to help me?"

"Because white men make a mess of everything," he replied, and though he adopted a friendly smile as he said it, the great sadness in his eyes told me the truth of his statement.

Sharpnose and I began our journey toward Boulder Spring, our speed substantially hampered by his laden donkey. We passed several dozen more people fleeing the town ahead as we went, and we stopped anyone with a wagon to be sure they carried no dead with them. Slowed as we were, the sun dropped below the mountains while we were still some miles out. Neither of us asked the other if we should stop for the night.

We rode into a quiet, darkened town that seemed vacant of any life at all. No one walked the main avenue, which was abnormal until the latest hours, and no one had lit the lanterns that hung on posts every fifteen feet or so. No light issued from the windows or open doors of the hotel, saloon, or any building at all, neither business nor home. I wasted no time investigating, but instead led Sharpnose through town to my land.

In so doing, we passed by the church, and there we found the only sign of life in the God-forsaken town that Boulder Spring had become. Although, I do not think it was life as God had intended it. Orange light spewed into the night from its few windows and from a crack around the closed doors. I could just barely make out a voice booming from within, strong and resonating. I had heard it before, often on Sunday. We did not stop to listen or investigate as whatever Michael Spratley had become gave its infernal sermon.

My home was dark, and none of my men stood watch around it or the mine. Someone had readied a team of horses to a wagon, one of those we used to transport our golden produce to Santa Fe and bring back supplies, and they snorted and neighed, their shod hooves stamping the dirt and dust nervously. I tried stroking their faces and whispering calmly in their ears, but the horses would not be drawn away from whatever disturbed them so. Quickly giving up, I moved around to the side of the wagon and lifted the canvas within it so as to take a peek at what hid underneath. A gleaming, golden reflection of the moon's cold, blue light met my eyes.

"Let me check inside," I said to Sharpnose, who hadn't yet dismounted.

No light shone from within the house that I could see, and with no shortage of trepidation, I lightly traversed the three front steps and onto the porch. I waited silently outside the door for a moment, listening for any sound or movement, but all was as still as a grave. I had drawn my pistol at some point, holding it toward the door with my right hand as I slowly turned the knob with my left. New and well oiled, the hinges made no sound as the door swung slowly inward.

"Tom?" I called softly as I opened the door, but neither he nor anyone else answered me.

I stood on the threshold, unable to will my feet forward into my own home. Nothing seemed amiss, except for a soundlessness that spoiled my calm the longer I waited in that doorway. It wasn't just the lack of sound in the house, but outside around it as well. Sound is often created by motion, and not even the air moved anywhere in Boulder Spring. I realized that all was unearthly still.

I finally entered and went through the doorway to my right, the hard soles of my boots on the wood floor the only sound. I avoided a collision with a small table next to the door only through my own memory of the placement of the furniture combined with the minimal, pale moonlight that filtered inside. Unwelcome darkness filled the room, and I could only just barely see the outline of my desk and chair and the wood burning stove.

I stopped when I stepped in something. My boot met the floor with a wet squish, rather than a clap on a floorboard. I froze in place as I slowly lifted my foot to remove it from the wet stickiness on the floor and looked down toward my feet. I felt sick to my stomach when I realized that a body lay there, and I knelt slowly to investigate, though I had little doubt of what I would find. My fingers searched my pocket and retrieved a match, which I struck on the floor.

The orange light flared brightly into existence for a moment before settling into a tiny, uniform flame, but it was enough to reveal Tom's face. It registered surprise, and his wide-open eyes stared lifelessly at the ceiling. A pool of sticky blood surrounded his head and upper body, obviously having issued forth from the wicked slash at his throat. Perhaps I should've felt either more alarm, sadness or both at this find, but his was not the first such corpse I had seen in recent days.

It was only when I lay my hand on Tom's chest and hung my head in silent prayer to an Almighty I had never spoken to before that the true horror of it struck me. It was not Tom's chest I felt under my hand, nor the buttons of the front of his shirt, but rather smooth fabric, under which I could feel the man's spine and shoulder blades on either side. I opened my eyes and inspected him closer. Not only had Tom's throat been slashed, but his head had been wrenched all the way around! The flesh of his neck was not only cut through but twisted as one may wring water from cloth!

"Tom... poor man, what did you do to deserve this?" I whispered.

Of course, I expected no answer, as there was no one alive within earshot to hear the question. Regardless, an answer came from out in the darkness, from some fell force. I heard a sharp exhalation from a source I couldn't see, and yet it had to be right in front of me. It was no different than the sound one makes when blowing out a match, and sure enough, my meager flame went out, allowing darkness to flood back in to fill the once lit space. A slight breeze arose outside, and to this day I'd swear on the Bible that I heard laughter on that wind.

A floorboard creaked behind me, and visions of a razor wielding Pops in my mind caused me to fall off my haunches to my left and land on my ass, facing the direction from which I had entered the house. At the same time, I raised my pistol toward a vague outline of a man in the doorway. I don't know if I meant to pull the trigger, if it was an accident or simple instinct, but my pistol's report in the small room deafened me for just a moment. The form at which I fired dropped to the floor instantly as my bullet embedded itself in the doorjamb to his left, splinters flying.

"Jesus! Stop shootin' at me!" cried Sharpnose with more feeling than I had ever heard the man express.

"Christ!" I replied, holstering my weapon hastily. I climbed to my feet and helped him up from his hands and knees. I said, "I'm sorry. It was just... You probably shouldn't sneak up on a man like that. I could've killed you."

"Not with that aim," Sharpnose replied. His studied calm had returned, but the hint of humor at my expense was unmistakable. I smiled briefly, but the smile disappeared as he asked, "This is your man?"

"Yes. Tom," I said quietly. I steeled myself, struck a match and lit a candle on my desk. Moving quickly and with a hand cupping the flame, I passed through a dark doorway into the room that served as an armory of sorts.

"What are you doing?" Sharpnose asked from behind me.

"Stocking up," I answered as I shoved several pistols into my belt and slung a pair of rifles over my shoulder. I took my new Greener double barrel shotgun in my free hand for good measure.

"I don't think those will help us much."

"Probably not, but they make me feel better."

"Is that dynamite?" Sharpnose asked, his eyes resting in a corner of the room.

"It is. Gonna' need it to cave in the mine."

"Is it wise to keep something so dangerous in your home?"

"Well, we're going to burn it down, anyway, so what does it matter?" I asked rhetorically, and then I adopted what I believed to be a sloppy, lopsided smile. "Besides, no one ever accused we white men of being wise."

"Yes, that is true," Sharpnose agreed. It was hard to see by the candlelight, but I think he too smiled at my self-denigrating jest. I had known William Sharpnose for far less time than many of my other acquaintances, especially back home in Omaha, but I found that I trusted and liked him easily.

I passed him to head back outside to my horses and wagon, placing my firearms on the driver's seat. I returned inside for four-gallon barrel of lamp oil, matches and as much ammunition as we could carry.

"Now," I said with a pause, organizing my thoughts and my plan, such as it was, "we need to make sure the town is clear. We'll go door to door, calling out for anyone who is hiding indoors. They have to leave. If they don't have a horse, they can wait here, and I'll take them back to Santa Fe. We'll fire each building as we go. As dry as it has been, should be easy. A little oil doused on a wall oughta' do the trick. We'll start at the far end of town and make our way back this way."

Sharpnose nodded and said, "If we find anyone dead in the streets, we must burn them also."

"Right, and one last thing – we know Pops and Reverend Spratley are… about. We have to be sure they burn with the town. By God, I hope we find them indoors and can just burn the town down around them."

We started toward town on foot, leaving our horses hitched up behind us. I was afraid that the horses may be spooked enough as it was, and I feared how they might react to a run in with a walking, talking corpse. Besides, we were about to fire the entire town around us, and I had no desire to be reliant on a skittish animal at such a time.

I stopped just inside the town limits, holding my hand out toward Sharpnose to tell him to do the same. We approached the church, the only sign of activity in Boulder Spring, and chills ran up my spine from it. The doors were open now and a sickly, flickering yellow light spilled out from within. With no small degree of apprehension, I slowly plodded toward it, and as we neared it, I heard a voice straight from Hell raised in some sort of ecstasy.

We dared to look inside, and I was nearly blinded by the illumination of hundreds, perhaps thousands of lit candles, surely every candle in town. The pews were completely full, every available seat taken by townsfolk, maybe as many as two hundred men, women and even children. None of them moved at all. Though I generally avoided church, I had seen any number of sermons over my years, and never did a full congregation sit completely still while a quality preacher ranted on. At the least, there would be head nods, and depending on the denomination, one may see as much as persons standing and shouting. This service was still as the grave, except for the preacher, and as I looked, I saw appendages twisted the wrong way, necks that slouched so much they must have been broken and terrible wounds caused by an edged blade.

My eyes found Sam at the end of one of the pews, his eyes wide open in sudden alarm, though there was no life in them either. It almost felt like a dream, or rather an horrific nightmare, and I hadn't realized that I actually stepped foot into the church, slowly traversing the middle aisle. The church had gone silent, excepting the cry of a babe from somewhere amongst the dead in those pews. I stopped when I realized that was the only sound, that I no longer heard the rasping screams of a Hell-preacher.

"Welcome, Mr. Landis. I knew that you would find yourself in my place of worship eventually," said a twisted voice from ahead of me. I tore my eyes away from Sam's dead face and looked up the aisle toward the altar and pulpit. The twisted, possessed visage of Michael Spratley leered back at me, his slit throat a disturbing second smile below the vicious grin of his razor widened mouth. His corpse wore the same clothes he had when Pops had made that cut, stained almost wholly with the reverend's blood.

I averted my gaze from Spratley, as I couldn't stand the look of him. With both the bisection of his mouth and that I knew he was dead, his animated corpse reminded me of some demonic marionette. He chuckled at my obvious disgust, and it was a terrifying, almost whistling sound as the air escaped his sliced neck as well as his mouth. I found I could focus on the sound of the crying baby, but I couldn't locate the child in the dead congregation. I thought it came from the far end of a pew to my right, and I began to move that direction.

"Touch that mewling infant, and both of you will join the flock," he rasped, and he stepped from behind the altar menacingly. I eased backward, careful not to trip over my own feet. I closed the church doors once I cleared the threshold, and they nearly muffled his infernal laughter.

"Mr. Landis?" Sharpnose asked after me, placing a hand on my shoulder.

"Let's get to work," I said and brushed past the Apache.

We moved quickly through the night, checking for signs of life in every building – homes, businesses and even outhouses before setting them ablaze. The recent dry spell, combined with a slight, warm breeze aided us in this endeavor, fanning the flames as it were. Sharpnose and I worked well together; we moved quickly with me checking the next edifice as he lit the last one I declared empty. We found no one as we worked, and I began to mentally count both the number of people I remember seeing on the road to Santa Fe and those who were dead in Spratley's church. I concluded that there was likely no one left, which made our task easier even though the pitiful crying of a lone babe still rang in my ears. Before long, most of the town burned, no doubt lighting up the night like a beacon for wayward travelers, and I imagined it could be seen as far as Santa Fe. I hoped it would draw no one's attention.

Coming out of our apothecary, I paused for a moment to stand on its porch as I stared at the next building in line. It wasn't so much in any form of consideration, but rather I found myself somewhat frozen with the memory of what had happened inside and out of Pop's barbershop. Sharpnose joined me, breaking my reverie. He seemed about to speak, and I hastily held my finger up to my lips. Understanding came over his face when his eyes fell on the red, white, and blue striped pole in front of our next victim.

I left Sharpnose to set fire to the apothecary, while I approached the barbershop, taking care to step as quietly as I possibly could. Pops always kept a few chairs in front of his shop, and these were of course vacant. I cautiously, quietly tread the steps to his closed front door, though one groaned slightly in protest, causing me to freeze for a moment. Something tugged backward at my sleeve, and a sudden image of Pop's blade wielding visage came to mind. I jumped several feet in the air and landed with the thud of my boot soles on wood, fumbling to draw my pistol. I met Sharpnose's gaze as he pulled his hand back from me.

"Out of matches," he whispered. I smiled sheepishly, partially for my terrified reaction, but also for the idiocy of needing matches at all. Once the first fire had been lit, a few simple torches would have surely sufficed. I reached into my jacket pocket, produced a small box and tossed it to him.

All opportunities at stealth now lost, he nodded and turned away, leaving me to brave whatever I found in Pops' shop. I could see nothing through the windows, as very little light filtered in through them from either the moon or our growing conflagrations. I think I held my breath while I turned the doorknob. The unlocked door swung open easily with just the smallest hint of a squeal from the hinges. My heels clopped softly with each slow step as I entered, leading with my gun. My eyes adjusted quickly to the lightless room, and I quickly concluded that it was empty of razor carrying corpses.

With a somehow relieved sigh, I turned to leave the shop. Out front, orange light and heat began to permeate the town, and a steady flame began to lap up an external wall of the apothecary. And then I started, my stance going wide as I turned and pointed my pistol in all directions. My Apache companion was gone.

"Sharpnose!?" I called urgently, but with a lowered, almost raspy voice. I moved toward our latest burning creation and called out again, anxiety building in my gut. "Sharpnose! William Sharpnose!"

But no one answered me. I spied something on the ground, as if water were mixed in the dry, dusty dirt. I knelt to investigate, though my recent experience made it almost unnecessary. The sight of blood had become all to common in the last few days, and as I looked, I found quite a bit of it making a macabre trail around the backside of the apothecary.

I stood and followed it, as I was sure I was meant to, with a sick feeling growing exponentially in my stomach. I don't know why I did so, because even as I did it, I was certain both of what I would find and that it meant my inevitable doom. I reached the back corner of the building, and before I turned it, I swallowed with some difficulty, the gulp seeming terribly loud in my ears. A body lay on the ground some six feet away, and I didn't need to look closely to know it was Sharpnose. I approached and stood over him, and even in the dim light, I could see the telltale slash across his throat. Even worse, the poor man had been scalped!

A familiar sound came from behind me, just barely audible over the growing fire of the apothecary –

the low, wheezing laugh I had come to associate with pure evil. I turned quickly and just in time to see Pops blade cut through the air toward me. I stepped backward out of instinct and tripped over Sharpnose's body, and it was probably this lack of awareness that saved my life as the blade passed just over my head. I landed on my ass end and scuttled backward as Pops stepped toward me with no concern for alacrity. I let loose with my Colt, burying round after round into his rotting torso, opening new holes near those I had made in him the other day. He laughed aloud even as the shots pushed him back a few steps.

"You can't hurt me, Landis," he taunted, resuming his slow approach. "Just give in and join us. As the one whom liberated us, you'll have a place of honor among the brethren."

The gunshots combined with his words, gave me a few scant seconds. I gave no reply, except to scramble to my hands and knees, and then my feet as I ran the other way and around the far corner of the now fully aflame apothecary. Coming back around to the storefront on the main thoroughfare, I found the oil barrel Sharpnose had been using, still upright. I twisted and popped out the stopper, which the poor man obviously had the forethought to replace after every use and rocked it from side to side to determine it was still at least half full. Using my pistol, I tried to pry apart the barrel further, hoping to widen the opening by which oil would come out, but I had no success.

My time ran out as Pops' corpse came out of the alley toward me. The flames of the burning buildings outlined his form, absolutely anchoring him in my mind as a minion from Hell itself. "What are you doing?" he amusedly asked, laughing almost maniacally as he approached.

I hefted the barrel as he came close, and I dodged what I'm convinced was an almost half-hearted attack. But it gave me an opening, and I jerked the barrel toward Pops, splashing a small amount of oil on his unclean clothes. He slashed again and missed, though I had no time to douse him as the weight of the barrel began to tire my arms. I timed his next attack perfectly, countering his razor with the wooden barrel itself. The blade sunk into the wood with a *thunk*, and I jerked away as quickly as my arms would allow. Pops' hand slipped off the razor's handle as I did so, and I retreated a few steps with his weapon in my possession.

"Fisticuffs it is, then," Pops said, adopting an almost comical fighting stance.

Dead muscles and sinews are substantially faster than one might think, and I had to work hard to keep my distance whilst trying to douse the corpse with as much oil as possible. He pushed me back into the alley between his shop and apothecary as he threw punches and lunged my way. He overthrew a roundhouse, and I used the opportunity to pour as much oil on him as I could. Unfortunately, I didn't realize the ruse, and as I lifted the barrel over my head, he took ahold of either side of it. I couldn't break his grip on the thing; it was like iron as he brought the barrel down between us. He jabbed it forward, and the barrel struck me in the chest, knocking the wind from me and sending me sprawling.

"Now is the time," Pops said with a tone of finality, and he tossed the barrel somewhere off into the darkness, razor and all. He moved toward me as I staggered to my feet, fighting for breath. I stumbled away while he approached, and I finally stopped, doubled over and leaning on my knees. Pops came to stand perhaps only five feet away, his mangled features obfuscated by darkness and framed by the blaze behind him. "Welcome, Mr. Landis."

Bluffs and feints are key to being an accomplished card player and gambler, as I was prior to coming to Boulder Spring. It is a delicious thing to convince one's opponent to fold when one's hand is weak, but even better, luring one's opponent into a large bet when they cannot possibly win is something else entirely. And just as whatever demon-controlled Pops lured me into overplaying my hand, I now did the same to it.

With all the might I could muster, I took one step toward the corpse, and launched myself sideways into the air. Both of my feet struck the perplexed looking dead man squarely in the chest with all my weight. The force of it knocked him back heavily and into the burning apothecary. The wall must have already grown weak, and with a crashing of breaking lumber, Pops' corpse fell through and into the burning building.

I had neither smelled such an evil scent in my life, nor heard such a vile scream as what came from the flames, and to my horror, a shambling mass lifted itself from the inferno, even as the screams ceased. It somehow found the strength to come out of the fire toward me, though its steps had lost all sure-footedness as the flesh blackened, cracked, split, and began to sizzle and slough off with the flame. I backed away in horror as the muscles and tendons burned next, and as they did, so did the thing lose its powers of movement. Finally, it fell to the ground, and all that was left was a small burning pile of bones.

After regaining my wits, and being absolutely sure Pops was truly dead, I destroyed the chairs in front of the barbershop and used them, strips torn from my own jacket and the remaining oil to make as many torches as I could carry. I proceeded to fire the rest of the town without bothering to check for life in the remaining buildings, adding Sharpnose's body to one of the bonfires. Later I would consider that his people surely had their own burial rites, but at the time I was both numb of thought and set on my course.

At the church, I rounded it once to make sure of what I already knew – that there were no other doors leading from the now accursed temple. I retrieved a heavy rope from my supplies and tied the doors together as tightly as I could by the doorknobs. Then, blocking both the sound of Spratley's voice rasping and lilting its infernal sermon and the incessant crying of the infant child, I circled the building again, pouring oil upon its external walls intermittently. The last circuit I made of the building was to set it aflame.

I stood in front of the church, watching my own devilry. The sermon had stopped, but the cries of the babe, oh those piteous cries, continued to forever make their mark upon my soul. Something began to forcefully beat on the doors, and I heard Spratley's voice demand that they open. The entire building became engulfed, and still he threw himself against those doors. The ropes held for a time, and when they finally gave way, a fiery form burst forth just as the church's roof caved into its consuming fire. With insanely waiving arms, the burning entity made it only perhaps ten feet before it too collapsed to burn.

From my home, I retrieved perhaps a dozen sticks of dynamite and tied them together into a bundle. I wasn't well-versed in the usage of TNT, but I was fairly certain that if I lit the fuse on one stick, it would explode when the fuse burned down to the dynamite itself. I also believed that if one exploded, they would all do the same. I stood outside the mine with my highly explosive bundle, and the calm evening breeze rose to a frightening gale, causing my final remaining torch to flicker wildly. To this day, I swear the forceful wind came from the mine itself.

"I don't know which devil you are or from whence you came," I said to the mine. "I may not be able to kill you, but be sure you'll never be found again."

I dropped to my knees and lay the torch on the ground next to me. I had a few matches left, and I used these to spark the fuse. It took several tries as the gale somehow found a way to extinguish my matches, but finally, after huddling over the tiny flames and cupping them protectively, I finally managed to catch the fuse. I tossed the dynamite down the mine in an underhand motion, hoping the momentum would cause it to roll well into the Earth. I took up my torch and ran from the mine's mouth as fast as my feet could carry me.

A great tremor knocked me to the ground as the dynamite exploded, blasting air, dust, and debris out of the mine before it. I turned over to watch as the very hills beyond my mine seemed to heave and then fall into themselves as the mine's supports collapsed as did, I hope, the cave of gold itself. I tried to regain my feet, but the ground shook so that it was impossible. After what felt like an eternity, but I expect was but a few minutes, the rumbling of the ground ceased. Upon inspection, the mine's entrance still existed, though it was nothing but earth and rock just a few feet inside. The night was calm and still, no wind disturbing the land's tall grasses and weeds.

Before leaving Boulder Spring, I retrieved from my house any records of value as well as large sums of money, both of which were kept in a large safe Tom had purchased in Santa Fe. I set fire to the house as well before climbing atop the wagon and driving away.

Securing ownership of all the property in Boulder Spring was easy and only a matter of time. No one wanted anything to do with the place after such wild rumors circulated through the territory.

I continued west and one day found myself in San Francisco. The climate was much to my liking, and I settled down with a large home and all the fine trappings I could afford, which were great and many for one of my wealth. Over the years, I became a bit of a hermit, rarely choosing to leave my estate. Occasionally out in the city, I would see a hooded beggar or some other miscreant, and I couldn't help but wonder if some burned mass of flesh hid under those rags, just awaiting its chance at revenge.

I was nearly forty before I married, not for lack of prospects. Such wealth affords plenty of options in those regards. I merely hadn't felt the need until I realized that my age advanced, and I would need someone to carry on my legacy. You see, every few years I paid for surveyors to return to the land upon which that once accursed town was built, just to be sure that no one had encroached upon the land. At least, that was my apparent motivation. Truly, I just need to be sure that nothing had been, or ever would be, disturbed.

To that end, I needed an heir, and my wife – a lovely young woman named Meredith – did in fact provide me a son. William Samuel Landis, named after the two of the best men I had ever known, was our only child, for I could not bear having another. For the first two or three years of his life, I was stranger to him, having sequestered myself in a separate wing of the house. His cries, the normal cries of a newborn infant, threatened to tear my mind asunder with the memory of that night so long ago. They reopened a deep wound in my psyche that I hadn't known existed, a terrible penance for what I had done, what I had to do in the summer of 1883.

Hunted

Thyss awoke at the sudden pressure forced over her mouth, a hand as strong as iron that kept her from screaming and also pinched her nose shut to obstruct the airflow into her lungs. Her eyes bulged momentarily in panic at the lack of breath, but she calmed herself quickly to assess her suddenly treacherous situation. There was little light by which to see, only that of a half-moon and stars mostly obscured by huge leafy plants, but two shadowy forms hovered over her. One was clearly that of a man with short shorn hair, and it was his hand clamped down upon her mouth. The other, a woman from both the smaller size and outline of other assets, seemed to have her knee on Thyss' chest. She also held something near Thyss' face, that she could not see, but Thyss felt the cold edge of a blade at her throat.

"You should be more careful, Your Highness," the man said in Dulkur's lower tongue, and he eased the pressure around her nose just a bit to allow her to breathe more easily.

Thyss' eyes narrowed dangerously as they began to adjust to the faint, silvery moonlight. The black shapes now had faces, but they still lacked definition. However, she did not need to see details in order to set Hykan's fires to work on these two.

"I wouldn't," said the woman, her voice the dulcet tones of a breathy lover. "You may get him before I slit your throat. By the hells, you might even get me, but the six men over there where you cannot see will hack you to bits for it. We pay them well for loyalty. And yes, we've already taken your sword."

"You see, Your Highness," the man continued as his round features began to take form, "there are those of us who take notice when one such as yourself appears alone in a common shithole tavern. Actually, everyone notices, but when you left alone, we realized we had an opportunity. Striking out alone across this jungle is dangerous to be sure." He glanced toward his partner and asked, "Can you tell whom she serves?"

"She is blessed by Hykan."

"Perfect! A fire witch!" he exclaimed. "There is a king on the other side of this jungle who will pay us handsomely to add this whore to his harem. I am going to uncover your mouth now to bind your wrists. Please don't try anything stupid."

The hand left her mouth, and Thyss spat as it retreated, receiving a mocking laugh in response. He grabbed each of her wrists in vise-like grips to bring them together. She resisted slightly, just enough to keep it from being too easy for him as he wrapped a leather cord painfully tight around her wrists.

"Now, none of your fire tricks, witch, or this will go very badly for you," he commanded as he tied the cord off. "And I promise you'll never work out of that. I've tied up more people than you've ever known."

"I am no witch, you shit!" Thyss lashed out. "I am Chosen by Hykan."

"I know, I'm counting on it," he nodded, and as he turned to walk away, he said, "Bring her."

"Come on," the woman said, helping Thyss to her feet by pulling on the bonds. Thyss refused at first, and they cut deeply into her wrists. The woman kneeled next to her and spoke quietly, "Look, make this easy on me. I know what you're thinking. You're going to burn your way through us, kill us all and escape. That's not going to happen. So, do you want to make this easier or harder?"

Thyss grudgingly nodded, hearing the wisdom in the woman's words despite the desire to kill and maim her way out of the situation. She knew the time would come, and she would have to act quickly. But the time was not now, and she allowed herself to be helped to her feet. The stranger was strong, easily Thyss' physical match. As they stood, a beam of moonlight struck the woman's face, and Thyss recognized the pretty features of the mixed Dulkurian woman she had seen gambling in the tavern that evening.

"That's better, thank you," she said. "You've nothing to worry about from us. You're a commodity to Lahn, and damaged goods bring less gold."

"I'll be no one's slave whore," Thyss hissed, her defiance beginning to wax again.

"Of course, you won't," she replied, "but you can't fight us either. We really don't want to kill you, but Lahn won't put up with any trouble from you either. We're going to sell you to King Chofir, and then you can escape all you want. By the hells if you play the game right, maybe we can even cut you in and do it to some other king somewhere else or maybe a rich merchant. I'm Ulinae. What's your name?"

"Go burn in your hells, bitch."

"Have it your way," Ulinae replied with a shrug.

"What in the blazes is taking so long?!" Lahn called from some twenty paces away, deeper into the jungle.

Ulinae pushed a large leafy plant out of the way as she led Thyss in the direction he had gone, led her toward his voice. Such foliage was everywhere to be seen at every level one looked, both close to the ground and far above, and all manners of vines, some with leaves and some without, hung down from above to create draperies of green that, often, one had to cut through. Brightly colored flowers were everywhere, smelling sweetly and adorning plants. A young child, knowing no better, may easily run to such a flower only to find it to be most poisonous or containing an imminently dangerous denizen.

When she'd decided to penetrate the jungle, heading east, Thyss steered clear of these as well as the numerous insects and arachnids she'd seen. She had no real knowledge which were venomous and which were not, but she had heard stories all of her twenty-three years of swarms of ants that could take down a rhino, as well as brightly colored spiders smaller than a fingernail that could nearly instantly kill a man with a single bite. She had also seen any number of frighteningly weird bugs with hundreds of segments and thousands of legs, and these she actively avoided as well. The larger creatures of the jungle seemed intent to ignore her, though she heard them moving about through the dense plants and foliage. She crossed paths with one enormous snake that was easily twice as long as a man was tall. Thyss gave the serpent a wide berth only to nearly stumble over a great cat, so black that it almost appeared purple. She had less interest in facing this wonderful foe, and it seemed the feline felt the same as it looked away in a most apathetic fashion.

Thyss had wondered how one was to find a place to rest in such a jungle, someplace safe from all of its flora and fauna. When she finally found a tiny clearing that seemed mostly bereft of anything living upon which to lay a thick wool blanket, she never expected men to be the greatest threat.

A few dozen feet into the thick of it, they came out into a small clearing that somehow Thyss had completely missed in her own explorations. The jungle seemed to be able to hide almost anything within a few feet of her, and she would never see it. A patch of roughly circular ground about ten feet across greeted them. It was completely bare of any plants of any kind, and it looked as if a fire had raged in just that particular spot, clearing it of anything living. Seven men stood here, all of them armed, including the one she already knew to me Lahn, who wore her rather plain scimitar on his belt along with his own. Two of the other men carried flickering torches, the flames providing a rather frenetic orange light in contrast to the constant silvery blue of the moon.

Just like Ulinae, Lahn also looked to be of mixed Dulkurian blood. He had the light brown skin that often arose when those of Thyss' own class mated with the dark brown skinned peoples of the lower villages. He was ugly to look upon, with exaggerated round nose, lips and chin, and the beautiful, almond shaped eyes much like Thyss' appeared completely out of place with irises so dark brown as to be almost black. He wore an angry expression, one of vexed exasperation. The other six men were all darker skinned Dulkurians, tall and well-muscled much like the palace guards her father had employed when she was young. They wore their steel with quiet confidence, leaving her no doubt as to their competence as killers.

"I'm sorry, love," Ulinae cooed as she turned Thyss over to two of the henchmen. She fingered the edge of her curved dagger for just a moment before sheathing it at her waist. She hung her arms about Lahn's neck and said sweetly, "I had to... coax her a bit."

"Get off me, witch," Lahn replied, shrugging her arms off of him, "This is neither the time, nor the place."

"Hopefully your attitude will change later," she replied to the leers of their hired muscle.

Lahn stepped over to stand before Thyss, looking her over thoroughly before saying, "Allow me to explain fully the situation you've found yourself in. You belong to me now. You're a product, a good to be traded for gold, and quite a lot of gold at that, if Ulinae is to be believed. As much as a slut as she can be, she's a damn fine healer and a good seer, which is perfect for my line of work. I fully intend to sell you, and you're simply worth more in an undamaged condition. I will protect you, and I will feed you. But don't you think I will tolerate a moment's bother from you. I know you don't need a sword to hurt or maybe even kill someone. The moment you use your fire witch powers on me or my men, your head will be rolling away from your neck. If you think you can escape, I'll just catch you. I'm the best tracker in Dulkur, and I know jungles. I already know you don't. The first time you escape, I'll just bring you back. The second time, I'll have my way with you, allow my men to do the same and then cut you open from your throat to your womanhood. Am I quite clear?"

Thyss said nothing, nor had she any intention to do so. She was a princess, a sorceress of Hykan, and this half-breed deserved no reply or validation of anything he said. She merely stood stone faced, her jaw clamped tightly shut and stared back at him with the fires of hatred burning in her pupils. She would kill this man, soon, but for now he had control of the situation. She pushed her ire downward to her gut where it could fester, but not erupt.

"I'll take your silence for assent," Lahn concluded. He then announced, "We will camp here for the night and head east tomorrow."

"This jungle has many legends," Ulinae said softly. "Should we not leave it and skirt the edge?"

"No. It will take three times as long, and we will be close to the hot sands of the Sha'qa Desert. We don't have the supplies for either. The eight of us can handle anything we may come across. You men – take shifts watching the camp tonight, two at a time. Stay alert. Keep an eye on our… guest and wake me at the first sign of any trouble."

"I hope you're right," Ulinae sighed, worry in her eyes.

Thyss slept poorly that night. Her predicament preoccupied all her thoughts as she mulled over the situation time and again only to come back to the same conclusion. Without a sword, she simply didn't have the strength to fight all eight of them at once; one of them would cut her down, and then there was Ulinae. What manner of witch was she? These thoughts caused her to toss and turn most of the night, and when she finally began to doze, the raucous sounds of the jungle – the growls of huge cats, calls of brightly feathered birds, gibberings of monkeys and the crashes of unknown things through the plants – which had not bothered her at all in her previous repose now kept her conscious mind racing. Her wrists bound together in front of her helped none. She felt as if she had only slept a few minutes when Ulinae lightly shook her awake.

"Quickly, now. We breakfast, and then we're on the move. You may relieve yourself over there," she said with a point at one edge of the clearing.

The going was slow as they headed toward the rising sun she could only just barely make out through the vast, leafy canopy overhead. Thyss had been in jungles before, but never one so dense as to require Lahn and two of his men to stand in a united front against the wet greenery, hacking their way through as efficiently as they could manage. She nearly snarled when she realized that he used her scimitar for the work rather than his own sword, but there was little she could do about it from her place next to Ulinae and surrounded by his other four mercenaries. At a leisurely pace on open ground, Thyss would be able to cover three, maybe even four miles over the course of an hour, but here she had no sense as to their pace except that it was slow. Every part of the place looked much like the last, and even the sections they just hacked through seemed to close and reform behind them, all adding to a sense of hopeless lack of progress. Still, they trudged, and at least the creatures that called the place home seemed to have no interest in impeding such a large group, indicating some degree of familiarity with mankind and its capabilities.

Eventually, Lahn called a stop to rest, as he was apparently unable to continue swinging Thyss' blade, and when they continued, he placed three of his fresh men to clear the way while he and the others escorted her.

"I don't understand why you can't just use some of your liquid fire to make this easier," Lahn mused.

"I have very little of it left," Ulinae replied, "and this place doesn't have the ingredients to make more. You could let the princess here help."

Lahn chuckled sardonically. "She would just as soon try to burn us all instead of the jungle."

The corners of Thyss' mouth upturned slightly at the thought, and she thought it ironic that Ulinae and Lahn both appeared to share the grim smile. The three of them looked almost like a trio of old friends enjoying each other's company rather than captive and captors. If it weren't for their intention to enslave her and profit from it, she might have even come to like this pair. Maybe she wouldn't kill them both after all, but instead just scar them terribly.

Eventually they stopped for the evening. The jungle's gloom, omnipresent due to the trees overhead with their giant green leaves almost entirely blocking the sun's rays, darkened considerably, indicating that full on night would soon be upon them. They hadn't found a reasonable campsite, so Lahn set his men to creating one, clearing away the foliage from a circle about the same size as the previous night's. With their vegetative habitats removed, most of the insects and other tiny creatures quickly vacated the area.

By the time it was done, exhaustion claimed them all. One of Lahn's men had not participated in the clearing of the path, so he was given the first watch for the evening while Lahn and the others rested sore and tired limbs. Thyss thought that this might be her best opportunity to effect escape, but she was no less tired than the others. The jungle terrain was uneven and difficult and caused more than one turned ankle amongst their group. Also, it surprised Thyss how much free hands and swinging arms aided with one's balance, and her hands bound in front of her required substantial extra care while she walked. As such, her legs and feet were just as tired and sore as everyone else's. In no immediate danger, she determined it would be best to stay with her abductors for now.

The next day brought more of the same. They slowly stepped their way through ever thickening growth, hacking and cutting their way through whatever they could to continue their easterly progress. Even with protection from the blazing sun, the distortion of heat played with one's sight, and the air was like steam when Thyss breathed. The group's existence turned completely miserable as they soaked their clothes with sweat and the air's moisture. They found they had to stop to rest more often. The following day, the heat grew completely unbearable as the sun reached its zenith, and Lahn called for a stop.

"We'll halt here and rest," he said.

The air continued to grow hotter over the next hour, and they all settled onto the cool ground, content to perform as little activity as possible. Ulinae sat to one side, busying herself with all manners of herbs, roots, vials, and liquids that she pulled from uncounted pockets and holds of her plain, white tunic. Three of the guards sat and spoke in hushed tones, while Lahn simply leaned against the tree and watched them all. Thyss lay on her stomach and stretched out, laying her face on her hands as a sort of pillow in an attempt to conserve her strength.

One of the guards stood from his place and stepped to squat down next to Lahn. The largest of them all, he was nearly a giant at halfway between six and seven feet tall, and he had one of the most muscled bodies Thyss had ever seen. She opened one eye to look at the two as they conversed quietly.

"How long will we stay here?" the guard asked, and his voice rumbled deeply like the greatest of war drums.

"We'll continue after the sun starts its way down again. It'll be cooler then, and it may be easier to continue into the night than during the middle of the day."

"The animals are more active at night," the huge man said.

"Perhaps, but there are nine of us. We'll be cautious," Lahn nearly agreed, and then he adopted a sly smile. "You're not afraid, are you, Huma? Surely not you."

"I do not like this place," Huma replied, "It unnerves me. That town a few days west – those people do not come here. When they must go east, they travel around the jungle."

"Superstitious peasants," Lahn replied dismissively, "Besides, you're more frightening than anything… out…"

Lahn's words trailed off as he suddenly shot to his feet, his eyes searching the jungle as he slowly turned where he stood. Ulinae quickly put her all her ingredients and such away, causing them to disappear into pockets that couldn't even be seen, and all of the guards stood. Hands were on weapons as all stayed perfectly still with their eyes on Lahn. Thyss sat upright, her legs crossed, as she too watched him with interest.

"What is it?" Huma whispered, and even his low tone seemed to make the earth rumble.

"Do you hear that?" Lahn almost whispered back.

"I hear nothing."

"Nothing," Lahn repeated in a hushed tone.

Thyss' eyes widened as she began to understand the full meaning of the word. She tilted her head just barely to the left while turning her face to the right, as if presenting her left ear to the jungle would better help her hear what was not there. Gone were the sounds of all the emerald jungle's fauna. No animals moved about in the brush, neither large nor small. The ever-present voices of monkeys and their conversation had died in the trees above. Even the squawks of birds and the quiet but constant rustling of insects had completely vanished. For all its life, the jungle was now as silent as a tomb.

The most ear piercing of screams split the air, exploding through jungle like the sudden eruption of one of Dulkur's many volcanoes. Thyss had never heard anything like it, and its entirely unexpected magnitude forced her to reflexively cover her ears, an action she found impossible with her hands still bound together. All of the others did the same, but it wasn't just the pure volume of the scream which demanded that it be drowned out from one's hearing. It was like the greatest, most powerful war cry from the strongest giant ever in history had combined with the roar of a male lion, confident and powerful at the head of his pride, but with the added hiss of one of the five-foot-long lizards of southern Dulkur.

The cry lasted a mere second, and as it ended, Thyss heard the tortured cries of another voice, some animal that sounded as if it were being ripped apart. The men heard it too and immediately formed a circle with weapons drawn, with Thyss and Ulinae in the middle of the ring. The second voice from the jungle faded away, leaving them again in dead silence.

"Sword," Thyss said, "Give me my sword."

"Not a chance, Your Highness," Lahn replied.

"Gods damn you, give me my sword."

"Shut up," Lahn snapped, and Thyss very nearly set the man aflame at that moment. It was only the obvious and dire danger that she was quite literally in the middle of that spared his life.

Everyone stood so completely still, that a random passerby might have thought them to be the most lifelike statues ever created, a true masterpiece of art. Thyss strained to hear any sound, any indication of what creature waited for them in the foliage beyond what they could see, but only the rapid thumping of her heart filled her ears. She doubted she would have heard anything over it, even another frightful scream. They stood for several minutes, or perhaps it was hours, and the sounds of the jungle suddenly returned as if they had never been absent.

"We should leave, now," Huma rumbled.

"We're almost halfway to King Chofir. We're not turning back now. Besides, how will those villagers back there respond when we walk into their town with her as a captive?" Lahn asked pointing his own scimitar toward Thyss. "No, I'm not risking it. Whatever it was, it's gone now."

"I have never heard such a thing," Ulinae breathed, and Thyss noted the witch shivered despite the oppressively thick heat.

"By the hells," Lahn sighed, "it was just a lion, or maybe a tiger, taking a kill. Nothing we cannot handle."

"You're a fool," Thyss blurted with little thought as to the way her captor might react. Lahn's face turned cold and hard, but Thyss spoke her mind anyway, "I grew up with lions. No lion made such a cry and not so loudly. That was something I have never heard before."

"You're barely off your mother's tit," Lahn sneered.

"She is right," Huma boomed his agreement to the nods of the other men.

"Superstitious low people," Lahn spat, bringing an angry grimace to Huma's face. Thyss was certain he was not a man she wanted to anger.

"Give me my sword," Thyss demanded again.

"Absolutely not. Even if I did, I would need to cut your bonds for you to use it, and I'm not about to do that. There are seven sword arms here already. One more is not going to matter, and Your Highness, I do believe you should have some sort of magick to protect yourself, anyway. So, if I am wrong on that account, I'll consider giving you your sword. Otherwise, shut your gods damned mouth before I force it shut with a leather strap.

"Now, if you're all done," Lahn sighed, "I will take Huma with me. I'll see what I can find. I'm sure I'll find tracks of a large animal and the remains of a kill. Then we can continue on our way. Come, Huma."

Lahn, with a stealth that the numerous jungle plants should not have allowed, strode cautiously away from the group, the enormous Huma practically crashing through the growth behind him. They had gone no more than ten paces before the greenery seemed to swallow them entirely, and they were gone. The remaining men watched all around them anxiously, with a nervousness born of the sense of life and death situations, though Thyss found solace in the fact that the other creatures of the jungle had resumed their noises.

"What is your name?" Ulinae asked, bringing Thyss' attention back to her. The witch was most definitely of a mixed breed of High and Low Dulkurians, something forbidden that happened all too often, and in sharp contrast to her compatriot, she had seemed to pull the most beautiful features from her parents.

"Thyss."

Ulinae's dagger was unsheathed and in her hand, its curved point dangerously close to flesh. Thyss started at the blade, nearly following her instincts to burn, but something about the woman's pose gave her pause. Why would Ulinae ask her name if she only meant to kill her?

"Thyss, I don't know what is out there, but I fear no animal. It's something else, something ancient, I feel. I learned long ago to follow my feelings, as they tend to come to fruition. I feel we will need your hands free before this is over."

In a swift motion, Ulinae brought the blade down, severing the leather cord wrapped around Thyss' wrists. As it fell to the ground, Thyss rubbed at each wrist in turn where the leather had rubbed the flesh an angry red and had only just barely begun to cut into it.

"Thank you," Thyss said.

"Don't make me regret it," she replied, sheathing the dagger again. Then she motioned at Thyss' wrists, "I can give you a salve for those, if you like."

"It's not so bad," Thyss dismissed the offer, unwilling to show weakness, and dropped her hands to her sides.

After a while, they grew bored as the anxiety eroded away by the lack of any further occurrences, and the air had begun to cool somewhat. The men maintained their circle around Thyss and Ulinae, but it had relaxed with boredom. One of the guards squatted, and two even sat down completely as the wait continued. The sounds of movement behind her caused Thyss to turn quickly to find Lahn and Huma returning out of the jungle's depths.

"What did you find?" Ulinae called to them.

"Nothing really," Lahn replied with a moment of raised eyebrows, but the hard grimace on Huma's face made her doubt the veracity of his statement. He asked with a motion toward Thyss, "What in the blazes is this?"

Ulinae answered simply, "I made a choice."

"You made a bad one. Bind her again. Now."

"You do not command me, lover. Remember? We're partners. She has nowhere to go, and somehow, I think Thyss isn't very interested in leaving our company right now."

"Then, I'll do it myself," Lahn replied coldly. He moved toward Thyss, another leather cord suddenly produced from nowhere apparent.

"No," Ulinae said, stepping between them. "We need her. We have far more to fear from what's out there."

"There's *nothing* out there!" Lahn shouted, spittle flying in his outburst. He turned to Huma, "What did you see?"

Huma sighed as he looked away for a moment before grudgingly admitting, "Not much. What was left of a wild boar, I think. A big one. Torn apart."

"That's it! A fucking pig," said Lahn, his head bobbing in feverish agreement.

"You found tracks," said Huma from behind him. "Big ones."

Lahn shot a hard, annoyed look toward the warrior, one that promised a price to be paid later. "Yes, tracks," he agreed, "we already knew it was something big, like a lion or tiger."

"No cat has ever made that sound," Thyss disagreed.

"Maybe not. A rhinoceros then."

Ulinae spoke, "I've seen rhinoceros on the savannahs south of here. They do not live in places such as these. Even if it were, I've never heard a rhinoceros make such a sound, and it couldn't have possibly come and gone so silently. Whatever it is out there, we never heard it until it attacked, and it was gone just as quietly."

"*D'kinde*," said one of the guards under his breath.

"No, absolutely not," Lahn responded, seeing the fear growing wide in Ulinae's eyes. "There's no such thing. They don't exist."

"Lahn..." Ulinae began, but he cut her off.

"No, they're just some legend that you low people created to keep your children from running into the jungles by themselves," Lahn said, shaking his head back and forth emphatically. "It's just an animal, and it has no interest in us or it would have come after us already. Either way, we're only a few days from being out of the jungle. We just need to keep going."

Despite their fears and regardless of their driving motives, none would argue the soundness of Lahn's statement, and with the day beginning to cool, they made good time cutting swathes through the foliage. Every slight breeze causing the motion of a leaf and every sound beyond their expectations of normality caused them to look over shoulders or even draw weapons. Thyss found it to be a nerve-wracking business, but it kept them moving quickly.

"Was it *D'kinde?*," Ulinae asked Huma quietly at one point when the man's turn to clear had ended and he sauntered back to the others.

"I saw nothing," Huma tried to whisper back, but his voice was so deep and strong that everyone surely heard it, "except…"

"Except what?" Ulinae pressed.

"The boar was not killed for meat. Much of it was still there. It was something else. It smelled of… pleasure. I… don't wish to speak anymore of it."

They continued until the darkness made it too dangerous to swing blades about each other, and then Thyss lit torches for them. The light was not easy to work by, throwing strange shapes and shadows about them as it flickered yellow and orange, but they made progress. None wanted to stop for the night despite exhaustion, the need to escape this place pushing them onward. It was only when thunder sounded far above and torrential rains came to put out their torches that they stopped. Even Thyss' magical fire could not burn for long in the rain, and they did their best to set up a camp. Though, none slept very long or very deeply.

At some point the rain stopped and even those left to stand watch drifted into a doze when all were awakened by a shout from the middle of their makeshift camp. Warriors jumped to their feet, immediately awake with swords drawn, to find that the pained outcry had come from Lahn himself. Thyss watched as he brought the blade of his scimitar down upon a red and black snake whose head seemed attached to the man's leg. Ulinae was immediately upon him to dislodge the snake's mouth and fangs from his thigh, and she closely inspected the blood red markings that looked like four skulls connected at the cranium as the chins pointed away like the points of a compass rose.

"Damn," she whispered.

"Is it?" he asked, not finishing the question.

"Very, and I can't stop it with what I have." She reached into a pouch and produced a tiny wooden box. She slid open one side and looked upon its contents with dismay. "Damn," she said again. She pressed a brightly colored blue and red flower petal into his hand. "Chew this. It won't stop the poison, but it will help the pain."

"I hate this jungle," Lahn replied sullenly as he did what he was told.

Ulinae stood and announced to the group, "Within an hour, he will be in terrible pain. I can combat the venom, but we need to make it to a town or village. Lahn can't walk. That was my last kemala petal. It will help his pain, but we need to find more to help him rest more easily. We'll carry him out."

"Kemala?" Thyss asked.

"So much you Highs know about the magicks of the gods that you know so little of the magicks of the world," Ulinae replied. "They are not plentiful, but there is a jungle orchid whose flowers start scarlet when they bloom and turn to blue from the center out. When the blue has consumed about half of the flower, a single petal will relieve pain if eaten. Two will put someone into a deep sleep, but that is all that can be eaten safely. Eat many, and you will stay asleep until your body simply starves to death."

His scimitar still drawn, Huma pointed it at several of his fellow mercenaries and said with an air that demanded no discussion, "You three, you know what she needs, yes? Go out there, try to find the flowers and bring them back. Stay close to each other, and don't go beyond earshot."

The men nodded, glanced at each other meaningfully and began to hack their way into the jungle, disappearing quickly. The gloom began to lift a bit as the sun had most certainly cleared the horizon, and after the previous night's rain, the day promised to be less hot. Although, the rain had certainly added even more vapor to the air, giving the entire jungle an almost steamy aspect.

"By the gods," Lahn moaned, "it burns. Huma, take the leg off and let us continue."

"It won't work, lover," Ulinae admonished. "The venom is in your blood, all through your body. They'll be back soon, and then you can rest. We'll be out of here shortly."

Thyss watched all this and almost felt as if she dreamed. It was like a play that had been scripted and put on just for her enjoyment, but she received none from it, for she was in the middle of this drama the end of which she both anticipated and feared. She eyed her plain, steel scimitar and longed to feel it in her hand. Simply having a weapon made most persons feel much more confident, whether one knew how to use it or not, and she was no different. Except that Thyss did know how to use her sword. She sighed and crossed her legs as she sat to wait.

"Maybe I should leave," she mused aloud.

"You're not going anywhere," Lahn called.

"I don't think you can stop me."

"No, he can't," Ulinae agree, "and I won't. So, if that's what you want, you can go."

"My sword," Thyss demanded, and then the jungle fell suddenly silent. She whispered, "By the gods."

"*D'kinde*," whispered one of the other men whose name Thyss didn't know, and all eyes were again on the jungle around them.

A voice called out from the growth to the west. It could have been ten or a hundred paces away, as the jungle seemed to have a way of distorting such things. It asked, "Huma? We have flowers!"

"We're here," Huma shouted back, and his hand balled into a massive fist to pump the air in victory.

"Are you mad?" Thyss hissed at the huge warrior. "You'll give us away."

"Lahn, tell them," Huma said to the prone man, who turned his face away from them.

"I tracked it long before we found the boar. It..." Lahn's voice trailed off as if he had no desire to finish his thought.

"Tell them," Huma commanded, and even Thyss started a bit at the man's forcefulness.

Lahn turned his face back to Thyss and the rest as he said, "It circled us, over and over and over, at least four times before it killed the boar. It didn't even try to hide its tracks until the boar was dead, and then it just disappeared."

"What is it?" Thyss asked.

"I don't know," he replied, and he turned his face away from them again.

A shout came from the east, causing all to look that way into the deep green. It was the voice of a man to be sure, but it was also a cry of alarm, of warning. Two other voices joined it for an instant before the horrible howl, the high-pitched scream of an unseen death overpowered them all. Huma made to leap into the jungle, to charge headlong into battle, but he was suddenly stayed by Ulinae's gentle hand on his massive bicep. Within moments, the cries ended, and silence again reigned.

"Too late," Ulinae said somberly, "*D'kinde* took them already."

"By the Gods, what is *D'kinde*?" Thyss asked.

"By the Gods is right, for They are to blame for *D'kinde*," Ulinae nodded. "Long before we became beloved of the Gods, they created other creatures, abominations that they cast from their sight only to become horrors to men."

"That means nothing!" Thyss almost screamed. "What is it?!"

"A creature born of man and dragon. It uses the jungle to hide itself, to hide the wicked intent of jealous men mixed with the raw strength and ferocity of the dragon. Should a man run afoul one, it will hunt him," Ulinae explained softly.

"Why?"

"It wants revenge for its existence, for being abandoned by its creators in favor of us."

"Horseshit," Thyss spat. "Give me my sword."

When no one moved toward the scimitar, which still lay attached to Lahn's belt, Thyss sauntered over to it herself. She didn't bother removing the sheath and buckle from his belt, but instead just drew the blade and turned to leave, her course leading away from the sun in the west behind her.

"Where are you going?" Ulinae asked.

"I'm going to get those flowers."

"Don't," Ulinae spouted, and she ran to stand just in front of Thyss. "It's suicide."

"Well, I don't seem to have a choice. I can't get out of here by myself, and you won't come without him," Thyss replied with a jab of her scimitar toward Lahn, who appeared barely conscious in his soft moaning.

"Be careful," Ulinae whispered, and she leaned forward to place a soft kiss on Thyss' cheek. "May that protect you."

"Bah," Thyss waived her away, and she pointed at her steel as she said, "I rely on this."

"Go with her," Ulinae said to one of the remaining men.

The mercenary neither answered, nor moved before Huma roared at him, "Go, or you'll need not fear *D'kinde*!"

Sullenly, the swordsman followed a few paces behind Thyss as she pushed away plants and pried apart leaves to make her way toward the dead men she expected to find. She quickly realized how exhausting the work of getting to this part of the jungle had been as she began to use her own scimitar to clear some of the more resilient plants that wouldn't bend to her will. She cursed them and the gods for her predicament, and the only reason she didn't burn her way through the plant life was for fear of needing her strength for a more dangerous confrontation.

They couldn't have gone more than a hundred feet from the campsite when Thyss and the warrior stumbled across one of the most gruesome scenes she had ever looked upon in a slight dip in the terrain. She had found the three missing men, or parts of them at least. Entrails had been flung in a wide arc to the left, and two arms and a leg lay strewn about in the depression. A head with no face stared up at her, open mouthed in horror, and the torn open upper half of one man was pinned to a massive tree trunk, two scimitars thrust through his ribs to hold the vile decoration in place. The stench of death permeated the air, and the entire jungle floor was drenched in blood.

"By the Gods," Thyss breathed, and she fought to hold down her gorge, though she hadn't eaten since the previous day.

"Let's go," the warrior said, having come to stand beside her.

"One moment," Thyss replied, as she stepped carefully amongst the gore.

While she had more than once stepped a sandaled foot in mud or even excrement, she didn't know if she could handle having so much human remains on her skin. On the far side of the depression, she spied what she came for – a long green stem apparently cut at its base with five of the flowers Ulinae needed. One had been crushed, but as she picked it up, Thyss was gratified to find four intact.

"Let's go," she said, and she turned to head back the way they had come.

"Thank the g-," was all she heard from him, followed by a disgusting gurgling akin to drowning.

She turned to find something had lifted the warrior over a foot off the ground, and he hung there, blood gushing from both his mouth and a wound in his chest. The blood spattered on something in front of the dying man, that she just couldn't completely see, a thing that was there and yet seemed to blend with the horrific scene about them. Her eyes focused as she blinked once, and she could then make out a forearm, so well-muscled and powerful as to be twice the thickness of Huma's. A terrible hand ended the arm, with powerful claws impaling its prey. The arm attached to a body that was difficult to see, for she couldn't easily tell where it ended and the jungle began, but the spattering of spilled blood helped add definition to the form. It easily stood eight feet tall, counting the head, whose details she could not make out, except for the eyes. Bright and baleful eyes stared back at her, full of eldritch intelligence and hatred, and they froze Thyss in place.

And then that horrible howl broke the silence, the preternatural shriek born of everything that made this thing what it was, and Thyss ran. Wild eyed, she crashed through the plants, sprinting as fast as she could with the flowers in one hand and her scimitar in the other. She could feel the thing following her, storming behind its human prey that dared attempt an escape. Somehow, either for her natural agility or the grace of Hykan, she managed not to trip or lose her footing even once. She burst upon the others, finally, and skidded to a halt on the ground still wet and soft from the rains.

"The flowers!" Ulinae exclaimed, and she took the growth from Thyss to begin peeling the petals, one of which she immediately fed to Lahn.

"Where's –?" Huma began to ask.

But Thyss cut him off, "He's dead. It killed him."

"Then you led it right to us!" accused the other mercenary.

"Did you hear nothing Lahn said?" Huma shouted. "It's known where we are the whole time!"

Thyss stared at the mercenary as he fumed, as Huma's words began to make an impression upon him as her breath began to slow from her feverish run. The man opened his mouth as he began to form his next words, and two great, clawed hands appeared out of the jungle from behind him. One clamped itself around the left side of his neck, driving the claws deep into the flesh, while the other wrapped the right side of his head, tearing skin, ears and eyes from the skull. Just as he began to emit a strangled scream, his entire body lifted from the ground to be pulled into the jungle and out of sight. Nothing remained of him except some blood and his right ear.

Ulinae, tears rolling down her cheeks, placed an open hand on Lahn's forehead and announced, "He's asleep."

Huma slumped forward a bit as he considered who remained alive. "Very well," he said, "we make a run for it. I'll carry Lahn. We run west, back toward the village we all came from. Run as fast as you can, don't stop to see if I am behind you."

"Huma," Thyss began, but a snapping of twigs from a few feet away pulled her attention from what she was about to say.

There it was. The *D'kinde* didn't even attempt to hide itself anymore, stepping toward them ominously, crushing leaves, plants, and insects underfoot. Its reptilian skin shifted slightly with the colors of the jungle, and Thyss understood how if the thing didn't move, she likely wouldn't see it, even if it was only ten feet in front of her. Its razor-sharp claws, each four or five inches long clicked together as its eyes feasted on the four remaining kills.

But Thyss was having none of it. She asked Hykan for strength and raised her arms to the heavens. A pillar of white flame came into being, scorching leaves and branches as it came down to engulf the malevolent thing before them. She felt the heat and the power within Hykan's fire, and she reveled in her strength to face any foe. After a few seconds, the magick dissipated, and the *D'kinde* was completely unharmed. Thyss even thought she saw sick amusement pass through those all too human eyes.

Huma leapt to the attack, bringing his own two-handed scimitar at the beast in great swinging blows, but the *D'kinde* was quick on its feet, easily dodging them. However, the constant onslaught kept the thing from mounting its own assault, and Thyss thought she saw her chance. She rushed in to get her blade into the fray, but as smart as it was strong and quick, the creature saw her coming. It somehow avoided Huma's attack, while deflecting Thyss' sword off claws that were as strong as steel. It ducked Huma's sword again and brought its arm up in a mighty back handed blow. Thyss knew a moment of weightlessness before she impacted some extraordinarily solid object, and her sword caromed somewhere into the foliage. Purple lightning shot through her vision, and then everything turned black for a moment. It cleared just a bit as she lay on the moist ground, small pinpoints of light in the center that slowly grew.

She saw Huma, fighting valiantly, but in that moment of hazy clarity, Thyss realized that he could not beat the *D'kinde*. The warrior knew it, too, as his strokes began to slow. She tried to sit upright, but the motion was too much, and she fell forward onto her chest, her head turned so she could face the scene of slaughter. Huma missed another attack, but he couldn't recover quickly enough, and the creature's claws flashed to slice neatly through the man's forearm. Thyss heaved herself up on her hands and knees, the world spinning crazily, as the point of Huma's huge scimitar dropped to the ground, no longer supported by two strong arms. Huma reeled backward and put all his strength behind a final back handed swing of his sword, which missed wildly.

"No," Thyss croaked as the *D'kinde* buried both sets of its claws directly into Huma's chest, punching through his sternum with a nauseating crack. She nearly collapsed again, unable to regain her balance, and she watched the monster rake eight claws downward through Huma's body, rending muscles, bones, and innards. The thing yanked its claws right through Huma's abdomen, and then pushed the still standing body off to one side as it closed in on Ulinae and the sleeping Lahn.

"No," Thyss repeated. The ground beneath her was just beginning to stabilize, but she couldn't seem to will her limbs to move. She finally pushed herself up so that she stood up on just her knees.

The *D'Kinde* was mere feet from Ulinae, well within the striking distance of its claws, but it chose not to attack, seeming to relish the moment. Tears poured down Ulinae's face, and she sobbed as her death approached. She took a handful of the flower petals she had picked and shoved them all into her mouth at once, chewing and swallowing laboriously. Ulinae fell from her kneeling position onto her backside, and her eyes stared wide and vacant at nothing somewhere off in the distance.

"No!" Thyss screamed with strength as the creature buried its maw into Ulinae's neck. The thing lifted its blood covered jaws from its kill to acknowledge Thyss' presence with another of its hateful shrieks.

The need to survive strong among all living things, her strength and balance returned immediately, and Thyss waited for nothing. She turned and ran west, back the way they had come through the jungle as quickly as her feet could carry her. She sprinted in blind terror, ignoring anything that came between her and escape, tearing through plants, some of which tore through her clothes in return. More than once, she tripped and fell on some vine or unseen root, but she never stopped her forward motion. She crawled forward, scrambled on all fours and regained her feet to continue her flight. It couldn't have even been a minute before she heard a terrible crashing behind her, as the creature no doubt took up the chase.

It was faster than she and seemed more agile as well, for it knew this jungle better than she or any human being, and somehow Thyss knew she could not escape it. She didn't turn to look, or even hazard a glance over one shoulder, but she knew it drew closer. She could hear its labored breath, and as she began to tire, she thought she could even feel its hot, rancid exhale upon her back.

Thyss knew it to be just behind her as a vine found her ankle, and she sprawled headlong forward. She wiggled forward like a worm, futilely trying to regain her feet as it stalked just behind her. She very nearly managed to stand again when she walked headlong into a massive tree that she hadn't seen in her terror. She fell again and turned so that her back was against the great trunk. Thyss would die with dignity, but she refused to look at the thing that would take her life. The stench of rotten meat caressed her face as the stifling breath blew upon it over and over again. She braced herself for a blow, for an horrific rending of flesh driven by claws, teeth and hate, and she whispered a final prayer to Hykan and any gods that would hear it.

But the blow never came.

Thyss hazarded opening one eye only, and immediately screamed at the *D'kinde* that stood only inches away. She scrambled backward in panic, trying to escape the thing, but it did not follow her. She forced enough reasoning calm upon herself to quell her shock, but her breathe still came in the shortest of inhalations. Her heart thundered in her ears. The *D'kinde* did not move, but only stared blankly ahead with the same blank stare Thyss had seen in Ulinae's eyes just before her death.

Several days later, Thyss emerged from the southern edge of the jungle to brave a desert. She had no interest in returning to the village that started her misadventure, nor continuing east toward Lahn's destination. She chose her own path. Draped across her body from head to toe was a reptilian skin that both kept the heat of the sun off of her, as well as made her difficult to see for any large predators that may have been about. Behind her she pulled a makeshift sled made of bones, upon which was stacked meat not too dissimilar in taste to that of many birds. It was well cooked, because fire burned away the potency of the kemala petals and helped preserve the meat.

The Lady in Yellow

A Novella

Chapter 1
The Dame in My Office – Early Wednesday, December 14th

The dreams are on me again. You'd think that, twenty years after the Great War, I would not be dealing with the same nightmares night after long night, especially with my recent troubles giving me something else to dream about. But no. Here I am again – in the trenches with freezing rain pouring on me in constant unforgiving sheets, the clouds overhead blocking out the moon's light. It's all I can do to stand, leaning against the trench's wall, mud slowly seeping in between the wood planks. My boots slide in the mud mixed from both the rain and blood of men. The sounds of machine gun and rifle fire fill the air constantly, and I cannot distinguish the difference between the rumble of the big guns in the distance and the crashes of thunder. I can't tell if the flashes of light are from lightning or the explosions of shells.

Death surrounds me; bodies of men lay everywhere, a reminder of the last ordered charge that met an onslaught of machine gun fire as soon as the men rose out of the trench. And it isn't just the bodies I see that is so sickening, but also the parts of bodies – dismembered limbs and entrails that cause my gorge to rise, though I haven't eaten in at least a day. At least the rain helps keep the stench down. When daylight comes, we'll regroup and charge again to be butchered yet again.

We all thought this would be fun. They shipped us over to France by the thousands, crammed into tin cans like sardines, off to the greatest adventure of our lives. Honor and glory awaited us; we were going to show Germany what American muscle was all about. We were going to march in heroically, and the Central Powers would just lay down their weapons. We all thought.

I'm shocked out of my daze as something explodes nearby, a sharp report like a door slamming in the room. I start, realizing that I am indeed in a dream of past times, something that happened twenty years ago, something that I've worked hard to forget and yet never leaves me alone.

With a groan, from both the chair and my throat, I lift my head from the pillow it rested on – the backs of my folded hands – and focus on getting my eyes to open. Sweat dampens my shirt, not that it's particularly hot in my office, and I'm vaguely aware of a more viscous substance on the back of one of my hands. I absently wipe it off on my shirt, and by happenstance, my tie as well. I reach up to loosen the latter and find the knot has already been pulled down and my shirt's top button is undone.

I fumble around in the dark, reaching for the bottle of Dewar's I know is here on my desk somewhere. Clinking its mouth loudly against what I know to be a filthy glass, I upend the too light bottle of scotch, and it rolls lazily across my desk as I throw about five drops of fire down my parched throat. I slam the monstrously heavy glass down on the hickory tabletop, only because my arm refused to hold it aloft any longer.

My eyes finally, slowly begin to clear, though I wish they wouldn't, because it is obviously still night. My office is dark apart from the moonlight streaming in through the window behind me, and the soft orange glow of the lamp hanging outside the frosted glass of my office door helps outline the reversed letters of my name, Thomas McAvoy, and the words Private Detective just below.

My Colt forty-five, my trusty 1911 rests quietly on my desk, moonlight just barely gleaming off its barrel, and my palm suddenly itches to feel its weight. But not in the way I've held it recently, not like how just a few hours ago I was considering pulling the trigger with that beautiful barrel in between my teeth. No, this feels like a need to defend myself, and the hairs on the back of my neck stand up on end. I think I know exactly how a spooked antelope feels while the lion waits nearby. That explosion in my dream, the one that woke me up – a door slamming shut in this very room.

My hand shoots to the pistol grip, and I train it on the black corner of my office next to the door, a viper ready to strike at the first hint of movement. Someone's sitting there I am sure, and the longer I peer into the darkness, I barely make out the shape of a form, someone wearing a hat. But it's the lower part of the shapely legs, lit up by the moonlight to appear as alabaster that lets me know my visitor is of the fairer sex. I put my weapon back on the desk, almost as quickly as I had picked it up.

"It's nice to know you're not gonna shoot me," a silken tone says dryly from the corner. A brief flame pops into being as she lights a cigarette, the yellow light giving me the shortest of glimpses at a pretty face.

"I haven't shot a broad... Yet," I reply, "but I wouldn't sneak into an armed man's office at..." I fumble for my pocket watch, peering at length at it, but there's not enough light. Or maybe I'm still too drunk. When's the last time I wound this thing?

"It's about four in the morning, Mr. McVey."

"McAvoy."

"If you don't want visitors this early, Mr. McAvoy," she says with a pause – I hear the faint burning of her cigarette, and the reddish orange tip glows brighter, "then perhaps you should lock your door at night."

At this point, my father's Irish blood starts to rise, and I'm about ready to slap her. "Lady, tell me what you want or beat it."

She sighs softly and stands, the orange light from the hallway outside outlining her thin shape. The lady's tall, probably every inch of five foot ten, but I'm glad she's leaving. I close my eyes, deciding that I'm just going to doze off again right here, but instead of the door opening and shutting, I hear her heels clicking on my wood floor as she approaches my desk, floating through the blue haze of moonlit cigarette smoke. In contrast to her, I sigh loudly, making my annoyance plain.

"I need your help, Mr. McAvoy."

"I'm not interested," I inform her, opening my eyes to see her standing right at the edge of my desk, less than six feet away. Between the scotch and lack of light, I can't see her too clearly, but I'm pretty sure she's a looker – dark hair, maybe black, everything with the right amount of curve in the right place. She's got a hat on – looks like something nice, but inexpensive – a light colored purse under one arm, and she's holding something.

"I think you could use the work," she argues.

She tosses the thing she's holding onto my desk. It lands with loud flop, and a dust cloud billows up, obscuring what little vision I've got with fine, gray particles. I wave my hand back and forth to clear them, resisting the urge to sneeze from the tickle building in my nose. I lean forward to grab it – a newspaper, *The Detroit Free Press* – and see the headline, "Private Dick Exonerated". A smaller headline on an article to the side says, "Detective Voss vows to find the killer".

"Mr. McAvoy," she continues, "I don't expect you'll be having many clients in the foreseeable future. You may want to hear what I have to say."

I don't know why her voice commands my attention so well. She enunciates clearly, so much so that I'm sure she is highly educated. She sounds young, less than thirty to be sure. Despite the sarcasm, her voice flows mellifluously, without the weariness the world brings as we age.

"No, thanks." It sounds half-hearted even in my own ears.

"Please," she pleads, "It's a matter of life and death."

Of course, it is. She's not going to take no for an answer, and now I've got this good-looking dame, practically begging for me help with dulcet tones. There's that feeling in the pit of my stomach, the one I've felt many times before, as a soldier, a cop, and a private investigator. You might think it's the scotch rumbling around in an empty stomach, but I recognize it as the tingling before I do something stupid. For some reason, I never can resist being a damn hero.

"All right, you have my attention," I say, feeling far more sober than I want to be.

She calmly, deliberately sits in one of the empty chairs across from me, and I wonder if she's aware of the amount of collected dust she just got all over her dress. Leaning back slightly, she crosses her legs, right over left, and her dress pulls up slightly to reveal her legs again. I try not to stare, pulling my eyes to her face. I can't see her well due to the silvery moonlight and the hat, but she's definitely pretty with dark hair and eyes, the latter of which holds a twinkle.

"So, what is it?" I ask.

"Mr. McAvoy," she replies slowly, "I need you to find a child, a missing child."

"I'm sure it's something the police can handle, so if you don't mind -"

She curtly, almost forcefully cuts me off, "The police don't have a clue, and you of all people should know that."

"Fine, who am I looking for?"

"I... I don't know, exactly," she answers quietly, all strength gone from her voice.

"So, how does that work?" I fire back, ready to kick the broad out.

"It's hard to explain. I don't know the child's name; I don't even know if it's a boy or a girl." Her voice is so soft, so needing, as if she's ready to open her soul to me because she needs help so badly.

"All right, let's start with what you do know," I reply, unable to keep up my angst against her vulnerability.

She sighs softly, her right hand moving up to her face; I think she's wiping away tears that I can't see in the gloom. Frankly, I'm glad that I can't see them, because I never could handle a woman crying in front of me. That's why I swore off dames years ago.

Chapter 2
Looking for Leads – Wednesday, December 14th

Have you ever awoken because someone in the room is snoring loud as all Hell, and when you wake up you realize that person is you? My vision and my head clear pretty quickly, and there is absolutely no doubt in my mind that I am woefully sober. I look down at my pocket watch and tuck it away in disgust since its hands are still stuck at just after four, as they have been for days. I can only guess it's about ten in the morning, just based on how clear my head is quickly becoming.

Everything around me is just like it's been for days, maybe even weeks, except for a few things that make it clear to me that I didn't hallucinate, or even dream, my visitor in the small hours. First is the newspaper the broad, Helen, tossed on my desk and all of the dust it dislodged from a perfectly good resting place. I don't think she realizes that I was perfectly happy with where the dust was.

Next is the handful of notes I scrawled out on a scrap of paper, reasonably and rightfully expecting that I wouldn't remember come the morning. They're barely legible, either from the scotch or the lack of light, but in addition to Helen's address, I can make out the initials "H.P.L.", the cryptic identity of a child, an infant who may be either a boy or a girl and has gone missing in the Detroit area within the last day or so.

How in the name of Hell am I supposed to find a baby based on just that information? For that matter, how does Helen come up with the initials of a baby that's gone missing without having at least the baby's last name?

And why did I let myself run out of scotch? My eyes rest mournfully on the empty bottle of Dewar's, still on its side as if discarded in the most vulgar fashion. I'm definitely going to need more before this whole thing is over, and that's one thing the pile of cash she left me will help do. In one final attempt at ending the whole conversation, I charged her twenty dollars a day plus expenses, and I'll be damned if she didn't cough up a hundred and ten bucks on the spot to cover me for five days plus.

"Screw it," I say to my friends assembled throughout the office – my gun, a bunch of old pictures and lots of displaced dust.

I stand up from my desk, skidding the chair with a screech on the floor behind me, and fold the cash while stuffing it into my right pocket. I shove the gun into my pants, tightening my belt to help hold it in place, and I reach up to push my tie's knot back up to my neck, not bothering to again button my shirt. I cast a longing look over at the empty scotch bottle as I toss on a matching but ragged suit jacket. I head for the door and slam it behind me.

In the hallway beyond, I go to lock the door before I realize how much of an idiot I'm being. I throw the door back open and return to my office long enough to grab the notes I scribbled almost illegibly last night as well as a dangerously short pencil. I again close the door behind me, maybe a little more gently this time, and walk to the stairwell at the end of the hall.

I push open the door at the bottom and emerge onto a cold Detroit street. The air is cold as Hell, so much so that your nose wants to start dripping the moment you breathe it in. Red bows, green wreathes, holly and mistletoe adorn doors, shop windows and lamp and telephone poles. The blocks around my office are further decorated with short trees every fifteen or twenty feet, trees that are only about twelve feet tall and bloom beautifully in the spring. They stand naked in the breeze, their leaves brown and crumbling about their trunks or on the street, a stark contrast to the apparent joy of the coming season, which is itself oblivious to the tensions building an ocean away.

"God damned cold," I swear as frigid air blows through my too thin jacket, and I light up a Lucky Strike as if that itself will keep out the cold. Should I go back up for my heavy coat?

"Screw it," I say again and set out west down the sidewalk.

Walking briskly and moving through the December air, I realize just how damn cold it is, and I keep from shivering only through sheer willpower. The smoke dangling from the right corner of my mouth might be helping a bit, but there's a damn deep chill in the air. The smell of steel, gasoline, and smoke – the smell of Detroit – tries to overpower an underlying scent, but anyone who has lived north of the Mason Dixon won't mistake the smell of snow in the air. To complement the point, I look at the sky as I traverse the four blocks, the cold gray of a winter storm blocking the blinding orb of the sun.

I'm standing in front of the police precinct, a three-story brick building of the most unimaginative architecture possible. A blue double door stands facing the street, flanked by a pair of ten-foot-tall windows. To the left is two overhead doors and another single door leading into the garage. A couple of the newest and best '37 Fords, solid black with the Detroit Police emblems emblazoned in white on the doors, sit out front. I understand these new models come with two-way radios. Amazing.

I step right up to the front door and turn one of the doorknobs. I completely ignore the glances and the stares of the cops outside, all of who I know and some of them I once considered friends, as I step over the door sill. It's a quiet day inside – the normal action of cops hustling from one end of the precinct to the other or hauling street toughs around by their collars just isn't happening today. I spot just a few cops around, mostly pretending to be busy with paperwork of some sort or another, certainly paying no attention to me.

I walk up to the desk sergeant, a burly middle-aged guy with receding red hair who is sitting behind an oak desk atop a raised platform. A lone plume of smoke trails lazily from a source I can't see, obscured by a raised wooden lip designed to shield paperwork and logs on his desk from curious onlookers below. I can barely see his forearm moving slightly, and I hear the scratching of a pencil.

"One moment," he says uninterestedly without even looking up.

"No problem, Jimmy," I reply, leaning one arm casually up on the desktop.

The scratching stops almost immediately as he glances up with a slight squint. He leans forward and almost whispers, "You shouldn't be here, Tom."

"Why not?"

"Come on, don't start any trouble."

"I'm not. It's a public place. I've got as much right to be here as anyone else."

"Tom," Jimmy pauses, "if Voss comes down here and sees you…"

"He'll what? I didn't do anything."

In a quick motion, Jimmy rolls his eyes and tilts his head slightly at an argument he can't combat, though all of his peers would expect him to. He opens his mouth slightly, grinding the points of his right-side incisors against each other. He glances around briefly, seeing the eyes of cops pretending not to be watching him.

"What do you want, Tom?"

"I need some information, Jimmy."

"Informa -," Jimmy replies with an almost incredulous whisper. "I can't give you nothing," he mumbles and picks back up his pencil.

"Come on, Jimmy, it's just a simple thing," I implore quietly. "I don't need you to tell me much."

Jimmy tosses the pencil in disgust, and it rolls across his desk. He reaches forward and produces the already burning cigarette and leans back as he takes a long drag from it. He searches my face as I wait patiently while he blows the smoke up into the air slowly. He takes another long pull while I produce one of my own cigarettes. Jimmy leans forward and lets the smoke out slowly as he says, "I can't tell you anything, Tom."

"Jimmy," I say, cupping my hand over my cigarette lighter, an affectation that is completely unnecessary when inside, "a kid might be in trouble."

We lock eyes for about ten seconds before he finally looks down at his desk. He forcefully stabs out his cigarette over and over, his forearm pounding his desktop. "Goddammit, Tom. Okay, follow my lead."

He raises his voice loud enough that cops on the third floor can hear him, and I almost flinch as he points a finger at me shouting, "I told you to get the hell outta' here. Hey, Robinson! Watch the desk a minute while I take care of this guy."

Jimmy almost upends his chair when he jumps up and bounds down from the platform. I'm surprised at how quickly such a bulk can move, and he's right behind me within moments, an iron grip clamping down just above my left elbow. I feel his other hand grab my jacket by the back of the collar like I'm some common criminal.

"Easy," I breathe.

I lose my cigarette as Jimmy manhandles me back toward the door, and I almost trip over my own feet several times. One of the other cops scrambles over to open the door for us as the big sergeant almost carries me outside. Before I know it, he's got me around the corner into an alley, out of sight, but I can still hear the cheers and jeers from Jimmy's fellows.

"Dammit, let go of me," I grumble.

"Had to make it look good," he says, but when I turn around, his face shows a little too much satisfaction. "I can't let those guys think I'm helping you."

"I'm one of those guys!"

"Not anymore, you're not. Not after…"

"I wasn't even indicted," I protest, "I didn't do anything."

"Tom, you and I both know that you're guilty as far as most of the cops in this town are concerned," Jimmy explains as reasonably sounding as he can. "Now, this is already taking too long. What's this about a kid?"

"I got a lady telling me a child has been kidnapped. She paid me to find him."

"It's a boy?"

"Well, I don't actually know," I reply, suddenly feeling like an idiot. "I don't even have a name."

"I must be dreaming," Jimmy mumbles.

"All I have are initials. Have you seen any abduction of a child, maybe an infant, with the initials H.P.L.?"

"This is ridiculous," Jimmy complains, and he turns to leave me in the freezing alley.

I reach out and just barely snag the sleeve of his blue uniform before he gets away. He whirls toward me, an incredulous glare in his green eyes, as if he is truly aghast that I would dare sully his person with my touch. I see his eyes, and the look of someone who's about to throw a stiff right cross, and I let go just as quickly.

"C'mon, Jimmy. This is serious. This broad contracted me last night, gave me cash and everything. She said a child is in danger, kidnapped. Just tell me, have you seen any abductions come across the desk in the last few days?"

Jimmy's face almost seems to ball up, as if he is squinting at a ledger that only he can see, maybe even a logbook imprinted on his brain, and his eyes are reading it on the inside. Finally, he simply says, "No."

"May not be reported yet," I mumble. I pull out a ten-dollar bill. "Can you let me know if something comes across? The kid may have the initials H.P.L."

"Jesus, Tom. Yeah, I'll keep an eye out." Jimmy sighs, takes the ten from me and almost surreptitiously folds and slides it into one of his pockets. Then it's like something suddenly occurs to the ginger haired cop with the physique of a prize fighter. "Oh, there is one thing."

"What is it?" I ask, my interest suddenly piqued.

Somehow, I don't see coming one of the hardest punches to the jaw that any man on Earth has probably had the forethought to block with his face. I'm thrown backward with the force, like a damn doll, and I fall into a pile of crates and trash left forgotten to rot in the alley. Instinctively, my hand flies up to rub at my jaw just to make sure it wasn't knocked clean off my face.

"Dammit, Jimmy, what the hell was that for?"

"Like I said – I had to make it look good," Jimmy chuckles as he leaves the alley, his shoes *clacking* on the street.

"Son of a bitch," I groan as I sit up, my legs splayed out in front of me.

I spit on the pavement right between them, my attention drawn to the red tint of the saliva. I reach into my mouth to assure myself that all my teeth are still there and solid enough, and my fingers come back red from the blood issuing from a wound in the inside of my cheek. I must have bitten myself when the bastard socked me.

So, it's my first day on the case, and it's going oh so swimmingly. So far, I'm not sure there's even a case, and all I've managed to accomplish is give up some of my cash and get cold cocked by a friend. There's a bar just a couple blocks back toward my office, and as I sit there, I'm thinking that I would very possibly like to head that direction. I slowly find my way back onto my feet, and I step out of the alley, ignoring the almost laughing gazes of the few cops hanging around outside. The bar is two blocks to my right. I turn left instead, pass the precinct, and continue on my way.

About an hour later, I'm standing in front of an ugly, red brick building that has the words "Wayne County Clerk" emblazoned in black writing on a white sign across its front. Its architecture is so blunt and pointless, with a complete and total lack of form and beauty, that it could only be a practical public building meant to service a practical public. The only thing resembling style is the five or six columns that support the front of the building, also of red brick and very geometric. They could have been easily substituted with a wall, giving the building a little more usable space on its ground level. Hands in my pockets and my jaw hurting mightily, I stroll into this edifice whose existence I couldn't despise more.

A receptionist sits behind a desk just inside with short, business appropriate hair – a bob just above the shoulders with waves that flow through the hair laterally. It's so perfect – like what a woman in a picture show would have – that I think she could hang upside down like a bat and it wouldn't move. She looks busy with paperwork of some sort, or perhaps she just wants me to think she's busy, so I don't dare interrupt whatever it is she's doing. It doesn't really matter, because a directory mounted on the wall tells me that "Birth and Death" records are to be found in 201.

The interior, receptionist and all, feels much like every other office building I've ever been in, not to say

I've felt the courage to enter many, but it looks different enough. The floor is made of that new-fangled stuff I think they call vinyl. It almost feels like walking on hard rubber, if such a thing exists, both solid and squishy at the same time. The ceiling is suspended from the floor above with a gridwork of interlocked tiles. I don't really know the purpose or reasoning behind it, but it's all very modern and new. It has me longing for the comfort of my old oak chair and my office's hardwood floor. My shoes squeak on this floor as I walk.

I continue to stroll, maintaining such an air of nonchalance that no one would look at me twice, a difficult thing to do with what had to be a massive bruise forming across my jaw. Only a few yards down the hall, I find an elevator, complete with an attendant in a cheap black suit just ready to take me up into the heavens. No thanks. Its only one floor, and I trust my legs and good solid steps a hell of a lot more than a damn wire and steel framed box supported by ropes, cable and pulleys, or whatever they use to make those things move.

I'm about halfway up the flight of stairs, taking the steps two at a time, when I realize that I'm not nineteen anymore. My thighs are burning, my feet hurt, and my heart is pounding so hard I think it's about to divorce me and find someone who'll treat it right. I need a drink. Bad. At least the stairs are of a good, old fashioned wood construction.

The second floor is more of the same, and I find the door I need just as soon as I exit the stairwell, the number 201 printed on a tiny tile at the top of the doorway. Inside is a huge room, a suite of rooms actually, and the vinyl floor gives way to thin, but rugged carpet. Several large desks greet me almost immediately, and beyond them are rows upon rows of file cabinets that go from the carpeted floor to the drop ceiling, whose contents and system of filing go well beyond my comprehension at a mere glance.

I easily walk right up to the first person I see – a thin, pasty and rather short man that's walking past the front desks on some task or another. He's wearing a cheap, light gray suit, with a darker gray vest and an even darker gray bowtie. No, cheap isn't right – that's unfair. On closer inspection, the suit is decent quality, it's just inexpensive. It fits him well, though, which really only accentuates his complete lack of athletic build. He doesn't want to talk to me. I can tell he's going out of his way to pretend I don't exist, because if I did in fact exist, I would just be an annoyance to him with whatever request I may have.

"Excuse me, sir?" I ask, practically throwing myself into his path.

He looks at me disdainfully and wrinkles his nose ever so slightly. I hope I don't smell. But I might. I don't remember the last time I had the joy of a hot shower or even a good soak in a tub. For that matter, I've been wearing these clothes for at least twenty-four hours, and I was knocked down into trash just a short time ago. The poor man's brown eyes look at me, almost pleading for me to just go away so that I don't insert my chaos into his perfectly ordered existence. He gives in to his fate, and his shoulders slump in defeat.

"Yes, may I help you?" he asks, and I know he would love nothing more than for me to just say, "No," and leave.

But I don't.

"I sure hope so!" I say cheerfully, my jaw tightening in complaint. I throw my hand out there. "I'm Tom McAvoy! You?"

He tentatively shuffles a file folder into his left hand and takes my hand with his right, saying, "Christopher Jones."

Of course, that's his name. This man's name couldn't possibly be any more inventive or unique than he himself – a perfectly boring name for a perfectly boring man. I shake his hand enthusiastically, adding even more tonnage to his discomfort, and Christopher's hand is like a damn dead fish in both temperature and firmness. He has to be somewhere around thirty – too young to have fought in the Great War, and probably too old to fight in the one that everyone feels coming, if America even gets involved. That's good because this man is not a fighter. Though, maybe the army might want him as a stenographer or something. He's got a ring on his finger that tells me he has a wife at home – probably a rather round woman who is good at cooking and raising little Christophers.

"Pleasure to meet you, Chris!"

"Christopher."

"What? Oh, sure," I reply dismissively. "Look, I need some help, and I have a feeling you're the man who can help me. I'm looking for birth records."

A pained expression crosses his face, and he fearfully asks, "Ummmm... whose birth records?"

"No one's in particular," I half lie, still holding his hand. I've stopped shaking it, but I'm slowly increasing the firmness of the handshake. "I'm doing a survey on modern baby names. So, I'm really looking for the name and birthdate of every child over the last... say... oh, ten years."

"You can't be serious."

"Oh, I'm very serious, Jonesy."

I still haven't released his hand, and I can feel the knuckles and other bones begin to squeeze together. I'm going to hold him right there. I don't want to hurt the guy, even a little bit, but by the time I'm done, he's going to feel so terribly uncomfortable, and he'll be so relieved when I let him go that he'll do anything I ask.

I heard a guy talking in the bar one night. He was a zookeeper or something – I don't know, but he was drunk and prattling on and on and on about dogs, wolves and packs. I must not have been completely gone yet, because I remember him talking about the alpha and the betas. You see, the alpha intimidates and exerts its dominance over the betas, and the betas follow the alpha's lead. The alpha eats first and, generally, decides everything for the pack. Once in a while, a beta gets brave or strong enough to challenge the alpha for leadership of the pack, but Christopher here is not that beta. However, like most betas, he is of distinct use to the alpha; the alpha needs the betas to keep everything running smoothly.

"Ummm, well," he trails off as something seems to occur to him. "What is this all about?"

"I told you, Chris, I work at the Free Press, and I'm doing a survey on baby names for an article."

"I don't remember you saying -"

"You should listen more carefully to people."

"You don't look like a reporter."

"How many have you met?"

"Well, none," he admits.

"No two are alike," I reply quickly with an ear to ear smile.

"Well, ummm… things are somewhat of a disaster right now. You see, the birth records are supposed to have two copies, one in order by last name and the other by birthdate."

"And?"

"Well, my predecessor who just retired, well he… uh… didn't really do much the last couple of months."

"It sounds like you have quite a task ahead of you," I agree with a bobbing nod.

"Well, I already have the alphabetical order section completed, except for the new records the hospitals have brought over since I started."

"You see, Chris? The county absolutely has the right man for the job!" I laud, throwing the beta a bone.

"I guess we could start with that?" he asks.

"Absolutely," I reply, and I finally let go of his hand. It shoots back to the file folder he's carrying, so now each of his hands holds a side of the folder in front of his torso, as if it were some kind of shield against my onslaught.

"Follow me," Christopher says, and he turns to walk toward the back corner of the room. We come to a halt in front of an imposing wall of filing cabinets that seem to stretch off to the right to eternity itself. Christopher turns back to me and says, "This is where it all starts – every birth record in Wayne County for as long as we've gotten them."

"That's great, Jonesy," I reply with gusto before he can say anything more. "How about this – if you'll start here at the 'A's, I'm going to go start at the 'L's. Just right down the first, middle and last name of every child born in the last ten years."

I turn and walk away, ignoring his open mouth and bewildered stare until I found a placard upon which was printed "La". I immediately pulled the drawer open and began to make a show of thumbing through the mass of paperwork with a pencil and scrap paper in hand. After a few minutes, I look up to find with no small amount of satisfaction that Mr. Christopher Jones has resigned himself to the task and had transported a step stool over to help him reach the top drawers. Meanwhile, I pretend to write something down every now and then, but in reality, if the child's first name didn't start with an "H", I thumbed on to the next.

I quickly come to the realization that if this were my life, day in and day out, I would have shot myself long ago. There couldn't possibly be anything so dramatically boring, so life draining as spending eight hours a day organizing records. I was all the way through the "La"s and into the "Le"s when I found a Lester, Harold. My heart jumps with the joy known only by the ending of an horrific torture before I realize that the middle name is Mark. Also, Harold Mark Lester was born in 1902, making him almost my age – certainly not a child. I keep looking.

I'm nearing the end of the "Lo"s when Christopher's understated voice calls across the room, "Ummm, Mr. McVey?"

"McAvoy," I reply, not looking up.

"Yes, sorry, Mr. McAvoy – the office closes here in thirty minutes, and I need to start locking some things up."

"Sure, Jonesy."

"Well, ummm, did you want to come back in the morning?"

"I'll be done in the 'L's in just a few minutes, and I'll come back tomorrow," I lie. Having found absolutely nothing of any use, I have no intention of returning to this mundane, stab-my-eyes-out-with-my-own-thumbs existence.

He nods and asks, "What do you want me to do with the names I've collected so far?"

"Just hold onto them. I'll get them from you when we finish all this," I reply and slide the last drawer shut with a bang that causes Christopher Jones to wince.

I glance at a wall mounted clock on my way out, seeing it's almost five, so I'm not at all surprised when I reach the crisp air that its almost dark outside. The new electric streetlamps in this area are already beginning to hum to life, not that their sickly orange glow illuminates the streets or alleys too terribly. A light, fluffy snow has begun to fall lazily from the gray sky – the kind of snow that you don't really expect to amount to much. I've got some walking ahead of me to reach my office, and I definitely need to find a bottle of scotch to keep me company.

Chapter 3
Edgemont Place – Thursday, December 15th

I generally find the cheap, but serviceable, couch that rests against the left wall of my office to be far more comfortable than sleeping hunched over my desk, but I don't always make it that far. It's not uncommon for me to simply pass out from exhaustion – and maybe scotch – sitting in my chair, but it looks like I managed to stumble over to my preferred sleeping area last night. I wake up from just a slow, general increase in the room's ambient light from the orange sun shining through my window, the empty glass from my last drink still in my hands, clasped across my chest.

Through some strength of will, I manage to push myself up to a sitting position, almost losing the heavy glass to the floor in the process. I stand and stumble my way to my desk and slam the glass down with far more force than I intended, right next to the empty half pint bottle of Dewar's. Maybe I need to quit drinking. Maybe I'm not drinking enough.

The street down below my window bustles with activity – men in suits walking, a group of dressed up women on their way to brunch, people Christmas shopping, cars driving and honking. Looking over this panorama of American life, it's hard to believe that somewhere around the corner there's a breadline a mile long. Detroit had been making half the world's cars while I was a cop here, and when a quarter of the country had gone out of work, no one was buying cars. It has been easy for me. I've got no one counting on me but myself, and I don't need much.

My door is still locked, so I go into the adjoining room, strip down and wash myself in the sink like a common prostitute. Standards are for people who need to impress other people, and I'm not one of them. Certain most of the stench is gone, I take a hard look in the mirror and decide four days without shaving isn't bad. I can go at least six. At least sometime in the last few days I had enough foresight to wash some clothes out and hang them to dry.

Dressed, though not exactly presentable for Mass, I find the notes I made when the mysterious Helen visited me the other night. It's shocking if one considers how drunk I was at the time, but I remember the entire affair clearly. I'm not missing anything, but the fact is, I have absolutely no leads at this point, nothing to follow up on. She gave me her address, and something about it is vaguely familiar. I don't think I've ever been to the street before, but I swear I've read something in the papers.

It's time to pay Helen a visit. I lock my door behind me, head down to the street and hail a taxi. It looks like an older model, a barely running heap from maybe '29, a sharp contrast to the clean cut and very young man behind the wheel. Through the window, I see his khaki army uniform, complete with a black tie tucked into his shirt and the single echelon on his arm denoting him as a private. Perplexed, I open the rear door and sit inside. The uniform has disappeared, replaced with a fairly common jacket, shirt and tie.

"Where can I take you, mister?" he asks with a deep baritone, almost bass voice.

I pause, blinking to make sure his clothes don't change back. I hand him the address and ask, "Do you know where this is?"

"Thirteen hundred Edgemont Place? Yeah, I do," he replies and runs an appraising eye over me. "It's a little out there. I'm sorry to ask this, sir, but do you have money?"

I reach into my pocket and just flash him my wad before shoving it back down.

The kid wasn't exaggerating. It took us about twenty minutes to get off the city streets, and we drove another twenty minutes or so toward the edge of Wayne County. We're heading into the rich section of the county, marked by huge Victorian homes, acres of lawns so perfect they could be golf courses and expensive new cars. The driver doesn't attempt to engage me in any conversation, and that's absolutely fine by me. I'm avoiding even looking at him.

He finds the place we're looking for, a mansion by any standards I have, and he turns into a gravel driveway. An eight-foot, black iron fence surrounds the entire property, and the gate across the driveway stands wide open. He carefully rolls the car up several hundred yards before stopping a stone's throw away from the house, a giant Victorian complete with huge windows, columns and a spire.

He takes the car out of gear, turns and says, "That'll be two sixty-five, mister."

"Here's two bucks," I say, handing him the money as he stares back at me with a glare that says he thinks he's about to get cheated out of his fare. I pull out a five-dollar bill and hold each end of it tautly. "Wait for me, because I got a feeling this won't take long, and this will buy my trip back with a little extra for you."

His eyes follow the bill as I jam it back into my pocket and get out of the car. As my feet hit the ground, I realize the driveway isn't gravel as much as tiny white and semi-clear river stones. I close the door and survey the amount of ground covered by the rock, and whistle slightly at what the cost must have been. I head up toward the house, and my estimation of the cash investment in the property continues to increase. I don't see any cars, but they could be hidden in what I think is a huge garage just off the house.

A stone walkway – made of something like marble but more opaque, less polished – curves away from the driveway up to the wide and rounded brick steps leading to grand front door of polished cherry. Standing in front of it, the thing absolutely dwarfs me, and the doorjambs are wrapped in mahogany, hand carved with a rope design.

I press the small button offset to the left, and less than a half second later, the clanging of a bell sounds several times just inside. While I wait, I turn to look across the enormous lawn, at least three times the size of Briggs Stadium. I notice my taxi driver staring at me, so I turn to ring the doorbell one more time. After what felt like maybe ten minutes and was more like thirty seconds, I try the door to find it locked up tight.

I come back down the walkway and hold a finger in the air, asking the driver for a minute, and I make my way across the front of the house to the garage. It has a side door, which is far from impressive or ornate, but is also locked. Getting around the side and back of the house seems to take forever, since it just seems to keep going and going, but I finally find a raised back porch with a set of glass double doors. These two are locked, brass doorknobs not moving the slightest bit. I hold my hands across my forehead to shield my eyes from the bright sunlight and peer into the house. All is still and dark, no sign of anyone at all inside, and I'm not about to break into this place to snoop around.

I settle back into the car, and the driver asks, "I guess no one's home, huh?"

"Guess not," I reply absently, staring out the window at nothing. I reach forward, toss him the five, and we head home.

Chapter 4
My Office – Morning of Friday, December 16th

I feel like I'm standing in a living newsreel. All around me, people are screaming and cheering, waiving triangular red flags with black swastikas emblazoned in a circle of white. The Austrian people are actually happy; this is not hundreds, maybe thousands of people forced by fascist soldiers to pretend joy. As gray uniformed soldiers march in perfect Hessian unison through Vienna's streets, as Adolf Hitler himself stands above with his arm raised in salute, pretty Austrian girls in the front row of the crowd swoon over their German liberators.

I stand alone amongst them, in my dirty, rumpled suit, and I shout at the top of my lungs. But no one hears me because no sound issues from my mouth. I tug on the jacket sleeve of a man next to me, but he completely ignores my advances. I'd do anything right now for a weapon – a rifle or even just a handgun – because I know I could take him out from here. Why am I the only one who knows what this man is? Why can't the world hear me?

And then the shots ring out. It's the staccato deep base of a heavy weapon, like maybe a twenty millimeter. It fires off four, five, maybe even six times, and people in the front row have huge holes ripped into them or even lose limbs. Blood and gore spatter the people further back in the crowd, and yet they keep cheering on the Nazi troops. The gun fires off again, and even more people go down. Even in their death throes, they continue their ecstatic support.

Another burst fires into the crowd, and a woman in front me whirls, propelled by the impact of a high caliber round. The right half of her face is torn off, everything below the cheekbone just simply gone. I can see into her mouth as it fills with blood, her shattered teeth and ruined right eye. It's…

The pounding on my door sounds again, this time with an angry male voice saying, "Damn you, McAvoy, I know you're in there."

"Damn it, hold on!" I shout back, sitting up to hold my head that I'm pretty sure would have been throbbing even without some asshole doing a number on my office door. I rub my eyes, feeling a glorious, painful burn like they've been staring at the sun and then drag my fingers down with a sigh.

Someone bangs on the wood door one more time as I approach it. I throw open the lock, shouting, "What the hell is -" as the door flies back toward me to allow two men to enter. First through is a balding man in a suit, blond hair turning silver as it recedes backward. He's about my height and a little heavier. Jimmy trails in behind him, and my jaw suddenly hurts again.

"Detective Sergeant Voss!" I exclaim as cheerfully as I can manage, especially with these two ruffians interrupting my hangover so early in the morning. What time is it anyway? "To what do I owe your pleasant company?"

"Cut the crap, McAvoy," Voss says shortly. He sounds like he's about to follow up with something else, but he closes his mouth instead.

I gently swing the door shut, closing it with hardly a sound while I search the two men for details. Jimmy has a pained look across his face – whether from my quick attempt to aggravate Voss or some other reason, there's no way to tell. He's definitely here as a cop, but his body is relaxed like he doesn't really expect anything untoward to happen. There is an odd look in his eyes though – something akin to worry. Robert Voss is a completely different story. He's wearing a long beige overcoat, which he has pushed back with his hands on his hips – all the better for making sure I see his revolver. He looks like he's been fuming over something, but I can't tell if his pressure is waxing or waning.

I drop the pleasantries. "What do you want?" I ask, strolling over to my desk.

"You need to come with me. We're going down to the house for a little talk," Voss replies with his best hard cop voice.

Honestly, it's either not very good, or it doesn't bother me since I was one of them less than a year ago. To prove the point, I pull my chair out, nonchalantly sit and cross my legs. "This is beginning to constitute harassment."

"You haven't begun to see harassment," Voss shoots back, and he charges up to the other side of my desk. "I know you killed that man, in cold blood no less. I know it, and I'm gonna' get you."

"You don't know shit," I snarl back, and I drop my comfortable pose to lean forward on my desk. "I didn't kill anyone. The D.A. knows that, because he won't even pursue an indictment your evidence is so weak. You forget, I'm a detective, too."

"A 'private detective'. Damned mercenary cop. Scraping by just enough to keep drunk," he says, his tone softer, more insulting as he flicks the empty bottle of scotch sitting on my desk. "You're probably so drunk, you don't even know the things you do, but I've got you now. You're going away, McAvoy, even if it's not for murder."

"What in the hell are you talking about?"
"Where's the baby?"
"What?"
"You murder him already?"

I lean to the right to look past Voss at Jimmy, still silently hovering in the background like an impending storm cloud. I appeal to him, asking, "What the hell is he on about?"

Voss moves to block my view. "You were at the station the other day. Jimmy here threw you out. Remember that or were you too drunk?"

I pull out a cigarette and light it, answering through the corner of my mouth, "I remember. Jimmy's got a hell of a punch."

"So, you remember what you were asking him about?"

I blow a lung full of smoke right into Voss' face, breaking his intensity as he coughs slightly. "Why are you asking me about this? Jimmy's obviously told you everything already. Thanks, Jimmy."

"Leave Sergeant Barnes out of this. He's a police officer acting in accordance with his duty. Where's the baby, McAvoy? I'm sure not here, or we'd hear him crying," Voss says, and he leans forward with both sets of his knuckles planted on my desk.

I breathe out another plume of smoke slowly, deliberately right into his face again, but he doesn't flinch this time. His open right hand comes up fast, its target not my face but rather the cigarette hanging out of the corner of my mouth. Before I know it, I'm on my feet. I catch him fast by the wrist, making it plain that I'm much stronger than he is. Voss' face turns bright red, and he looks like he's about to explode when I fix him with a cold stare, my face just six inches from his. My free hand delicately takes between two fingers the less than half smoked cigarette out of my mouth and stamps it out in my overflowing glass ashtray.

"Easy, Detective Sergeant," I breathe in a lowered tone, "you don't want this to go south."

Before Voss can say anything else, Jimmy appears out of nowhere to be standing at the right side of my desk, a sudden and unexpected mediator in my and Voss' little dispute. He says soothingly, "Come on, Tom, let him go. The detective just wants to ask you a few questions about this case. Right, detective?"

Voss' eyes shoot to the left at Jimmy's words, and he seems to consider them for a long moment. Finally, the tension in his arm breaks, and the red begins to drain from his face. He nods, "That's right."

I let him go and settle back into my chair. "Jimmy if you've filled Mr. Voss in," I say, actively avoiding Voss' title, "there's really not much else to say. You know as much as I do at this point."

"Go over it with me," Voss demands. However, he eases off my desk and keeps his voice low, calm.

I'm such an idiot. In my need to prove whose dick was bigger, I ignored the most blatant and obvious fact. It struck me like a bolt of lightning, and I swear my hair stood up on end. My eyes narrow as I lean forward again. "Wait a minute. What's happened?"

"There was an abduction last night," Jimmy says, and I can almost hear Voss' neck snap as he fixes Jimmy with a glare.

"Damn it, Barnes."

"Detective Sergeant, if Tom's guilty like you think he is, then I'm not telling him anything he doesn't already know. If he's not involved, then maybe just the basic facts will help him help us."

Voss sighs. "Fine. McAvoy – Sergeant Barnes said you came to the precinct two days ago, looking for information about an abduction."

"Yeah," I reply.

"He said you don't know the name, but just a set of initials."

"Yeah."

"Those initials are H.P.L."

"Yeah."

"So, it wouldn't surprise you to know that a ten-month-old boy named Harcourt Pennington Larew was abducted from his home in the middle of the night last night?"

"Whew," I exhale, and honestly, its half English, half whistle. I look down at my desk for a second while I consider the implications, and then I glance up at Jimmy for confirmation. He almost imperceptibly nods with a worried half-smile. Back to Voss, I say, "Yeah, actually it surprises me quite a bit. Before this minute, I just assumed I was set on some wild goose chase by a half crazy, half pretty dame."

"What's her name?" Voss asks.

"Helen Smith."

"Sounds like baloney."

"Maybe, but it's the name she gave me."

"She's the one who gave you the initials?"

"Yeah."

"And you actually took this case?" Voss asks, incredulously.

"It was four in the morning, I was drunk, and she had cash – something I've been terribly short on lately. Some asshole put me in a situation where the lawyers sucked me dry," I grumble.

But Voss doesn't take the bait. "You don't expect me to believe this, do you? She give you a way to contact her?"

"Just an address."

"What is it?"

"Confidential."

"You better stow that nonsense, McAvoy, or I'll haul you down just for fun," Voss threatens, and Jimmy's uncomfortable shifting of his weight tells me Voss means it.

"All right. It was thirteen... hold on," I make a show of closing my eyes and rubbing them for a second in thought. "Thirteen twenty Edgington Drive."

"You're sure?" Voss asks, not trusting my drink addled brain.

"Absolutely."

"In Wayne County?" Voss asks, but before I can answer, he adds, "Have you been there?"

"I assume, and no," I reply, both answers more or less truthful. I assume Edgington Drive is in Wayne County, and I have never been there. "I figured she'd come back here eventually."

"If she does, be sure to let us know. Come on, Sergeant Barnes," Voss says, and he turns to head for the door. He opens it to leave but stops and turns. "McAvoy – you're still on my list for this. You know that don't you?"

"How stupid would that make me, Voss?" I fire back. "I'm going to ask around about a kidnapping two days before I perpetrate it? Common sense says that gives me an alibi."

"Or maybe, that's what you want us to think," Voss argues.

"Oh, for Christ's sake," I curse with a roll of my eyes. "Are we really going to play knowing-that-you-know-that-I-know-that-you-know?"

"Come on, Barnes," Voss says again.

"Give me a minute with Tom here," Jimmy replies.

Voss stares at him long and hard before saying, "One minute." He turns and heads down the hall.

Jimmy watches out the door for a minute, probably until he's sure that Voss has started down the stairwell before turning back toward me. "You sure you're clean in this, Tom?" he asks, a curious Irish accent in his voice.

"Yeah, Jimmy," I call back, and he turns to leave. "Hey, Jimmy! I have one question."

Jimmy turns back again, and asks with a tired voice, "What is it?"

"What's the address? Of the Larew house?"

"It'll do you no good," Jimmy answers.

"Help me out here. You know I can just go down to the clerk's office and find out. Save me some time."

"Six fourteen West Cedarwood," Jimmy says, and he shuts my door behind him.

I turn to look out my window into the sunny morning. Voss stands on the sidewalk below next to a car parked on the curb, staring up at me as if he's waiting for me to do the one thing that gives him a break in the case. After a moment, the heavy frame of Jimmy strides into view. He walks around the rear of the car to the driver's door and gets in. As he does so, Voss finally breaks his gaze, and enters the car's passenger side. A moment later, the car speeds off.

Chapter 5
West Cedarwood & County Clerk's Office – Friday, December 16th

After finding my cleanest, least rumpled suit, I take a taxi over to West Cedarwood, though not straight to the address Jimmy gave me. About four blocks away I pay the driver (I'm really debating buying a car; even just a cheap heap) and jump out, heading south down a side street for a block. I then turn left and west for three more blocks before turning left one last time to come back north. As I approach the intersection with West Cedarwood, I'm already seeing police everywhere. This is not good.

I skulk my way in broad daylight as close to the street as I can to see what I can see. The six-ten block of West Cedarwood is one big building, a gothic style brownstone that seems to dwarf the street with Paleolithic greatness. I see steps leading up to eight different front doors, but only one of these is the center of activity, the third from the start of the block. I count at least four cars and five officers out front. Who knows how many are inside?

There's no way I'm getting by that many cops without someone knowing who I am or, at least, that I'm not a detective on the force. If I want to get in there, I'm going to have to figure something else out, or maybe wait until things die down a bit.

All right – new plan. From here, I could walk to the county clerk's office, but it would take me close to an hour. I really should consider buying a car – if this case turns out to be as big as it's starting to look, it could be a real windfall for me. I already know Helen is loaded. I think I can get a brand-new Ford for about six hundred bucks. Musing over this, I backtrack a few blocks away from the scene and find another taxi.

Sixty-five cents and ten minutes later, I'm back at the ugly building from two days ago. I suppose it's possible that I might cross paths with Christopher Jones, but I'm not heading for his section. I need property records, which are up on the third floor. Already remembering my discomfort climbing the stairs, I take a ride in the infernal contraption that I'm fairly certain will one day kill a whole bunch of people, but today is not that day.

An older woman with stone gray hair, thick glasses and a no-nonsense dress that looks like its straight from the 1890s sits behind a counter just inside. There's no way past for me, excepting a door to the right with a sign that says "Clerk Employees Only", which I assume would take me to the promised land of all the records beyond the intervening barricade. I stroll up to the counter with by best boyish good looks kind of smile, but she doesn't even stop typing to look up at me.

"Hello," I call softly.

"Yes?" she asks without looking up or pausing her work.

"I was hoping you could help me."

Finally, her fingers stop, suspended in mid-air over the typewriter, and she lifts her head slightly to regard me silently. I widen the smile, fully expecting my strong, youthful appearance, as well as my obvious interest in her, to melt away her all-business façade and unleash the woman inside. She'll be like a sculptor's clay in my hands, ready to be molded into any form I desire, and she will happily let me through the door to find what I need. She has no idea what is about to happen; she's not by any means the first fifty or even sixty-year-old woman I've wooed to get what I need.

She hands me a sheet of paper and says, "Fill this out. Five cents per inquiry."

"Oh, we can do without the bureaucracy, I think," I reply, my eyes locked on hers. "What I need is so simple, and so easily supplied by such a lovely woman as yourself."

She stares at me.

"I'm Tom. You are?"

"Miss Williams," she replies with the efficiency of an United States Army sergeant. "Fill out the form. Five cents per inquiry."

"*Miss* Williams? So, there's no *Mister* Williams I have to compete with," I reply, leaning in. I reach forward to take the paper from her, and oh so clumsily and accidentally land my hand directly on top of hers. I gently caress the back of her hand with my thumb.

"If you will kindly remove your hand from mine, sir, and fill out the form. Five cents –"

"Yes, I know," I admit defeat to the old model refrigerator sitting before me, "five cents per inquiry."

Ten cents and a half hour later, Miss Williams types up two records for me, the originals of which she found back in her icy catacombs. Honestly, I should have just come at her straight on what I needed; she's probably the most effective county employee I've ever met. I wanted to know who owned six fourteen West Cedarwood, but something else occurred to me as well – who owned thirteen hundred Edgemont Place? That's the address Helen had given me, but I found no one home upon my first visit.

Of course, I didn't even know her last name. My calling her Helen Smith… well, that was the one honest lie I'd told Voss.

When Miss Williams hands me the paper, I wander off to one side of the counter to read the newly typed words. Six fourteen West Cedarwood is owned, has been owned for two years, by a company called Mississippi Freight, Incorporated, which would make the Larew family tenants. A Howard and Wilma Shanaberger have owned the house at Edgemont since they bought it in twenty-two for *eighty thousand dollars*. Eighty thousand; I could live the next forty years on that kind of money and never run out. Something's familiar about that name, but I don't know what it is. It seems like I've read it somewhere maybe.

I have one more hunch.

"Miss Williams, can I ask one more thing of you?" I ask pleasantly enough, but all business. "The address on West Cedarwood I had you pull for me is part of a brownstone. There's four other addresses in that building, on that block. If you'll just look at those other addresses, see if they're all owned by this Mississippi Freight, I'll be happy to pay another twenty cents."

She starts to hand me the form, but I put on my best oh-God-please-no face. She sets it back down, the corners of her mouth upturned ever so slightly at the knowledge that she had more than bested her good-looking assailant. "One moment, please," she says, and Miss Williams glides away into rows of records. In only a few minutes, she returns and, with a polite nod, says, "You're correct, sir. They're all owned by Mississippi Freight, Incorporated."

"Thank you so much, Miss Williams," I say genuinely, and I slap a crisp one-dollar bill on the counter as I leave. I hazard a final glance back at her and grin like a sixteen-year-old boy who was just told by a sixteen year old girl that he could kiss her. Miss Williams glanced around once and slid the dollar into a fold in her dress.

Chapter 6
Question for a Friend – Friday, December 16th

I need to get back to West Cedarwood, but it's too early yet. The activity has to die down before I try to get in there to talk to the Larews. If Voss catches me in there, it'll only add more fuel to his fire. At the least, I'll get outright arrested for interfering in his investigation. I won't be able to do much from a gray metal cage. The Detroit Free Press building isn't far from here, maybe a half hour hoofing it, and I have a buddy there that may be able to shed some light on a question I have. He takes lunch between noon and one, so I know right where to find him.

Eugene Miller stands in line outside the hot dog stand across the street from the Free Press. He's a little guy, no more than five foot three and a hundred twenty pounds. He wears a black suit and a brown overcoat with a matching oversized fedora, as always, and like all his suits this one is immense on him. He compensates by tucking his shirt in and constricting a black leather belt way too tight like a snake trying to kill its prey. Also, he cuffs his pants and keeps the top button of his shirt undone, tie pulled down loosely from his neck. To me it just draws more attention to the fact that no one makes suits in his size, and he doesn't make enough to pay for tailoring. I quietly slide in next to him in line, with a friendly nod at the guy behind him.

"Good afternoon, Gene," I say with an outstretched hand.

"Barely," he replies, warily taking my hand without looking at me, "You getting up before noon these days?"

"Not by choice. You would think I'm still in court."

Gene snorts ever so slightly as we step forward in the line. God, he looks young. He has to be coming up on thirty, but he only has to shave about once per week, making him look perpetually fifteen years old. The constant dark shadow on his upper lip does nothing to dispel the image. I think he likes it that way – people tend to underestimate the young, but Gene here is as slippery and savvy as they come.

"I thought you would be covering that abduction up on Cedarwood," I say absently.

"Was late this morning, missed the call."

"That's not like you."

"Was up late," he explains absently, a half-smile appearing for just a moment. "You heard about that?"

There it is. It's the most innocuous question – simple, innocent, and right off the cuff. There was absolutely no hesitation before he asked, his lightning wits making it sound like he didn't even think about it. That's why he is such a good reporter – no one sees him coming. He would have made such a great investigator, such a great interrogator.

"News travels. Hey, I've got a quick question for you."

We step forward again to face the short Jewish guy that owns this particular curbside establishment, and Gene says, "Two. Just mustard, please," as if the guy doesn't know what Gene eats every damn day.

"Make it three," I say, pulling out some cash – otherwise known as the universal exchange medium for information. "It's on me, Gene."

Gene sighs softly, "What do you need?"

"It's not much of anything," I reply, paying the vendor and taking all three hot dogs.

As we step away, Gene's realizing that I full intend to hold his daily lunch as hostage. He asks again, "What is it?"

Making sure we're out of earshot of anyone that might possibly be paying attention, I ask in a voice lowered to be just audible over the street noise, "Does the name Shanaberger mean anything to you?"

"No, I don't think so," he answers thoughtfully as a hand absently scratches an imaginary itch at the top of his forehead. "Is it local?"

"Yeah. Howard and Wilma Shanaberger. Own a house out on Edgemont. Big place."

Gene tucks his lower lip in between his teeth for a moment as he looks down and away, sorting through his own personal archives. After a couple of seconds, his eyes widen just a bit, and his face lifts up to mine. He says, "I know the name. So do you."

"I'm sure, but I can't quite place it."

"The *Shanabergers*," he says as if the emphasis alone will make me remember. "Rich people. Got rich on the import business. You know, back in the *twenties*."

I roll my eyes with a long sigh, cursing myself for being a moron. "How could I of all people forget something about booze?"

Gene laughs at my expense, "I was wondering."

"I wonder what they're up to these days," I muse, handing Gene his hot dogs. How does such a scrawny little runt like him put away two in one sitting.

"The same thing. Importing. It's just legal now. Where do you think that fine product of Scotland you like so much comes from?"

"You remember my brand!" I exclaim, moving a bite of my own lunch to the side of my mouth. "I cannot help but be touched."

"I bet."

"They have kids, to your knowledge? The Shanabergers?" I ask. I really hope Gene knows. I don't want to go back and face Christopher Jones and his collection of birth records, not after I left him high and dry a few days ago.

"Yeah," Gene nods enthusiastically, "they got one son. Went east somewhere. He's a lawyer of all things."

"You sure?"

"Absolutely."

"Thanks a lot, Gene," I reply and quickly turn on my heel. I know he's just staring after me, and I'm one step away from praying to the Almighty that I make a clean getaway.

"Hey, Tom?" Gene howls after me.

Shit.

"What's this got to do with the Larew case?" he shouts across half a block, letting everyone in the damned world know I'm up to something.

"Nothing," I call back over my shoulder, and I pick up the pace, endeavoring to make it look like I'm not running away from him.

Chapter 7
The Larew Residence – Friday, December 16th

It's a nice day for a walk back to the office. I think that if I head back to Cedarwood and arrive around four or five, the police should have mostly dispersed. Which means I have at least three hours to occupy my time before I start the trek down there, assuming I walk and don't take a taxi. That's fine. I need some time to think, some time to go over what I know so far, which, unfortunately, is next to nothing.

Who the hell is Helen, and what is her involvement in all this? How could she possibly have known about an abduction that hadn't happened yet unless she is somehow in on it? If she is involved, why would she come to me and not just the police? Why wouldn't she give me more information? What is her connection to the Shanabergers? I'm willing to accept that my visit to the house was just bad timing, but if she's not related to them in some way, why would she give me their address?

Maybe she has nothing to do with them, but they're somehow involved. And she knows that. So, she gave me their address, knowing I would look into them further. I'm going to have to go back there – maybe tonight – and see if she is there. If no one is home, I can snoop around a little…

I find something else strange – it's not uncommon for a company to buy up property in a city. Property is one of the few investments that in the long run will only go up. After all, there is only so much land. What is bothering me is the company that bought a brownstone taking up an entire city block, apparently as a rental property, is called Mississippi Freight. I'm assuming, just from the company's name that they're some sort of shipping or logistics company, but why would a shipping company buy property to rent out in Detroit of all places? It's an oddity in this affair of oddities, but probably not my biggest worry in this case. I'll see what I can find out about Mississippi Freight tomorrow.

Reviewing these facts, or rather lack thereof, I completely ignore that I've made it all the way to my office, have been seated for some time, and the room has gotten fairly dark. Of course, my window faces east, lighting the room up at a time of day when I'd rather not be awake (poor forethought on my part). This time of year, it gets dark in here fast when the sun passes overhead and into the west on its daily rounds. A quick glance at my pocket watch tells me it's a little after three thirty. Time to get a move on – I grab a fedora that I hardly ever wear and head out.

I pace myself getting down to West Cedarwood, and I arrive at the corner of the block close to five, which is just about perfect. I see two police cars still and only two cops, one who is sitting behind the steering wheel of one of the cars and looking down. He may be filling out paperwork of some kind; more likely he's reading the newspaper or the funny strips. The other cop is a young man I don't recognize, and he's just standing next to the front steps, staring out at nothing. Gloom floods the street itself, the sun having already dropped low enough that the brownstone's roof blocks its barely warm light.

I've got a chance if I do this right.

I pull my hat down tightly, hoping that it blocks as much of my face as possible, and I stride purposefully right down the sidewalk. I pass by the first two addresses and keep walking without any hesitation at all. If I falter or pause in any way, I'll draw this young cop's attention, and the jig will be up. I go right by him without a look, a motion or anything, and he doesn't even seem to notice. I take the steps quickly, like a man on a mission, but not too hurried. I open the door, my peripheral vision telling me he hasn't moved at all, and I step inside.

I find a narrow wood stairway heading up as it hugs a wall on the right, bordering a hallway that moves straight ahead into the home. To the left is a doorway leading to a sitting or family room. Someone stamps around upstairs, and it looks like the hall empties into a kitchen. I cautiously peek into the other room to see two chairs, a long couch and a freestanding radio all clustered cozily around a dark fireplace. I see the back of a man's head with neat brown hair poking out just above the back of the couch. I step lightly into the room, the hardwood floor giving way to a thick rug, and his head turns slightly in recognition of my presence. No choice but to go for it now.

I purposefully come around the side of the couch and take a seat opposite the man in one of the chairs. A small table separates us. All the furniture, though somewhat plain, is of a solid, quality workmanship, just on the precipice of being expensive. The man has a woman leaning against him, her face streaked with tears that have mixed with makeup to stain his shirt. Her eyes are closed, but the speed of her breathing tells me she's not asleep. He's regarding me quietly.

"I'm sorry, Mr. and Mrs. Larew, to put you through this," I say softly. I want to keep my voice as low and calm as possible, partially because I think there's at least one cop upstairs, but also to sound as sympathetic as I can. Reaching into a pocket to pull out a few pieces of paper and a stubby pencil, I ask, "But could I ask you a few more questions?"

"Again, sir?" he asks. "Can you not just talk to your friends upstairs?"

"I'm sorry," I repeat, "but sometimes it's better this way. It lets us all compare later. Sometimes, we come up with something that way."

The wife sits up, wiping at her eyes delicately with two fingers while nodding. "Yes, okay."

I put on my most concerned face. "Thank you. Just tell me again what happened."

"I woke up because I heard Harry crying. He's a good baby. He wakes up every night to eat just once," she starts, her voice trembling just a little.

"Harcourt?" I ask, receiving a nod. "About what time was that?"

"It's always about two. I don't know why, but I just couldn't wake up right away. I saw a person standing there, just over his crib," she says, her voice starting to break.

"It's okay," I say, as soothingly as I can manage. "Can you tell me what he looked like?"

After a moment, she collects herself. "No, it was dark, and I think he was wearing black. I'm not even sure it was a man."

"What did you do?"

"I... I thought I was dreaming... or still asleep. I think I rubbed my eyes, blinked a few times. The person was gone. I got out of bed to check on Harry in his crib, and he... he..."

She sinks like the Titanic then, full blown sobbing and tears flowing everywhere. Mr. Larew wraps his arms around her protectively, rocking ever so slightly back and forth like he might a small child and every few seconds whispering out a long "shhhhhhhhh". He's a pretty straight up looking guy – clean cut brown business hair, clean shaven with a slight shadow and definitely west European descent. He just stares back at me with dark brown, grief-stricken eyes, and I find his gaze unsettling for some reason. It's like his is an older sorrow, the grief of someone who has finally come to terms with their loss, but it still pains them, not at all what I would expect from a man whose son just went missing. He may just handle pressure well.

"She screamed," Mr. Larew continues for her, "and it woke me up. Whomever it was, I think they ran down the stairs and out the back door."

"Where's the back door?"

"The kitchen," he says with a nod of his head that direction. I follow the motion and see a doorway adjoining the sitting room with a small dining room. "There's an alley back there."

"I'll take a look in a minute. Mr. Larew, was Harcourt born here in Detroit?" I ask, not looking up at him. I pretend to write as he answers me.

"No, we moved here six months ago for my job."

"And who do you work for?"

"Mississippi Frei –," he starts but cuts it off quickly. I look up, and his eyes are almost boring holes into me. "What does that have to do with any of this?"

"Just collecting basic information, Mr. Larew," I reply quickly, almost with a shrug.

"Mr. Larew?" a familiar voice calls down from the top of the stairs.

"I'm going to go look at your back door, sir," I say quickly as I stand. "Thank you very much for your time."

"I think we're about done here for the day," the voice proclaims.

I'm already through the dining room and turning the doorknob in the kitchen. I'm moving so quickly, that I nearly trip down the three wooden steps that lead into the world's smallest back yard – a ten foot deep, maybe thirty-foot-wide patch of packed down dirt surrounded by a ten foot tall wooden fence. The rear gate is hanging open, and I push through it quickly to find myself in a narrow, paved alley. Trash and debris litter the area between the brownstone and the building behind it. I pick my way quickly through it all to exit into the clear air of a side street. I start heading home in the least direct way possible.

But first, I think I need to visit Charlie.

Chapter 8
Charlie's – Friday, December 16th

I push my way through the blue gray haze that permanently hangs in Charlie's. It's like the Red Sea, the cloud parting momentarily as I approach it just to fall back into itself once I pass through. The lights are low, as they usually are, and it must be Friday night, because a broad in a red dress with bright red lipstick and fancy done up brown hair stands on the stage singing some lonely sounding song to a piano's accompaniment. I call it a stage, but that's really giving it way too much credit. It's little more than a slightly raised wood platform that someone slapped some blond stain on real quick. A half dozen lonely guys sit by themselves at a half dozen lonely tables crowding the dame, pouring their money and souls into the toilet bowl known as booze. A lone waitress moves between them doling out their solitude in shots and doubles.

The broad is pretty, I'll give her that. Her voice has a sweet longing to it as well, but she'll never get anywhere. Acts like hers run on Friday and Saturday nights in bars, pubs, and restaurants all over the country. If she's lucky, she'll pick up a few bucks from some poor broke schmuck just long enough to survive. Then, once she realizes that life isn't all sunshine and rainbows, she'll marry some hard-working guy who can provide her a home and give up her figure to give him some kids.

And it will all start again. Welcome to 1938 – really no different from '28 or '18 or even 1878... We live in such an age of technological wonder, scientific advancement, and progressive thinking, and yet the cycle of our lives just repeats endlessly as it has for thousands of years. The futility of it all, if everyone truly realized it as I do, would cause worldwide mass suicides. Jesus

Christ, I haven't even started drinking yet today (I'm late), and my head's already going south for the winter.

I saunter up to the bar, which is mostly vacant except for two guys at the far end, closest to the music, and Charlie, of course, who is leaning on his side of the bar watching, listening, and chatting softly with his two patrons. The bar itself is dark mahogany, wrapped by a brass arm rail. I slide one of the matching bar stools out just enough to climb up onto it, resting my feet on the matching brass foot rail. I look down at Charlie, and he's just gazing back coolly. I hold up a finger, and he straightens up, removing his weight from the bar as he sighs and throws a white towel over his left shoulder. He meanders cautiously my way.

I've known Charlie for twenty years, ever since I came home from the war, and I swear he hasn't aged a day, or changed at all. He looked fifty when I first met him, which should make him look seventy now, but no more or less lines crease his face. He's over six foot, and his back hasn't become stooped with age. Most people have become a lot thinner over the last few years, with work and money being so tight, but not Charlie. His roundness, every bit of two hundred fifty pounds, has not lightened a bit, though I imagine Prohibition letting up in '33 has helped with that. He wears his normal black slacks, vest and white shirt with a black bow tie. A big, bushy black mustache, that matches his oiled so-black-to-be-almost-blue hair, twitches a little as he comes to stand before me.

"Evening, Charlie. How's business?" I ask warmly. "Could I get a double?"

"Business is fine," Charlie replies gruffly, "but it'd be even better if I could get people to pay their tabs."

"Oh, come on, Charlie. Don't be like that. You know I'm good for it."

"No," he argues with half of a head shake, "I know you *were* good for it. After everything recently, I'm doubting you can pay up, much less afford more."

I endeavor not to sigh or show any hint of my thoughts at all. Looking in his unblinking eyes for a moment, I almost get lost in the hard gray stare, and it's suddenly very clear that Charlie has no intention of budging an inch. Instantly aware that I've eaten almost nothing today and that the money would be far better spent on food rather than liquor, I look down at the bar in defeat.

"What do I owe you?"

"Fifty-three dollars and twenty seven cents."

"Holy shit! That can't be right. It was just a few drinks."

"Tom, I let you drink for free for about a month," Charlie answers shortly. "You wanna' see the ledger?"

"No…" I reply mournfully.

I turn away from him to reach into my pocket and thumb through my remaining money, blocking his sight with my body. The dame gave me a hundred and ten bucks, and I'm down to about eighty-five. I can make this work. I slide a very recently crisp but getting quickly worn twenty from the pack and shove the rest back into my pocket. I turn back to face Charlie and hold the bill up for him to see.

"How about you bring me two doubles and put the rest toward my bill."

Charlie's eyes light up a moment, and his gruff mood seems to suddenly brighten as he takes the cash. I watch woefully as he slides it into his pocket. He turns away from me, reaching for a bottle and says, "Tom, I'm out of Dewars at the moment. Will Macallan do?"

Crestfallen but desperate, I say, "Yeah, that's fine. You knew I'd be back eventually. How did you run out of the good stuff?"

"Mississippi didn't show today," he replies as he sets the two doubles down in front of me.

As he begins to float back to the other end of the bar, I call after him, "Hey, don't forget to apply the change to my tab!"

"I won't," he replies as goes back to talking to his more important patrons at the bar.

The lady in red finishes her song to some muffled and halfhearted clapping, Charlie being the only one to throw her full applause. She says something about being right back and steps off the stage to head for the bar. Meanwhile, the pianist starts playing something that feels like it should sound familiar, but either he's butchering it or I don't know music very well. In the end, no one cares, because they're not here to see him pound horse teeth. They're not even here to listen to Red.

She's singing something suitably depressing again by the time I finish the first scotch and light up a cigarette. Charlie slides a cheap ash tray down my way. I don't turn to watch Red; I just hunch over the bar to enjoy my Lucky Strike, feeling suitably morose. I nurse the second double a little bit, unsure whether I want to throw more cash at Charlie. About halfway through it, I set it down to smoke again; I'm going to make this last all night if I can.

I hear the barstool next to mine slide out, and Charlie comes over. I neither look up at him, nor over at this newcomer that dares to sit next to me. To do so is the universally recognized sign that you're ready to engage in conversation, and quite frankly, I'd rather kick a litter of puppies than talk to some asshole right now.

"What can I get you?" asks Charlie.

"I'll have whatever he's having," some dame says, and I hear the scratching flick of a cigarette lighter.

That voice…

"Are you sure?" Charlie asks. He pauses, then adds at my expense, "Why would a fine lady like yourself want to drink that piss?"

"Piss matches my dress," she says as she blows a plume of smoke into the air in front of us. "Bring him another one, too."

I glance up at Charlie. Just before he turns away, I see the half smile of a man who appreciates a stabbing wit, especially when hurled at him by a dame. He returns a moment later and *clops* two more glasses on the bar. I quickly drain what's left of my second double scotch, and Charlie efficiently swipes away both glasses as he leaves us alone.

"I went by your office, Mr. McAvoy," Helen says. I know it's her, though I have yet to look her way.

"I'm not there."

"I figured that out for myself."

"So, you're a looker and a wise guy," I say, lighting another cigarette.

"How would you know?" Helen asks. "That I'm a looker, that is. I'm not sure you could really see me in your liquor induced stupor the other night."

"Leave my stupor out of this. She's a close friend, and she visits me often. You came to me. Remember?"

"I remember. What have you found?"

"I found that you came to me over a kidnapping that hadn't even happened yet. A boy, about ten months old, was just taken early this morning. How did you know it was going to happen? And how did you know the baby's initials before it even happened? You're holding something back from me, lady, and that's no way to start a relationship."

I drain my third scotch, and the glorious warmth is spreading through my whole body. I put my cigarette back into the corner of mouth and turn on the barstool to look at her for the first time since she sat down. I'll be damned if she isn't one of the best-looking creatures I've ever seen. She's definitely tall for a broad, sitting as tall on the barstool as I do. A bright yellow dress, visible even in Charlie's gloom, falls in straight lines down just past her knee. It has large lapels of white that come down from her neck to form a "V" right where her curves start. Perfect dark brown hair spills out just slightly from a matching yellow slouch hat all the ladies like so much these days (thank you, Greta Garbo).

Her cigarette had gone out, and when she lights it again, the deepest, darkest brown eyes regard me, silent and intense. A man could get lost in those eyes, and my cold resolve, my frozen heart, starts to melt under their gaze.

I take in a deep breath and say, "All right," with a sigh, but before I can say more, I see the door to Charlie's open. Based on how the moment with Helen had progressed, the fact that I felt like I might just get at the heart of something real, it just stood to reason that Detective Sergeant Voss would walk in at just that instant. It sometimes amazes me how much the universe is out to get me, but truthfully, I should have guessed he'd look for me here once he didn't find me at the office. I look back at Helen and tell her, "We have to go. Now. Stay behind me."

We stand and head for the door, which is of course blocked by Voss – the guy saw me at the bar the moment he walked into the place. I have no idea what I'm going to do or how I'm going to do it, but I'm pretty convinced I can do just about anything and get out of this. It's probably the piss talking, as Charlie called it.

"Evening, Detective Sergeant," I say curtly with no intention of stopping to talk to him.

"McAvoy – we need to talk."

"I'm out with a friend, right now. Come see me at the office in the morning," I reply, and I take an evasive course to get around him to the door.

"No. Right now," Voss says as he forcefully puts a hand on my right shoulder from behind.

Now, it should be understood that as a former cop, I don't generally make it a point of assaulting a police officer, nor do I recommend it, but it seems to me that Voss isn't going to take a simple, "Talk to you tomorrow," as an answer. I certainly could turn and talk to him like a reasonable human being, try to convince him that I have nothing to do with whatever he's here to accuse me of, but I just don't see that as providing the outcome I'm after. Maybe the scotch is clouding my thinking, maybe it's giving me more courage than I may normally have, or maybe I just figure I'm going to end up with the exact same grand finale regardless.

So, the obvious and inescapable conclusion is just to turn around and sock the guy in the jaw just as quick and hard as I can, and Voss never sees it coming. As I turn, I just happen to notice him look at Helen, and his eyes widen with some sort of recognition right before my fist crashes into his face. With a grunt, he flies backward onto a table, upends it and falls to the floor with a shattering of shot glasses and surprised exclamation from patrons.

"Run!" I shout at Helen, and right before the door shuts behind me, I call out, "Sorry, Charlie!"

Once outside and into the dark city street, I take Helen by the hand. "This way," I shout again, adrenaline fueling my vocal volume as well as my desire to run left down the sidewalk.

She takes my hand but pulls the opposite way. "No, my car's this way!"

"You have a car?!"

"Of course, I have a car!"

I let her lead me right, and we break into a full run at the astonishment of the small scattering of people out and about. After just a few steps, we reach Jimmy Barnes as he leans up against one of the new police cars. "Hey, Jimmy," I yell cheerfully as we pass by, and he just shakes his head slowly and knowingly before staring at the sidewalk under his feet, hands in his pockets. Helen lets go of my hand and runs over to the driver's side of a God damned, brand new '38 Cadillac V16. She jumps in, and its massive engine roars to life.

"Is this your car?!" I almost scream at her as I pull the heavy door shut behind me on the passenger's side. I've never been in an automobile so finely appointed and equipped as this, the most expensive Cadillac ever made.

"Don't ask stupid questions!" she shouts back as she throws the car in gear, mashes the accelerator, lets out the clutch and screams down the street.

Chapter 9
M&P Diner – Friday, December 16th

I've never seen a Series 90 Cadillac up close, much less been inside one, and I'm actually rather pleased with myself for recognizing it so quickly having only seen it from afar at the Detroit Auto Show last year. It's everything one would expect from a Cadillac, especially the newest top of the line Cadillac. The front seat, which is far more comfortable than any couch I've ever sat on, is covered in a rich, burgundy leather, matching the leather inset on the inside of the doors. Heavily polished lacquered rosewood accents the leather on the doors and makes up most of the dash. And that says nothing of how quiet the sixteen-cylinder engine is.

"Get out of the way," Helen screams at pedestrians as she presses the horn button, narrowly missing a young couple who had stepped off the curb.

"You are a terrible driver," I inform her, watching her struggling with the steering column mounted gear shifter.

"If these people would just open their eyes," she replies, almost frantically, swerving around a slow-moving vehicle. "I almost didn't see him."

"Try turning on your headlamps."

"What? Oh…" Her crazed grip on the wheel relaxes a bit now that she can actually see what is in front of her. After a few minutes, she asks "Where should we go?"

"Well, we can't go back to my office, so I suggest your house, but let's stop someplace first," I say, relaxing into the car's plush seat.

"Where?"

"Well first, get off this street. If Jimmy got a good look at your car, he'll know there aren't many of these around."

"Oh, no?"

"There aren't many V16 Cadillacs driving around, even in Detroit," I explain. Then I point at an upcoming left turn. "Cut down a few blocks, and double back the way we came. Do that a few times, then we'll find a place to eat."

"What time is it?" Helen asks.

"Coming up on eight, I think. We'll find a lounge or someplace, and then we can go back to your place."

Helen becomes very quiet as she begins weaving through city blocks, and I'm sure I see her briefly gnawing on her lower lip between two teeth. I could be wrong – darkness floods the car, and the soft orange glow from the streetlamps or the headlamps of other cars doesn't allow me to take in a lot of details. At one point she takes her hat off and sets it on the seat between us. After about a half hour of this, we pull up onto a curb outside a place with a big neon sign on the front called M&P Diner.

"How much was this car?" I ask as she turns off the lights and cuts the engine.

"I... I don't really know."

"Let me see the keys," I say. She hands them to me, and I turn the lock for the glove box. I reach in and find what I'm looking for, what I was hoping to find – a bill of sale. I unfold it and hold it closer to the window to give me just a tiny amount of light to read by. I whistle. "Seven thousand bucks!"

"Is that much?"

"Well, it's about what I made total my last three years when I was on the police force," I explain. I fold the receipt back up and restore it to its proper resting place. I lock the glovebox and hand her back the keys. "Shall we go inside?"

As we exit the car and walk to the restaurant's front door, my mind is racing through the fact this woman doesn't know how much money seven grand is. Admittedly, I don't know much about her. I don't even know her last name or how old she is, but surely a grown woman has a sense of money. And for now, I'll certainly keep something else to myself – the car was sold back in April to Howard Shanaberger.

The diner is narrow as a bowling alley. High backed, cushioned wooden benches create booths on the left, a table placed between each pair. The right has a long counter separating the kitchen, and leather upholstered spinning barstools allow seating at the counter. A radio plays softly somewhere in the background, and a gray haired, older lady – my guess would be coming up on sixty – is standing behind the counter adding up the day's take.

"Excuse me, ma'am," I call over to her, "Are you about to close?"

She looks up from her task, sees us standing there and flashes a smile at what she probably thinks is a good-looking couple, "Not quite yet. Have a seat. I'll be there in a minute."

I walk down the row of booths and select the last one, sitting with my back up against the wall behind me so I can see the door. I know there's next to no chance at this point that Voss will find us here, but I still want to be able to see who comes in the place. Helen sits opposite me, and we both politely remove our hats to sit them next to us. I realize just how perfectly defined her face is, how perfectly symmetrical, but her eyes take hold of me yet again. They're deep and dark, intelligent, and knowledgeable, and yet a degree of naivete hides within them. I have so many things to grill her over, but somehow her eyes just melt my resolve. Or maybe the scotch has worn off.

"Shall we talk or just keep staring at each other?" Helen asks, breaking the moment.

"Yeah, I think we need to have a talk."

"What have you found?"

Before I can answer, the woman behind the counter has appeared. She wears an understated light blue dress covered with a white apron, and her gray hair is wrapped up on top of her head. "Need menus?" she asks.

"I don't think so," Helen muses. "Do you have any steaks?"

"A good t-bone. How do you like it?"

"Very rare."

"What else do you want with it?"

"I'm not picky," Helen replies with a smile. She has the whitest, most perfect teeth. "Could I get a glass of water?"

"No problem, young lady. What can I get you, young man?"

"Is it too late for bacon and eggs? Scrambled?"

"Not here, it's not. I'll bring you hashbrowns with that. Do you want anything to drink?"

"I guess scotch isn't on the menu," I half mumble, receiving an eyebrows raised look in return. "Just coffee, please. Black."

"Be out soon," she says with a smile and heads for a break in the counter, hollering, "Pop, pull out a t-bone!"

M&P? Mom and Pop Diner?

"So, you want to tell me your last name?" I ask Helen.

"I'm paying you," she says. "You answer my questions, not the other way around."

"All right." I'm about to get mad, so I lean forward across the table and lower my voice. I want to make sure she hears my feelings on the matter without declaring them to the entire damned world. "The other night, you told me the police don't have a clue. Well, you were right. They didn't know a damned thing because the abduction of ten-month-old Harcourt Pennington Larew hadn't happened yet. It happened maybe eighteen hours ago, almost two days after you came to me."

Helen doesn't move a millimeter, doesn't even seem to breathe. She's so still, you might think she's the most lifelike statue anyone had ever created, a living, breathing woman just frozen in time by some witch's evil spell. Except... I swear a flicker of light flashes through her eyes for just an instant, those dark brown eyes trying to disarm me of my anger.

"But you're not surprised by that, are you? How did you know this was going to happen?" I growl.

"I," Helen starts, and then holds back to smile at the old lady bringing my coffee and her water.

"Food will be out in a few minutes," Mom says and glides away.

"I can't tell you," Helen says.

"The Hell you can't."

"I don't know any more about Harcourt," she pauses as if she's searching for her next words.

"Pennington Larew," I repeat.

"Pennington Larew than you do."

"Maybe not, but you're holding back on me, lady. I need to know what you know."

"What I know," Helen says slowly while pulling a cigarette out of a pack, "won't help you find the boy, and that's what I hired you for."

"Why? Why do you care?"

"He's just a baby," Helen breathes, almost convincingly.

I lean back in the booth, lighting my own cigarette. I breathe in deeply, then blow the smoke straight up in the air, my eyes locked on hers the entire time. She's not giving it up that easily. I almost want to believe that she's just a concerned innocent bystander in all this, but the unanswered questions in my gut overpower this façade she would have me believe.

"To paraphrase Elliott – bullshit," I finally respond. "What's your full name? How are you related to the Shanabergers?"

"Who?" Helen asks, and response is quick, natural.

"The address you gave me – the house is owned by Howard and Wilma Shanaberger. What's your connection to them?"

"I don't have one. I'm watching their house while they're out of town."

"Housesitting? I was there the other day, and no one was home."

"I have other things to do, too," she replies, putting out her cigarette before its finished.

I look up and see Mom coming our way with a plate in each hand, and I'll admit the food looks glorious. I haven't had a good, real, home cooked meal in what feels like forever. Within moments I know it tastes as good as it looks, and I consider that maybe a steady diet of scotch and Lucky Strikes may not be the best way to live. Helen dives into her steak with a gusto the likes of which I don't expect from a pretty, young woman, her knife and fork squeezing juice one step removed from blood from the meat. She wanted very rare, and she got it. With apparent disgust, she pushes some broccoli off to the side and tears a roll in half, laying the split bread inside down on the plate to soak up the juice. Honestly, I've never quite seen a woman eat so aggressively.

"All right look," I say around a mouthful of the best, buttery, fried hashbrowns I've ever had, "you have secrets, and you're not ready to tell me what they are. But let me tell you one thing – if its pertinent to my investigation, I need to know. For that matter, I'll find out eventually anyway. So, tell me now, tell me later, or don't tell me at all. I don't care. You want to know what I've found so far, here it is."

I stop short as the door to the diner opens with a jingle of a bell hanging from the inside handle, and two uniformed cops stroll inside. I make a point of nodding to them politely, and then returning my eyes back to Helen's face. She doesn't even pay attention to me or that I've stopped talking, so intent she is on her meal. The police officers don't pay me any mind at all as the saunter up to the counter.

"Hey, Mom," one calls into the back from the counter. "Any coffee on?"

"For you guys? Always," Mom replies, coming back to the front with a full pot. "On the house."

Everything is silent for a moment as the police officers taste their coffee, and Helen and I focus on our meals. For me, it was about remaining unseen, but she seems to be genuinely starving. The radio seems to have moved on to some news. A voice says, "In international news – at the opening ceremony for a new section of the Autobahn yesterday, Joseph Goebbels announced that the Reich's territory is still too small to meet the German people's vital needs."

"Jesus," says the cop on the left, the one who called for the coffee, "those madmen are going to start a war."

"So what?" replies the other.

"I'd think we all learned our lesson last time."

"Let it stay over there. It's not our problem."

"God, I hope so," Mom chimes in. "Pop just missed the Great War, but I know we lost so many young men. You don't think we would get mixed up in that, do you?"

"Of course not," right says at the same time left replies, "Probably."

I try to ignore the two cops, because I really don't want to hear any more of this conversation. Just hearing talk of a war anything like twenty years ago is making my ears ring. Helen has nearly picked the t-bone clean, meat, fat and all, and is savoring her reddish-brown soaked bread, the broccoli still completely ignored. I stare back down at my own plate, my appetite suddenly gone. After another minute or so, the cops bid Mom goodnight and head out.

"Jesus, I thought they would never leave," I mumble.

"Who?" Helen asks, looking up as if she forgot the whole world was there.

"The police. Never mind."

"You were about to tell me –"

"Oh, yeah. So, a baby boy with the initials H.P.L. was abducted, just like you said. His mother woke up in the middle of the night and caught a glimpse of a figure, maybe a man in dark clothes, as he took the baby. I couldn't get much more out of the Larews. I had to go unless the police found me there. That's what Voss wanted back at Charlie's, I'm sure."

"Doesn't sound like you found out much," Helen comments with an annoyingly matter of fact tone.

"Yeah..." I agree with resignation, staring at the ceiling. "I'd like to get back in there, the house on Cedarwood, to look around. I'm sure the police dusted for fingerprints, but I want to snoop around myself. If the police match the prints to someone, my part of the investigation will be over pretty quickly."

"I'm sure they won't," she replies, and the certainty in her tone forces my eyes back to her face. Something on her face tells me that she's absolutely right, but after just a second, whatever it is disappears, leaving me with mystery yet again.

After a few seconds of silence, I tell her, "Eventually, you're going to have to tell me what you know. Why not right now?"

I don't even hear her answer, except noting that it was something negative yet again pushing me off, because a realization strikes me like a lightning bolt. I can't believe I missed it, and now I've got three things on my to do list. I already mentioned to Helen my need to go back to the Larew residence, but now I really want to get inside the Shanaberger house. The third thing, as well as the easiest to accomplish? I need a phone directory. I realize I've been silent for a few seconds, Helen regarding me without a word.

"How about we go back to your place?" I ask.

"I don't think our relationship has come that far yet, Mr. McAvoy," she replies sardonically.

Mom shows up rather suddenly, a protective matriarch hovering over a young woman's honor. "We're about to close up for the night. Would you two like anything else or just the check?"

"The check is fine. Thank you," I reply, and Mom tears a receipt out of a carbon book. She begins to hand it to me, and I hold up my hands like someone's pointing a gun at me. "Oh, no. The lady will be handling this one. Plus expenses, remember? Consider this an expense."

Helen betrays nothing as she reaches into her purse. After a moment, she hands Mom a five-dollar bill and says, "Keep it. Thank you, very much."

After a few minutes, we're back outside at Helen's car, and I've made a point of not saying a word or showing any surprise whatsoever. I saw the total for our meals – three dollars and twelve cents – which made that five bucks one hell of a tip. It's becoming extremely apparent that, whomever Helen is, she has absolutely no clue as to the value of money. Maybe she's rich.

"By the way, I didn't mean it that way – what I said about going back to your place. It's just that I can't go back to my office right now."

"I see," she replies coldly. "Tonight is not a good night, and I have to get back."

"So, I guess I had better find a hotel with a room."

"I guess you had better," she echoes.

"I'm going to need some more money."

"I paid your fee for five days," she disagrees, opening the door to the Cadillac, "It has only been two.

"It's essentially been three – Wednesday, Thursday, Friday," I reply, popping up a finger as I count each day. "Besides, I said 'plus expenses'. This is another expense. Your little case has me spending money on lodging, now."

Helen sighs, but she has absolutely no problem finding me another fifty dollars. "I'll meet you back here tomorrow at five o'clock," she says before she speeds off.

I know I saw a place a few blocks back on the corner of Randolph and some other street – a big place called Hotel Mason or something. I doubt I'll have a problem getting a room there; as well as Detroit has weathered the last ten years, business just isn't what it used to be. But I have a short layover to make first.

I stop at the nearest phone booth, a cherry-stained wood box with glass windows. Finding it unoccupied, I pull open the door and shut myself inside. I reach down into the deep pockets of my overcoat until my fingers feel the cold metal of my battery powered flashlight. I flick it on, revealing one of the new Bell phones with a slot for change, but that's not what I'm trying to find.

On a recessed shelf under the phone itself, I find a thick, bound book, whose contents are printed on paper very similar to that of a newspaper. The flashlight held by my shoulder in the crook of my neck, I flip to the second half of the book, where I find businesses in alphabetical order by category and sort through to the Fs. My finger drags down page after page until I find the heading "Freight Companies". Down to the bottom of the page and on to the next, my finger finally stops on Mississippi Freight at twenty-three nineteen Gordon Street.

"I'll be damned," I grumble.

I tear the page from the book, so I don't forget the address, slide the phone directory back in place and let myself out of the phone booth while pocketing my flashlight.

So, Mississippi Freight has an address here, and based on the address, I'd say it's down near the docks between Lake Erie and Lake St. Clair. The Larews moved into the city just a few months ago, right into the brownstone that Mississippi Freight bought shortly before. Okay, so he works for them, and they needed him to come to Detroit. So, they gave him a place to live; I'll bet everyone in the brownstone works for Mississippi Freight – nothing terribly outlandish about that. But…

When I asked for Dewar's, Charlie said he was out, because Mississippi missed his delivery. A freight company missing a delivery isn't the strangest thing I've ever heard of, but a freight company that just happens to deliver liquor in the same city where there is a family that made themselves very, very rich importing liquor from Canada during Prohibition? Now, that is very interesting.

Chapter 10
Larew Residence – After Midnight, Saturday, December 17th

Freezing air permeates the night, and under the general odor of automobile and factory fumes that flood Detroit, I smell the snow that's starting to move in over the city. Heavy snowstorms aren't particularly common this early in the year, but that's not to say it won't happen. If nothing else, maybe we'll get a white coating that sticks around just long enough to get the kids through the holidays. I'd give anything to be one of them again, to forget the things I've seen men do to other men. Of course, I've got a foreboding feeling that some of these children are going to see the same types of things soon.

It's a long, slow, and damned cold walk from Hotel Mason to Cedarwood, and again I curse not having a car. I'm sure the hotel concierge could have called me a taxi, but I want to keep as much money in my pocket as I can. Besides, hoofing it all but guarantees that I'll show up at the Larew residence well after midnight. I don't know that I'd be able to sleep if I were in their shoes, but on the other hand, eventually exhaustion gets the better of anyone. I should know – twenty years ago I slept in places that normal men would deem impossible, and the Larews have good reason to be exhausted. Still, I walk the city blocks with my coat wrapped tightly around me, somehow keeping warm with my gloved hands in my coat pockets, arms pulled in close.

The electric streetlamps have already gone out for the night, and there's very little natural light by which to see. A week, ten days ago, a full moon shined down on the city, but tonight it's just a sliver of crescent. The stars can't even penetrate the light cloud cover that drifts northeast. I'm glad for the darkness.

I cross West Cedarwood, peering into the night for any activity in front of the Larew's home. Seeing none, I keep going and find my way back to the alley behind the brownstone. I hadn't noticed it before when I left in such a hurry, but it really stinks of garbage, waste, and rot. I slow my pace to be as silent as I can manage. Coming close to the gate leading to the rear of the Larew's, my foot kicks a glass bottle I couldn't see. It spins and clatters deafeningly in the paved alley before coming to a stop. I freeze in place as a dog somewhere further down the alley begins to bark, the only sound in the night. After only a few seconds, the mongrel seems to lose interest and goes quiet again, leaving me standing absolutely still in the alley for an eternity. Not one beam of light from any source pierces the inky black of the alley, so I'm pretty sure I've avoided complete catastrophe.

The gate is closed, so I push lightly against it. It feels like it wants to give, but something behind it forces it to stay in place. I think back to my flight through this very gate earlier, trying to remember what sort of lock the gate has, but nothing comes to mind. I retrieve my flashlight from deep inside one of my coat pockets and outline the gate in search of any locking mechanism or even just a simple bar. Seeing nothing, I drop to the ground and look under the gate, endeavoring not to think of the filth lining the alley, and I see it – a simple wooden board, wedged into the ground up against the gate an angle, probably against a cross member.

While the fence itself seems solid enough, the gate is rather rickety, almost like it was added to the ten-foot fence as an afterthought. I'm sure I could break through it, but that's probably not my best plan, considering I'm trying *not* to make noise. I could lean down, get my fingers under the gate, and lift it just a little. It wouldn't take much play to make the board fall away, I think, but again, how much noise do I really want to make here. There's got to be another way.

I continue down the alley as silently as I can manage, and try the next two gates, finding them to also be closed and locked in some manner. I return to the Larew's gate and backtrack the way I came, and I'm rewarded as the gate to the neighbors' just silently swings inward. I look into the miniscule yard, swing my flashlight around once to make sure all is clear and enter. The fence is a standard picket style with heavy four by four posts and two by four cross members. I gently press some of my weight against it, and it neither moves a hair nor groans against me.

I return to the alley and remove my flashlight from my overcoat. I then remove the coat, fold it and lay it in the cleanest place I easily spot in the dark – on top of a crate. I then take off my suit jacket and lay it on top, but not before I retrieve a small leather pouch and slide it into my back pocket. Finally, I remove my fedora and place it atop the coats. Damn, it's cold. I consider leaving my gun behind, but it seems secure enough in the holster wrapped around my shoulders. I make sure I still have a pencil and a scrap of paper in one of my pants pockets, and I return to the fence, jamming the flashlight as far into the other pocket as it will go.

Scaling the fence is easy, and I land on a thick layer of moss that muffles my drop to the ground as well as I could hope. I pause and count to fifty, just to be certain I've alerted no one.

I try to look through the window of the back door but can see nothing but black. I check the doorknob, but of course it's locked. Breaking the window clearly isn't an option. I quickly shine my flashlight onto the doorknob; it's a simple lock. I kneel down in front of the door and pull the pouch out of my back pocket. I quickly select a couple of tools and set my gloved fingers to work on the lock. The tension in the doorknob disappears in just a few seconds.

I swiftly enter and close the door silently behind me. I stand very still, listening for any sound inside the townhouse, and after a few seconds, I again swing the beam of my flashlight around the room. I am in the kitchen through which I fled just eight or nine hours ago. The silence and stillness of it all feels surreal and disconcerting even as specks of dust flow lazily through my ray of light. There's really not much that strikes me here, but I see where the police dusted the door and several other surfaces for fingerprints. How nice of them to clean up after themselves…

I stick my head through the doorway to my right to look around the dining room I paid no attention to in my flight. A simple, elegant cherry table with six chairs surrounding it fills the room. A matching sideboard and hutch stand in the far corner to my right. Another open doorway to the left leads to the sitting room where I interviewed the Larews.

I turn around and scan the kitchen again. Across the room from the home's back door is the narrow hall that leads to the front door and the stairs going to the next level. A three quarters sized door, probably to a pantry, is just to the left of the entrance to the hallway. What do I actually expect to find here? Probably nothing except for the gnawing in my gut when I think back of the look in Mr. Larew's eyes. Before I head down the hall, I almost absent mindedly try the doorknob to the pantry. Who locks a pantry door?

The lock is surprisingly more difficult to pick than the first, but I still manage to open it with minimal effort. Perhaps I missed my calling as a common street criminal? I gently pull it open, wincing at the slight squeal of the hinges, and peer into a blackness that could lead straight to Hell as far as I can see. I shine my flashlight down a narrow set of unfinished wooden steps with a low ceiling that end at a dirt floor. I have to turn my body slightly sideways to fit in between the walls, and the wooden plank steps groan softly as I cautiously make my way down. I'm glad to reach the dirt floor at the bottom; I felt like those steps were actively trying to wake the dead as I traversed them.

The room below me looks like an unfinished basement. It's one large room, essentially the same size as the entire floor above, though there are some columns and two partial walls made of concrete blocks in places. My guess is they bear part of the load of the townhouse above. A riveted steel furnace sits in one corner, a black pipe leading out of it into the ceiling above me. Nearby is a three-foot-tall pile of coal, and a shovel stands on its own, imbedded into the black mound.

Apparently, this lark into the cellar is a waste, and as I turn to head back upstairs, my flashlight catches something I hadn't noticed shoved into the corner behind the steps. A writing desk with a matching chair hide under the stairs. It looks ancient, like something that belonged to Thomas Jefferson in the eighteenth century when he penned the Declaration of Independence. Feeling the wood, I'm certain it is made of oak and very, very old. A cover, also wood, on some sort of track is pulled down over the front of the desk, shielding its contents. I gently pull up on it but find it to be locked and solid.

I sit in the chair to get a sense of the desk's size. I would think the surface on which one would write is thirty inches to three feet from the floor, but the shield – I don't know what else to call it – seems to pull out of the top of the desk, probably a good six feet tall. How did they even get the damned thing down here? I drop to my knees on the dirt floor and shine my flashlight up underneath the thing, but it is all solid wood construction with no apparent way in from below or behind.

I pause a moment in consideration of this find, still kneeling in the dirt, when I spy a rather modern, red painted wastebasket. I slide it out from its corner and look inside, seeing a single, lone piece of paper that was apparently balled up when it was discarded. I work it open, careful not to tear the delicate paper, and I find the beginnings of a letter written in script with a fountain pen. I climb up into the chair to read it.

> Exalted One,
> I find I am having misgivings in regards to our latest endeavor. I know the honor you have shown me by choosing me for the greatest of sacrifices, and I know the importance that we not fail. Regardless, I could not have known how this would weigh upon me as

The letter ends there. Apparently, whomever wrote it, my guess would be a man based on the vertical nature of the script, changed his mind at that point. The date written in the upper right-hand corner – December 15th, 1938 – is the day before Harcourt Larew was abducted.

Who addresses a letter "Exalted One"? And whom in the name of Hell goes by such a title? Did Mr. Larew write this, and why did he change his mind and throw it away?

Every damned thing I learn in this case seems to give me even more questions, but I know one thing for sure – I need to get into this desk. A small knob protrudes from the front of the shield, and I pull up on it a bit more forcefully. It moves just slightly, but immediately returns to its place. It feels like a fairly ordinary latch and tension clasp type system, which would mean there's a release for it somewhere. After a few minutes of fumbling around to no avail, impatience gets the better of me. I pull up on the knob – I guess it is meant to pull the cover down - as hard as I can manage, standing in the chair to increase my leverage. I lean hard to the right, causing a miniscule gap to appear on the left – just enough to get a few of my fingers inside. The damn thing tries to crush them for a moment, and I almost yelp out in pain before I get all my strength up under the lip of the cover. With a loud splitting of wood, the cover finally releases, and I push it up out of the way.

The desktop is wide and smooth with ample room for just about any project. There is a half dozen cubbyholes with various contents, but my eyes immediately go to the one containing a small stack of paper that looks just like the sheet in my hand. I gently slide one piece out, and it feels just as delicate as that with the half-written letter. A fountain pen sits to the side. I again wedge the flashlight between my neck and shoulder and write the name Larew on my blank piece of paper. The ink appears to be the same as that on the balled up, half written letter which I shove into one of my pockets.

Above the compartments full of writing supplies is a bookshelf, laden with a number of heavy tomes. I scan my light over their spines – *King James Bible*, *Complete Works of Shakespeare*, *On the Origin of Species*, *Moby Dick* – all pretty normal at first. But then comes the bizarre - *The Necronomicon*, *Astronomy of Yag*, *Creation and Destruction and the Yellow Sign, Nexus of Insanity*. There are several others with no discernible titles, but they appear absolutely ancient. Most of the books I don't recognize are leather bound, and something about their very existence makes my skin crawl.

I missed it before, but now I see in the cubbyhole furthest to the left a small stack of what appears to be opened letters. I reach forward to take a look at them when I suddenly hear footsteps upstairs. I grab the letters quickly and kill my light. I should have closed the door behind me when I came down. Now, someone up there knows there is someone down here.

"Who's there?" a man's voice echoes down the steps. I'm pretty sure it's Mr. Larew; he must have heard me either on the steps or breaking open the desk.

An electric light set into the middle of the room's unfinished ceiling suddenly turns on, driving gloom into the corners. As quietly as I can manage, I stand from the chair and hunch under the steps, trying to somehow blend into the shadows. The steps above me begin to creak slowly as he cautiously begins to descend. I hazard a glance upward, and I'm certain I see the barrel of a revolver in Larew's hand.

He reaches the bottom of the steps and searches the room from his left to his right. I wait until the last possible second, until he's looking through the gaps of the steps at where his desk should be. After a moment, his eyes widen, suddenly realizing that he's staring right back at my own. I don't know if he recognizes me or not, and I don't wait to find out. I charge out from under the steps, perhaps just a half second before the gun goes off and the slug passes behind me to embed into the desk and block wall beyond. Before he can fire again, I bull rush him and bowl him over. Larew crashes backward into the corner, and I kick my foot out to connect with his wrist. The gun clatters against the wall, hits a wooden step and then falls in behind the stairs.

Before Larew can recover, I fly up the steps two at a time. As I rush out the back door for the second time in less than a day, I'm vaguely aware of a woman screaming from the upper level of the house. I kick the board wedging the fence's gate shut and rush out into the alley to grab my effects. As I run off into the night, I wonder, besides my growing list of crimes – breaking and entering, burglary, destruction of personal property and assault – in what sort of mess have I gotten myself mixed up?

Chapter 11
Cantigny, France, 1918

I make sure to breathe in through my mouth instead of my nose to avoid the scents of the trench. France, cold up until recently, had warmed well with Spring, and the new warmth brought rain, heavy and sloppy. I can't tell if the low, distant rumble comes from the depths of the clouds above or from the firing of artillery guns. I lean up against the side of the trench, boards doing everything they can to hold back the seeping mud that still managed to pass and settle on the trench's floor. They told us to keep our feet dry and warm, to change our socks as often as necessary to avoid trench foot – good damn luck finding a dry pair of socks or boots that aren't full of water.

As we were being shipped out, we all had these beautiful ideals of what France would be like – idyllic, sun showered fields, hills and plains, good wine, and even better companionship. Millions of French men would congratulate us on victory assured, and the millions of French women? Well, they would most certainly swoon and indulge us in our search for love. None of us really believed France would be wet and full of blood and death, and yet, here we are.

"Hear that?" my pal, John Tomansky from Cleveland, says from the corner of his mouth. He's trying, most unsuccessfully, to light a cigarette in the downpour.

"Thunder," I mumble, unconvinced.

"Not thunder," John disagrees, flicking his cigarette off into the mud, "Those are guns. Something's happening."

I listen intently, as do dozens of other men throughout the trench, and I'm fairly certain that he's absolutely right. The constant low rumbling isn't thunder at all, but rather a rolling artillery barrage that seems to fire continuously some miles behind us. Such a sudden mass of artillery fire means that an attack is about to happen – either our guns are firing to soften the enemy position or they're firing in response to the German's firing to do the same. I peer down the trench and see the captain talking to two lieutenants and some non-coms. Yep, we're about to attack. The small meeting disperses to organize the men, and one of the NCOs – I don't remember his name – starts pulling together my platoon.

"Get ready. We're about to go take Cantigny," he says in an obnoxious Minnesotan drawl.

"Cantigny?" one of the men asks.

"It's a village up there on the hill. Can't see it from here for the trees around it. Germans are using it for artillery observation. Everyone ready, we go in fifteen."

As the sergeant moves off, the other men and I exchange knowing looks. We're about to charge out of this trench across over a mile of open ground toward an elevated position. We've heard about these sorts of attacks before, and it generally ends a whole bunch of guys getting machine gunned down just feet out of the trench. All fairy tales forgotten, I know now that this is France.

"To Hell with this," John says, and he again works to light a cigarette.

I don't think much of his comment as I make ready, which really means little more than gathering my sodden pack and my Springfield rifle. After less than a minute, I'm as ready as I'll ever be. The guns continue to fire behind us, but now the ground shakes ever so slightly. No, it's more of a steady vibration that I can feel through the mud and planks that make up the trench floor. I hear a growing, dull roar underlying it all, and it seems to be in tune with the vibration. After a moment, I recognize the sound of engines and tracks of thirteen-ton Schneiders.

"I'm not going," John says.

"Don't be ridiculous."

"Charging that village is ridiculous. Germans'll cut us down."

"We have orders," I tell him. "We'll be fine. Do you hear that? The French are giving us armor. Just stay behind the Schneiders."

"To Hell with that."

The men form around the many ladders that lead out of the trenches, our platoon no different. John doesn't seem to want to move forward, so I stand with him near the back of the line. Time is almost up. A nearby explosion rattles our brains, a German artillery shell that struck ground maybe only five or ten yards away from us. Sod and mud rain down on us from above. The German artillery has started up in answer to our own guns, or perhaps their spotters saw the French armor coming forward.

"I'm not going," John says again, receiving a couple fearful glances from the other men.

"We'll stay together. Stay behind the armor. We'll be fine."

"I'll be fine," John agrees, "because I'm not going out there."

"The Devil you're not!" shouts Sergeant Minnesota, storming toward us.

As if to punctuate the tension and complement the twisted look upon the sergeant's face, guns in the distance begin to fire again. A lot of them. As he crosses over to me and John, there is a brief pause in the firing as azimuths are adjusted before the guns blast off again. My guess is the French artillery is conducting a rolling barrage – it's a common tactic where they completely plaster a line across the battlefield and then adjust their firing so the next round of shells lands a hundred or two yards behind the last. They'll do that all the way to Cantigny, and if they've started, it means we have precious seconds before we leave the trench.

As if I need any more confirmation of this, the sides of the trench rumble and shake, and a clacking of metal slaps the ground. Men yelp and duck instinctively as thirteen-ton metal beasts, little more than glorified, steel sheeted tractors cross more narrow portions of the trenches. The 28th Regiment and I will fall in behind them for protection from enemy machine gun fire. We haven't much time, only seconds at this point.

"Fall in, soldier," says Minnesota.

"No thanks, sarge," John replies nonchalantly as he tries to puff on an increasingly soggy cigarette. The non-com from Minnesota's face turns bright red in moments at the disinterested disobedience as he grows more and more furious.

There's really no time for this as the Schneider tanks are already in position and idling waiting for us infantry to clamber out of the trench one by one like an army of ants. As we start to form up, they'll begin to march slowly forward while more men climb out to form long columns behind the tanks to protect us from the machine gun fire that would surely be coming. Eventually, they would push up to their top speed of four or five miles per hour, causing us to jog or run behind them. Some of us might still get hit, but a bigger fear is tripping or just plain losing my balance in that column of men; either I'd slow down the whole column, making us a better target for the guns, or I'd just get trampled to death.

The sergeant pulls out his forty-five revolver and checks to make sure it's loaded. Whenever I see one of these, I wonder if the user has a romanticism for cowboys or if the army was just out of the 1911 pistols when he was issued his weapon. "You're under arrest, private," he says.

"No, sarge, I don't think so," John replies, still just leaning against the side of the trench. I hear the Schneiders beginning to move.

Sergeant Minnesota points his revolver right at John's face, his own screwed up in anger as he shouts over the armor, "Fall in or report to the stockade. Those are your choices, soldier."

"You're really gonna shoot me, sarge?" John asks, to which the non-com merely responds by cocking his weapon. John tries to look nonchalant, but his eyes betray him.

"It's okay," I exclaim, almost jumping between the two with my hands up. "Come on, John, this is what we signed up for. There's French ladies up there right now just waiting to be rescued by a big, strong American."

John's resolve crumbles, likely caused more by the gun pointed his direction rather than my promise of feminine companionship. He sighs and drops his cigarette into the mud, turning to pick up his soaked pack. I turn back to Sergeant Minnesota with raised eyebrows, who uncocks his revolver and holsters it.

"Form up!" he shouts, and he takes his place at the head of the platoon, ready to urge the men up and out of the trench when our time comes.

"Screw you, Tom," John mutters as he wanders toward the ladder.

I shoot him a friendly smile and put a hand on his shoulder. "Just trying to keep you from getting killed, pal."

"Shot by him or shot by the Germans is still shot," he replies glumly.

"Maybe," I concede, "but at least this way you have a chance."

Shockingly, we stood in the village merely a half hour later, having faced hardly any resistance. We had run up hill carrying our forty or fifty pounds of gear, through mud, every second ready for a German artillery shell that would disable one of the tanks, forcing the men behind it to find a new column, likely getting mowed down by machine gun fire while doing so. Or worse – maybe the shell misses and lands behind the Schneider, turning a score of guys into an explosion of dirt turned red with bloody mist and body parts turned shrapnel.

There was some of that, but nothing compared to the wholesale slaughter this war had been. When we reached the village, there were a handful of guys from the German Eighteenth Army, but not a lot of fighting. We lost a few of our boys to be sure, but once the Germans realized they were up against almost four thousand Americans and dozens of French tanks, they lost their stomach for fighting. Once the village was secure, we moved on an artillery spotting position less than a half mile away. They even hit us back early the next morning on our right flank, but we knocked them back easily.

John and I hold a post next to a beaten-up French house overlooking what once was a grassy, picturesque slope, something that might have appeared in a famous landscape painting by some French or British artist. Now, it was nothing but brown dirt torn up by tank tracks and impact craters. The Germans had been hitting us with artillery all day, keeping us on our toes. I am sure the officers expect an attack any moment, and the NCOs are keeping everyone sharp and alert. Fortunately, John and I are on the extreme left of the line, nearly facing back the way we came.

"I told you we would be fine," I finally say to John. I had held back the obligatory I told you so until now, until I felt pretty safe in saying it.

"The war isn't over yet. Any minute those Germans are going to send a whole army back on this village. You know that don't you?"

Almost on cue, a streaking sound cuts through the sky. Someone shouts, "Take cover!" and an explosion lands somewhere in Cantigny. A few more shells land, but nothing within fifty yards of my position with John. Even still, I drop to the ground and keep myself as compact as possible. The chance that a shell lands right on me is much, much lower than being hit by flying shrapnel because I'm dumb enough to be standing up during an artillery barrage. A hazard a glance over at John and see that he's just leaning up against the house like nothing's happening around him, his hand cupped around a flame while he lights a cigarette.

"Goddammit, get down!"

John just shrugs and puffs on his cigarette. "What's the point? We're all gonna' die anyway."

"Not today," I shout back over another impact somewhere nearby. I begin to scramble to my feet; I'm gonna force the bastard to get down if I have to, even if I have to lay down on top of him.

He stops me cold when he says, "Why, Tom? Why do you keep coming back here?"

"What?" I whisper, somehow knowing that this isn't the way the conversation is supposed to go, not the way it went twenty years ago. Somehow, John hears me despite the constant hurtling screams and explosions of the German artillery.

"Why do you live in this place? Why here? Now? The world is moving on without you."

"I can't do anything about the world," I answer despairingly. "The world is going to destroy itself no matter what I do."

"Maybe," John concedes with an almost knowing nod, "but right now there's a baby boy that needs your help."

"Why bother?" I ask.

"Because it's who you are."

John flicks his cigarette away and pushes away from the side of the house, apparently having finally made the decision to take cover or at least get down. He takes one step forward, and that horrible screeching of a shell cutting air drowns out all other sound. The shell lands at John's feet just as I put my face down in the dirt, and an explosion fills my being. My hearing just blacks out, replaced by a high-pitched whine, higher than any violin could make. I lift my face and look around, finding nothing but smoke choking my vision. I'm vaguely aware that my helmet is gone, probably blown right off my head. I sit up, still unable to hear anything but the damned accursed whine, and I grope around my face and body until I am satisfied that everything is where it's supposed to be, that I'm not bleeding or worse.

"John," I say, as my fugue state starts to subside, though I can't hear my voice except in my own mind. I look toward where John should be, and the smoke begins to clear. There's nothing there except an impact crater easily six feet across, the edge of which is no more than three feet away from me. There's no John. The house, mostly made of stone, seems to have held up against the explosion, and I suddenly avert my eyes from the spray of black dirt and something red spattered across the gray stone.

Chapter 12
Hotel Mason – Before Noon, Saturday, December 17th

The bright morning permeates my hotel room, blinding me through my eyelids, and I curse myself for not asking for a room without windows or at least one whose windows don't face east. I slide the pillow out from under my head and shove it over my face, relishing the dark and the cool surface against my face. Then I realize that my brain feels like it wants to explode straight through my eye sockets. I try to ignore it just long enough to drift back into oblivion, but it's just not happening.

I usually sleep late into the day to make sure my hangover doesn't make me wish I would die, and I endeavor never to rise before noon. Today it's just simple lack of sleep, having been out late the night before, combined with one hell of a nightmare that's already fading from memory. I remember it was about when John Tomansky was killed, since I have that one fairly often, but there was something surreal and disturbing in this one. I can almost get my hands on it, and the memory leaves me forever.

Well, I'm not going back to sleep, that is one thing I can be sure of, and I toss my pillow with disgust at one of the windows. I'm hoping for the satisfying sound of glass breaking, though rationally I know it's impossible. Sure enough, the down and cotton pillow hits the window with a muffled *wmpfff* and falls to the carpet. Screw it. I throw my legs over the side of the mattress, force myself into a sitting position and rub my eyes for an eternity. What now? Coffee. The lounge has a number of large wingback chairs that offer their occupants at least an illusion of privacy, and I find that the brown leather is substantially suppler than I originally expected.

It's while I'm nursing my third cup of black coffee (the first two disappeared with neither trace nor memory) that the rusted gears of my mind begin to turn again, though that says nothing of the splitting headache that I somehow know won't dissipate until after the sun has gone down. I most definitely need to pay a visit to Mississippi Freight. They're probably closed, which yet again puts me in the awkward position of trespassing, but I have to get in there. I'll bet my next bottle of Dewar's that Mississippi Freight is owned by the Shanabergers or owned by a company owned by the Shanabergers. I don't know any other way on a Saturday to secure that connection except to poke around inside to see what records I can find.

But even so, what does that connection mean? Anything at all? Assuming I'm correct on that, what difference does it make? All I have is that Larew moved his family here for work, into a home owned by the company, the same company that just happens to be owned by the family whose home my employer is housesitting. There's something missing there, but I can't grasp it.

I reach down into my pocket and retrieve the balled-up piece of paper that I truly didn't mean to pilfer the previous night. I open it, the paper crinkling in a shockingly noisy way and reread it, mulling over the implications. Larew is the key. He can tie up all my loose strings; he even knows who has his son, I have no doubt. I'll beat it out of him if I have to, but after my escapades from last night, there is no way in Hell I'll even be able to get to him. I doubt I can even get a message to him at this point. Voss will have all my contacts on lockdown.

For a brief moment I consider if I should send my only piece of evidence to Voss with a note saying where I found it. I'm sure I could find some kid off the street to run it down to him, but would Voss even believe it? The guy's got it out for me, so he'd probably just decide that I'm trying to cover my tracks. I doubt there's any more evidence in Larew's cellar – if the guy has half a brain, and I think he has more than half, he has already torched everything down there, desk included.

"Excuse me, sir?" a haughty, almost British but not quite sounding voice address me. I hadn't even realized that I was staring right at a pair of highly polished shoes. My eyes trail upwards to find the concierge standing right in front of me in not quite a tuxedo but something nicer than a suit, his mustache and black hair oiled to a high shine.

"Yes?"

"It is well past our checkout time, sir. I assume you will be staying another day?"

"I will."

"Very well, sir," he replies and holds his hand out flat in front of him.

I stare at it for a moment before I realize the man is expecting payment for another day up front. Realizing I probably look like a disheveled mess, I figure I would too, were I in his shoes. I find him a bill from the cluttered contents of my pockets that should more than cover an additional day's lodging and place it in his outstretched hand just as my stomach grumbles, my coffee having obviously awoken more than my brain.

"Thank you, sir, and if you hurry, you can reach the restaurant before they close for the afternoon. They will not reopen until five," he says before disappearing from my sight.

Jesus, how long have I been sitting here?

Chapter 13
Mississippi Freight & the Shanaberger Residence –
Saturday Afternoon, December 17th

It's almost two in the afternoon before I get myself out of Hotel Mason and onto the street. The sky is clear today, but the air is bitter cold, the cheerfully shining sun doing nothing to shake off the deep chill of a Michigan winter. The dame wanted me to meet her back at the diner at five, which gives me a little time to look into something. For a moment, I consider going on foot, but I don't really want to be in plain view if Voss is still trying to find me. I hail a taxi and give the driver, a burly Italian with a nearly bald round head, Mississippi Freight's address.

"Why you wanna' go there on a Saturday?" he questions with a thick Chicago accent.

"Why do you care? Capone needs to know everything us little people do all the way up in Detroit?" I fire back, affecting my father's Irish accent. Realizing I sounded more like an asshole than I planned, I toss the guy a few bucks before he moves an inch.

The cabby doesn't seem to be much of a conversationalist, and that's fine by me. I don't really feel much like talking. The fact is, I'm feeling like an ass. He's just some working stiff like me, probably trying to feed a litter of little Italian kids, and I just lumped him in with one of the most notorious criminals alive based purely on who his parents are, to say nothing of continuing the us against them of the Irish and Italians.

"Hey, pal, sorry about that back there," I apologize, receiving just a grunt in return. Screw it, I tried.

The taxi works its way into a decidedly industrial section of town as we head toward the lakes. The number of homes, hotels, apartment buildings and brownstones decrease and give way to wide, squat warehouses and many windowed factory buildings completely unadorned except for some company name stenciled on in a flowing script. As I expected, there's almost no one out and about through here; factories just don't run on Saturdays any more like they used to before the crash. I smile inwardly at that – if I've got to break into a place in broad daylight, I really don't want anyone around to see it.

We make a hard right turn onto what a street sign proclaims is the twenty-two hundred block of Gordon Street, and I physically sit more erect with the knowledge that we're almost there. The fact is, I'm checking out everything ahead, every detail so I can make a quick plan when the cab stops. We're coming up on an empty intersection, the line of demarcation between this and the next block, and see the street ahead is almost completely empty. Almost completely empty. A police car sits parked up against the curb directly across from a huge brown warehouse building that I am absolutely sure is Mississippi Freight.

"Hey, pal," I lean forward, thinking fast, "Don't bother stopping. I don't see my buddy's car here. Just take me back to the hotel."

"Hey, *pal*," he replies with an animosity that leaves me no doubt as to where I stand with him despite my heartfelt apology, "Dis is where you wanted to go, dis is where you get out."

He's coasting up the street, ever closer to the cop car. I can't be spotted here by Voss' goons, much less risk being arrested. At the very least, I'm facing a heated and desperate footrace, and I'm not really looking forward to all that frantic huffing and puffing. Running marathons has never been much of an interest to me.

I pull a crumpled ten-dollar bill from a shrinking wad in my pocket and wave like a flag in front of the guy's face. "This should be double what I owe you *after* you drive me back."

"Whatever you say, Mick," he replies as he hastily grabs the bill and shoves it in a shirt pocket.

I guess I deserved that. I lean back in the seat, keeping my head low, and just for good measure I cock my hat toward the cop car to hide my face.

So, I got to give Voss credit – he's smart enough to stake out Larew's place of employment on the off chance I might come snooping around there. But that means he can't possibly think I actually have the baby; if I had the kid, why would I be investigating the abduction. He's just using me to do the work for him so he can come out on top as some kind of hero.

I stop the driver and get out of the cab over a mile from Hotel Mason. If that cop down at Mississippi Freight is doing his job correctly, he's writing every detail down about anyone or anything that comes down that street, and I don't want anyone tracking down my Italian friend here. I'm sure he'll gladly lead the police right to my doorstep at the hotel. I glance furtively around as I step onto the sidewalk, and I can't help feeling like there's more cops out and about than is the usual on a Saturday. I'm probably just paranoid. Even still, I turn up the collar on my overcoat and lower my hat as I start heading up the block. To a casual onlooker, I hope I look like a guy trying to keep off the cold air.

A couple blocks up, I approach a kid hawking a stack of newspapers. It can't be much past three, which makes it a little early yet for *The Detroit News* to have hit. "Special early edition!" the kid yells. "Hot off the press! Abducted baby's father murdered!" I nearly trip and fall flat on my face at this, something the kids notices right away. He shouts right at me, "Just three cents, mister!"

As casually as I can, I stroll over to the kid and flick him a shiny nickel as I take a paper off the stack. It rings slightly as it comes off my thumb nail, and the kid catches it in midair with a muffled slap, that I am sure is a highly practiced maneuver of a hand protected by fingerless wool gloves. For an instant, I think I see some sort of recognition come over his face; as his eyes widen, I hurry off, and I'm less than a few steps away before I hear him back to his business.

A horrible feeling seeps into the pit of my stomach, like a bizarre mix of emptiness and way too much booze. I almost feel like I want to throw up as a strange sense of foreboding begins to make my skin crawl. I turn right into an alley, taking just a few steps in before I lean up against a mossy brick wall to take a long hard look at my acquisition.

Well, I'll be damned if it isn't right there in black and white for the whole Goddamned world to see. "Father of Kidnapped Baby Murdered!" says the headline, but that's really not what draws my attention. In a sidebar built right into the article is a picture of me in a suit. It looks like it's one of the pictures from last year during my trial, and a bolded caption reads, "Private Detective Thomas McAvoy Wanted for Questioning". It goes on to say that I am armed, and that anyone seeing me should contact Detective Sergeant Voss immediately.

Well, shit.

I fold the newspaper back up under my arm and exit the alley. The hair on the back of my neck stands on end with the sudden sensation that everyone on the street is staring my way. In truth, I don't think anyone is paying me any mind, but I figure I need to get off the street pretty quickly. Another taxi idles nearby. I stride over to it, consciously trying not to run, and hastily climb inside.

It's time to pay a visit to the Shanabergers, or rather to their house. Helen promised to meet me at Mom and Pop's diner at five o' clock, and whether she's still at the house or not doesn't really matter. If she's home, I can finally get some answers, even if I have to slap them out of her. If she's already gone, then I can follow my nose through the house. I have no doubt that somewhere in that house, I'll find proof of ownership of Mississippi Freight. Maybe I'll even get lucky and find some weird named books or some handwritten letters.

I walk up the driveway toward the house just a few minutes after four, having already paid and dismissed the taxi. The sun is setting, deepening the chill in the air, and an ice-cold wind cuts across the open lawn and right through my overcoat. In contrast, the trees in the distance don't move at all in the wind, their leafless, lifeless limbs furthering an impression of death around me. For just a moment, they're replaced with bones, appearing as skeletal fingers jutting from the countryside. I blink them away to again find the trees. The house looks just as empty and lifeless as before. The front door is closed, and the windows are completely dark. I get the impression that the lack of light from within the house battles with the fading sunlight outside, as if it's forcing the spread of its gloom into the outer world.

I have a clear view of the garage now, and one of its giant doors stands open, the stall that should hold a massive Cadillac empty. I couldn't ask for more, except maybe an engraved invitation; there's no better way to announce that no one is home than an open and empty garage.

I hasten my step to the front door but hesitate before pressing the button that would announce my presence to anyone inside. I gingerly take hold of the doorknob and give the slightest, stealthiest of turns, and it rolls over slowly with a slight click. I gently push, and the door silently opens just a bit. With a furtive glance around the property, a nervous and useless act since I would have surely seen anyone about, I quickly open the door another foot or two, slide inside and close the door behind me.

It's definitely dark inside, with just a faint, failing blue glow coming from behind closed curtains. I wait a moment for my eyes to adjust, details of the opulent interior coming into focus. I stand in a cherry floored hall with an expensive, burgundy runner covering the center of the floor. Two wide sets of solid wood stairs flank the hall, their curved paths leading upward to meet at a landing area above.

As stealthily as I can manage, I follow the runner, and the hall opens up just past the stairs. To my left is a six- or eight-foot opening into a large sitting room, complete with a dormant fireplace and furnishings that I couldn't buy after three solid years of sobriety. A set of folding doors seals off another room on the far side. Still in the hall, there's a single, narrow door to my right and a set of dark stained oak doors at the end. Turning the doorknob shows the single door to be locked. The double doors open right up into a lavish dining room with mahogany furniture, crystal chandeliers and a rug that I can only assume to be direct from Persia.

Pondering my options for just a moment, I enter the sitting room. Nothing seems abnormal here or out of place, not that I know much about the lifestyles of the super-rich. Another luxurious rug fills the room, and upon it sits three leather chairs and a couch. Two solid, ornate wood end tables separate the chairs, and matching coffee table stands in the middle of all the furniture. A half dozen curio cabinets, wood framed with glass faces, line the walls of the room. The room seems impeccably clean, and I run my finger across the coffee table's surface just to prove that there is barely a speck of dust anywhere.

With a general feeling that whatever is behind the folding door should be my next point of investigation, I choose to delay and fish my flashlight out of my coat pocket. I'm pleased that it comes to life, realizing that I haven't replaced its batteries in recent memory. I used the yellow-white circle of light to peer into the curios one at a time. The first cabinet is full of normal, family mementos – photographs of people I've never seen, an open jewelry box containing someone's diamond rings, a Victorian cameo, and various other items. The next two apparently contain items bought from various shops throughout the world, making it plain that the Shanabergers are wealthy enough to travel wherever they will and buy whatever they wish.

I move to the fourth such case and nearly jump backward when my light is reflected by a pair of reptilian eyes. My skin wants to crawl right off my bones and hide in the corner when I realize this case is full of the dead and somehow preserved remains of spiders, scorpions, and snakes. I focus my light on what I know to be a typical black widow spider, waiting for any number of the creatures inside the cabinet to leap toward me as I lean close to the glass. A small card reads:

Latrodectus Hesperus
Western Black Widow

I count about a dozen spiders, six snakes and a dose of other creatures contained within the cabinet, all with cards proclaiming what they are and, in some cases, where they are from.

I hastily move on, and while the next cabinet causes me less physical anxiety, it does make me wonder exactly what kind of people the Shanabergers are. I find a long mass of silky, black hair that a similar name card proclaims to be the scalp of a Lakota tribesman. Slightly less disturbing is the array of five shark's teeth taken from an unknown species, each tooth the size of my open hand.

There's also something proclaimed to be a lip plate (whatever that is, exactly) from Ethiopia; my stomach turns at the dark piece of flesh displayed next to the plate. One shelf down, I find a small skull of some animal the likes of which I'm not sure I've ever seen, and associated card claims:

> Deformed Infant's Skull
> New Zealand

I turn away from the curio cabinet, unwilling to see whatever comes next in this case of horrors. I breathe deeply several times, expelling the air from my lungs forcefully as if it carried whatever demon turned my stomach so.

This room reminds me of something my mother used to tell me about – places that existed closer to the turn of the century and before, prior to natural history museums. People, mostly rich people, would display artifacts of all kinds, from historical to geological to the fantastic and charge entry. My mother told me children especially loved these displays, though they sometimes bordered on the terrifying. She called them cabinets of curiosity.

My composure regained, I investigate the last of the curios, though my better judgement is telling me to move on. The final case is divided into two sections, the bottom of the two consuming maybe three quarters of the curio cabinet. A sculpture of stone sits upon a sturdy wood base, and for a moment I cannot even comprehend what I am seeing. I look at a three-inch-long brass plate that is screwed into the wooden shelf, upon which is engraved:

> Avatar of Yag the Creator
> Unknown Artist, 1841

Almost unwillingly, I look back to the sculpture. It's nothing but a solid piece of flat, polished gray stone perhaps four feet tall and eighteen inches wide. Most of it is featureless, but in the center is a gaping maw, a perfect circle with a row of frightening teeth lining the entire mouth. Another row of circular teeth seems to be set inside of that one, with another and another and another, continuously decreasing in size as it retreats into the sculpture itself. It has the incredible illusion of depth, and I can barely pull by eyes from the maelstrom of terror that is the mouth (mouths?) of the thing. Jutting from the center of the terrible display is a trio of tentacles that seem to twist this way and that, each one with a long row of suckers on one side not unlike an octopus and ending in a triangular appendage.

My eyes burn as I try to take in the sight, try to understand what crazed mind sculpted such a thing, and I blink to clear them. I fall backward onto my ass, certain that the stone sculpted tentacles had moved in the fraction of a second. I scuttle backward like a crab in an almost crazed terror that has no basis in rational thought. This is ridiculous; it's only a sculpture, a statue of stone, and yet what had to be a trick of my flashlight and tired eyes scared the God-loving shit out of me.

I stop when I find myself backed against one of the leather chairs, and I close my eyes for a few seconds and just breathe. There's a glorious burn between my eyes and eyelids, and as it abates, I open my eyes to again behold the thing. It seems to be exactly what I first saw – a sculpture, bizarre and even grotesque to be sure, but just a piece of stone.

"I must be losing my Goddamned mind," I deride myself as I climb to my feet, dusting myself off uselessly.

I should just continue to the folding door set against the wall to my right, yet for some reason, I come back to the curio cabinet and inspect the two items on the upper shelf. The first is a leather-bound book that lays open about halfway. The pages also appear to be some sort of tanned leather, and the words and symbols penned upon these is of a reddish-brown ink. Based on some of the other contents of these cabinets, I shudder to consider of what the tome is actually made. The other item is a small statuette of some faceless monstrosity. While vaguely shaped like a man, its arms and legs are too long, seemingly stretched to unnatural angles, and I get the impression that each hand ends in some sort of claws. I call it faceless, but yet there is no mistaking the gaping jaws and teeth.

My better judgement is now telling me to drop the whole damn case and go find some scotch. I seriously doubt whether or not I should be involved in a case about a kidnapped baby with a murdered father in which I'm suddenly the prime suspect. And let's add to the shit sandwich that these Shanabergers have some truly bizarre interests. Then again, I'm sure there's plenty of other eccentric rich people out in the world.

I turn to the folding door – a cherry wood job made of six sections, each just under a foot across – my shoes clopping loudly as I leave the rug. The door opens in the middle, folding up in opposite directions, and two knobs flank the crack in the middle where the sections meet. Wedging my flashlight between my neck and shoulder, I gently try to pull them apart only to find the door securely locked. I shine my flashlight between the knobs to see a miniscule keyhole. Kneeling down for a closer look, I realize it will take me just a moment to pick it.

The room beyond is tiny and windowless. A five-foot wide, dark stained wood desk of exceptional quality occupies most of the room, with a high backed, leather upholstered wood chair behind it. Both seem heavy, expensive, and ornate, even with what little light I have to see them by. A quick swing of my beam shows the wall to my left and the one behind the desk are wall to wall, floor to ceiling bookshelves, and the remaining wall to my left is plain red brick, though obscured by a quartet of five-foot-tall wooden filing cabinets.

I shuffle around the desk's perimeter, oddly loathe to brush up against it, even though have I no reason for such a reaction. Standing before the cabinets, it's clear to me that the room's contents have been exactly measured out. I figure there's just barely enough room to open the lower cabinet drawers all the way without hitting the desk. Even the drawer pulls are wood, perhaps cherry or something similar, and nothing adorns the drawers' fronts to lead me in the right direction. I pick one at random and pull, finding that it opens smoothly, easily, and quietly.

I breathe easier at the silence of it and then smile as if beholding an idiot who doesn't understand how unfortunate is his lot in life. Why should I care about making noise at this point? Clearly, no one is home. In a momentary panic, I check my watch. Twice in a matter of seconds, relief washes over me. I've only been in the house for about ten minutes; it's only about twenty past four, and Helen wouldn't even be looking for me at the diner for at least another half hour. I have all the time in the world.

Which is fantastic, because after a few minutes, I begin to realize the enormity of the task in front of me. I see no obvious system to the contents of the file cabinets, though I am sure there is one. In fact, I am sure the Shanabergers, either Howard or Wilma, know exactly where every scrap of paper can be found in these drawers. Unfortunately, they weren't kind enough to leave me map. Next time I sneak around someone's house in their absence, I really should let them know I'll be coming and what I'm looking for. This family has dealings all over the world! I see land records, telegrams and letters going back over a hundred years from all over Europe – Scotland, England, France, and Romania to name a few – to Australia, Shanghai, Cairo and all sorts of places I have never heard of. I find promissory notes, financial contracts, and bills of sale.

I'm beginning to lose hope, and I glance at my watch to find that it's five 'til. I've not found what I'm after, and I have somewhere between thirty minutes to an hour before Helen arrives, of course assuming that she comes straight back here when she doesn't find me at the diner. With renewed vigor, I open the eighth or ninth drawer in my search, and I immediately stumble into contracts and land deeds registered to Mississippi Freight. I'm not surprised that I was correct – that the Shanabergers own the company that Larew works – worked – for, but I still don't know the connection to my dear Helen.

Regardless, I slowly make my way through each piece of paper. It appears that Mississippi Freight has not always operated in Detroit, which I guess makes sense. Otherwise, the company would probably be called a rather unimaginative Detroit Freight. In fact, the company bought its warehouse and yard down on Gordon only three years ago in thirty-five. A whistle when I find the contract on the sale – it looks like the Shanabergers shelled out forty thousand for the place! I don't know much about commercial real estate, but that seems ridiculous. I move on, finding more and more deeds, more and more contracts, and bills of sale on property throughout the city, including the brownstones on Cedarwood. The place the Larews are in? They paid eleven grand for that, which I know is probably double what the place is worth. So, why in the middle of this economic Hell, when a quarter of people are out of work would the Shanabergers suddenly choose to move or start a business here in Detroit, no matter the cost?

Why does each answer bring up more questions?

I close the drawer and turn to consider the desk. I make my way behind it and slide the exceedingly heavy chair back away from it so that I can sit down, precariously perching just on the edge of the leather cushion. The heavy drawers slide out easily enough, and they're surprisingly empty of anything of importance. All I find is pencils, fountain pens, even some antique quill pens and ink wells and all sorts of paper, stationery and envelopes.

I lean back against the chair and sigh heavily at my current lack of progress. All I've managed is to confirm something I had already assumed. I half-heartedly scan the bookshelves to my right, slowing moving my flashlight's beam across hundreds of bound spines, but nothing catches my eye. I'm really not even looking. I could still explore the rest of the house, but what do I really expect to find but a kitchen and some bedrooms. There is the one locked door in the hall... Screw it. I'm not moving another inch on this investigation without some answers from the person who knows more than she's letting on.

I stand and leave the claustrophobic office, not even bothering to push the chair back into place. I pull the doors shut behind me and stride over to one of the hefty wingback chairs. Wrapping my arms around it, I heave backward. The chair's monstrous weight pushes back against me, threatening to topple and crush me to death. My face flattened sideways against the leather back of the chair, my breathing labors as I manhandle the chair into the hallway, banging a leg up against a wall as I go. I drop the chair with a thud on the carpet runner and a skid on the wood floor, angled to point directly at the front door.

I settle into the chair, which is extraordinarily supple and comfortable, to wait. I turn off my flashlight and rest it on the chair's left arm, my forty-five resting on the right.

Chapter 14
The Shanaberger Residence –Saturday Night, December 17th

A huge engine rumbles in the distance, a powerful one, probably a Liberty truck bringing reinforcements or supplies to our position. It's strange that it would be coming at night, and it must be night, because I can't see anything at all around me. I must have fallen asleep in the little house on the hill of the French countryside, exhaustion having finally taken its toll. I look around, trying to make out my surroundings, but there's just nothing at all to see. The engine is closer, though oddly muffled as if something fairly solid is interposed between me and the truck. It doesn't sound like a Liberty Truck engine; it sounds… modern.

And then it's just simply gone, erased from existence, and I start to doze again into wonderful oblivion. Ever since the war, truly deep, dreamless sleep is the only place I can find real peace. Dreams bring nightmares, horrific reenactments of battles, blood and death, faces that once belonged to friends and fellow soldiers, blown apart like piles of leaves during autumn when the shells fall or when the machine guns tear them apart. It's that quiet, dark space in between the dreams that I can finally rest.

One might think that daylight would bring respite from the terror but being awake is little better than the nightmares. I spend most of my days trying to forget the dreams, trying to bury the memories of the war – the tanks, guns, shells, gas and death – but I can only manage it for a short while. It's probably why I prefer to stay drunk as much as possible.

There's a whole generation of us boys who fought in that war, tens of thousands that made it back alive, and most of us don't dare tell anyone how horrifically evil the whole affair was. Maybe some of us liked the attention – the conquering heroes, returning from foreign lands having kept the flames of freedom burning – liked being branded heroes. It's more likely that most of us just want to move on, just want to live and not relive those days. I might be doing my fellow man a disservice by running from it all. If I and all the others who lived through it screamed from the hilltops of the horrors that were the Great War, well maybe the world might just try to avoid it again.

A banging report from outside the house breaks me from my self-indulgent, philosophical repose, and it brings me to full attention. I realize now that I'm not in a forgotten house on a forgotten battlefield, but I'm slouched in a comfortable wingback chair in a house owned by Howard and Wilma Shanaberger. A house that as yet has yielded no answers, and whose contents have only served to bring about dark thoughts with its bizarre contents. The place is deathly still and completely pitch black. No light at all penetrates the inky blackness from the windows in the next room, and I can't help but feel my skin crawl at its contents. Maybe staying here wasn't such a good idea.

The engine I heard in my reverie was not a Liberty Truck at all, but that of a new, expensive Cadillac. The sound that brought me to my senses was in fact the wide wooden door to the garage being slammed closed. Silently, I straighten my back against the chair and rest my hands on my flashlight and pistol. I hear the front door's knob turn and click, obviously manipulated by someone outside, and I hold my breath, steeling my nerves. The door swings open, and a dark form whose outline is only barely illumined by the most faint, muffled moonlight outside cautiously steps into the house with a click of a heel on the wood floor.

"Close the door," I demand, keeping my voice as calm and even as I can manage.

The figure whose outline I can barely see stops moving but doesn't make a sound. I can barely see it, but the figure is vaguely female, tall and thin with curves in certain places. An amorphous blob seems to make up the head, and suddenly the visage of that horrible little figurine in the next room superimposes itself onto the shape. I gasp as a terror takes hold of me, and I nearly fumble and drop my flashlight to the floor. I manage to flip the switch and shine a bright beam of light right onto Helen's face, causing the terrible vision to instantly dissipate. She stares directly back into my light, her dark eyes lit up eerily. After a moment she squints and shields her eyes with a hand held up against a large, floppy yellow hat.

"Mr. McAvoy?" she calls uncertainly.

"I said, close the door."

She does as she's told, pushing the door shut behind her and then putting her back up against it for good measure, and I stand, keeping both the flashlight and my gun trained on her. As I gently step a little closer so that we stand about ten feet apart, her eyes begin to adjust to the flashlight, and she looks back toward me. The whole scene would appear that I have her trapped, but something in her eyes makes me feel like it's the other way around.

"This seems familiar. Do you plan to shoot me this time?" she asks.

"I told you once, I haven't shot a woman yet. Yet," I repeat for emphasis.

"Put that thing away," she says.

There's an edge to her voice I just don't particularly care for, and to be honest, I'm just about done with this particular broad. She's done nothing but make my life Hell since she arrived, and I was a perfectly happy drunk before she showed up in my office. To prove my point, I swing my gun out to my right and fire off a round. The powerful bullet goes right through a wall, and I hear glass breaking beyond. Helen's face and body register a cringe, but her eyes flash in anger for just a moment.

"All right," she says softly, "What now?"

"Now, it's time for the truth," I reply. "Who are you? What am I mixed up in here?"

"You wouldn't believe – hey!" she almost yelps as I charge forward and grab her hard by the wrist, squeezing it painfully in my hand against the flashlight. For a moment, her arm tenses up like she's going to resist, and she's definitely stronger than her skinny frame would admit. The tensions slacks, and I drag her back down the hall toward the chair and fling her into it.

"Damn, that hurt!"

"I don't give a Goddamn!" I shout at her, channeling my father's Irish temper. I put my light back in her face, and I see that she's rubbing at her wrist. A twinge of remorse hits me, but I force it away. "Lady, don't you tell me what I will and will not believe. I'm wanted for murder, now, in addition to being a suspect in the kidnapping of the baby you asked me to find. So, I want to know who you are, what this is all about, and what is your damned angle in the whole thing. And I want to know right now!"

"All right. All right," she softly repeats, her resignation to the situation plain. She stops rubbing at her wrist, reaches up and takes her hat off, letting it drop onto her lap and the fabric of a yellow dress. Is it the same dress she wore the other night? I'm not sure, and as someone who has been wearing the same clothes for days, I suppose it really doesn't matter. She looks about her and asks with those big, brown eyes, "Can we at least turn the lights on?"

That does it. My resolves softens just enough, and I sigh as I almost turn around to the light switches that I saw next to the front door. A suspicious tingle on the back of my neck, just a hair standing on end I suppose, gets the better of me though, and I just backpedal to the door. While I fumble to my left for the light switches, Helen calmly reaches into her purse and lights a cigarette, sitting in an almost bored way with her legs crossed one over the other. Even as the lights come up, forcing both of us to squint for just a moment, I get the distinct impression that she has been prepared for this very moment probably since she met me.

"I think you can put the gun away, Mr. McAvoy," she admonishes as she breathes out a plume of smoke.

She's using that tone again, that tone that says she's in complete control of everything around her. We're about to find out just how in control she really is, but she is right about the gun. I holster it, as well as turn off the flashlight, which I had almost forgotten about, before dropping it into my coat pocket.

"Where do I begin?" Helen muses.

"I would say at the beginning."

"It's a long story," she replies with upraised eyebrows.

"I'm a patient man."

"I'm not so sure about that, but I hope it's true. Like I said, it's a long story, and we're about to find out just how much you know about the world."

"Just what in Hell does that mean?" I ask, stepping forward to stand just a few feet away from her. I hope that, as my shadow falls over her from my body blocking the light behind me, I am an imposing sight, but all she does is blow a cloud of smoke my way. Wordlessly, she offers me one from her cigarette case, and I take it, realizing that I am admitting defeat.

She begins, "This is not the first disappearance of a boy sharing Harcourt Pennington Larew's initials. Little Harry is just one of many. If you know where to look, you can trace this back about a hundred years. After that, the records aren't very clear. If you were to look at the dates, or the locations, you wouldn't find a pattern, but there most certainly is one. The –"

"That's all very interesting," I interrupt, "but you're not really answering my question."

She purses her lips, and her eyelids drop just a bit. I suddenly feel like I'm being regarded by an infinitely superior and substantially annoyed housecat. She takes a drag off the cigarette and blows it off quickly to the side.

"May I continue?" Helen asks, to which I just nod. "You would need to know something of ancient astronomy to know where the next abduction will be. My father has been tracking them for years – well, decades – his whole life."

"Is Shanaberger your father?" I ask. She blurts laughter, and I feel suddenly foolish. "Okay, fine then. Who is your father?"

"Just an old man who would rather stop the abduction and sacrifice of innocents."

"So, what is your connection," I start to ask something, but my words just evaporate when her last sentence solidifies in my mind. A chill tries to run up my spine and wash over my body, and my voice drops almost to a whisper. "What do you mean by 'sacrifice'?"

Her eyes open wide, drawing me into the deep brown of her irises, and she looks away as she takes a long drag. When she looks back at me, her haughtiness, her cool control of the world is gone, and I see the eyes of a woman who wants to cry.

"They're murdering children, because they need the blood of an innocent for –," and her voice breaks.

She drops the cigarette to the floor, lowers her face and covers it with her hands as she begins to cry softly. My heart, which I've been working so hard to keep frozen solid, just absolutely melts seeing a good-looking young woman cry. I step closer to her and hunch down to her level, putting my right hand on her shoulder in the hopes that it feels comforting. With my left, I retrieve the cigarette that is starting to smolder on the runner, and I stamp it out. Screw the Shanabergers and their carpet. Helen's crying slows after a moment, and she produces a handkerchief from somewhere to wipe at her eyes.

"It's gonna' be okay. We're gonna figure… this… out," I say, not very believably I admit, but my words falter as something catches my eye at the end of the hall, something I wouldn't have seen in the dark. For that matter, I wouldn't have seen it with the lights on, were it not for the fact that I must have kicked over the end of the runner when I huffed and puffed the chair into the hall. A tiny crimson stain stands out from the brown oak of the floor.

I stand and circumvent the ill-placed chair, snatching the handkerchief from Helen's fingers as I did so. The action only calls to her attention that something has changed, and she suddenly looks up and follows me with her gaze. I approach slowly, hoping to God that what I see is some imperfection in the wood, but of course I know better. I kneel down and touch the red with my index finger, using the handkerchief as if it is some sort of inviolate barrier. It's sticky, like it has been here for maybe a day. I sigh.

"What is it?" Helen asks, her face peeking from above the chair. She must be kneeling in it.

"Blood."

I hear her heels on the floor as I examine the underside of the runner to find it slightly stained but certainly not soaked through. The blood had been sitting for a bit before the carpet runner was just thrown over top of it. I take the fringe of the runner and toss it backward, revealing more mostly dried pools of blood, some just mere droplets and others quite large. I look back down at my first sanguine discovery as I consider. Helen comes to stand behind me just as I lift my gaze to the locked door in front of me.

"Oh, Hell," I whisper.

"What?"

"Where does this door go?" I ask.

"I don't know," she replies. I stand, turn and fix her with my best I'm Goddamned Tired of Bullshit stare. She says, "Okay, I think it's a cellar, but I don't have any need to go down there. I stay in a bedroom upstairs."

I check the doorknob again, confirming its locked status, and ask, "Key?"

"No idea."

"All right… just… stand over there, okay?" I sigh with a pointing finger at a place about eight feet down the hall.

"Why?"

"Just, do as I say."

I take a good look at the lock on the door, and its not much of anything, really. I reach into my coat pocket for my tools as Helen finally does as I asked, carefully stepping around any of the blood. I nearly stop to check my own shoes, and I even wonder about my pants and coat from where I fell on my ass in the next room. Putting the thought out of my mind for now, I choose my weapons and go to work on the lock. It clicks after just a couple of seconds, and I allow myself a small smile of satisfaction as I begin to turn the doorknob. Someone once told me it's the small victories in life…

The door opens inward, revealing a gaping maw of darkness, yet another gateway to Hell that the light from the hall absolutely refuses to penetrate. Cool, musty air assaults my face, which certainly suggests cellar to me, but there's something else – the stinking draft of a charnel house, a salty-sweet stench of murdered meat. I fight to keep my stomach right side up, reaching into my coat to replace the lockpicks with my trusty flashlight. Clicking it on, I shine a beam down at an angle, down a set of wooden stairs that end at what looks like a cement floor. A wide trail of red, like some poor bleeding soul was dragged down those steps, leads me downward.

"Sweet Jesus," I blaspheme, and I pass through the yawning portal.

I go down the steps half sideways, keeping to one side of them and endeavoring to make sure my shoes step in the sticky blood as little as possible. The further I go, the less successful I seem to be. About halfway down, a triangular opening appears as the right wall of the stairwell gives way to the ceiling of the room below, and a few more steps down, it's open enough that I am tempted to crouch down to look around the cellar. The idea of my coat dragging in sticky gore quickly changes my mind. The growing stench of death pushes me to just go back upstairs, close and lock the door and move to Nebraska, maybe Iowa or one of those other big, square states.

I soldier onward, downward, ignoring the sticky peeling sound my shoes are making as they pull away from the wood steps. I drop another five steps or so, and now I can see easily into the open cellar. I shine my beam of light through the pitch-black from left to right once and then back again. I stop and hold very still as my mind makes sense of an image I had just seen but hadn't completely assembled yet – a black, curved triangle jutting upwards from the floor. I bring my flashlight back, slowly until it touches the point of a man's shoe pointing toward the ceiling.

"Good God," I whisper.

"What's down there?" Helen's voice calls from the top of the stairs.

I glance up and see her shape outlined in the doorway by the light beyond, her features dark and blank, and I shout more aggressively than I mean to, "Don't come down here!"

I turn back, and my light illuminates a scene of brutal carnage as bad as any battle in war. Two people lay dead. A woman in a pink dress is on her stomach, a wide pool of clotted blood beneath her. The dress is ripped and torn in several places, one of her shoe's heels broken. The man lays upon his back in a full suit, but something is most strange. I cautiously approach the bodies from the side, and when I try to shine my light on the man's face, all I see is matted down, short brown hair. It's almost as if... oh God, the man's head is twisted full around on his neck to face the floor. Hiking up my coat so it doesn't touch the floor, I squat down for a closer look, and I see wide gashes and wounds in the man's chest and belly and across his throat, and the woman seems to have some of the same, though I don't dare turn her over to look. It's as if they've both been mauled by a bear or perhaps a tiger, the latter of which aren't exactly natives of Detroit. Bears? Maybe, but unless we're talking about the football team from Chicago, I don't think bears are capable of hiding bodies.

I really don't want to do this, but I gingerly slip my hand under the fold of his tattered jacket. Finding what I seek, an almost square lump contained within a pocket, I carefully slide out the dead man's billfold. Knowing what I'll find, I inspect it for any form of identification, perhaps a driver's license.

"Howard Shanaberger," I mumble resignedly.

A sharp gasp comes from behind me, and I stand and whirl to find Helen at the bottom of the stairs, hand clasped over her mouth. She turns suddenly to face the corner, likely to avoid the ghastly sight on the floor than to avoid my light.

"I told you not to come down here," I say forcefully, striding over to her. I take her by the arm. "Upstairs. Now!"

Suddenly heedless of watching my step, I push her upstairs, steering her by the arm in my grasp. As we emerge into the lit hallway above, I grasp the edge of the door with my free hand and slam it shut behind us with a resounding bang. Twisting her arm firmly, I whirl her back around to face me, catching her other arm in my free hand. I hold Helen face to face with me for just a moment, her features registering surprise, fear, and something else.

"Let me go!"

"No. Not until you tell me what's going on here."

"I was trying to, but then you found..."

"All right, let's go," I say, releasing her arms.

"What? Where?"

"I don't know, but we can't stay here," I reply, ushering her back to the chair to get her bag. We close the heavy front door behind us as we hurry toward the garage, where we're about to borrow a dead man's car.

Chapter 15
The Shanaberger's Cadillac –Saturday Night, December 17th

I haven't driven a car in a long time, especially not something large, expensive, and powerful, and I'm a little rusty. I grind the gears the first few times I shift; I'm just not used to the weight of the car. Or driving at all really. At least a three-speed transmission is pretty much a three-speed transmission anywhere you go. I push the clutch in as I brake near the end of the driveway, and then I opt to head right – back toward the city. I goose it a little too much, and the rear wheels throw rocks out behind the car as the rear end swings out a little on me. I pull back, and the tires squeal when they hit the asphalt and catch hold.

I realize I should've had the broad drive so that I could keep a close eye on her. I really don't know why I took the keys from her and jumped in the driver's side, but there's not much I can do about it now. Oh well, I doubt she would actually try anything while we're in a moving car together. Then again, what am I worried about? There's no way she did that to the Shanabergers.

"Where are we going?" Helen asks shakily.

"I have a place at the Mason. You should know that; you paid for it. You know something? I'm about done with you and this whole mess. Start talking."

"Were those people...?" she begins to ask but trails off.

"The Shanabergers, yes. One Howard and one Wilma, I presume. They've been dead down there at least a day or two. You expect me to believe you didn't know they were down there?"

"I've only been down there once. I've been sleeping in a room upstairs. I usually don't even turn the lights on while I'm there."

"So, you didn't kill them," I say with raised eyebrows, and it's definitely a statement, not a question.

"Do I look like I could do something like that?" Helen asks incredulously.

I must admit that no, she doesn't.

"No, you don't," I admit, "but you didn't hear anything? See anything? There's too many coincidences going on here, and I want answers. Let's start with why you are at their house."

"Because the Shanabergers had a business interest near every abduction that has ever happened or, at least, their family did," she replies.

I slam on the car's brakes, causing all sorts of screaming and squealing of rubber on asphalt, and I steer the car off the right side of the road. It comes to a stop amidst a cloud of dust illuminated by the headlights. I put the car in neutral, set the brake and turn off the engine. I turn to face Helen, whom I think has a look of surprise on her face, but it's awfully hard to tell in the darkness. I may have overreacted to her words, but something else occurred to me rather suddenly – I can't go back to the Hotel Mason with my name and picture splashed on the front page of the newspaper.

"What was that about?" she asks.

"Don't worry about it. How do you know that – about the Shanabergers and their business interests?"

"I can read, and I know how to look up records, too," she replies, almost condescendingly.

"So, you lied to me about housesitting for them?"

"No, well, a bit. My father determined that Detroit would be the site of the next abduction, so I came here to try and stop it. It just happens to be where they live. I called on the house and found it empty, so I poked around. I was going to confront them, but they never turned up."

"So, you just naturally helped yourself to a bedroom and their car," I say dryly.

"Naturally." I can actually hear the smile come back to her face.

"Okay, the Shanabergers have business interests near where these kidnappings have happened in the past -"

"Had."

"What?"

"Had business interests. Past tense," Helen clarifies. "They pack up and close whatever business it is after the sacrifice."

"How do you know they're killing these kids?"

I can barely see Helen turn to face forward, staring out the windshield of the car. I wish I could see her face, could see what emotions are playing out across her features, but the car is almost pitch black. She sighs – no, rather she breathes out in slow, controlled way as if steeling her nerves – before taking a deep breath.

"Isn't it enough that the children are never seen again? What other proof do you need?" she asks. After a moment of utter silence, she says, "I am sure that the Shanabergers are part of an ancient society called Praesidia ex Yag."

"What?"

"Praesidia ex Yag," Helen repeats patiently.

"What in Hell is that?"

"It's Latin."

"Okay, but what *is* it?"

Light suddenly floods the car from behind as a car comes up the road. It seems that my heart both stops and leaps up into my throat as I wait for it to approach and finally, slowly pass us. For a moment, I am sure that I see a face turned towards our car in the passenger side window, but the car doesn't slow or falter in any way as it continues on its journey. The thought of some local county cop or sheriff deputy driving by makes me start the car again. The engine roars to life, and I gently ease it into a U-turn and start heading back the way we came before turning the headlamps on again.

"Where are we going?" Helen asks.

"I'll figure it out when we get there. So, what is this Praes…"

"Praesidia ex Yag is a society that goes back as far as the Roman Empire, probably further, though the history is almost impossible to track."

"How do you know about it, then?"

"My father knows almost everything about human history," she answers, and I suddenly get a mental image of a skinny, frail, mid-fifties bookworm surrounded by thousands of dusty old tomes. "The name means 'Protectors of Yag'. Before Christ or Moses, before the pagan gods of Europe or even the multitude of gods worshipped by the ancient Egyptians or Sumerians, there were the Elder Gods who ruled over the Earth and all of the heavens. Yag was one of these, the one most capable of creation. When the younger gods of mankind came into being, they locked away the Elder Gods, so they could jealously protect their world. Yag wishes to return, so that he can create everything anew."

"What does that mean?" I ask, and I'm resisting the urge to guffaw at the whole story, despite the chill that ran up my spine as Helen spoke. The fact is, it doesn't really matter if the whole thing is a steaming pile of mythology if these cult members, or whatever they are, believe it. People will do some truly inane and insane things in the name of beliefs.

"Everything this world is will be erased in favor of Yag's world."

"Erased?"

"Well, the legend has it that it would not be so simple. Every religion has its end of the world. Imagine the worst horrors from those, and you have a small idea of it."

"I've seen horrors," I reply disdainfully.

I see light up ahead from off the left side of the road, and I breathe a sigh of relief when I see we approach a motel. We couldn't go to the Mason and sleeping in the Shanaberger house was totally out of the question as far as I could tell. I could just picture Voss' grin, that I want to club you right in the mouth again grin, he gets when he thinks he's got you. He would most certainly have it if he stumbled on me in the house with two dead bodies in the cellar. Even if he couldn't link me to the murders physically in any way, possession is nine tenths of the law, and I would be in possession of a couple of corpses.

The motel has a wide gravel parking lot, with room for dozens of cars to go with the dozens of rooms. From the look of the lone car parked of to one side and the bicycle leaning against the outside wall of the front office, I imagine they have plenty of rooms available. I slow down as I pull in, steering the car to a spot not quite dead center in front of the office, but close enough not to arouse suspicion. I don't want to be spotted by whomever is behind the desk, just in case.

"Go inside and get us a room," I say.

"Just one?" Helen fires back with a sly smile.

"Well, it would be strange for a married couple to rent two."

"We're married, now?"

"Well, it sounds better than asking for a room for you and your gentleman friend. People talk about things like that. We'd rather not invite any loose lips or prying eyes. The car is enough to catch attention for anyone who knows cars," I answer reasonably enough. The truth is that, now that I'm somehow implicated in a triad of murders, I want the only person who absolutely knows that I'm innocent within my sight at all times.

"All right," she replies with a nod. As she opens the door, she looks back at me and asks, "Since we're married now, what should I call you, Mr. McAvoy?"

"Tom is fine," I reply. I endeavor to narrow my eyes and sound stoic, but I find my gaze lingering on that damn smile and her hair and the way her neck curves…

"I'll be right back, dear," she says, and she nearly bounces out of the car, pushing the heavy door shut with a thud.

"Tom," I say to no one.

I watch her glide to the office door, a purse on her arm and that great, big yellow hat to go with her yellow dress. I'm certain now that it is not the same dress from the other night, but I am very uncertain as to how I know or why I care. A bell on the inside of the door chimes when she opens it, clanging a jingle when the door is at its most open point, and I swear she shoots me a smile as it shuts behind her. It's almost an, "Hey, I caught you looking smile," but what else was I supposed to be doing while I just wait here in the car. A few minutes later, she emerges and flashes me a small brass key as she climbs back in the car.

"Mr. and Mrs. McAvoy are in room twelve just over there," she says, pointing generally in the direction of a bunch of red doors.

We find it easily enough, as they were numbered with room one being the closest to the office. I was gratified that the clerk or whomever ran the desk thought enough of our privacy to put us several rooms down from the motel's only other occupant. The room is small, but clean and well kept. My expectations had dropped considerably when I got out of the car and eyeballed the structure. It looked fairly old, and the wood siding was in serious need of a fresh coat of paint, if not complete replacement. The room contained two basic wooden chairs, a small round table no more than thirty inches across and one bed. One.

I close and lock the door behind us, leaning against it for a moment as I let out a sigh. Helen noncommittally seems to just mosey over to the bed, sits down on the side of it and crosses her legs. Her dress pulls up just enough to display her perfect legs. Pretending not to notice, I peel off my overcoat and toss it into the chair on the far side of the table. Kicking the other sideways just a bit with my foot, I fall into it and stare at the ceiling for a few moments. I hear the familiar click of a cigarette lighter, and I look down to see Helen lighting a cigarette.

"Would you like one?" she asks.

"God, yes please."

She hands me the one she just lit, and she reaches into her case for another. As I take it between my index and middle fingers, I note that a small red band from her lipstick wraps the butt. Screw it. I was in the army once – sharing a cigarette was commonplace there – and I really have no sense of pride anymore, anyway. I breathe in deeply, and it takes all of my willpower to keep from hacking my lungs up.

"Jesus this is awful! What brand is this?"

"Pall Mall."

"Absolutely awful," I grumble, but that doesn't stop me from smoking it and going back to staring at the ceiling. "So, you're telling me this cult -"

"Society."

"Society is abducting small children, infants, to murder them in some ritual to their satanic god?" I ask, to which Helen almost blurts laughter. I look back at her, and she cuts it off. "What's so funny?"

"Yag has nothing to do with Satan. Yag is an Elder God of destruction and creation. Satan was an angel kicked out of Heaven for questioning Almighty God. He's just the Christian Prometheus."

"What?" I ask, my head almost spinning now.

"Prometheus was punished by Zeus for eternity for bringing fire to mankind. The myth isn't literal – fire means knowledge and civilization. Satan did much the same thing when he convinced Adam and Eve to eat from the Tree of Knowledge."

"What does any of this have to do with Yag?" I ask, feeling both exasperated and like a lectured primary student.

"Yag exceeds both of them in power and deed, a god so powerful that a man's mind would shatter upon looking at him."

"Wonderful. Look, whatever. The point is, they think they can bring this about by murdering innocent children in some sort of ritual?"

Helen merely shrugs back at me, possibly the most unhelpful thing she could do. It certainly contained the least number of words. A silent, physical response seemed out of character for someone who hasn't been at a loss for words since I first met her.

"So, we don't know where the Larew child is, but we know one thing for sure," I conclude.

"And that is?"

"He'll be wherever the ritual is. How do we figure this out and stop them?"

"Well for that, like I said before, you would need to know something of ancient astronomy. Fortunately for us, I do."

"Wait," I say with a squint, "how did you know the initials of the baby?"

Helen's smile turns somewhat down, almost regretful when she answers, "They've all had those initials. Some sort of significance to the sacrifice, I suppose."

"Wait!" I say again, bouncing to my feet, and I point a finger right at Helen. "Astronomy of Yag! That was the name of a book hidden in Larew's cellar!"

Helen nods, "That makes sense then. Mr. Larew was a member of Praesidia ex Yag. I wonder about his wife."

"No, I don't think so," I muse, and it's all starting to fall into place. I sit down, but I can barely contain my excitement. "Okay, so Larew works for the Shanabergers, for a company called Mississippi Freight that they own. The Shanabergers are at the head, or at least very high up, in this Yag cult. Larew is, was part of the cult also, and he was chosen or volunteered to sacrifice his own son. He names a son Harcourt Pennington for the initials and then moves his family to Detroit, where the Shanabergers have been buying up property under their company name for the last few years. They've known for years that this would be the next place for their next... ritual."

"You've got the gist of it all now," Helen nods approvingly, tossing her hat to the table where I catch it before it slides off the far side.

"Why didn't you just tell me all of this from the beginning?"

"Would you have believed me?" she asks with big soul-searching brown eyes.

"No probably not," I admit, "but I go where the money is. So, how do we stop this."

"Well with help from my father, I've determined the time of the ritual," she says, and I realize we both seem to be avoiding the word sacrifice or anything close to it. "It must happen between six-twenty and six-twenty-three tomorrow night."

"That soon?" I ask, surprised.

"Did you have somewhere else to be?" she shoots back with a lopsided grin. She stands up from the bed and reaches into her purse, pulling out some folded paper. She leans over the table, close enough for me to smell her perfume and the scent of her hair and unfolds a map of Detroit that dwarfs the table.

"Where did you get that?" I ask.

"I stole it from a library," she answers and gives a melodious laugh at my semi-shocked visage. She placed a finger on the northern edge of the map and began tracing it down through the city. "I've figured the longitude and latitude down to the minute. That gets us within a square mile of the location, and we have to determine how to pinpoint it from there."

I watched her fingers as they moved across the map, one going from north to south and the other from west to east. As they closed in on the destination, I spoke up, "I know exactly where it will be. The Mississippi Freight warehouse building at twenty-three nineteen Gordon Street."

Chapter 16
A Motel Room in the Small Hours

I should let it be known that while I know my way around well enough, I am certainly no lady's man, never have been. In fact, Three Finger Mordecai Brown could count on one hand all of the women I have been with throughout my illustrious tomcat career, and I've never made a point of bragging about them, even while in the army or when I was on the force. Other young men would walk around the barracks or the station house and brag about this or that dame, some could-be starlet that they slept with, just one of many conquests in their long Casanovian history. I would just sit quietly and smile inwardly, knowing on some level that he is probably about as full of shit as a West Virginian outhouse after Thanksgiving.

There was that one girl right before I went off to war – we dated for about two weeks before I spent the night with her, and I'm pretty sure I saw her smooching on some other kid as my ship left the dock. After I got home, I had an on-mostly-off-again fling with Maryjane something or other; I hate to admit I don't even remember her last name. Every time she talked about settling down, I would manage to disappear with work for a couple of weeks, and eventually she moved on. And then there was Doris, a blonde beauty I ran into while she was singing at Charlie's. I was quite taken with her, as was pretty much every guy in the joint, and for some reason, she repaid that attention to me. I think she wanted more from me than I was ready to give.

To look back on it, I've never really been that interested in striking up any sort of romance with some broad, much less a long-term thing with marriage bells and little McAvoys in the long-term picture. I seem to have fallen into my few relationships, no pun intended, always having been the pursued instead of the pursuer, which seems to be quite the opposite from general expectations. I imagine women find my oh so warm exterior rather off putting, leaving only those seeking a challenge to show any interest.

I explain my rather unimpressive history with the fairer sex for one simple reason – to make it very clear that I had absolutely no designs on Helen. Why such a good-looking woman, and a smart one as well, would have any interest is completely beyond me, and I would most definitely think that we hadn't known each other long enough for feelings of romance to sprout. For Christ's sake, she isn't but, I don't know, twenty-five? Maybe twenty-seven? For that matter, our relationship had been strictly one of business, though like most dames she seems to know how to tug on the strings of a guy's heart when she needs to. Or maybe I'm just a sucker.

How I ended up in bed with her completely escapes me. I was snoring happily, slumped in a chair with my feet up on the table as I have done many, many times, and before I knew it, we were kissing fiercely. As I've somehow known all along, she is certainly no innocent. Maybe she just needed some company, or something to take her mind off what the coming day would bring. Shit, I don't know. Maybe women aren't too different from men after all, and she just had an itch to scratch. Just laying here, staring at the ceiling as she begins to snore ever so softly, I can't figure out exactly what just happened or why, and I suppose it really doesn't matter at all.

And I will reiterate that I am not a braggart of any kind, nor am I one to generally throw a woman's honor into the street for all to see, but I will say one thing. She really does like yellow. Every article of clothing Helen has is yellow. Every single one.

Chapter 17
Sunday, December 18th

The roar of a big, expensive Cadillac skidding to a halt and throwing gravel wakes me up. It's yet another item on the list of unpleasant things that have woken me from my slumber as of late, ever since I took this damned case. Gray light tentatively peers in through the drapes, as if the clouds themselves know what today will bring, and they simply cannot allow the sun to warm the world. The door to our room opens, and Helen bounds inside, bringing an errant snowflake with her. She's just as fresh and yellow as ever. She smiles at me briefly, and I self-consciously pull the bedsheet almost to my chin.

"I let you sleep as long as I could, Mr. McAvoy," she says as she brushes snow off her hat.

"I think we can dispense with last names," I reply with furrowed eyebrows. Can you believe the nerve of some broads?

"For now, let's keep things professional."

All right, fine. If she wants to act like it didn't happen, I can manage that, but I swear it's like she's two different people sometimes. I ask, "What time is it?"

"Almost eleven."

"Eleven? Shit!" I nearly jump out of bed, quickly forgetting or simply ignoring my nudity. I start to wrestle my clothes together from around the bed like some kind of damned goat herder chasing his flock. "Why didn't you wake me up sooner?"

"I figured you needed the sleep. You don't look like you sleep much, and I needed some coffee."

"Do you mind?" I ask as I stand in front of her, the crumpled ball of my clothes held strategically to protect my dignity from onlookers. "Let's keep things professional. Remember?"

That slight smile touches the corners of her mouth as she turns around to face the door. As I dress, I realize that I'm really in need of a shower and a fresh change of clothes. My wrinkled shirt and pants make it fairly obvious, but I'm aware that there may be an olfactory hint as well as the visual. I supposed there is very little time, certainly not enough to swing by my office anyway. Besides, Voss will probably have someone camped out there.

"I wish you'd woken me up sooner," I chide as I button my shirt.

"It doesn't matter. It won't even take us an hour to get to the warehouse."

"Maybe not," I reply as I fix my suspenders, "but I need to snoop around the place, find a way in. Last time I tried, there was a cop waiting outside."

"I'm sure we can figure something out."

"Must be nice to be so sure of things." I check my weapon, holster it and put on my suit jacket as Helen turns back around. I grab my hat in one hand and fold my overcoat over my other arm. "Let's go."

"You should put that on. It's cold outside."

I restrain a snort as I fenagle my arms into the coat and pull it up on my shoulders. "What are you, my mother?"

"I certainly hope not," she replies with upraised eyebrows, and we leave the motel room behind.

The ride back into the city is scenic, like some idyllic representation or painting titled "Christmas in the City". Stone gray clouds overhead pour tiny white flakes down through the air, most of which melt on contact with just about anything. Even still, a thin coating of white layers the grass and trees, though the road stays clear. The falling snow rushes to meet us as we drive.

Since the car itself is enough to attract attention, I keep the speed down as we rumble through the streets.

There are very few people out and about, even though it's close to noon, but why should there be? No one works on Sunday, no stores open, no factories, no businesses with the exception of the odd diner trying to capture some after church money. Though, I've heard some talk about the New Empire Photoplays opening up for Sunday matinees. Wouldn't that be something? To go see one of those new color talkies on a Sunday afternoon?

I mosey the car down to Gordon Street, an easy task with the nearly complete lack of traffic. The one point of congestion is at the new St. Aloysius Church, the new Romanesque style Catholic church they built back in thirty. They had torn down the old one and built this new one in its place to increase access to parking. I navigate carefully, watching for cars, families, and errant children. Running over some poor kid probably wouldn't help my progress. I take a long look at St. Aloysius as we pass by, and for just a moment, I almost give in to a sudden instinct to run inside and ask God for strength. I've got this feeling that I'm going to need some help from on high very shortly, but I keep driving.

Keeping an eye on my mental map, I turn off two blocks up from Gordon so that I am driving parallel to it, counting off the intersecting streets until I know I'm just up from the warehouse. We're still very much in an industrial area. With the docks nearby, warehouses, textile mills and machine shops surround us. I furtively look up and down the street to make sure no one is around, or at least no one around who is paying attention, and I pull the car up to the righthand curb and park.

"This isn't the right place," Helen says with a slight frown.

"I know, but I want this to go right."

"What do you mean?"

"We've gotta be careful. First off, Voss had a cop outside the warehouse keeping an eye on things the first time I tried coming down here. Second, if you're right about these people and what they think they're doing, we may only get one chance to save this kid. What time is it?"

Helen looks at a silver, oblong watch on the inside of her left wrist. "Almost one."

"Perfect. We have about five hours before they perform their ritual or whatever it is. That means I've got some time to go check the place out."

"And what am I supposed to do?" she asked as I open the door and step into the snowy air.

I turn back to her and smile, "Well, your yellow dress makes you visible for miles, so why don't you just wait here and look pretty."

"I do not care for that," she replies. She stares straight ahead through the windshield, and the edge in her voice combined with the deepening frown really damages her looks.

"Do you want me to leave this with you? I mean, do you know how to use it?" I ask, holding open my coat to show her my gun.

Without so much as blinking or even glancing at me, she coldly replies, "No, thank you. I'll be fine."

Dames.

I push the heavy door shut and pull my coat back tightly around me as I step off the road onto the sidewalk. The snow starts to stick, now, and the air feels colder than it did just two hours before when we left the motel. I hurry up the sidewalk as quickly as I dare while still taking care not to slip. I wish I had a scarf as a frigid wind blows right down the street, freezing my face and blowing snow into my eyes. I adjust my hat and walk with my face pointed toward the sidewalk to keep the deathly cold wind out of my eyes. I head up one block before turning right down the next street to head towards Gordon.

At the intersection of Gordon, I quickly and discretely peek around the corner of a building, keeping my body pressed against it. A two second glance confirms that there is still a cop sitting outside of the Mississippi Freight building. I'm not sure if it is the same guy as yesterday, and it really doesn't matter at all. The fact is, he's there, and he seems to be maintaining one hell of a vigil up and down the street. There's no way I am getting past him. There isn't anyone around this part of the city on a snowy Sunday, and I'm sure my appearance would arouse some suspicion.

Still, I need to make my way to the backside of the building to see if I can find another way in. I backtrack and cut down an alley, ignoring the putrid stench of garbage and piss. It's darker in the narrow space, the soft diffused light of illuminated snowy clouds almost completely blocked out by the three and four-story buildings surrounding me. The alley ends, and I continue by way of one of the main streets. Finally, having traversed five city blocks, I head back to Gordon Street. Taking a long look down the street, I can barely make out the police officer at his post in the continually increasing snowfall. I doubt he will see me this far out, and even if he does, I can't believe that he'll go to the trouble of chasing me down, especially if it means leaving his post. I cross to the other side of Gordon and quickly continue down the block to the next street down before heading back toward Mississippi Freight. This street feels decidedly emptier than Gordon because it is barely wider than an alley. Fences line the street, protecting the rears of buildings from prying eyes. Some of them have gates or other entryways, probably to allow freight to and from various industrial or commercial destinations.

After five blocks, I see the brick building of Mississippi Freight, the company's name so very helpfully emblazoned in white-washed letters on the buildings rear so that one can see it from the street over an at least twelve-foot-tall panel fence. I'm suddenly surprised by the width of the building, as its fence easily runs a third or more of the city block. At its center, two portions of the fence open inward, obviously to allow trucks and other traffic in and out. I peek through the crack where they meet and see that they're chained together on the inside with a heavy lock threading the chain's links.

I step back and consider the fence. It's made of relatively new wood planks, nailed onto crossmembers on the inside of the panels. It's over twice as tall as I am, and the exterior is very solid. There's nothing to grab ahold of, not even cracks between the panels. I walk up and down its length, looking for boards in bad repair that I can easily pry apart and begin to make an entry for myself, but I'm out of luck. Short of finding enough junk nearby to stack and stand upon, I'm not getting over or through this fence. I can probably do that. The nearby alleys and side avenues probably have enough pallets, crates, and other junk for me to stack and scramble over. But that will take some time, and the longer I tarry here, the better chance I'm spotted by someone. One call to the police about some man trying to scale a business' fence, and I'll be neck deep in shit.

I check my watch. Damn, I've lost an hour already, and I still have to get back to the car.

"What did you find?" Helen asks me when she sees me approaching.

She's leaning against the Cadillac, smoking, a brilliant vision of yellow in the ever-increasing snow. I'm beginning to think we have a real storm on our hands. Maybe I should take some time to look at the local weather reports. I hold my hand out for a cigarette, and she simply hands me hers as she opens her case in search of another one. Yet again, my complete lack of pride allows me to ignore the red ring around it and that it's almost half gone already.

"Not a damned thing. The whole rear of the building is pretty tightly locked up. There's no easy way in without making a ruckus."

"We have about three and half hours," she states, as if I don't know the situation, "so what do we do now?"

"I've got to get in there. We're going to have to distract that cop."

"Why don't you just knock him out like you did the cop in the bar?"

"Well first, I don't think I knocked Voss out, I just knocked him down," I reply, extending fingers as I count off my reasons. "Second, Voss is an asshole, and this poor guy is just some working stiff doing his job. And third, I've already committed several crimes working this case, and I don't really want to add a *second* charge of assaulting a police officer."

She frowns at this before exhaling a plume of smoke. "It's not really going to matter much if they succeed, is it?"

"No, I suppose not," I concede, leaning against the car next to her.

The ensuing moments are silent, just the soft pitter-patter of snowflakes hitting the ground, the car and my hat, and it has a most calming, almost mind clearing effect. What did she mean by that? Surely, she just meant that if we don't save the Larew child, it will all be a waste. Helen doesn't actually believe in this whole Yag shenanigan mess, does she? I flick the cigarette into the snow several feet away and push myself away from the car.

"Let's go."

"Where?" she asks, looking at me sharply as if she forgot I was there.

"I'm going through the front door of Mississippi Freight. You're going to have to distract that police officer."

"I have an idea," she says with a smile.

The Cadillac rumbles to life, the throbbing of American made power vibrating through its steel body. I ease the car down the street, with no intention of picking up any real speed. Things are getting slick with the snowfall, and we really just don't need any mishaps at this point. I turn right to head down to Gordon Street, but I pull the car over to a stop on the sidewalk just before reaching the intersection, while the buildings still block view of us from Mississippi Freight.

"What are we doing?" Helen asks.

"I just want to be sure he's still there."

Climbing out of the car, I nearly slip and fall on my ass. I cautiously shuffle my way over to the sidewalk and near the edge of the corner building. I pull my hat off, feeling the freezing snow on my head, my hair getting cold and wet, and hazard a glance around the corner. Our young police officer is still there, ever vigilant, but now there's another car. The driver's door opens and a man in a beige overcoat and fedora climbs out and greets the cop.

"I'll be damned," I whisper.

"What?" Helen's voice sounds from behind me, *right* behind me. I hadn't even heard her get out of the car, and I very nearly jump three feet in the air.

"Jesus Christ, don't do that!" I whisper-yell.

"What is it?" she asks again.

"It's Voss," I reply, peeking back around the corner. The uniformed cop produces a key from one of his pockets and unlocks the door. Voss shakes his hand, says a few more words to him and disappears inside before the officer resumes his vigil. He didn't lock the door again, and I turned back to Helen. "Voss is here, inside."

"The policeman you…"

"Yes, him. He just went inside. Maybe I was wrong about him, he's not as much of a moron as I gave him credit for. Somehow, the son of a bitch has followed the same trail here that we did."

"Maybe he's just investigating Larew's employer?"

"Maybe, but he's had plenty of time to do that before now. Okay, here's the plan. I'm going to go down that alley. It ends as close to the Mississippi freight building as I can get. When you get the cop's attention, I'll cross over and get inside. How do you plan on managing that?" I ask with a sudden twinge in my gut. The thought of her using her feminine wiles to lure the cop away makes me strangely sick to my stomach. Or maybe it's just that I haven't had a drink today.

Helen smiles again and turns away from me, heading back over to the car. She pulls her purse out of the front seat and squats down in front of the passenger front wheel of the Cadillac, her purse obscured from my view in her lap. She jabs her arm forward and retracts it just as quickly. When she stands, the mournful exhale of air escaping the tire competes softly with the sounds of falling snow.

I smile back with a nod, "Good thinking. Do you always keep a knife in your purse?"

"A lady has to be careful," she says back with the odd mix of a playful wink and a deadly serious tone.

"Let's hurry. That tire will go flat quickly," I explain as I rush into the alley.

I barely make it to the end of the alley, watching from behind a stack of empty crates when the very large, expensive – and I suddenly realize – very stolen Cadillac comes slowly into my view of Gordon Street. The front tire has completely caved in on one side under the weight of the car, causing the car to lift as the tire rotates off the flat spot and then thump downward back onto it again. Helen maneuvers the car dangerously close to my position, causing me to duck as the cop's eyes follow it before she parks it against the curb on my side of the street only about fifteen feet down from my alley.

She climbs out of the car and walks around the backside of it, smiling slightly at me as she does so. She moves out of my range of view, and I don't dare try to see what she's doing. In my mind's eye, I can see her inspecting the flat tire and adopting a woe-is-me-whatever-shall-I-do sort of expression. I can barely hear her make a sort of disgusted sound, and then her voice calls out with a pleading tone, "Sir, I need some help. Can you help me, please?"

The young officer hesitates for a moment, taking a long look down each way of the street. He then turns slightly to glance towards the door behind him. Deciding all was well, he carefully steps his way through the snow and across the street to the yellow clad damsel in distress. "Hold on, miss, I'm coming."

So valiant he is. I roll my eyes and suppress a chuckle as he nears the car and passes out of my view. I slowly emerge from my hiding place and edge closer to the alley's exit onto Gordon.

"Yes, ma'am, you have a flat tire."

"I know. Can you help me? I don't know what to do!"

"We'll have you fixed up in a jiffy. Do you have a spare?"

"A spare what?" she asks, and I'm not sure if she's just laying it on that thick or if she truly didn't understand the question. For someone who knows so much, Helen sometimes seems to know very little. It must be the difference between a book bound education and education by life.

"A spare tire. Never mind, I saw it right there on the side. This'll take a few minutes."

I wait until I hear the sound of a jack, and I peer out at the car. The policeman kneels in the snow on one knee, like some sort of gallant white knight before his princess as he jacks the car up off the ground. Helen stands to his right and sees me watching. The smart girl that she is, she comes around behind him to stand on his left, blocking his peripheral vision my direction. I leave the alley and tip toe my way past them and into the street while they converse.

"That looks so difficult," she gasps. "I could have never done this myself. Can I help you somehow?"

"No thank you, miss. I can do it."

"This is a very nice car," he complements, adding "Cadillacs are expensive."

"My father's rich."

I pick up the pace suddenly wondering if we've just made a terrible mistake. If this cop knows cars, then he knows there are almost no Cadillac V16s around. If Voss knows the Shanabergers own Mississippi Freight, he may also know they're dead and their car is missing, a car that just happens to be the very same kind of car that got a flat tire in front of this policeman. I can't stop now. I have to assume he's just making idle conversation, perhaps working up the courage to ask for a reward of some kind from a rich and beautiful young woman.

I make it to the door and give it a light tug to verify that it's not locked. It gently opens a few inches, and I shoot a last look at Helen before stepping inside. She just nods in return. I hate to leave her behind, but there's just not much I can do about it at this point. I need to look around, maybe even find Voss. If he has tugged the same loose thread that I have, he may have come to his own conclusions. I'm sure he doesn't have the inside track like I do, but he should have enough that I can convince him that we have a real problem here. We can work together and save the child. He can have the honor and glory; I just want a clear name and maybe some cash to go along with it.

Inside is a small room maybe ten feet deep and a little wider, and there's really nothing here except a wooden counter almost bisecting the room, a wooden door set into the paneled wall behind the counter and a phone next to the door. I move around the counter, and gently try the doorknob to find that it turns smoothly and silently. I pull it open to reveal a dark passageway, only barely illuminated with some soft gray light somewhere off in the distance. I enter the passage and pull the door shut swiftly, slowing it just before it closes to make sure I elicit no sound at all.

I find my flashlight and turn it on to reveal that I'm not actually in a passageway or hallway, at least not of the usual sense. Instead, large stacks of crates, pallets and wood boxes surround me. They make high walls to either side, and they're stacked close together to give the illusion that I stand in a hallway just wide enough for one person to pass. I shine my light from side to side, millions of dust particles reflecting it back toward me as I begin to step softly forward. My shoes make no sound on the floor, as it's not a floor at all, but just packed down dirt. As I walk, I sometimes find small breaks in the stacks of freight, just enough to allow me to shine my flashlight into and see more such passages beyond.

I come to an intersection of sorts as two paths come together, and I ponder which direction to go. I can see more easily now, and I turn off the flashlight to save the waning battery power. Also, it may be best to not announce my presence by shining a light all around. The freight at one corner of the manmade intersection is stacked a little more haphazardly than in the aisles, and I venture a guess that I can climb these to, hopefully, get a clearer idea of the warehouse's layout. I step tentatively at first, careful not to catch my coat or pants on a rough board or nail, gentle with my weight until I am sure that it will hold me, but I quickly realize that I can easily reach the top with little fear.

The warehouse is truly immense, seemingly larger on the inside than the exterior dimensions would have me believe. I can't get a good eye for the dimensions in the low light, but I see labyrinthine passageways in all directions. Off to my left is what I think is the rear wall of the warehouse with large, smoky windows set into it thirty feet in the air, the only apparent source of light as they filter the soft gray light from outside and make it somehow colder and darker. Some distance ahead and against another wall is a clearing of sorts in the forest of crates. It seems out of place, as if this one section of the warehouse was not intended to hold freight.

Before I climb down, I make note of one more thing – an ancient, thick layer of dust seems to coat the surface of the stacks of crates and containers. How long have these been here without having been moved?

I reach the floor, dust my hands, and set off down the passageway that I think most directly leads to the empty area I had spied from above, as it seems to be the one thing most out of place. I find that my chosen path doesn't lead straight there, but instead stops and splits to the left and right. Every time I choose a direction it either branches off, comes to a dead end or doubles back upon itself. I pick up the pace, as does my pulse, an irrational fear gathering in my gut. I suddenly can't help but feel as if I may never escape these tunnels, and what minotaur awaits me at the wrong turn?

When I finally burst into an open area, I trip over my own feet and fall to my hands and knees on the dirt floor. I breathe deeply, gulping air greedily, as if it is somehow less polluted by dust than that of the passageways. My pistol is in my hand, and its cold presence gives me something to focus on, something on which to center my attention so I can regain my composure. I hadn't realized I had even drawn it until my eyes rest on the barrel. I look to my left and right and stand to my feet as if to regain my pride. I make a show of dusting myself off, not that anyone is there to see me do it, the action also brushing away my sudden feeling of foolishness.

Despite completely losing my sense of direction, I somehow ended up at my destination. This section of the warehouse has been completely cleared of freight, creating an open space that I'm guessing is about thirty feet in each dimension. There are six metal stands spaced evenly around the perimeter. I'm not sure what the word for them is – stanchions, maybe? Each is about five feet tall, looks to be made of blackened iron and holds an unlit torch, an honest to God medieval looking torch! A brick wall forms one side of the area, and I can barely make out something painted upon it. I flick on my flashlight, and in the faltering light I see some sigil or glyph whose meaning escapes my understanding and comprehension. It is painted upon the wall in yellow, and its very presence makes my gut uneasy in a primal way. I slowly reach toward it and, after a long pause, touch the yellow sign to find the paint completely dry. I draw back my hand quickly.

The sickness in my stomach doesn't ease, however, as it dawns on me that I saw one other thing in the dead center of this space, though my mind chose not to acknowledge it at the time. I turn slowly to consider the bassinet, a baby's sleeping place, sitting dead center. I take one hesitant step after the other, somehow finding the will to move close to it. It's old, completely made of solid, brown-stained wood with rockers for feet, unlike the modern ones that just stand and seem to be made of white wicker and lace fabric. I cross the last few feet with trepidation and breathe an intense sigh of relief to find the cradle empty.

A door slams from somewhere in the warehouse. I turn off my light and dash to my left, into one of the shadowed passages, almost knocking down one of the stanchions in the process. Pressing myself against the wall of boxes, I hold as still and silent as possible. I hide my pistol in my coat pocket, though I keep my hand wrapped around its grip. An eternity passes and nothing happens.

Just as I relax, I hear far off voices, oddly echoing through and yet muffled by the narrow passageways. I tense up and wait, listening intently and yet unable to make out the conversation as at least two men continue to approach. I realize that I'm essentially leaning into the open as I strain to hear, and I yank back into the dark just as two men emerge from what I think to be the same passage that I had come from as well. Fairly certain that they didn't see me, I shrink further into the gloom as they talk.

"Do you think it was a Yaggoth?" asks a voice that cracks as if its owner is still in adolescence.

"No one has seen a Yaggoth in five hundred years," replies his bass voiced companion.

"Yeah, but something tore Larew apart, limb from limb, I heard. How is his wife?"

"She is fine, doesn't remember a thing," Bass-voice replies, almost with a sigh, and I hear them more clearly than before. I begin to walk backwards, slowly and quietly, further into the passageway.

"She's an innocent."

"As far as we know," Bass confirms, and the vague outline of two forms the size of grown men appears at the mouth of my hiding place. One is tall and thin, while the other sports a wider frame about my height. I freeze as they pause, wondering if I have been seen, but then the larger of the two pushes past the other, saying, "What are you waiting for?"

"Then it *was* a Yaggoth."

"How could you know that?"

"Yaggoths can't touch innocents."

The larger man whirls around to face his lanky compatriot, which buys me some time to retreat further. I find a stack of boxes that jut partially into the aisle, and on the other side of it is a gap between two great stacks of wooden crates just large enough for me to squeeze into. I shrink down as much as I can, suck in my gut while breathing out and cram myself into the dark hole, endeavoring not to think about the spiders or other crawling things that may inhabit such a space.

"Even if it was a Yaggoth, the brotherhood has dealt with their kind before. We'll do so again if we need to," Bass berates his companion. "Besides, a Yaggoth would have shown itself by now."

"Okay, okay, you're right," says the other, and an image of his hands in the air to placate Bass-voice comes to my mind. They continue walking my direction, and just as they pass, Skinny asks, "What about the Exalted Father?"

"We know what to do. We'll have to go on without him. Let's go. Most of the others should be here by now."

I cautiously stand as they disappear into the darkness. This section of the warehouse is particularly dark, I suppose because it's so far from the windows. On the other hand, the day is probably coming to an end. I hear the two men some distance ahead, and I follow them. I walk as silently as I can while trying to match the rhythm of their gait, so their muffled footsteps cover mine as much as possible. I stop after taking maybe ten steps, at most, realizing that I no longer hear motion from in front of me. I freeze, holding as still as I possibly can.

Suddenly I'm blinded by light. I shield my eyes with a hand just enough to be sure that the one of the two men points a flashlight directly at my face from less than ten feet away. Just then, stars explode into my vision as something solid impacts the back of my head. I fall, turning as I do so, to hit the back of my head against a wooden crate as I hit the floor. A man – Voss? – stands over me, partially revealed by the lanky man's flashlight. I struggle to speak, but before I can put any thoughts into words, his lead sap cracks the left side of my skull.

Chapter 18
The End of It All

I never knew the world contained so much pain, which is funny if you think about it. I've seen thousands of men riddled with machine gun bullets, blown apart by mines and artillery and reduced to a coughing, vomiting mess by mustard gas. But I am fairly certain that the throbbing, lancing pain that fills my very being is worse than any pain anyone else in the world has ever felt.

A slight orange blur pierces the black, just a lance of unfocused light that contrasts heavily with the excruciating blackness that is my existence at this moment. I try to focus on the orange, and I realize that it is light just barely shining through my cracked open eyelids. With all the effort I can muster, I move closer to the orange, forcing my eyelids to open. I groan.

The room spins and rotates wildly, jumbling the entire scene together in a way that I cannot make sense of any of it. My stomach churns with the motion, and I close my eyes. I try again after a few breaths, after my stomach settles a bit. The scene that greets my gaze starts off jumbled and sideways, but it abruptly rotates ninety degrees to settle right side up.

The orange light comes from the torches that are now lit, flames undulating and flickering smokily. About a dozen figures stand arrayed in a semi-circle around the bassinet. They wear purple, hooded robes that completely obscure them and seem just an inch or two too long, so that they would drag as they walk. Their faces are turned down toward the floor, causing the hoods and the torchlight to cast bizarre shadows across their faces, but I am fairly sure they are all men. One more robed figure stands away from the rest, toward the center and just in front of the bassinet. The cry of a baby issues from the bassinet.

I close my eyes for a moment, as the torchlight seems to make them burn. When I reopen them, the room again rights itself for just a moment. I reach up to feel a huge and painful knot on the side of my head and find that my hands are cuffed together in front of me. At least they're not cuffed behind my back.

"He's awake, Exalted One," intones a familiar voice.

"We have little time," replies the central figure. "Keep an eye on him."

One of the robed men near me turns to face me. He produces a gun from under his robe, and I catch a glimpse of a suit underneath. The gun, my gun, is aimed directly at my face, less than two feet away. I look up at him, blinking several times and squinting to make out his features under the hood.

"Voss!" I exclaim. I pause before adding, "I guess you know I didn't abduct the baby."

"Safe guess," Voss nods. "What did you do to my man out front."

"Nothing. Last I saw him, he was changing a tire."

"Bullshit. How did you get in here?"

"I'm sneaky," I explain with a wink. I don't know if it's my tone or the wink that makes Voss lift the gun as if to hit me with it.

"Enough!" shouts the Exalted One. "The time is upon us."

All turn their attention to the robed man in the center, who steps to stand less than a foot from the bassinet. Even Voss backs away a step or two from me so that he can watch his leader while still keeping one eye on me. His arms escape the fold of his robes as he holds them well into the air, and something in his right-hand glints in the chaotic torchlight. I squint to sharpen the image of a wicked, curved blade held in that hand. The baby's cries grow louder, at least they seem to as if beckoning to me personally to intervene in the surreal scene. I can't just sit here as the child's wails touch my spine, building a need to do something, anything. Voss must sense it as well, for the moment I begin to appraise how I might take him down, his full attention turns right back toward me.

"O terribilis Yag, factorem interitum, colligitur ante te, sicut et nos fecimus, quia omnes historiae et erit in saeculorum saecula," the Exalted One says. I don't understand the words, but I've heard enough Latin in church to recognize the language.

"How can you let this happen?" I ask Voss desperately.

"Let? It must happen," he replies, and he sounds oddly somber or even mournful.

"Nomina illorum, qui ante nos tolle hoc vitae."

"Jesus Christ, Voss, we have to stop this."

"No, we can't. You'll understand afterward."

"Nos effundet sanguinem potenter nomine innocens, quem non tangere."

A flurry of motion in my peripheral vision draws my eyes to the right, behind the middle of the semicircle. I'm not sure what I saw, if I saw anything, or it may have just been wishful thinking. I'd swear that a flash of yellow had appeared suddenly and disappeared just as suddenly. I can only hope that it is Helen, and she'll find some way to stop this madness, or at least make enough of a distraction that I can sucker punch Voss below the belt or something. I really wish I had made her take my gun earlier.

"Super hoc murum, imago tua erit lucrum eius potentia a sanguine offerens."

"How did you get mixed up in something like this?" I ask, jutting my chin toward the knife wielding man. Harcourt Pennington Larew's screaming cries permeate the air, almost drowning out all other sound. The sound of such unknowing terror, such mournful noise that wants nothing more than the very basics of human contact, of human warmth. I can't fully describe the amount of nervous anxiety building in my gut.

"I was born into *Praesidia ex Yag*," answers Voss.

"*Et servabit te in carcere inter mundos, donec vires muros deinde volutpat.*"

The cultist ceases his speech, and I know I'm out of time. I tense up to spring at Voss, but stop short as, with a screech of rough wood sliding across rough wood and a groan, a huge crate comes crashing down from my left right on top of Voss. It flattens him against the hard-packed dirt floor. The sickening sound of cracking bones accompanies the crash, the commotion distracting all of the robed men, including their leader, for just a moment. Voss' hand and part of an arm extend out from under the battered wooden crate, my gun just inches from his fingers. I lurch forward toward the gun, almost falling forward as I try to grip it with my wrists cuffed together. The robed cultists see it happening, but they're too slow to react as I sit back on my haunches and squeeze the trigger twice. Their leader, the Exalted One who had half turned to face me whirls to the left with the impact of my bullets and falls face first onto the floor.

Then comes the blur of action that always happens in these kinds of moments. A man leaps toward me, and I fell him with a quickly and well-placed shot. A yellow streak comes from a passageway just behind me to the right. I shoot twice more, once at a cultist diving for the fallen knife and once at another robed figure. I'm not entirely sure who I hit, but the sounds of yelps tell me I hit someone.

As quickly as it started, everything stops. I'm sure my willingness to shoot at anyone who moves has garnered me some immediate respect. Another cultist lies in a growing puddle of blood next to their leader, near the wickedly curved knife. The man immediately in front of me seems unharmed, though another just behind him cradles an arm while on one knee. My eyes rest on Helen, held roughly by each arm, her yellow dress ripped. The baby continues to cry terribly.

"All right. Now," I start as I edge to my right.

But I'm cut off by an immense crash of thunder, a boom that drowns out all sound, even the incessant cries of the baby in the bassinet. It shakes the entire building and its contents, shatters at least one of the massive windows on the warehouse's other side. Men's faces grimace and convulse momentarily, and some move to cover their ears to protect themselves from the pain of the wave. My reaction is to do the same, but the cuffs prevent it of course. I almost drop my weapon as a result.

Thunder during a snowstorm? I served in the Great War and have seen things most people wouldn't believe – the lush plains and rolling hills of France turned to craters of mud, ash and blood. I've watched men do terrible things to one another over a few inches of land. I've done terrible things in the name of duty and survival. When I was on the force, I had seen the remains of a man struck by lightning several days previously, his burnt corpse blackened and bloated in the summer heat. I once arrested a woman who drowned her own children, possibly the most impossible to understand act of all, but I've never heard thunder during a snowstorm.

A second cracking boom sounds, but this one much closer and not nearly as deafening. I waver, and my hands fall to point the gun at the ground as my attention is drawn – as all of our attention is drawn – to the painted sigil on the wall. I've never seen anything like this before, as the yellow itself begins to glow as if it were a shade over an electric lamp. Within seconds, it's so bright that it practically sears my eyes, forcing me to look away and blink several times, almost like I had been looking at the sun. The glow waxes and wanes every couple of seconds, building and turning purple and then white before fading back to the slightly illuminated yellow.

Someone breaks from the astonished bewilderment and shouts, "Kill him! Now!"

I start forward to realize that the man I shot at and missed just moments before stares me down. He's burly and wide like a football player, and he may be one of the men I eavesdropped on before. I raise my gun deliberately, knowing that I cannot miss at this range. He knows it, too, and he charges at me. I fire once, twice, three times and his crushing weight falls on me. I struggle for a moment before I realize that he is just dead weight, and I heave him off me with a titanic push, ignoring the blood now staining my suit and coat.

I still hear the cries of baby Harcourt as I struggle to my feet, a sign that I still have not failed, at least in this moment. A throng of the robed figures surround Helen, and I can't see her, only the flashes of yellow in half second breaks in the wall of purple robes. I begin to charge to her aid, but stop when I hear her cry out, "Save him!"

As if on cue, a cultist breaks away from the group for the bassinet. I aim and squeeze the trigger, only for my .45 to go *click*. I made a rookie mistake – I didn't count the rounds as I fired. With no time, or real ability with my hands so restrained, to find a clip and reload, I charge the man just as he bends down to pick up his fallen leader's knife. He doesn't see me coming until the last second when, at a full run, I bash my knee right into his face. I feel the cartilage of his nose give way just before my momentum bowls him over and causes me to go sprawling.

I push myself up to my knees as thunder sounds for a third time, a boom so deafening that it makes the six-inch field artillery guns of the Great War pale in comparison.

The circle of cultists around Helen opens, as they all stare open mouthed at something past me, but I cannot pull my eyes away from the monstrosity in their midst. There is no Helen, but some creature standing nearly seven feet tall with grossly elongated arms and legs. I follow the gray flesh of the arms down to its hands, and where unnaturally long fingers end, begins six-inch curved claws that almost look like steel. The face of this horror is non-existent, just a blank slate of nothingness, save a pair of dead, black eyes not unlike those of a shark and a mouth. Oh, that mouth... Stretched unnaturally, twice as wide as a man's at least with blackened lips pulled back in a terrible rictus of death, it's terrifying grin reveals dozens, maybe hundreds of razor-sharp teeth. It wears a dress of sorts – a yellow tunic that falls below the waistline to end mid-thigh to reveal more unhealthy flesh. The garment is old, moth eaten and tattered.

"Helen?" I ask, unwilling to accept what I see. None of this can be true – it can only be the diseased meanderings and nightmares of a sick mind.

"Save the child!" a voice screams that shakes me to my soul. While it is Helen's voice on the surface, it has layers and depths from outside of human tones. It almost seems to reverberate in on itself, giving it inhuman dimensions.

Regardless of what this thing is, its words are still right! I whirl away from the monster and the cultists toward the bassinet, and I see what had drawn all of their attention. The symbol on the wall had vanished, replaced by a purple, swirling mass I can hardly describe. It seems to be part of the surface of the wall itself, yet it has indescribable, immeasurable depth within that flat, two-dimensional surface, as if what I see before me extends into and behind the wall itself. Yet, somehow, I know it does not. The swirling maelstrom is clear in the center, as if the layers of existence themselves have been pried apart almost a foot by the two tentacles, not unlike those of an octopus, that struggle through the aperture.

"Yag comes! You must save him!" screams the inhuman voice from behind me, and it is accompanied by a sound I have heard many times before – that of men dying.

I look down into the bassinet to see soulful eyes staring back at me. Shockingly, he no longer cries and screams, despite the pure Hell that rages around him. My soul seems to still at his calm, and I find calm within it. At this moment, I wonder what the tiny creature, the baby known as Harcourt Pennington, is thinking as he looks back at me. Does he understand what almost happened to him? Will this moment live on in his mind and feelings for the rest of his life? Or will it fade into obscurity as time does to all memories, especially those of a child?

I begin to reach down to awkwardly to scoop him up, but something tugs on the end of my overcoat. I stop and look down to see the man whose nose I crushed, and it looks like one of his knees is bent out sideways as well, just a bit of luck from running him over I suppose. He has the knife in one hand, though he is not brandishing it threateningly, but rather as if he wants me to take it. I resist kicking him in the face for just a moment.

In a gargling voice caused most likely by blood running down his throat to match that running down his face, he says, "No, stop. We must *kill* the child to stop this! Kill him or Yag -"

He stops short with a scream as a tentacle with a huge diamond shaped head slaps down onto his back. My

God, I can hear the thing sucking at his body as his eyes roll back into his head in a grotesque display. Suddenly, his body is yanked into the air and back toward the wall with lightning quickness. The wall – Opening? Doorway? – has been pushed further open, the tentacles continuing to strain against the purple maelstrom. An alien eye stares back at me, like nothing I have ever seen or heard of. It has concentric rings of red and yellow, turning to orange where the rings meet and a black slit that threatens to devour me in all of its knowledge and hatred of everything on Earth. The thing pulls the cultist through the wall's opening into a gaping maw of thousands upon thousands of teeth, and I cannot watch as he meets them, his screams ending abruptly. The knife clangs slightly as it drops to the floor.

The diamond headed tentacle returns, and I duck instinctively but needlessly as it latches onto a corpse and yanks it through. It comes again, this time grabbing the wooden crate resting upon Voss's corpse, as it seeks to feed a seemingly boundless hunger with anything it can find. All I can do is stand there as all of existence turns maddeningly around me.

"Yes! Yag comes! Feed my Father!" says the inhuman caricature of Helen's voice, this time little more than a whisper and just beside me.

I turn slowly, my body barely responding to an addled brain, to behold the vile thing in yellow next to me. Its frightening mouth is open and raised to the sky, its back arched in some sort of ecstasy, an ecstasy I feel I've seen before. For just a second, the beautiful face and body of Helen morbidly superimposes itself over this thing, bringing about an image that makes me feel sick. My God, what did I do?

What must I do?

I bend down slowly to retrieve the ceremonial knife, the weapon meant to sacrifice this child. My movements are clumsy like I'm drunk, and I almost fall over when I wrap my hand around its metal handle. It's cold and smooth, plain, and unadorned. I regard the blade for a long moment. Evilly curved, it looks so sharp as to cut one who merely looks at it. My gaze rests on the baby, as maddening tentacles of all sizes whip around the warehouse seizing corpses, boxes, a stanchion and even the grotesque Helen-thing to drag into its maw.

 Must I do this? I don't have long to decide.

 This ancient monstrosity will destroy everything I know, all of mankind and all of man's world. I can stop it now – I need only slaughter this innocent child as he lay here, watching me with unknowing eyes. But maybe this world isn't meant to exist any longer. We continue to find more and more terrible ways to kill each other – swords, guns, cannons, machine guns, bombs, gas. What will be next? We've killed millions, and yet I know the next war will kill more. The evil of men knows no bounds and will never stop until it destroys everything it has built anyway.

 Must I do this? I don't have long to decide.
 Perhaps Yag is the better way?
 Must I do this? I don't have long to decide.

Fin.

Eyes of a Madman

My head throbs as I wake up, like I have been hit with something heavy. Gray fills my vision, tinged purple at the edges, but it slowly clears. Even still, everything appears double, and it takes several minutes of blinking my eyes before the world coalesces into one image.

I sit in the back seat of a car, and my feet and hands are bound tightly together with rope and that polyethelene tape we used back during the war for quick field repairs. More tape wraps completely around my head and covers my mouth. Bing Crosby's new hit, "It's Beginning to Look a Lot Like Christmas", croons from a radio, and a brown-haired man sits in the front seat, facing out the front window so that all I can see is the back of his head. Panic rises within me, and I struggle to no avail against the bonds.

"Be still," says the man behind the steering wheel. His voice sounds familiar, though I'm not sure why. "You're not getting free anytime soon, so be still lest you hurt yourself."

I force myself to breathe deeply, in and out, through my nose, and I look around to get my bearings. We are parked against the curb on the right side of a snowy neighborhood street. No one is out and about, which doesn't surprise me for a Monday and also Christmas Eve. I can't be sure of the time, but it may be late afternoon or early evening – that time on a snowy day when the sun has mostly gone down but still illuminates everything with an eerie gray light.

"Good. I'm gratified that you awoke in time to bear witness."

My gut reaction is to ask him what he means, but the tape of course prevents me from doing so. Then I realize that he stares at me via the rearview mirror, wide and unblinking, bulging brown eyes watching me intently from the front seat. Red blood vessels course through the whites of those eyes, a contrast that somehow chills me to the bone. He looks away.

"You see that house over there?" he asks with a nod of his head across the street.

I peer out the partially fogged up window at a snowy street and sidewalk beyond. At least four inches of snow has fallen already, blanketing the lawn of a perfect American ranch style home. The curtains are still open wide to allow an easy view through two triple windows, one on each end of the house. Through the left window, I see a cherry dining room table with festive red and green place settings. A pretty, young blond woman passes by the table and through a door on the far side of it. On the other side of the house, someone sits in a chair, hiding behind a newspaper. A Christmas tree, gaily decorated with tinsel and ornaments, stands in the corner, while the heads of two small children bob in and out of view.

"Such a wonderful life," the man sighs. "I wonder if they'd allow me to partake?"

Bing Crosby comes to a close, to be replaced by a tinny voice, a newsman with some announcement. "Now hear this," he says, "there has been an escape from the Cook County Hospital for the Insane. The man, named Lou Williams, is five foot nine with short, brown hair, brown eyes and may be wearing a beige or brown coat. He is considered extremely dangerous. Stay in your homes and lock all doors and windows while police and state officials work to recover Mr. Williams."

"How unfortunate," he whispers, and I look back to the mirror to again catch his unsettling gaze. "I really wish they hadn't done that, put me out there to everyone. It may make this much more difficult than it needs to be."

First, I try to speak to him, demand my release. In the space of just a few seconds, I order, threaten, and beg, but with the tape across my mouth, all I manage is some pathetic, muffled utterances. Then I struggle, fighting against the bonds around my wrists and ankles, and all I manage to do is fall over sideways in the backseat of the car.

He pivots around in the car's front seat to face me as he chuckles at my undignified predicament, adding damaged pride to the list of trespasses against me. He has an unassuming face that somehow looks like no one in particular and everyone at the same time. There is nothing special about him, except perhaps his strength which he uses while leaning over the seatback to push me upright again and those terrible, almost protruding eyes.

"That's enough of that," he admonishes, and he finally blinks one time. "It's important to me that you see this. You need to know."

With that, he is gone, out of the car and into the snowfall. The car door slams shut behind him as he calmly but quickly crosses the white covered road, pulling a camel-colored trench coat tightly around him. He doesn't walk up to the front door, but rather follows the sidewalk just a bit until he's even with the left side of the house. He then trudges into the yard, and peeks into the dining room window for a moment. He turns toward the car one last time with a broad, almost friendly smile across his face, and he gives an exaggerated wave, his hand held high in the air, before continuing down the side of the house.

I must do something. Once again, I fight against the rope and tape, though I know it's a lost cause. However, I still have some use of my hands. I pull up on the interior door handle, and the door releases with a loud click. I begin to push it open and very nearly lose my balance to fall into the snowy road, but I stop myself just in time. What help could I be to anybody, laying there, tied up in the road. If I don't freeze to death, or get run over by a car, the madman will just find me there. With disgust, I pull the handle back toward me with all my weight and the door shuts again.

No, the first step is to get untied, somehow, but nothing inside the car seems to offer any help. The beige back seat is completely vacant of anything except for me. I lean forward to glance over the seatback into the front and find it to be equally empty, except for one thing. I fought in the war, so I know it could only be blood, and it isn't fresh, having congealed into something between a pool and a stain. I also spot bloody finger and handprints around the inside of the doors and on the dash, but the car is devoid of anything I can use as a tool to free myself, even just a pen or pencil.

I lean in close to the chrome door handle, inspecting it for anything that may help. I run my fingers down the bottom edge of its length and then back across the top edge, finding, with some satisfaction, a slightly rough, jagged imperfection in the chrome. I place the tape around my wrists up against it and begin to saw back and forth. I make little progress at first; I have almost no room to work, not even an inch, but the tape begins to stretch slightly. It seems to take forever, but my heart jumps when I hear it tear just a tiny bit.

Motion catches my eye, and I glance up momentarily to see the lady of the house delivering a cup, coffee likely, to a small table next to the chair and its newspaper. As the tape continues to tear, she turns and leaves the room. I focus on the task at hand, but then it dawns on me that something is wrong with the picture in my mind's eye. I look up with no small degree of dread, and I watch the newspaper lower to reveal a young man in a business suit and a red tie, loose slightly at the neck. He reaches over for the cup, takes a cautious sip, and then places it back on the table.

On the other side of the house, the red dress again appears in the dining room, but it's not a blond-haired wife and mother who wears it. I see him, unmistakable with his short brown hair and bulging eyes, with the woman's dress stretched comically over his frame and looking uncomfortably tight around the shoulders. He stands there, smiling at me openly, a frightening and wicked grin that seems to stretch the width of his face. The dress has tears in it, no, punctures of some sort. Red stains, much darker than the dress' fabric, has spread around those perfectly shaped tears.

He waves again before bending down for just a moment, and when he stands upright again, he has something in his right hand. Gripping it by yellow hair, he holds aloft a woman's head, severed from her body. *Good God, no*, I think, and I turn my face away fast, clenching my eyes shut as if I can make the entire scene go away just by doing so. I hope when I open my eyes again, I'll find myself in bed, staring at the ceiling, the sweating victim of a terrible dream, but when I do, I see nothing but the street and the house. The madman has disappeared from my view.

I resume my work, having torn completely through the polyethelene tape, and I'm now working on the rope. Fortunately, the rope is only about thickness of my little finger, but with such a small edge to work it upon, I'm making no progress. After a few minutes, I stop to appraise my work, and I find just the smallest amount of fraying among the rope's threads. I resume my task but with reckless abandon, moving my arms forward and back as fast as I can manage. I pay no mind to the painful thudding of my hands against the inside of the door.

The man I assume to be Lou Williams appears, having entered the home's family room again, still wearing the red dress. I don't stop my attempts to get free, but I also cannot pull my eyes from the scene that plays out. He stands behind the husband and father, who has dropped the newspaper into his lap, and the madman reaches over the back of the chair to rub at the man's neck and shoulders.

I shout and thump my hands and forearms against the glass of the rear window, an absolutely idiotic attempt at warning the man or his children. Even if it weren't for the tape over my mouth, he'd never hear my cries. I cause as much motion as I can, waiving my still tied arms together and causing the car to rock slightly in the hopes that I can catch his eye, but it is to no avail. No, my only chance to save them is to get free!

The door's handle severs the ropes too slowly. As I work, the killer stops his massage, and the family man places his hand lovingly on the hand he believes belongs to his wife. A realization crosses his face, but not soon enough as the hand yanks away, grabs ahold of his hair and wrenches his head backward. Light glints off the blade of a large knife, seconds before it slashes across the man's throat.

"No!" I scream, the word almost audible even though my mouth is still covered.

As the father dies, Lou comes out from behind the chair, brandishing his bloody knife. The children stand now – a boy and a girl, neither older than eight, perhaps, and both dressed nicely for a holiday dinner that will never come. I can't bear to watch, and the car shakes as violently as my churning stomach while I continue to cut the cords around my wrist. I'm almost relieved when he violently draws the curtains against my view, and I ignore the shadows cast upon those drapes from the light behind them.

The rope breaks, freeing my hands just enough to finish untying and unwrapping my wrists. I nearly hyperventilate, air speeding in and out of my nose, as I bend over to work on freeing my feet. I kick franticly over and over until the offending bonds are gone, and, finally, I reach up to painfully tear the tape off of my face, pulling hair and skin simultaneously.

I dive over the seatback into the front of the car, almost impaling myself on the gear shift in my carelessness to move quickly. The keys are still in the ignition, and I start the old Ford, ready to speed off. I take one last glance at the house, but I can see nothing past the navy-blue uniformed man that now stands at the driver's side window. He knocks politely at the window, but I ignore him.

Throwing the car in gear, I floor the gas and spin the tires, the car's rear end swerving crazily from side to side in the slick snow. I ease off a bit to let the heavy car gain some traction and then speed away. After a few minutes, my breathing returns to normal, and I wipe heavy sweat from my brow, despite the cold. I don't even stop the car as I work my way, rather dangerously considering the road conditions, out of the camel colored, heavy trench coat that's causing me to sweat so profusely.

Satisfied that my night of terror is ended, I look into the rearview mirror to see behind the car, but it's angled downward, showing me a reflection of my own face. The bulging eyes of the madman Lou Williams stare back at me.

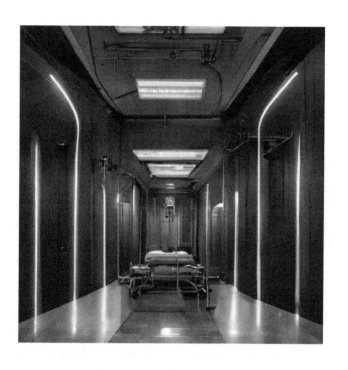

Containment

Dr. Tim Murphy leaned back in his chair and rubbed at his eyes. After a moment of enjoying the red glowing burn of eyelids shuttered over strained eyes, his mind started to wander. At last he looked, it was well after one in the morning, putting him on for seventeen straight hours, seventeen straight hours reviewing data from failure after failure. Despite all of his knowledge, experience and vast resources, he couldn't quite grasp why his team had been unable to grow functional human organs using stem cells. It seemed so easy after successes in the field with mice, then rabbits and then pigs. Human biology, though ninety nine percent the same as most animals on the planet, certainly had its idiosyncratic differences.

He knew he'd get there eventually, just as the pioneers of the past eventually transplanted organs or transfused blood even before that, but he needed to get there before eventually. Tim needed to get there now. There were other teams – companies, universities, and even governments – working toward the same goal, and his company had to be first. Director Chambers, the head guy of Engineered Biologic Solutions, demanded it, even to the extent of having multiple solutions researched by different teams under the same roof.

Three days ago, Tim had been called up to Gerald Chambers' office on the fourth floor, a place that persons rarely entered and left with their jobs intact. On his way up, he mentally prepared his resume and steeled his will to accept his termination with grace and dignity. The office was far less grand than he had expected, perhaps slightly larger than a dozen feet in either direction, most of the floor space taken up by a large cherry desk, a couple accompanying chairs and matching bookcases. A beautiful rug covered a hardwood floor – actual hardwood – and a door to the desk's right led to what Tim assumed was Chambers' private washroom.

"Dr. Murphy, thank you for coming," Director Chambers had said affably without standing from his own chair, but there was no warmth in his eyes or façade. The man was used to putting on a personality like a Halloween mask, and Tim could never figure out what the man really thought about anything. He wore a severely starched and pressed shirt with what looked like a two-hundred-dollar tie. Expensive looking cufflinks, a platinum wedding band and what was probably a four grand watch rounded out the attire of the pencil thin and somewhat hawkish looking Director Gerald Chambers.

"Please have a seat," he had said, and he waited until Tim slowly and most uncomfortably eased himself into a plush leather chair, the cherry desk separating the two men. "You're running out of time, Tim."

"I am?"

"You are."

"There's been some setbacks, Director, but we're close."

"You can call me Jerry," Chambers said with a smile, but Tim felt no comfort in it.

"We'll get it, Jerry," Tim assured the man. "The Chinese breakthrough turned out to be a hoax or, at least, unrepeatable. I know the Israelis are close to 3D printing workable organs."

"Yes, yes, but they're having trouble bridging the communication between the nervous system and the organs themselves."

"Right," Tim nodded, thinking he was somehow winning an argument, "and I know the Brits have had some success with biological robots, but I think they're a long way from anything close."

"Probably, as is Bio-Tex," Chambers agreed, mentioning EBS' primary domestic competitor, "but that's just the point, Tim. The field is full of competitors, and one of yours has made the move to a human trial."

Tim slumped back in the chair, his face registering open mouthed surprise. He hadn't thought anyone was nearly so close. "Who?"

"Kara."

"Kara?!" Tim asked incredulously with upraised eyebrows.

Dr. Kara Stout-Latham was extraordinarily secretive about her work, as he supposed they all were to an extent, but often teams attempting to achieve the same goal through completely different means tended to talk shop over lunch or at the coffee machine. Sometimes they found they had the same problems. But not Kara. All Tim knew was that her work had something to do with a biological compound that EBS owned. She worked in the containment section of the second floor, and all her helpers had been imported from elsewhere several months ago.

"Admittedly, it's a special case," Chambers had said, "her husband. Stage four pancreatic cancer."

Tim woke with a start when his glasses almost slipped from his fingers. He sighed and set them back on his face. He leaned in toward his bank of computer monitors and blinked a few times, trying to ignore the glare on his screens from the overhead lights. For a moment, he considered clipping on the anti-glare lenses Claire had given him, and he opened his desk drawer and stared at them for a moment before shutting the drawer again. Tim decided he was ridiculous looking enough as it was.

At five-foot-seven, Tim didn't exactly tower over anyone except for his five-foot partner, Claire – partner because she didn't much care for the social connotations of the word wife, and his once thin but not fit frame had thickened over the twenty five years since college, providing a positively dumpy appearance. He always had a hard time finding clothes that fit right, because pants that measured forty in the waist usually had legs large enough for a football player's, despite the twenty-eight-inch length he needed. His hair had kept most of its original brown color as he aged but had chosen to fall out on top. With Tim's general disdain of spending unnecessary time at a barber shop, he tended to let the remaining hair around the sides and rear of his head grow to an unruly length. Combined with bifocals perched on a narrow nose and the constant shadow of an unshaven beard that wouldn't go away no matter how often he ran his Norelco over it, he was the decided visage of a mad, German scientist from an old, black and white movie.

Tim rolled his chair back and stood to head over to one of the broom closets that served as a staff lounge. His shoes clapped and clopped on the black and white checkerboard pattern laminate floor in the double wide hallway outside of his office. The overhead lights were set to night at ten, so only one out of every ten of the LEDs were powered, making the hallway look like it came straight out of a hospital from an eighties slasher flick.

He pushed through the faux wood grain door to reveal an even darker room beyond. Normally, Tim would expect the slasher to be in this room, perhaps even behind the door, but fortunately there was only about three inches between the wall and the door, just enough for a doorstop to keep the interior handle from damaging the drywall. Tim didn't bother fumbling for a light switch as he entered, because the carbohydrate laden vending machine and the automatic Señor Cafe machine lit up white blue upon his approach. A quick tap of his phone to the payment sensor, and he was off to the races, punching in his favorite code - five nineteen - for an extra strong coffee with extra sugar and extra something white and powdery that they called creamer but he quietly suspected was somehow related to cocaine. That's how they kept him coming back time and again for such terrible coffee like a lab rat or some sort of Pavlovian dog.

As he nursed his scorching, taste bud murdering caffeinated beverage, Tim idly surfed his news feed on his phone, subconsciously deciding he would go for a walk to get his blood flowing again. It was less exercise and more of a vague saunter over to the elevator and letting it do the work of dropping him to the ground floor. He thought he might just stroll outside and breathe the crisp November air before going back to his office.

As he exited into his building's main hall, his phone chimed with an incoming text message. A bubble popped up on his screen from Claire, saying, "Going to bed. Gnite."

Tim sighed and tapped the bubble to text a response, but he hesitated for just a moment. She knew how important this was to him, to his company and maybe even the world, but was she mad? She sounded mad. He never could tell over text message what someone's mood was. A lot of people added emoticons, or emojis or whatever they're called, which helped quite a bit.

A banging from the front of the atrium drew his attention, and he dropped the phone into his slacks' pocket as he moved toward the vacant reception desk. There were people outside the front door, their silhouettes vaguely illuminated by the huge lamps in the parking lot. As he moved closer to see who it was, one of them pressed a palm to the external lock pad while sliding an identification card through the security strip. The lock light turned from red to green, and the door locks released. Four persons burst through the now unlocked doors, rushing by Tim without a second glance. He even backpedaled a step or two to be sure he stayed out of their way.

"Get him to containment!" shouted Dr. Kara Stout-Latham as she urged the other three men down the hall. Tim caught a glimpse of her husband, one Dr. Mark Latham, as he stumbled along. He was supported, more like dragged by two huskier gentlemen. They wore suits, and Tim did not recognize them.

His sense of awareness returned, and Tim sprang into action. Dropping his coffee, he hurried down the hallway after them, his lab coat fluttering in the breeze behind him. He made it around the corner just in time to see them disappear through a heavy door marked "Containment 2". The door shut and latched just as he reached it, and Tim fumbled to unclip his card from the coat. He didn't know from what acute affliction Mark suffered, because it clearly wasn't just cancer, but he would help anyway he could.

He swiped the card, and the lock simply beeped at him, the light remained red. He swiped it again to the same effect. He looked through the six-inch glass, or plexi or whatever material it was made from, to see Kara's palm on the internal lock. She then spoke to the terminal, running off a list of numbers or letters or words. Tim couldn't hear her; no sound would penetrate that room. Nothing could penetrate that room now, not even from the inside, without Dr. Kara Stout-Latham releasing the lock with whatever passcode she fed the mechanism.

She looked up at Tim with big brown eyes, full of sadness, maybe regret and mouthed, "Sorry." Maybe she actually said it. He would never know.

As Kara turned away, Tim looked into the room beyond. The two suits seemed to have Mark on an exam table and were working to secure him as he convulsed and fought with them. It didn't look like he was in open conflict with the two men, especially since Tim couldn't picture Mark Latham in a conflict with anyone, but rather as if Mark were in a brain fogging confusion caused by some immense pain in his abdomen. They had him tied down, but his struggles seemed to shake the entire table - a steel table bolted to the floor and wall so as to be unmovable. The largest earthquake the world had ever seen could hit the building, and that table would still be bolted to that floor and wall.

Kara hovered near his face, caressing his hair with one hand while she tried to calmly explain something to him, but her husband didn't seem to hear. She seemed to give up trying to speak with him and, with a face speaking at once of resignation and determination, used a pair of scissors to cut Mark's white t-shirt open from the neck straight down to his belt line. His abdomen was horrifically distended, as if the normally thin and fit geologist had an entire basketball shoved under his skin.

All Tim could do was stand and watch, and he may have even banged on the door, calling for Kara to open the door and let him help. The scene took surrealism to a new height as Tim could hardly believe it was all real, and yet he watched it all with his own eyes. And no sound accompanied the horror he watched.

One of the suits had his back to Tim, but he had angled just enough to show that he had drawn a pistol. The suit pointed it right at Mark's stomach while Kara seemed to hold her open hands up begging him to wait, to do nothing. She turned away to the corner of the room and returned seconds later, wearing a pair of elbow length cryo gloves. In her hands she carried a large alloy container. Tim couldn't read the markings on the cylindrical urn-shaped item, but the wisps of foggy vapor issuing from its mouth told him it could only be liquid nitrogen.

"For God's sakes, what are you doing?" he shouted as he renewed his banging on the metal door, but it was to no avail. No sound would pass either way.

And then, the worst possible thing that Tim could imagine happened, straight out of nightmares. Mark's belly split open right up the center, layers of skin and flesh peeling to the left and right not unlike a banana's own peel. Tim swore he heard a wet, fleshy sound when it happened, though he knew that was impossible. Splatter flung across the room, causing the other three persons to duck away, a natural reaction to be sure. Liquid nitrogen lapped up over the lip of the container and doused the floor. Droplets struck Kara's feet, but either they didn't penetrate her shoes, or her adrenal gland allowed her to ignore it.

Mark's eyes stared lifelessly toward the ceiling, but his hands still shook with a life of their own.

An alarm began to sound through the building, a blasting klaxon that drowned out all other sound, even Tim's own breathing and thudding heartbeat. Emergency lights began to flash red, a dizzying effect meant to tell everyone in the building that there is some sort of breach, and the building is going on lockdown. He had never experienced it before, and it seemed to evoke a primal panic from the pit of his stomach.

Motion caught Tim's attention, and he ceased his thorough beating of the door as something resembling a hand reached out and took a hold of the far suit. The fingers were bloated, almost tentacle like, each several inches thick and at least a foot long. It encompassed the man's thick neck fully, wrapping itself around him. The suit's eyes bulged outward, and his face turned blue.

The suit with the gun began to shout, at both his partner and Kara, his gun waiving around perilously. Kara continued her approach with the liquid nitrogen, with far less care than before. As she came close to Mark's corpse, for it could only be a corpse, her eyes widened in unknowable terror and disgust, and she hesitated for just a moment.

The alien appendage released its grip on the suit's neck and whipped to its left in a blur, striking Kara's hands and flinging the nitrogen container. The foggy liquid seemed to almost suspend in mid-air for a moment before splashing in a widespread across the gun-toting suit. The gun fell to the floor, and he fell out of view. The metal container struck the door, vibrating it ever so slightly for a moment. The strangled suit seemed to fall in slow motion to his right, his neck nothing more than a bloody, pulpy mess barely keeping his head connected to his body.

Tim could hardly make sense of what he next saw. An unspeakable mass of flesh and gore seemed to almost rise from the shell that was once Mark Latham, and as it did so, Mark's own flesh seemed to cave in or somehow fall into itself as if retracted from within. He couldn't bear to watch, yet his eyes wouldn't tear away from the grotesque scene as the mass fell to the floor in front of the table.

Kara had fallen backward against the wall, apparently dazed, perhaps from hitting her head. She cradled her right arm against her, and Tim could see points of discoloration across the skin. Her eyes cleared as she came to, and she tried to scurry backward even though she was already against the wall. She looked off to her left at something Tim couldn't see, and she dove across the floor.

The mass began to move again, a now humanoid shape of blood and flesh wobbling unevenly almost like a toddler learning to walk. Then Kara reappeared, standing with her back against the wall, the gun in her left hand. The thing ceased moving toward her and seemed to turn and regard Tim through the door for a moment with eyes he couldn't see. He pulled away out of sight as it moved off to his left.

Tim covered his ears with his palms, trying to block out the clanging siren. He closed his eyes as he did so, demanding to wake up from this nightmare, but he opened his eyes to find nothing had changed.

He hazarded a glance through the glass just in time to see Kara fire off the pistol several times. The containment room and the hallway outside of it, even the whole building rocked as if by an earthquake. Orange flame suddenly filled his tiny viewport, and Tim could even feel the heat against the door itself. He fell to the floor, partially out of instinct to protect himself from fire. He half expected to find his hair gone.

When he climbed back to his feet, Tim found his view in the room completely obscured by smoke. He pulled on the door, but found it still sealed tightly. There was no sign that the door had been compromised by the explosion, which it shouldn't have been based on everything Tim knew of the containment rooms. He swiped his card again, just in case, and nothing changed.

Tim felt his pocket vibrating. Someone called him, but he ignored it.

He stared into the room but could see nothing for the wall of gray smoke within. The fire system would eventually vent the room, removing all the smoke as well as most of the remaining oxygen inside. He knew no one could have survived the explosion. Even if they had, the fire control system and the smoke should finish the job. As the latter started to clear, Tim braced himself for the carnage. But it wasn't the carnage he saw; not the blackened remains of Dr. Mark Latham or the bodies of two men and Dr. Kara Stout-Latham burned and disfigured beyond recognition. It wasn't the aesthetic of the containment room that had been blasted away to reveal the supposedly impenetrable metallic walls underneath.

Dr. Tim Murphy found himself staring into the depths of a set of eyes. A man stood in the room, just a few feet from the door. He was completely nude and the perfect doppleganger or simulcrum of Mark Latham. Tim found himself chilled to his core, and it wasn't for the knowledge that Mark Latham was most assuredly dead, because after all, Tim saw the man die. It was the eyes that stared back at him. Mark Latham was a kind man, full of laughter and fun, even at his own expense at times. His eyes glowed with life. This man's eyes were dark, devoid of anything human or feeling. They held no regard for anyone or anything beloved by man, and Tim wasn't even sure they saw him as anything other than another obstacle, if they saw him at all.

Tim turned away and put his back to the wall, not daring to again make eye contact with the thing on the other side of the door. Again, he felt the phone in his pocket vibrating, and he realized that it had never stopped. He fished his phone out of his pocket and lifted his head up slightly so that his eyes could see through the lower part of his lenses, something he had affected well before he started wearing bifocals, to read the name Director Gerald Chambers lighting up his phone.

Tim swiped to answer the call, "Jerry, something's happened."

Chambers said something to him, something urgent and rushed, but Tim couldn't understand it. The alarm continued to blare at a hundred thousand decibels, drowning out the sound of Chambers voice through the speaker of Tim's phone.

"Jerry, I can't hear you! Hold on!" Tim shouted into his phone, and he began to head down the hall. Perhaps if he made it to the lobby, the siren would be quieter there. Maybe he could even make it outside the building. He only made it about three steps before the alarms suddenly stopped, though the lights continued to flash.

"There," said Chambers calm voice, barely audible over the ringing in Tim's ears. "Can you hear me now?"

Tim stopped dead just a few feet away from the door he wouldn't turn to face. "Yes, I can hear you."

"Is it contained?"

"Is *what* contained?!"

"Damn it, Tim!" Chambers nearly screamed as his ever present even demeanor suddenly evaporated. "IS IT CONTAINED?"

"Yes," Tim replied, taking a deep breath. "It's contained."

He reared back and threw his phone as hard as he could down the hallway into the lobby. It struck a wall and shattered into a thousand pieces, a storm of silicon, glass, plastic and metal. Avoiding a glance toward the containment door, Tim staggered backward toward a wall and slumped against it as if only it could keep him standing on his feet. The aftereffects of an adrenaline rush began to take him, and his legs lost all strength. His back slid down the wall, as his legs would no longer support him, until his ass hit the floor. He shivered as he wrapped his arms around his knees and began to cry.

Overslept

Some repeating sound slowly brought him from the darkness of his slumber. He may have been dreaming, at least at some point during his repose, but he never remembered if he had or what the content of his dreams were. The offending noise – noises – must have occurred no less than a dozen times before it even broke through the thick wall his mind erected when he slept, and he didn't start his rise to consciousness until he knew he'd heard the sound at least two dozen times. He was almost awake when his mind identified it as a shovel being driven into dirt and then said dirt being flung elsewhere, sometimes with an accompanied grunt.

Someone was digging nearby? What was the likelihood of that? *How odd*, he thought as he became fully awake. *How long have I been asleep?*

He opened his eyes to find everything dark around him. Puzzled, he squinted, his brow furrowed as he tried to work out why he was completely covered and surrounded by earth. He pushed his hands outward until the resistance disappeared and cool air touched his skin. He followed his hands with the rest of his body, pulling himself out of the darkness that concealed him until he stood on a wood floor of sorts in a rough tunnel that had been burrowed and dug through the ground itself. He had emerged from one of the walls in a heap of black dirt that coated him head to toe.

A hunched man stood some six feet ahead, digging steadily with a shovel. His clothing seemed largely unremarkable, though it was almost impossible, due to the poor light provided by a few small lamps, to see any details other than that he too was covered in dirt. He continued to dig in perfectly timed repetition, and he flung a shovel-full backward every few seconds.

Humans wore on the Yaggoth quickly, and tired of this one's incessant dirt throwing, the Yaggoth stepped closer so as to be just behind the man. He stretched, his body growing and extending, to raise himself to his full height. He hadn't noticed the low, also manmade ceiling, and he thumped his head solidly on the wood above him. At the same time, the digger apparently decided to adjust the angle of his discarding, flinging another load of dark earth over his right shoulder and into the Yaggoth's face and open mouth. The Yaggoth coughed and spit to clear his mouth, causing the man to cease his digging and whip around.

"Oh, sorry," he began to say, but the Yaggoth had no interest in the man's apologies. Before he could say anything else, a razor clawed hand clamped over his mouth and whipped his body around in a practiced motion that kept his head completely unmoving. As it twisted too far, the neck snapped, and the body went limp. For good measure, the Yaggoth simultaneously ran the claws of his free hand across the man's neck.

Feeling the warm human blood spill across his clawed hand made the Yaggoth's stomach grumble with anticipation of a warm meal. How long had it been? How long had he slept? There would be other opportunities to eat, but now he needed to find out how close he was to the next Conjunction. He frowned wistfully at the fresh meat that would be cooling too quickly and simply going to waste. Seeing nowhere to go, the Yaggoth turned around to find that the tunnel was relatively short, less than ten feet, and intersected another at a right angle.

"Mr. Wells? Are you back there?" a man's voice called from around the corner, causing the Yaggoth to stand perfectly still.

"Yes?" he called back in his human voice, something he himself hadn't heard in... well, in how long he didn't know, but it was at least ten years since before he went to sleep.

"Foreman says we're done for the day. See you at eight tomorrow."

The Yaggoth simply nodded in response, as if the speaker could see him, and he continued to stand absolutely still until he was sure the other man had gone away. He peaked around the corner and found another tunnel going left and right into darkness. Lamps were spaced every so often, and these had been put out. Fortunately, the Yaggoth had extraordinary eyesight, allowing him to see in near total darkness. There seemed to be slightly better lighting down the tunnel to his left, perhaps indicative of an exit.

What are they doing down here?, he wondered.

With popping and creaking sounds, and even some amount of disturbing suction, he shrunk his frame down in height, dropping to seven feet in total length, then another six inches, yet another six and then finally ending well below six feet. He could stand fully upright now, and he rubbed his chin as though in consideration. The points of the teeth in his giant, terrible maw poked at his human hands, and he rolled his eyes at his absent mindedness. His mouth shrank to that of a normal man's, and his teeth retreated into themselves simultaneously, completing his transformation.

Brushing himself off, the Yaggoth turned to his kill and appraised the state of the dead human's clothing. It was filthy, stained black from digging, but he had managed to keep the blood mostly off it. Of course, humans were filthy animals anyway, and one day he hoped to help liberate Earth from their heinous rule. With a slight snarl, he worked the dead man out of his shirt, pants, and boots, slightly dismembering him when necessary to make it easier. Finally, the Yaggoth kicked some dirt on the corpse, just enough to indicate his distaste more than cover his handiwork.

He made his way up the tunnel, following the illumination that even he could only barely see. He traversed three score feet or so, having seen no one else, before concluding that the light trickled in from above. The tunnel walls and ceiling and turned from wood to some sort of smooth, hard, gray stone. He reached a ladder that leaned up against this, and he climbed it toward freedom from the underground.

He emerged into cool night air, tinged with the stench of more humans in one place than the Yaggoth had ever experienced. He stood in the middle of an avenue of sorts that was blocked off at either end. The road had been paved with some sort of continuous black stone, the likes of which he had never seen. He'd seen volcanoes form such things in his years, but this pavement was dull and rough, unlike obsidian. People, paying him no mind whatsoever, walked on slightly upraised paths on either side of the street, and huge buildings of red, brown, or gray stone rose upward on either side. Light came from every window.

He felt suddenly bewitched at the feats these puny humans had begun to achieve, but he shook the marvelous feeling off almost as soon as it had come. While enough of them could harm or maybe even slay him, they were nothing to the Father. When He arrived, all would be ended, and there was nothing these things, barely evolved from single celled organisms, would be able to do about it.

To that end, the Yaggoth looked above, searching for the stars, but an ambient glow blocked them from his view. He snarled in disgust but cut the action short in the sudden fear that his real face may have shown through. He glanced around briefly and saw no reaction from the people around him.

Well aware of the dangers involved in walking down the middle of a street in New York, he stepped up to the sidewalk and started toward one of the intersections. Travelling in the flow of so much foot traffic was difficult to master. He had never seen so many people at one time, and somehow, they all managed to stay in step with one another. If he walked too slowly, the people behind him ran up upon him, but when he stepped to quickly, he did the same to those in front of him. Either way, they were the most mean spirited and angry human beings the Yaggoth had ever had the misfortune to meet. At first, he bore their swears and vile statements about his parentage with sheepish acceptance, but after the third or fourth time, it required all his restraint to withhold his true form.

At the first intersection, the crowd suddenly stopped and seemed to wait for some reason. He pushed up onto his tiptoes to get a good look around, only to find something that caused his breath to catch in his throat. It was a coach or wagon of some sort, in many ways little different from those he'd seen over the centuries, but this one gleamed of metal in the feeble light, instead of polished wood. More importantly, it traversed the city street under its own unseen power, no horses, or animals of any kind at all! What magic had these humans harnessed to create such devices? Like everything in this new version of the city, the self-propelled coaches too emitted light from round disks on their faces, and as the coaches went by, they spewed a vile, blackish smoke.

The Yaggoth decided he could handle no more. To the protests of those around him, he pushed his way from the crowd and went back the way he had come. He walked with huge strides, having grown just a few inches to lengthen his legs, purposefully driving himself from any large groups of people. He stared straight ahead, unwilling to find any new wonders, and continued until the numbers of humans began to thin. Eventually, he found himself virtually alone in a section of the city with incomplete buildings and streets of dirt. The Yaggoth sighed with relief and contentment that he had escaped the latest hellish incarnation of human civilization, at least just enough to feel more comfortable.

Needing to be closer to the sky, he entered one of the construction projects, found a set of stairs and began to climb. Four flights up, the stairs ended at a level with walls around its perimeter, but it stood without roof, open to the sky. He peered at the stars and constellations, his mind calculating the position and quantity of cosmic power. The Yaggoth determined that it would be nearly three decades, as humans tell time, before the next Conjunction took place. That was good; he had time, though it still didn't quite answer how long he'd been asleep.

He looked around the open level and spotted something of interest in the far corner. Crossing over to it, the Yaggoth ignored the various tools humans used to build their pathetic edifices but instead focused on what they called a newspaper. It was folded neatly next to an empty cup, and he picked it up to read the headline, "OFFICERS SANK WITH TITANIC, SAVING WOMEN TILL THE END". The date under the print declaring the paper to be the evening edition of "The World" read April 17, 1912.

"Well, shit," the Yaggoth mumbled as he tossed the paper into a heap near its original resting place. He'd been asleep for almost sixty years, having missed Yag's last Conjunction by ten years. Father may be angry if he managed to break through in the next one, so it would probably be best if the Yaggoth were nowhere nearby for a while.

The Yaggoth, like most males of his kind (how many were even left?), was inherently lazy. After all, when one didn't age, and therefore had an eternity to accomplish one's aims, why be in a hurry? If he missed an opportunity, another would present itself, and Yag Himself had no perception of time anyway.

The nameless Yaggoth yawned and scratched at his grumbling belly. It seemed like time to find a meal, and he certainly wasn't returning to retrieve his kill. Besides, the meat was long cold by now, and men weren't particularly tasty. He resolved himself to finding a woman, and the type he wanted were typically easy to find as night fell. A particular itch needed to be scratched, and human biology was, more or less, compatible with his, although he had never waited long enough to see if such a union produced anything. It was an interesting thought, as female Yaggoth were so bothersome to mate with, assuming you could even find one. Human women were much more accommodating, and besides, they had a wondrous flavor immediately after intercourse.

Calvin

"Are we there yet?"

"Almost, baby," Letitia Gordon answered her son as she turned her ten-year-old Chevy Malibu into their new neighborhood. It was a cool Wednesday morning for late June in Atlanta.

"Why'd we hafta' move again?" Tre asked for the millionth time since she broke the good news to him two weeks ago.

"Because I want you to live someplace safe with a good school."

"I like my school," he mumbled petulantly, and he began to pout. After a moment, he said, "Is Dad coming over?"

"No."

"Dad said he can come over any time he wants."

"Oh, he did, did he?" Letitia asked, though she doubted Tre sensed the tone in her voice.

"Yep. He said it be his money that let you buy the house, so it be practic'ly his."

She almost spouted, "Well, he's just paying for fucking that bitch at work for a year behind my back," but she settled for, "Grammar, Tre. You need to speak properly."

Letitia changed the subject, "You'll like your new school better. I've already met your teacher, and she's a nice lady," she assured him. They turned into a rectangular parking area bounded by rows of townhouses on three sides.

A large group of kids, ten or so elementary and middle schoolers, played a game of improvised football on a grassy common area to the left. She pointed at them, "And look at all the kids around here. This'll be awesome. We're here," she announced after pulling into a parking space directly in front of one of the two-story townhomes. They all had red brick first floors with vinyl siding of various colors on the second level; this one had beige.

"I don't like it," Tre mumbled.

"You haven't even been inside, yet."

"I wanna' go back home."

"This is home."

"Back to our old home."

Letitia knew this battle was coming, knew exactly what Trevon was going to say to her. She had practically scripted the whole thing out ahead of time. He was a little kid, and little kids don't like change, especially when that meant moving away from friends. But she had an ace in the hole considering that their "old home" was a shitty, little apartment with a kitchen-dining-living room and a tiny single bedroom where mother and son shared a double bed.

"Well, okay," she said with a shrug. "I'll just tell the realtor to never mind, then. That's all right. Some other kid will be really happy to have his own room."

She sighed as loudly as possible and slowly dropped her hand to the gearshift while she waited for it to sink in, while she waited for Tre to work it out. She put the car in reverse, checked her mirrors and turned to look out her rear window, about to back up.

"Wait!" Tre shouted, and his hand shot to hers on the gear shift. "My own room?!"

"Yep. We can paint it any color you want, and you can put up your Iron Man posters…"

Letitia watched as Tre's eyes grew wide and lit up at the possibilities. He hadn't enjoyed the comfort of his own space since four years ago when they moved out of the house, her ex-husband's house, and into the apartment. But this was *her* house, and it would be everything Tre needed and wanted it to be.

"Let's go," he nearly shouted, and he had his seatbelt off almost before she put the car back in park. In his excitement, he very nearly threw the passenger door open into the next car in, rushing to get out.

"Careful," she admonished though smiling.

Tre bounced on the sidewalk with excited energy while she extricated herself from the car, quite the change from his sullen attitude moments before. "Come on!" he called, and he turned and ran to the front door before she had even closed the car door.

"Okay, I'm comin'," she said as she walked toward the front door, keys in hand. Her son stood directly in front of her, leaning his weight backward up against the storm door. "Well, move out of the way if you wanna see inside!"

She barely had the door unlocked before Tre burst through it and into the townhouse. A white tile landing met them just inside and flowed into a beige carpeted living room. A staircase bisected the first floor, separating the dining area and galley style kitchen from the main room. Tre stood at the sliding glass door that opened to the rear patio.

"Mom! We got a backyard! With a fence!"

"I know, baby. You want to see your room?"

"Yeah!" he sprung away from the door and bounded up the stairs.

"Tre, let's not run in the house, okay?" Letitia called after him as she climbed the stairs.

"Sorry, mom."

"It's okay."

He turned right at the top of the steps, ignoring the bathroom in front of him. She found him standing in the middle of the master bedroom that sat directly above the living room. He leapt over to one of the windows and looked out onto the neighborhood, before turning to face her in the middle of the room.

"This room is huge. Is it mine?" he asked, wide eyed.

"No, yours is the other way."

He raced after her out of the room and to a closed door on the other side of the stairs. Opening it revealed another room, about half the width of the other with two windows that looked out over the backyard and the grassy easement between the row of townhouses and the row of the next court over. Centered against the wall to the right was a twin-sized bed with a simple mission style pine headboard.

"Mom, someone's already got a bed in this one."

"That's your bed. I bought it, and it was delivered yesterday."

"Really?" Tre asked softly, almost as if in awe of the simplest of luxuries - his own bed. He was on it in an instant, laying spread eagle with his arms and legs stretched toward the four corners of the mattress. A wide, silly smile stretched across his face, and he began to giggle as he moved his arms and legs back and forth as he would to create a snow angel.

Letitia smiled and laughed with him, ignoring her impulse to tell him to keep his shoes off the mattress. It didn't matter. Only his perfect moment of childhood joy mattered, and she fought to hold back tears. It helped when the doorbell rang, and Tre sat upright.

"Baby, that's probably the movers with our stuff. I'll be downstairs. No jumping on the bed, okay?"

"Okay, mom."

It didn't take long to unload a truck with two rooms' worth of belongings. Letitia left Tre in his new room, which he was still completely over the moon about, with the three measly cardboard boxes and the suitcase that represented all of his toys, clothes and other belongings. This left her alone with her thoughts while she pulled her cheap, yard sale dishes wrapped in newspaper from their boxes. She washed and dried each one in turn before placing them in a cupboard. The moving guys had done her a nice solid.

"Ma'am, do you want the mattress and box spring in the big bedroom?" the older white guy asked. He was probably in his fifties, overweight and smoked – heart disease waiting to happen if it hadn't already.

"Yes, please, thank you."

"Uh, okay, where's your frame? It's not on the truck."

"Just set it on the floor. It's fine," she told them.

"We still got that old one on the truck from that other move?" he asked the kid who couldn't have been older than twenty.

"Think so."

"Go get it for her, huh?"

"Thank you!' Letitia had gushed. "That's so sweet."

"Hey, my ma back in Jersey raised three kids by herself after my dad died in Nam. Don't worry about it."

She smiled as the image of Tre on his new bed came back to her mind. This was her moment. She did this, and she did it for him. They had both been through so much with the divorce and all - her working late at the hospital, sometimes picking Tre up from her mom's place at two in the morning to drive him a half hour to their place. She owed a lot to neighbors and Mom, but in the end, Letitia made this happen. She's the one who finished school, becoming a registered nurse. She's the one who saved every penny, lived as cheap as she could for both of them, so that she actually had a down payment. And that son of a bitch had the nerve to think his shitty little two hundred fifty bucks a month entitled him to tell their son the house was practically his? Who in the hell...

"Mom?" came a call from the dining room behind her, interrupting her thoughts.

"In here, Tre," she answered, setting their fourth and last plate on the stack in the cupboard with a clink. She turned, expecting to see him walking into the kitchen, but he wasn't there. She stuck her head into the empty dining area. "Tre?"

He didn't answer, but she heard slight thumps above her in his room, the carpet muffling his activities. She crossed the room to the stairs and made the turn to quickly climb them. She had taken only the first four or five, when a child's voice softly said, "Mom?" from behind her. Letitia stopped immediately and stood very still. She leaned between the railing and the ceiling, checking both the dining room and the living room, but both were empty. She walked over to the tiny half bath which was little more than a closet attached to the dining room and tucked under the stairs. She turned the knob and swiftly pulled the door open, expecting to find her son in there and snickering. It, too, was empty.

"Tre!" she called up the stairs, her voice echoing and reverberating off the walls. He didn't respond, except for a slightly louder thump through the floor. She shouted more urgently, "Tre?!"

Footsteps pounded upstairs, and he appeared at the top of the steps. "Yeah, mom?"

"What are you doing up there?" she asked.

"Just building my robot."

"Did you call me?"

"No," Tre replied with a brief, half shake of his head, and he went back to his room.

It wasn't long before Letitia's stomach started talking to her, and she glanced at her phone. It was half past twelve, and she realized the flaw in her master plan –

there was no food in her new home. She hadn't really thought about that. She'd go to the store tomorrow, but that didn't solve her more immediate problem. She quickly made a decision and went to get her son's opinion.

Upstairs, she found Tre's door closed. She almost opened it but stopped short for just a moment when she heard her son's voice from inside the room. He was mumbling, no whispering to himself from inside the room. His low voice and the closed door prevented her from hearing anything he said. She opened the door.

Tre sat on his new bed with a two-foot-tall robot monstrosity – a robot assembled from a set she bought him as a move-in gift. It looked like he had it all put together, even had the computer and power installed. It was marked for ages thirteen and up, but that hadn't stopped her from getting it for him. He was born to build things, and this whole move into a good neighborhood with good schools was all about giving him that chance. He'd go to college, to a good college, and start his life out right.

"Who are you talking to?"

Tre just looks back at her for a moment and then scans the room. When he looks back at her, his face adopts an odd blend of surprise and sheepishness, and he says, "No one."

"Please keep your door open. Okay, baby?"

"Okay, mom."

"Well, we have to go to the grocery store."

"Awwww, mom…"

"Not today," she interrupts his whine. "I'll order pizza. We'll go to the store tomorrow."

"Pizza?! Where from?"

"From where," she corrects him.

"From where?" he asks again.

"I'll get on the Padre Jose's app. I'm sure they have a store near us. What should I order?"

"Cheese and pepperoni!"

"Hmmmm," she mused, "I was thinking onions, olives, tree bark and leaves."

"Mo-ommmmm," Tre replied, making the word two syllables in disbelieving disapproval.

"Okay, okay. We'll split it. Half veggie, half pepperoni."

"Yay!" Tre chanted as if he were about to join a pizza conga line, "Pizza, pizza, piz-za!"

Letitia slouched on the loveseat in the living room – *her* living room – while she waited for their lunch and dinner to arrive. She hated this piece of furniture. It was some old, stained leftover from the nineties, or maybe even eighties, that she found on the street somewhere near her old place. She'd paid a couple of nice guys forty dollars to bring it up to her apartment. As a nurse, she doubted its sanitation very highly, and she had emptied two cans of Lysol on it.

It was okay, though, for its time in her possession was nearly over. One day next week, Havarti's Furniture would be bringing her a whole new living room set. It wasn't fancy, but they approved her for it, and they had it in stock, ready to deliver. Hopefully, the small, round oak kitchen table and matching chairs would show up at the same time. When she paid all that off, she would order a bedroom set and new mattress for herself. The cable would be turned on Friday, which meant she had to go buy a TV, probably just a cheap one from one of the big stores.

She dozed a bit while she waited for the pizza to show up. It had been a good day.

"Tre don't sit on the side of the bed," Letitia groaned.

Her mattress was literally the cheapest new mattress she could find at the time when she bought it two years ago. It was barely six inches thick, little more than a paper-thin quilted fabric stretched over steel springs, and it had no edge support whatsoever. So, when someone sat on the edge of it, the mattress almost bottomed out, making her feel like she was going to roll or slide to that edge.

"Either climb in or go back to bed," she told him, annoyance creeping into her voice.

Letitia opened one eye slightly and saw the early, early morning light just barely outlining the blinds. In terms of late June, that meant it probably wasn't even six yet, and she had really planned to sleep until at least seven on every day of her move-in vacation. She flipped over to face her son, expecting her clear aggravation to help Tre decide, but he wasn't there. Letitia sprung upright in bed and looked around her room. She leaned forward to peer through her open doorway toward Tre's room. She saw his feet sticking out from under his blanket.

She must have been dreaming. Still, her heart pounded, and she felt wide awake. She searched through the bedding for her phone and discovered that it wasn't even six yet. She flopped backward on the bed and covered her face with the pillow to block out the light. About five minutes later, she went downstairs in disgust to start the coffee maker, one of the few conveniences she had, and one that the hospital staff had given her when they replaced one in the lounge. It was almost eight when Tre finally wandered downstairs, his face only capable of conveying extreme grogginess, and by that point, her FaceGram newsfeed had started repeating the same stories.

"Good morning, sleepy head!" she greeted him with far more enthusiasm than he was clearly ready for.

"Hi," he replied. He stared somewhere past her, absently scratching his stomach. "What's for breakfast?"

"Toasted strawberry!" she called, continuing to imbue every word with sunshine as she held out a foil wrapper containing the carb-loaded breakfast food. "No toaster, though."

Tre just nodded, unblinking, then walked past her into the kitchen. She heard him open and close a cabinet, and then the beautiful sound of her refrigerator dispensing filtered water into a glass met her ears. That was *her* refrigerator that did that! Though, the sound still vaguely sounded like someone peeing. He returned to the dining room, took the offered rations and then just sat in the middle of the dining room floor as he tore them open.

"You awake?" she asked, holding back laughter.

"Yeah."

"You sleep okay?"

"Yeah."

"You want some coffee?" she asked, masking a knowing smile.

Tre perked right up, and his eyes took on sudden life. For some reason, her son had always been obsessed with drinking coffee, even though she had never let him have more than a sip. He asked, "Can I?"

"No, but I thought I'd ask."

He replied with the universal kid tone that turned a one syllable word into two, "Mo-ommmmm."

"When you're done, I need you to go get dressed, okay? We gotta go to the store."

"Awwwww..." came the standard kid reply to anything they don't want to do, especially going to the grocery store.

"What? You think we can just order pizza every day for lunch and dinner?"

"Yes!" Tre shot back, suddenly very awake and interested.

"Not gonna' happen, baby."

He slumped again as he chewed his breakfast absently, not quite dejectedly, but certainly less interested in the day's potential than just a moment previously.

Letitia set her coffee cup down in the sink and went back into the living room and her secondhand miniature sofa to compile a shopping list. She could cook for the next five days or so, but after that, she would be back to work. After a few minutes, she heard Tre trudge upstairs, hopefully to get dressed. She checked the time after some fruitless grocery soul searching and decided to make sure Tre was ready to go. Letitia stopped at the top of the stairs when she heard Tre's voice in his room.

"Yeah, I don't wanna' go," he said with a pause.

"I have to," he said with another pause.

"Because I have to," his voice took on a rather glum yet insistent tone, and Letitia felt anxious. She felt like she heard just one side of a two-person conversation.

"I'll be back. We can play then."

"I have to go with Mom, okay? I'll be back soon. I promise."

Tre came out of his room, and Letitia acted like she was just reaching the top of the stairs. She asked, "Were you talking to someone?"

"Just Calvin."

"Who's Calvin?"

"He's my friend," Tre answered, and he shouldered his way past her and down the steps.

Letitia almost turned to follow him but instead went into Tre's room. Except for his bed, the suitcase he used as a dresser and a few boxes of toys he hadn't yet unpacked, the room was empty. She walked over to the window and pulled the blind cord to double check that the window was locked. She turned to leave, and as she reached his doorway, a thump sounded behind her.

Letitia turned and saw Tre's constructed robot had fallen on its face. She stood it back up and left the room.

"Buckle up, baby," she said in the car while she sent a text to her friend, Christina, who was a child psychologist at the hospital.

It read: *Hey. You got a second.*
Sure. How's your move in?
It's good. Thanks. Can I ask you something?
"Are we going, Mom?"
"Yeah, give me just a minute."
What's up?
Call me.

Within a few seconds, her phone began to play Marvin Gaye's *Mercy Mercy Me*, and she said to Tre, "Hold on a minute. I have to take this."

"Okay."

She answered the phone as she exited the car and closed the door behind her, "Thanks for calling, Chris."

"What's up, girl?" Christina's voice registered a little worry through her standard greeting to Letitia. "Everything okay?"

"Yeah, I think so. I just... well... Tre's talking to himself."

"What do you mean?"

"Last night, I heard him whispering to himself in his room," she explained, "and then this morning, it was like he was having a full conversation with someone."

"Highly intelligent people, especially children, tend to talk things over with themselves. Sometimes, they even have arguments or answer their own questions. It's part of how they work through things. Did you ask him about it?"

"Yeah. Last night he said he wasn't talking to anyone. This morning he said it was someone named Calvin."

"Oh," Christina replied, drawing the word out extensively. "Tre has an imaginary friend! Sweetie don't worry about that. It's perfectly normal. Kids often find imaginary friends when they feel somehow isolated from children of comparable age and interests."

"Yeah?'

"Absolutely. It's no different than when a kid inserts themselves into a story or a movie as one of the characters. Calvin is just acting as an equal to Tre's personality. He'll be fine."

"He's never had one before," Letitia replied, worry obvious in her voice. "This just came out of nowhere."

"You surprised him with awesome news; he's just not reacting quite the way you expected him too. Sweetie, you just moved. He's suddenly realized that he's not going to see any of the people in the neighborhood or the kids at his school anymore. He'll be just fine. Once he makes a few friends, Calvin will begin to disappear, and then soon he won't need Calvin anymore," Christina assured her.

"Thanks, Chris."

"Any time, girl! I'll see you next week."

"Who's Calvin, Tre?" Letitia asked her son as they drove home from the store.

"What?" he replied, wide eyed.

"Who's Calvin?" she asked again, trying to keep her tone light.

"He's just a kid," Tre replied, looking at the window.

"How do you know him?"

"I just met him yesterday."

"Is he in the car with us?" she asked at a stoplight, half turning as if to scan the backseat of the Malibu.

"No, he stays at the house."

"Oh," she replied softly. After a minute or so, traffic began to move again. "This weekend is your father's weekend. He's gonna' pick you up about three tomorrow."

"Okay," Tre replied, somewhat glumly.

Her immediate reaction was to tell him he didn't have to go, but she worked hard to remind herself of what the lawyers, as well as Christina had told her. "It's important that you spend time with him. He's your father, and he'll always be your father."

"I don't like Chimere. She's mean to me."

"Don't worry. Chimere won't be around forever," she assured him, and then she realized how ominous the words sounded. "I mean, your father doesn't love her, and she doesn't love him. They'll break up, but he's always your father."

She hoped she had managed some damage control on what could have been mistaken as some sort of threat against that slut Tre's dad was banging, but it still sounded hollow. It would be best, she decided, if she just didn't mention it again and let it go away. She turned left into the neighborhood. A kid, probably a few years older than Tre, rode by on his bike.

"Well between now and tomorrow, I think you should get out and meet some of the other kids in the neighborhood," she suggested.

"No, I'm good."

"Just try, just go say hi to them."

"I don't need to. Calvin says the other kids aren't nice," Tre said, and then he added, "Calvin's nice."

She steered the car into the court's parking area and turned the car into the empty parking spot right in front of their house. She put the car in park, but she didn't shut it off just yet. She just silently looked at Tre as he leaned forward to look through the windshield, peering up at the windows of her bedroom on the second floor.

"Is Calvin real?" she asked after a few slow heartbeats, dreading the answer to the question, dreading that, despite Christina's expert assurances, something might be wrong with her son.

"I don't know," he said with a nonchalant shrug, and he jumped out of the car.

The doorbell rang twice in quick succession, echoing through the mostly empty house. Letitia checked her phone and saw it wasn't even two yet. It shouldn't be Marcus. Several of the neighbors had come by to say hello in the last day or so which was quite the change from the old neighborhood. She hoped it was more friendly greetings, but when she looked through the peephole, she saw Marcus' distorted image standing there, his fifteen-year-old Beamer that he thought made him look like a baller sitting in the middle of the court. *She* was with him.

Letitia opened the door but stood like a sentinel with one hand on the doorjamb, the other gripping the door itself, her arms barring his entry. "You're early."

"We got plans tonight," he said with a smile. His perfect, white teeth, perfect smile and dark skin had broken down a lot of women, but it didn't work on her anymore. The spell was broken.

"The agreement says between three and five."

"Can I come inside?" he asked, throwing his dark eyes into the game.

"Fine," she acquiesced grudgingly, backing up into the townhouse to let him enter.

As he stepped inside, he was careful not to let the screen door bang shut. He just barely came in, being careful to stand on the tile breezeway of the first few feet around the door. Letitia was sure he wouldn't leave that spot. He wanted to make sure Miss Chimere Slutbag could see him the whole time. That way, she couldn't accuse him of anything.

"I told you she isn't welcome here."

"She ain't in the house."

"You mean *my* house," Letitia clarified.

"Fine, she ain't in *your* house."

"Isn't."

"What?"

"She *isn't* in my house. I expect you will use proper grammar around our son," she reminded him of a subject they'd discussed before.

"God damn, Letitia –"

"Watch your language around him, too."

"What is your problem?" he asked exasperatedly. He had gotten just a little louder, proving she had gotten under his skin.

She was about to reply when telltale thumps vibrated through the ceiling. Tre's voice called from the top of the stairs, "Is Dad here?"

"Yes, baby. Go start getting ready," she called back without breaking eye contact with Marcus.

"Already?" he asked with a hint of kid-whine.

"I'll come up and help you in a second. Go on now."

"He ain't even ready yet?" Marcus' face twisted just a bit as his voice's naturally low register came up almost an octave.

"No, he *isn't* ready yet," she corrected, and he began to steam. She lowered her voice almost down to a whisper, "Do you want to know what my problem is? My problem is you. You're a player. All you want to do is drive around in your BMW, thinking you look good and making girls wet. It won't work on me anymore. You want to know why I correct the way he speaks and expect you to do it, too? It's 'cause I don't want him going through his life -"

Marcus interrupted, "Like he's black?"

"I don't want him to be judged wrongly by people because he sounds like he's from the hood."

"It's all those white people you work with."

"I've worked hard to get where I am, and you didn't do anything to help. I did it! Me!" her voice rose as she began to smolder. "I work at a hospital with people of all skin colors, with people from all over the world, and not one of them sounds like a damn gangsta'. And neither will Tre."

Letitia turned and stormed away from him, up the steps, to help Tre pack. Marcus was a dickhead, always trying to shame her "blackness" when she started "acting white". More than anything, he knew it got under her skin. By the time she reached the stairs, she realized she should've kicked him out to wait in his car until Tre was ready.

She found her son sitting in the middle of small mountains of clothes, trying to shove his robot into the suitcase.

"It won't fit," he almost whined.

"No, you can't take that with you."

"It's boring at Dad's house. There's nothing to do. I just watch T.V."

"I'll make sure he gets you some things to do, okay? Let's just make sure you have clothes to wear," she replied, counting out shirts, shorts, socks, and underwear. She would have to talk to Marcus about the toy situation at his place as well - another point for them to fight over.

Letitia whipped around at a painful cry that echoed up the stairs from the living room, followed by Marcus' voice shouting, "What da' fuck?!"

"Stay here," she said to her son, and she bolted back down the steps. Marcus stood where she left him, holding his left arm upright as blood ran freely down to the point of his elbow to drip on her tile floor. Four deep gouges ran half the length of his forearm as if a large cat had raked its claws to cause the wound. Letitia gasped, "What happened?"

"How da' fuck should I know?!"

"Let me see it," she said, her nurse instincts kicking in.

"Get away from me!" Marcus shouted as he turned toward the screen door.

"At least let me look at it."

"Naw," Marcus said as he threw open the door took huge strides to his car, where he waited until Letitia cleaned up the blood and sent Tre out to his father.

She sent a text to Christina: *You want to go out tonight? I need a drink.*

Letitia woke up groggy the next morning. She hadn't really overdone it, but she was a real lightweight when it came to alcohol. A couple margaritas and she was done for. The morning sunlight blinded her as her eyes cracked open, making everything unbearably bright and blurry. She groaned and pulled her pillow tightly over her head. Instead of going back into peaceful oblivion, her head slowly cleared. Finally, she tossed her pillow to the side and sighed in disgust when she read nine-thirty on her phone's lock screen.

The springs in her mattress creaked and then compressed suddenly, like someone sat on the right edge of the bed. Letitia shot upright in bed and stared at nothing - there was nothing there. Yet, the mattress was compressed almost flat. Letitia blinked once and then nearly jumped out of bed to stand on the other side of it, keeping it between her and whatever caused the edge of the mattress to flatten.

She just stared, and nothing happened. This had to be a dream; this wasn't really happening. "Wake up, Letitia," she whispered to herself once, then twice, but nothing changed. She closed her eyes, clenching them tightly as her heart thudded and she repeated it to herself over and over, some new kind of mantra. Finally, she peeked through her eyelids at the mattress, and everything was normal. She laughed at her own expense and declared, "Girl, you gone crazy!" Her heart slowed from its marathon pace, and she breathed deeply for a few minutes. Letitia even blinked a few times to make sure her mattress stayed normal.

She unlocked her phone and held it in front of her as she started the camera app. She accidentally snapped a picture before switching to the camera that faced her. She zoomed in and checked herself out in the camera for a moment - she didn't look bad for a chick who had gotten a little tipsy the night before and barely remembered the cab ride home.

She found some workout pants, shimmied into them and then made to leave the room, but she walked into something she couldn't see. It felt like walking into a wall that gave just a bit so she didn't get hurt but was completely and totally solid. Hairs on the back of Letitia's neck stood on end, and gooseflesh rose up on her arms. She shivered involuntarily, like she was suddenly freezing, and she stepped back instinctively.

Letitia didn't know what was going on, but she knew she wanted no part of it. She stepped back again and then to the left once, intending to go around whatever this was. Before she could go any further, it pressed up against her so forcefully that she almost lost her balance. Two invisible appendages wrapped around her waist and pulled her close, distinctly like an over enthusiastic bear hug. One of the "arms" dropped a bit, like it was grabbing her ass.

"Please stop," she blurted, and it was gone.

Letitia stood absolutely still for a moment as her skin began to warm. She glanced around the room once and then bolted, nearly tumbling headlong down the stairs in her rush out of the house. She ran to the blue Malibu and fumbled with the keys, somehow unable to find the right key, and then she dropped them to the asphalt with a jingle. She leaned over to pick them up and tapped the unlock button on the key fob as she did so. She jumped in the car and closed and locked the door. She just sat there, relishing the heat as it washed over her; it felt cleansing. After a while, she began to sweat, so she started the car and turned on the air conditioning.

She called Christina, receiving a belabored, "Girl, it is way too early after last night."

"I need you," was all Letitia managed to say at first. "Do you still do ghost stuff on the side?"

"Huh? Yeah. APIS," Christina supplied. "Why?"

"Listen," Letitia started, and she recounted everything she could remember, every detail of every odd thing that had happened since she had moved in. Christina seemed vaguely interested at first, but it wasn't until she heard what happened to Marcus that she sounded completely attentive. And then Letitia told her friend what just occurred in her bedroom.

"Are you there?" Letitia asked finally after she finished, and Christina said nothing in return.

"Yeah, I'm just processing. I'm gonna call Bob. He's the head of APIS. I don't know what he's going to say. A lot of this could be debunked -"

"I'm telling the truth!" Letitia almost screamed.

"No, no, no, sweetie, I'm not saying that. A big part of what APIS does is explain away most of what people consider to be evidence of ghosts. That's what we do."

"Please, explain it all way," Letitia almost begged.

"Let me call him and see when we can come out," Christina said. "Go shopping or something, girl. I'll call you back. Remember though, it's *your* house."

"Okay," Letitia said with a nod and ended the call.

She sat there silently, just staring blankly at the front of her townhouse for a while. If a stranger had just told her the story she'd told Christina, she wouldn't have believed it, but here she was, sitting in her car and afraid to go into her own house. Shopping? Maybe that was Christina's way of taking her mind off something, but Letitia didn't see the need. Not right now. Maybe Christina was right, and it's all just her imagination.

Letitia pulled out her phone to check her look again, to decide if she was presentable enough to go out. Looking at her image on the screen, something caught her eye. The bottom right corner showed a thumbnail of the last picture she'd taken. Confused, she touched it to bring the picture up full screen, and she'd never seen anything like it. She didn't even remember taking it.

She cocked her head sideways while considering the pic, trying to figure out where it was. There was a fuzzy green haze dominating the center, obscuring and distorting the carpet and plain wall of a room behind it. And then when she recognized the corner of a bed with its purple sheets, she realized when and where she took the picture. The longer she looked at the bizarre form in the middle of the picture, the more she realized its shape resembled a person.

Her fingers shook as she shared the image to Christina and sent her a text: *I took this picture by accident right before it happened.*

Bob and Shalonda will be over 9AM Monday morning, came the reply about ten minutes later. *Shalonda's a psychic.*

Letitia looked back at her house and snapped a few pictures before getting out of her car. She strode right back into the house, and she'd be damned if this thing thought it was going to scare her out of her home.

Something startled Letitia as she slept, and she sat upright, immediately awake. Dark blue light filtered into the room through its windows, the low glow of the early morning hours before the sun had started to rise. She felt the weight on the edge of her bed, the same place as the previous two times. She didn't need to see to know there was nothing to see.

As calmly as she could manage, the opened her phone's camera. She snapped two pictures without the flash, followed by two more with the flash on auto. The strobing light lit up the room for several split seconds in succession, just enough to show her the room was empty. She was about to look at the pictures when the screen went black. She tapped it a few times, her nails clicking on the glass, but nothing happened. She pressed the power button to no avail. She held it down for a couple seconds, and an image of a battery with a line slashed through it appeared on the screen.

Letitia steeled her nerves and turned to squarely face whatever sat on her bed with her.

"Now, you listen to me," she said, her voice low and firm, "I don't know who or what you are, but this is my house. You are *not* welcome here. Leave me alone. Leave my son alone. Go away, and don't come back."

She then just sat cross legged, unblinking, her jaw clenched as she waited for something to happen. It felt like a game of chicken between two speeding cars or maybe a standoff between two lions, one waiting for the other to flinch. It seemed to last forever, but finally, the weight lifted off of her bed. Letitia waited a little longer, listening to the thud of her own heart in her ears. She exhaled a huge breath and hung her head in relief, almost exhausted.

And then something grabbed her ankle, pulling her right leg out from under her. Letitia instinctively yanked her leg back toward her, but she couldn't escape the grasp of whatever held her. She kicked at nothing with her free foot, though she seemed to connect with a solid form that also had no substance. Her other leg was caught in mid-kick, her shin gripped by some force. It pulled her toward the edge of the bed, forcing her legs apart.

Oh my god, she thought, *It's going to...*

She couldn't fight it. She couldn't stop it. She couldn't escape it. She tried screaming, tried calling for help, but something covered her mouth, muffling every sound that came out. She begged and pleaded, she cried and eventually gave up, just whimpering as it all happened. She blacked out, and when she came to, cheerfully bright Sunday morning sunlight shone through her blinds.

She lay naked on her bed, curled into a fetal position. Everything ached, and she had bruises on her wrists, ankles, legs and other places. She began to cry, and it built to wracking sobs. She pushed her face into her pillow, wishing that she could just die. It wasn't enough that this thing ruined the single greatest achievement of her life, her shining moment. That was violation enough, but now...

She gained control over herself and sat up, wiping tears and snot across the back of her arm. She was stronger than this, and she had help. She needed help. Her hands quaked and trembled as she unlocked her phone and called Christina.

"Can't talk, girl. We're gonna' be late for church."

"Christina?"

"I'll call you later, okay?"

"Christina," was all Letitia could manage to say, but it was enough. Perhaps it was her inability to say anything else, or maybe the quiver in her voice gave her friend pause.

"Are you okay? Did something happen?" Christina asked, overwhelming concern in her voice.

"Yeah... I... I need your help," Letitia finally got out, and she began to cry again.

"I'm on my way," Christina replied, and just before the call disconnected, she said to someone else, "Just go without me."

Twenty minutes later, the knocker clapped several times through the house, breaking Letitia out of a long stare. She still sat on her bed. She hadn't moved, hadn't put clothes on, hadn't done anything but sit, wait and stare. She willed herself off the bed, ignoring the spots of blood on the sheets, and found her robe on the dresser. Wrapping herself up, she made her way downstairs. Just as she reached the door, her phone chimed with an incoming text message. It was Christina saying, *I'm here*.

It took the better part of an hour for Letitia to tell her friend what happened. Time and again, she found herself with Christina's arms wrapped protectively around her, even rocking her at times when she couldn't keep control. Her friend listened and held her, saying almost nothing. Letitia plugged in her phone to pull up the pictures, finding the same vaguely human shaped green distortion from the first picture. As one last point of proof, she opened her robe so Christina could see her injuries. Christina was on her phone in moments, pacing as she spoke.

"Bob, you know my friend I told you about? I'm with her right now. We need to get the team over here. This is a nine one one. No, Bob, I'm dead serious. Bob. Bob!" Christina lowered her voice and paced into the next room, but Letitia could still hear her. "Bob, it *raped* her for God's sakes. *Yes*. Okay. I'll text you the address."

Doctor Robert Vaanderhoeven wasn't a particularly tall man, maybe five foot eight, and in his forties with curly light brown hair and a scruffy beard. He stood in Letitia's living room in blue jeans and loafers with a black t-shirt that had APIS – Atlanta Paranormal Investigation Society screen printed on it. He had with him an older woman that Christina introduced as Shalonda. Her wise and gentle smile made her look like everyone's favorite grandmother, excepting the crazily arrayed gray hair going every which way and that.

"Ms. Gordon," Bob explained, "I've got two vans and two more people on the way. They'll be here in under an hour. We're going to set up a lot of advanced equipment – high end cameras that see in ultraviolet and infrared spectrums, electromagnetic field detectors, white noise recorders – just to name a few. We're going to find what's here."

"How do we get rid of it?" she asked, and the question seemed to make Vaanderhoeven suddenly uncomfortable.

"Well, you see, that depends on what it is, why it's here and what it wants," he explained, unconvincingly, and a shudder went through Letitia, causing Christina to wrap an arm around her.

"I can't stay here," Letitia said.

"I understand," Bob nodded. "It would probably be easier for the investigation if you weren't here anyway. Christina mentioned you have a son. Where is he?"

"At his Dad's."

"Can he stay there another day or two."

"No," Letitia answered more firmly than she meant to. "I have to pick him up today."

"All right, then it's settled," Bob decided, "I'll put you up in a hotel for a few days. Ms. Gordon, Shalonda needs to take a tour of the house. Are you able, I mean…

comfortable enough... to show her where different... things happened."

As a nurse, Letitia knew something of bedside manner, and she knew when someone didn't have it. She saw it in med students all the time – they just didn't know how to respond to certain things. Bob seemed to be an academic of sorts, a nerd, and talking about sensitive subjects clearly made him uncomfortable. She swallowed and just slowly nodded in response.

The tour didn't take long. After all, the townhouse only consisted of four rooms, plus a kitchen and two bathrooms. Regardless, Letitia took the three through her home, starting with what happened to Marcus in the breezeway. As they entered each room, Shalonda slowly scanned it from one side to the other after Letitia detailed the events there. She made no comments at all, simply nodded when she was ready to move on. Vaanderhoeven snapped several pictures from several different angles with his phone.

At her bedroom, Letitia stopped in the doorway and said, "I... I can't go in there."

Christina clasped her hand. "It's okay, girl."

"This is where you took the pictures?" Shalonda asked as she shouldered by everyone to enter the room, shivering once when she crossed the threshold.

"Yes."

The older woman repeated the same ritual she had in each of the other rooms, but this time it seemed to take forever. She stood to the side of the bed, staring at it for several minutes before scanning the entire room from left to right. She then, slowly, walked around the bed to the other side of the room, repeating the process. Finally, her gaze rested on the mattress again, and then she lifted her eyes to the group huddled in the hallway.

Everyone jumped when a car's horn sounded twice from the parking area outside. Shalonda peeked through the blinds and said, "The first van is here."

"I hate it when they do that," Vaanderhoeven muttered, "just announce to the whole neighborhood that something's up."

"We should go to lunch while they set up," Shalonda suggested.

Letitia followed Vaanderhoeven's car – something sleek and sexy called a Genesis – to a place called Tony's. It didn't look like much from the outside, tucked away as it was into the corner of a strip center, but the place was cute inside, homey. The standard restaurant booths lined the inside with tables in the middle, and she instantly recognized the smells of an Italian pizzeria style restaurant. She hoped they had a veggie calzone, though she guessed she could build one. Extra cheese sounded good right now. They took a corner booth, and all of a sudden, Letitia found herself alone with Vaanderhoeven as Shalonda and Christina went to the ladies' room.

"This place is great. Everything is good here," he said. "Ms. Gordon –"

"Call me Letitia."

"Thank you. Please call me Bob. Letitia, we're going to figure this out, okay? The place I'm going to put you up in is pretty nice. I know it's not home, but…"

"How long do you think we'll be there?"

"As long as it takes," Bob replied, his brown eyes soulful and empathetic. "My team works very hard on these investigations. If possible, we want to disprove your haunting."

"What if you can't?"

"We move to the next step. I… I don't want to say what that may be because I don't have any information yet. We investigate a lot of places – a lot of

313

them for P.R. purposes, investigations of high-profile historic sites and the like so they can claim to be haunted. But I've made substantial investments in people and technology, *lots* of technology, to help people like you."

"How do you get funding for all of this? The government?"

"Ha! No, I fund it all."

"What are you rich or something?" Letitia asked, crossing a line that would've made her grandmother blush.

"Ummm… yeah," Bob answered quickly as Shalonda and Christina returned.

A round, black haired man came over and took their order. Bob introduced him as the Anthony from which the restaurant took its name. He was as jovial as he was ponderous, making friendly small talk with the group. "I don't recognize you," he said to Letitia. "New to the group?"

"I'm Letitia," she said as cheerfully as she could muster, offering a handshake.

"Have fun working with this man," Anthony said with a pointed finger at Vaanderhoeven. "He's a good man."

"Ms. Gordon is… ummm," Vaanderhoeven paused as he searched for the right words, "a client."

"Oh," Anthony replied with raised eyebrows. "Okay well, meal's on the house."

"You don't have to do that, Tony."

"It's done," he argued, and he turned to go to his kitchen.

Christina leaned over toward Letitia and said in a low tone, "Bob helped Tony with something years ago."

"I see," Letitia said. "So, what now?"

Both Christina's and Bob Vaanderhoeven's eyes shot to Shalonda, who was about to take a sip of water. She apparently thought better of it and sat the cup down on the red and white crosshatched table. A small ring of condensation had started to form. She adopted a face Letitia had seen many times in the hospital; doctors always seemed to get it when they were about to deliver bad news.

"There *is* something in your home," she started.

"Yes, I know that," Letitia lashed out, a result of a flood of emotions that she just couldn't process.

"Sweetie," Shalonda said softly, placing her hand on Letitia's, "be patient with me. We're here to help you. Most people wouldn't know what you've gone through in just a few days. Some of us have gone through it ourselves."

She paused as she let that sink in, and Letitia's mood began to soften, her fear and anger beginning to subside. She felt like she'd just been chastised in the most loving and caring way.

"Now," Shalonda continued, "this presence in your home – it was hiding while we walked through the house. It didn't understand who we were or why we were there, but it did know you called us there because of what it did."

"Are you saying it's intelligent?" Bob asked.

"Oh, yes."

"Demonic?"

"I don't think so," Shalonda replied with a slight tilt of her head. "I think it's a child of sorts."

"A child?! It *raped* me!" Letitia blurted. For some reason, the psychic's words caused unreasoning anger to boil to the surface, but just saying the word – it was the first time she had said – felt somehow cathartic.

"I know, sweetie. I know," Shalonda repeated, patting Letitia's hand. "Children, especially those that are somehow wrong, are capable of evil no differently from adults. I'm not saying that this Calvin is truly the spirit of a child. I meant it seems very childlike, perhaps like an adult with mental disabilities."

"You said it was hiding?" Bob interjected.

"Yes. I think it was hiding under the bed."

"What does this all mean?" Letitia asked, trying very hard not to sound exasperated.

"There are different kinds of hauntings," Vaanderhoeven explained as Anthony began bringing food. "Residual is where a spirit is attached to a place and just repeats the same actions over and over. Poltergeists – forget about the movie – move objects and make noises but are generally harmless. Then you have demonic and intelligent. I think we can count out demonic. Beyond the violence, there has been none of the telltale signs of demonic activity."

"I think that makes me feel better," Letitia said as she cut into her calzone.

"It should. While Christian mythology tints our viewpoint somewhat -"

"Bob," Christina interrupted, stretching out his name as Vaanderhoeven sighed and rolled his eyes. She cut off his reaction with, "Be respectful."

"Am I wrong in that, at its core, all Christian beliefs and parables are little different than the myths and legends of most of the older pagan religions? We call them myths just because they're not the ruling ideology du jour."

"Your expression was condescending even if your words weren't. Besides, I don't think you should be invoking blasphemy while talking about demonic possession."

"I hadn't even gotten to possession yet. You're predisposed to that kind of thinking because of your Catholic upbringing and horror movies," he argued.

"Is it not true that demonic hauntings occur more in Christian households than any other?"

"Yes, but –"

She cut him off, "And isn't it true that we generally have to call in priests to exorcise said demon?"

"Yes," he agreed with a huff, but he held up a finger to stop her next interruption, "isn't it possible that demonic hauntings are simply reported more in Christian homes than other religions? The Western world especially is more predisposed than the Eastern because of the belief systems at work. If you look at Japan, China, India, Korea – just to name a few – their belief systems are much more intricate than ours, and they don't have as much fear of such entities as we do. Many of them just live with these demons as part of life, and they do other things to protect themselves and or appease the demons. Our response is to fight back. We view them as inherently evil."

"They are evil," Shalonda interjected.

Realizing that it was now two against one, Bob Vaanderhoeven smiled at Letitia and said, "Obviously, this is a very old argument, one which I won't win today. There are many different beliefs about demonic hauntings, but there are a few things we all agree on in our field. Demons are inhuman, meaning they've never had human form. They gain pleasure and strength from torturing us, emotionally and psychologically as much as physically. We believe their goal often is to break down your will so they may possess you – the ultimate in torture. They are extremely violent, which is also the case here, but they don't hide from human beings. They have no need to; they're not scared of us, and they certainly don't interact peacefully with children and give themselves human names."

"So where does that leave us?" Letitia asked.

"An intelligent haunting," Christina answered.

"Which means what?"

"The spirit has consciousness on some level. It probably knows it is a spirit, and it acts of its own volition. Most are not harmful, but some can be dangerous. These spirits used to be human which is how they're different from demonic entities. They want something."

"So, how do we get rid of it?" Letitia asked.

Bob answered, "We have to figure out what it wants."

"I wanted to talk to you in person," Bob Vaanderhoeven said as he stood outside Letitia's hotel room.

"Please come in," Letitia replied with an open hand.

Vaanderhoeven entered the room and looked around uncomfortably for a moment before settling in a brown wooden chair that matched the room's desk, probably provided for business patrons. "How's Tre doing?" he asked with a pointed look at her son who laid on the bed watching some superhero movie.

"He's okay, I guess. He's not happy about being here. When I picked him up, the first thing he asked was if we're going home so he could see Calvin."

"What did you say?"

"I told him the truth. I told him Calvin hurt me really badly while he was gone."

"Really?" Bob asked, and he seemed genuinely surprised.

"I've never lied to my son. I never will."

"Probably a good policy. I... I'm not really comfortable with children. I wouldn't know where to start being a parent, much less a single parent."

"Can we talk about why you're here?" Letitia asked, hoping to move along the conversation.

"Absolutely. Sorry," Bob answered, and he took a deep breath. "Twenty-four hours, and we've got nothing so far."

"What?"

"The entity, Calvin, is in the house, seems to stay in your room. We've caught it on our digital cameras, well on the pics we've taken. It doesn't manifest on any of the live cams. We've tried asking it questions, asking it to interact with us, and we get nothing. Nothing on infrared, UV or the white noise recorders, and we've been sure to keep plenty of charged devices and batteries all over the house."

"I don't understand what that means."

"There's a prevailing hypothesis and belief in my business – well it's not a business, because I don't make any money at it, but you know what I mean – that these spirits - ghosts, entities, whatever you want to call them – require energy to manifest. Einstein told us that matter and energy are interchangeable, so it stands to reason that they would require energy to manipulate matter. Ever since we've had rechargeable electronic devices, researchers have noted power drains right before manifestations."

"Like my phone going dead right before…"

"Exactly," Bob nodded, "and the coldness you felt was the entity drawing energy from heat."

"That's all very interesting, but why won't it interact with you?" Letitia asked.

"That's a question of the nature and psychology of the entity. Most intelligent spirits are attached or drawn to a person, place or object. We researched your home today. It was built twelve years ago, you bought it from the original owner, and there have been no tragedies in it. Everything in your home, you brought with you or recently bought brand new. Calvin didn't manifest to you before in your apartment, and brand-new belongings don't have hauntings by virtue of being new."

"So, that leaves what?" Letitia asked, turning to look wide eyed at Tre as tears began to build. "Tre?"

"No, we don't think so," Bob disagreed, pulling her attention back to him. "If Shalonda is correct, and she usually is, that this thing is a child or childlike, it likes to interact with Tre because it's comfortable around him. But you…"

He paused, taking a deep breath before continuing, "You're the one thing in common. You've been present every time Calvin has manifested, not your son."

Letitia stood in her living room amidst a half dozen people, most of who were busy watching banks of monitors and listening to headphones. She really didn't want to be here, wasn't sure why she had come except that she had worked so hard for this house, and she wanted this thing to be over. She really wanted to cross her arms protectively over her chest, but Tre held her left hand and stood slightly behind her. Christina had taken her right hand and held it supportively since the moment she walked in the house.

"What do I do now?" Letitia asked.

"We need to," Bob Vaanderhoeven replied haltingly, "coax the entity out, so that we can try to interact with it. I think the best way to do that – and I appreciate how uncomfortable this will be – is for you to go to your bedroom and lay down."

"No way, no fuckin' way," Letitia burst, causing quite a stir among the group. Christina squeezed her hand softly. "I'm sorry. I can't do it."

Vaanderhoeven swallowed and nodded slowly before making another suggestion. "Okay, I understand. What if we have Tre go upstairs and play in his room."

"I am not endangering my child," Letitia stated firmly.

"There's no reason to think he's in any danger," Bob argued, shaking his head. "Calvin has never done anything negative to Tre. There's no reason to believe that will change now."

"Ms. Gordon," interrupted a furry little white guy in an APIS t-shirt and ballcap. He stood as he pulled off a set of headphones. "I have every corner of Tre's room covered with cameras and mics. If he starts talking to Calvin, we'll know immediately."

"Then we'll go up there and see if it will talk to us. It's the only way," Bob finished.

"If anything happens to him," she warned.

"I'll never forgive myself," Vaanderhoeven replied genuinely.

Once dismissed with a parental warning not to touch any equipment he saw in his room, Tre ran upstairs eagerly to be back in his room with his toys. Letitia watched intently on one of the monitors as the first thing he went for was his pet project – the robot he had so painstakingly put together. He inspected it for a few minutes, pulled out a tiny screwdriver and wrench to make some adjustments and then turned on the power.

"Something's different. Tre's body language is different," Christina reported after about ten minutes. She pointed at the monitor, "See? He keeps looking up from the robot at something in front of him."

"The robot's not working right," said ballcap. "It stopped responding to his remote about a minute ago. He's tried turning it off and on a bunch of times."

Letitia moved away from the monitors as if to run upstairs, but Vaanderhoeven intercepted her, saying, "Just give it a few minutes. Okay? Just a few more minutes."

"He's talking!" announced Ballcap, and he unplugged his headphones so that everyone could hear through the speakers.

"No," Tre said aloud. He continued, pausing between sentences as if in a conversation with someone. "I don't want to talk to you. Mom told me you hurt her while I was gone. I love her more."

"Now," Bob said.

Letitia rushed upstairs, taking them two at a time with Christina and Shalonda close behind. Vaanderhoeven stayed downstairs with Ballcap to watch remotely. When she reached the top, she was met by the fourth member of the team, a heavy pink haired girl whose name she didn't remember.

"Easy. Easy," Christina warned as they converged on Tre's room, all of the activity drawing Tre's attention. She shouldered into the room with a digital camera and began taking pictures.

"What's wrong, mom?"

"Nothing, baby. Is Calvin here?"

"Yeah," he replied with a tone kids use when they're either bored of or not happy with something.

"I'm going to talk to Calvin, okay?" pink hair asked, but only received a shrug as an answer from Tre. She began to speak aloud to the room, pausing for several seconds after she asked each question. "Hello. We're not here to harm you, we just want to talk. Is that all right? We think your name is Calvin. Is that correct? How old are you, Calvin? Did you used to live here? Do you like to play with Tre?"

She continued for some time, asking question after question, most of them seemingly pointless or innocuous to Letitia. She grew impatient, crossing her arms, and she grew more and more angry with each passing minute. She shifted her weight from her left foot to right and back again, finally loosing a long sigh that caught everyone's attention. Why didn't they just tell the thing to leave?

"Because that's your place," Shalonda whispered in her ear. When Rosey finishes, you will need to take a stand, like you did the other night. Don't worry. I'm right here. Nothing will happen to you or Tre."

"Did you hurt Tre's father the other day? Why?" Rosey continued. "Why did you hurt Tre's mommy? Why are you here? We want to help you. How can we do that? What is it you want?"

Finally, the pink haired Rosey seemed to run out of things to ask, and she nodded toward Shalonda, who whispered into Letitia's ear, "It's your turn, sweetie. Remember – be strong. We're here."

Letitia stepped forward, facing the room, and everyone watched her expectantly, the seconds seeming to stretch into hours. She didn't want to do this. An uncontrollable shudder ran through her body. The last time she challenged this thing, it became violent, violating her, and yet here she was challenging it again. She wanted nothing more than to grab Tre's hand and run away. Christina came to stand next to her and clasped her hand with a supportive smile.

"Calvin, this is my house, not yours," she began while Rosey snapped pictures with a digital camera. "You're not welcome here. You aren't allowed to be here anymore. You need to leave, now, and never come back."

Something pushed up against her, almost knocking her back a step. A steady force leaned against her, and Letitia's body went suddenly cold. Her eyes opened wide as she began to shiver from the extreme temperature change. She felt like a panicked animal, wanting to do nothing more than run. Then an aged hand, Shalonda's hand lay peacefully on her right shoulder, and the terrible fright, the need to run instead of staying to do battle lifted away from her.

"You don't scare me," Letitia said to the unseen thing, and in that moment, it was true. "You can't hurt us. Go away!"

The force pushing up against Letitia eased and disappeared, and her skin began to warm. A tiny electronic beep sounded repeatedly, and Rosey stopped taking pictures for a moment to check her camera just as its power died. Both wireless cameras feeding picture digitally to the monitors downstairs also turned off.

"What's going on?" Letitia asked.

Before anyone could answer, Tre's robot levitated upward about three feet off the carpet. It held there by an unseen force, and time just seemed to stop for everyone in the room as they gazed and gasped. In a blur of motion, it shot to the left like an arrow shot from a bow and shattered against the wall. The drywall buckled and cracked, caving in at the center of the impact, and the thin metal pieces broke and bent, tiny screws, washers and nuts raining onto the carpet.

"Calviiiiiin," Tre yelled as he shot to his feet and ran toward his destroyed toy, but he collided with something unseen and fell back onto his rear.

Something freezing cold brushed past Letitia's left, and Shalonda half screamed from behind her. The older woman crumpled to her knees in apparent pain while she fought to hold back sudden tears. Audible stomping filled the hall, the petulant and angry gait of a child, and then the door to Letitia's bedroom slammed shut of its own accord, thundering through the house as it did so.

"Jesus," Christina whispered, and then she asked as she moved toward the collapsed Shalonda, "Are you all right?"

"My back."

Letitia, already in full nurse mode, knelt down beside the woman, checking her out. Gently brushing some of her hair aside, she found scratches just above the neckline of Shalonda's floral dress, disappearing behind the fabric. "I need to unzip your dress just a little. Okay?" Letitia asked softly, receiving just a nod as an answer. She pulled the zipper down just a few inches and saw that the excoriations, three parallel scratches that looked like human nail marks, continued downward. They didn't look deep, but blood rose to the surface in places.

"There's a first aid kit in the bathroom under the sink," Letitia said to Vaanderhoeven. She returned her attention to the psychic, taking the woman's hands in her own in an instantaneous juxtaposition of the two women's previous roles. "Let's go downstairs, and I'll get you patched up."

"I want to leave, now," Letitia told the team about a half hour later.

Shalonda had already left, gone home to rest. The scratches on her back had been almost six inches long, but Letitia's first appraisal had been correct. They bled a bit but stopped quickly with just a little dabbing pressure. A little hydrogen peroxide, some antibacterial cream and a bandage, and the woman was good as new. The signs of the attack would be gone in just a few days.

"Yeah, okay," Bob Vaanderhoeven nodded. "It's probably for the best, anyway. We can spend the night analyzing all that and meet you in the morning to review what we find."

"I can't. I have to be back at work tomorrow!" Letitia shot back, more aggressively than she intended. This whole mess had worn on her.

"I'll take care of that."

"What? How?"

"I went to medical school with your hospital's director," he explained. "It'll be fine, and you won't lose pay. Trust me."

Letitia couldn't get out of the house fast enough. She collected her son, and they rushed to the car. She drove entirely too fast back to the hotel, and once inside the room, Letitia went through her phone and deleted every picture of the townhouse she had ever taken, even those she snapped when she walked through the place in her initial walkthrough with the realtor.

She ended the evening with a text to Christina: *I can't go back.*

Letitia awoke in the hotel room thanks to a text from Vaanderhoeven at about seven in the morning asking her to come to the APIS office at ten to review some findings. She almost flipped out when she saw the time, realizing that she was late for her shift, even though it was supposedly "taken care of". A quick call into her manager confirmed that she was, in fact, still on paid vacation.

APIS apparently rented a small, three-room office about twenty minutes out of the city in a clean, well maintained office park amidst medical and other professional service businesses. She brought Tre with her, because there was no way she was leaving her son behind in the hotel room alone, and she had no one else to watch him – the hospital usually provided those services during her daytime shifts. The door chimed when they entered, and the ballcap wearing guy popped out from one of the rear rooms.

"Good morning, Ms. Gordon," he replied somewhat subdued. Huge dark rings ran under his eyes, and he squinted somewhat as if light itself bothered him.

"Hi. You look tired."

"It was an all-nighter," he replied, "but we have some things you should hear."

"We could've done this later," she suggested, and she was genuinely concerned. Of all people, she knew what lack of sleep could do to someone's health, both physical and mental.

"No, this was important," he said with a slight shake of his head. "Dr. Vaanderhoeven's in back. We have some things set up for you. I don't know if he should hear…"

It took Letitia a moment to decipher Ballcap's meaning, and then realization hit her – he meant Tre! She asked, "Is there a place he can wait?"

"Can he play video games?" Ballcap asked, and Tre's face lit up with excitement. "I mean, is it okay with you?"

"Please, mom, pleeeeease," Tre begged earnestly, while pulling on her hand.

"Okay, okay," she acquiesced. He deserved it; he was a good kid, and she hadn't been able to afford video games since the divorce.

"So how 'bout this," said Ballcap, moving past them, "I'll lock the front door, and then I'll set Tre up on my computer in my office. I'm sure I can find something he can play. Ms. Gordon, you can go see Bob in the office at the end of the hall. I'll be right there."

She found Vaanderhoeven seated on the far side of a foldout table that bisected a tiny room, little more than maybe eight feet in either dimension. Two monitors were situated at both ends, connected to computers on the floor, and an elaborate array of speakers were mounted around the room's ceiling. The doctor – Letitia just realized she didn't know what he was a doctor of – tapped on a wireless keyboard's spacebar intermittently while watching one of the monitors intently. She knocked quietly.

"Good morning!" he said, entirely too cheerfully as he almost jumped to his feet. "Come in, please, and have a seat."

Bob Vaanderhoeven wasted no time with small talk, immediately jumping into picture after picture taken throughout the first day of the investigation. He explained how none of their digital recording equipment had picked up any sounds at all, other than the team itself. For that matter, the pictures he scrolled through quickly displayed nothing out of the ordinary either, except for one still photo taken of under her bed.

"You can see right here," Vaanderhoeven said as he outlined something spherical with the eraser end of a pencil, "a green something, very pale, very light, but it is there."

"Under my bed?" Letitia asked with a shudder. She felt her eyes begin to water.

"Yes, but," Ballcap, whom she hadn't even realized had come back and sat right next to her, interjected, "we can't really use this as proof. Paranormal investigators often take pictures of what they call orbs. They tend to think they're proof of some sort of entity."

"You don't think so?" she asked.

"Too indistinguishable from dust particles," Ballcap shrugged.

"Now these pictures," Bob said as he closed one folder on the computer and opened another, "were taken during the EVP session in Tre's room when you were both present."

"EVP?" Letitia asked.

Ballcap explained, "Electronic voice phenomenon. We use digital recorders and white noise while we ask an entity questions. We don't hear it answer, but sometimes we find something when we check the tape. Sometimes we get a voice. Sometimes it's easy to hear, but it can blend into the background noise which makes it easy to miss. Then we have to clean it up."

"If I may," Bob said, recapturing Letitia's attention, "these photos are the originals. We haven't amplified them in any way."

Letitia felt the hair on the back of her neck stand up as he clicked through a dozen pictures, all of which were taken of Tre's room but from various angles. It was there – the light green translucent, almost transparent anomaly – low to the floor, almost as if it were sitting apposite Tre with the robot in between.

Bob continued as he clicked through a few more pictures, "I checked the time stamp against our video, and here's where you… stood up to it."

The form had shifted, grown taller as if it had stood from a sitting position. Then an appendage, a tentacle of sickly green, had reached out from the thing and enveloped the toy on the floor. There was nearly a dozen more pictures, and if Vaanderhoeven clicked through them quickly enough, they would have looked like a child's flipbook illustrating the robot lifting from the floor and then being flung against the wall. The entity's form seemed to darken as the scene progressed.

"So, that's it," Letitia concluded.

"Well, not entirely. There are a few things we caught on tape. I'm dating myself a little, huh? On tape…" he murmured as he backed out of a folder and opened a new one, double clicking a file. "I'm sorry, this is going to be a little loud."

Distortion and white noise roared from the speakers around the room, followed by Rosie's voice asking the questions of the previous night. Looking at one of the monitors, Letitia saw the audio file laid out like something from a movie, with peaks and valleys indicating volume, the peaks coinciding with the young woman's voice, but there was something else. As one of the peaks fell into a valley, there was a slight and momentary increase in volume for just a moment.

Letitia pointed at it and asked, "What's that?"

Bob smiled slightly back at her and answered, "You're a smart woman. That's an answer."

He clicked on the graphic just before the large peak, and Rosie's voice cut through the noise, saying, "We're not here to harm you, we just want to talk. Is that all right?" As her voice disappeared, all Letitia could hear was noise and distortion, like when someone turned their car stereo up all the way, but no music was playing. Bob highlighted the section between the end of Rosie's question and the beginning of the next and played it on a loop that lasted about two seconds. As it repeated over and over, she listened intently, and on the fifth or sixth time through, something caught her ear. It wasn't much, just a slight variation in the noise.

"Yeah," Bob agreed with a nod. "It's hard to hear, but it's there. Let me move ahead to the other two answers we found."

Letitia felt frustrated at this new evidence. The following replies were no easier to understand, though she heard them both on the first listen. Either her ears and brain knew what they were listening for, or the answers were clearer. In either case, they told her nothing. "This doesn't help," she told them, with no small amount of aggravation.

"I know, I know. Just let me show you this next file. It's the same recording, but we've cleaned it up. We've taken all of the extraneous noise out of it," Bob explained, and then he took a deep breath. "This will be difficult to hear, okay?"

The new audio file lasted for less than a minute, having been cut down to just the sections of importance. The volume in the office was much more manageable with the reduction of all the background and white noise.

Rosie's voice was crisp and clear as she asked her questions.

"We're not here to harm you, we just want to talk. Is that all right?"

"*No.*"

"Did you hurt Tre's father the other day? Why?"

"*He's mean to Mommy.*"

"What is it you want?"

"*Mommy to love me.*"

"Oh my God," Letitia whispered as she just stared unblinking at the monitor. Her eyes had watered up, and a tear from each made a slow track down her cheeks. Her face felt numb, and she began to shake and shudder, though the room was warm, even stuffy.

"I, uh," Vaanderhoeven started slowly, "haven't discussed these findings with Shalonda or Christina yet. I really want their input before –"

"I'm not going back," Letitia interrupted.

Bob raised his eyebrows, his face registering surprise, more for the interruption than the words themselves. He took a shallow breath in through his mouth and let it out through his nose with a slight whistle. He then said, "This is going to take some time. This is one of the more… interesting cases I've seen in a while, and if we're going to cleanse your home of –"

"I said I'm not going back!" Letitia repeated, and tears ran freely down her face.

"Okay, okay," Bob acceded softly, his fingers raised in the air though his palms seemed permanently affixed to the table. "Let me ask you this – what if we can make this entity go away and be sure that it's gone?"

Letitia started to wipe the tears away with her fingers, but Bob offered her a box of tissues, seemingly produced from thin air. He smiled gently as she pulled three or four from the box. She dried the tears on her face and then held tissues to her eyes, her head bowed as if to pray. After a moment, she turned away from the men and blew her nose.

Finally, she pulled herself together and answered, "I... I don't know. I don't know if I can ever go back with what it..."

"I understand," Vaanderhoeven said with a nod, interrupting Letitia so that she didn't have to finish the sentence, "but you can't keep living in a hotel room. So, here's what we're going to do. There's an apartment complex next to your neighborhood. They look pretty nice. Let's go check it out, and if you're comfortable with the area, I'll pay for a six-month lease. That will give us the time we need to figure this out."

"I can't ask you to do that," Letitia shook her head, and she felt the tears coming on again.

"You didn't ask. I offered."

"That's a lot of money."

"Not to me," Bob Vaanderhoeven replied nonchalantly. "I'm rich."

It took less than three days to arrange everything. The complex was clean and quiet, more or less, and they had several two-bedroom places available and ready to go. Letitia took one on the end of a row, which gave her one of the few two-floor apartments; the units contained within the rows were the same size but only a single level with two apartments, one stacked on top of the other.

Vaanderhoeven even had a couple guys run their stuff over with an old, beat-up pickup truck. She felt kind of bad for them – it was hot as Hell, and the truck obviously had no air conditioning considering they kept the windows down. It didn't seem to bother them much, but she gave them cold bottles of water from the fridge anyway. She supposed they were used to working hard.

Letitia sat on her decrepit loveseat, which she still intended to replace at some point in the relatively near future and closed her eyes with her head tilted backward. She breathed out a long sigh and just enjoyed the silence and calm of the empty room while Tre unpacked his things for the second time in as many weeks. She zoned out and drifted a bit, suddenly feeling very exhausted by the entire ordeal.

"Mom?"

"Yeah, baby?" Letitia answered, pulled back to consciousness just a bit.

"Mom?" came the call again, and Letitia shot upright on the couch. Pressure formed behind her eyes, and the hair on her neck and arms began to stand on end. She jumped to her feet and ran up the stairs into the tiny hall that led to the bedrooms, hers on the right and Tre's on the left. Tre's door was open, and he sat next to his bed, working to reassemble the shattered robot.

"Tre?" she asked. He looked up at her for just a moment, something akin to fear in his eyes, like when a child has to tell their parent something that they really don't want to talk about.

"Calvin moved, too," he said, and he returned his attention to his work.

Untitled And Unfinished

On the next page you will find a Prologue, the first few pages of a project that is exactly what the words above indicate it to be. It is something that I haven't yet wrapped my brain around but will be working on over the next few months.

While this is generally meant to be a modern story, the Prologue takes place in the 1950s, a time of great and well-deserved civil unrest, much like today. Some of the language used by characters in the following pages is vulgar and distasteful. Please understand that I do not personally use such language and find it to be stomach turning, but it is representative of the time in which the Prologue takes place.

Martin V. Parece II

Prologue
Back in the Day

I look around and realize that everything is suddenly different from what I remember, but the memory of what we were just doing fades quickly like a dream upon waking. I shake my head as I try to assimilate my surroundings, a sense of confused déjà vu attempting to cloud everything, and I of course know why it's happening. Thank God, Sarah's with me. I look at her, and I still know who she is. She looks back at me with both the same confusion and recognition, and I think that's helping lift the fog from my mind. We're still both dressed in our suits, and I can feel my weapon holstered underneath my jacket.

Sarah's wearing a black, kind of tight knee-length skirt and a matching suit jacket on the shoulders of which falls her dark brown hair. Sarah's a hottie with All American good looks, but I don't really see it anymore. We've been partners in the Bureau now for two years, and she's taken me down on the mat more than once. More importantly, I've found her to be a consummate professional, not to mention a damn good shot.

We're sitting in a car of some kind, me behind the wheel and her on the other side of a wide black leather, or maybe vinyl, bench seat. The interior, dash and all, looks ancient. No – correct that – it's an antique design, but it looks and feels brand spanking new. The gleaming dash is kind of a putty gray with an analog clock dead center and an antique looking radio below it – the kind that has a big black dial for your stations, two round knobs and four big, chrome contact switches between them. Looking out the windshield that meets the dash at an almost right angle, I see a huge black hood and a chrome V8 emblem at the end of it, the old school kind where the V and the 8 intersect and overlap each other. The steering wheel is white and shiny, well over a foot in diameter, but the ring of the wheel itself is perhaps only an inch thick at most. The word "Ford" is emblazoned in chrome on the end of the steering column, which is connected to the skinny wheel in only two places. Looking through the gaps, I see an antique analog speedometer that reads up to only seventy miles per hour.

We're stopped in traffic on a city street surrounded by antique cars, most of which look fairly new despite the fact their models must be sixty years old. I really don't recognize any of them, but all the cars from the fifties look the same to me anyway. We're in the fifties? I continue to look around, and the buildings that line the street seem to be of an older style of architecture, not too dissimilar from what I've seen in any number of small towns across the country.

"Do you get this?" I ask my partner.

"No," she replies. "Do you remember where we were?"

I pause before answering because I can almost say it, and then the memory just drifts out of my reach. "No," I admit, "but I know it wasn't sixty years ago."

The Ford's windows are up, and I suddenly realize how stiflingly hot it is in the car. Jesus, it must be summer. I look around the dash for something resembling air conditioning, and I sigh in disgust when I realize the thing probably doesn't have it. I reach for the handle at the lower part of the door and crank down the window.

There's a cop standing there, perhaps only eight feet away right next to a blue mailbox. He's not overly tall, maybe just below six feet, but with him standing on the curb and me in the car, he looks huge. He's white and skinny (no – more like wiry), with a bony facial structure that I've seen to be common in the deep south. He has light brown hair in a crew cut, and his face is completely clean shaven. He returns my gaze for a moment and then takes a long, hard look down the side of the black Ford.

"Excuse me, officer," I call out the window, "could I speak to you?"

He takes another long look at me before stepping cautiously off the curb toward the car. As he approaches, he rests his hands on his belt, and the fact that they're near his gun and stick isn't lost on me. I can read the words on his badge that say "Montgomery Police" with "AL" centered underneath them. I change my mind on something else – it's not so much that he's clean shaven as much as he has a baby face and hardly ever has to shave.

"Officer, can you tell me what's going on here?" I ask, motioning forward at the jammed up street.

"It's one of dem cibil rats marches," he replies in what must be the thickest southern accent I've ever heard. It takes me a moment to piece the words together in my head.

"Civil rights," I repeat, and I look over at Sarah, who shrugs with only her eyebrows in response. "Maybe we should go have a look."

"Scuse me sir, I'd recommen you stay rat in yo car until it's all ovah." Ovah? Over…

I turn my face back toward the young cop and search his face for a moment. "Is something wrong, officer?"

"I jus don't wanna see any trouble made, is all," he replies.

Trouble? "Officer, I'm going to reach into my jacket pocket for my identification. I'm informing you so you don't think I'm going for a weapon."

"Alright," he says, though it sounds like "all rat" to me. His right hand is still near his revolver, and he takes my wallet from my outstretched fingers with his left hand. He peruses my I.D. for a few seconds and then, without taking his eyes from it, says, "Sir, I'm pretty sure that impersonatin a federal agent is some kinda felony."

"Excuse me? Son," I say, putting on my fatherly authoritative voice, "my name is Special Agent William Lane with the Federal Bureau of Investigation, and this is my partner Special Agent Wilcox."

It worked; I can see his confidence beginning to waver as he says, "I ain't ever seen no F.B.I. drivin' no car lookin' like that."

"A black Ford?" I ask.

"One that's got, 'Niggers are great, everyone should own one' painted down the side," he clarifies.

"Oh," I reply, thinking quickly on my feet, "we were vandalized back in Tuscaloosa, and I didn't have time to requisition a new car. I guess people around here aren't too happy with the federal government right now. Do you mind if we take a look?" I ask, reaching for the interior door handle.

"Oh, not at all sir," the cop replies quickly, backing away from the door to allow me out.

Sarah just slides across rather than risk opening the big steel door into the car next to her. Once out of the car, I look up the street briefly, and I see huge throngs of people gathered. There's a lot of angry people up there, shouting, and some have signs. I look at the car as I close the door behind Sarah, and I see the words painted in bright red. They turn my stomach.

"Is the car fine here for now?" I ask.

"Yes sir. Traffic ain't goin' nowhere for a while," he replies as he hands me back my wallet.

"Thank you, officer."

We shake hands, the firm handshake of two men but not so much that it's a competition of wills, and I feel a jolt enter my hand and go up my arm. It's like static or an electric shock but different, and I've experienced it before. We hold the handshake as the sensation fades, and I search the young officer's face. There it is – a slight smile or smirk, a cat ate the bird face.

"Thanks again," I say as I release his hand.

I turn to step up the sidewalk toward the commotion, and Sarah falls in beside me. "Tuscaloosa?" she asks.

"Only Alabama city I could think of," I say with a lopsided smile. Once I know we're out of earshot, without looking at her I say, "He's one of them."

"Who?" Sarah asks. "The cop?"

"Yeah, I felt it when I shook his hand."

"You wanna take him out?" Sarah asks, and I shoot her a sidelong glance.

"In front of all these people?" I ask back, slowing our gait.

"They're not real," she replies.

"We don't know that. They could be caught up in this as much as we are," I reason.

"If he's the one causing this, one bullet could end it."

I stop and turn slightly to look Sarah in the face, her pretty face with its well defined angles that please the Western eye. She has big brown eyes to match her hair, and those big brown eyes are deadly serious. It's not that she's violent per se. It's just that Sarah pieced this all together and brought it all to my attention. Somehow, she saw through the veil these things pull over our eyes. I've learned how to do it myself, but it comes naturally to her. It has something to do with the force of her personality, her simple unwillingness to accept the things she sees or is told.

"If he's not the one, a bullet will do nothing, except maybe land us in a cell for shooting a police officer. I shook his hand, and we're still here. I'm still me. Whatever they want to do to us will happen right here, right now."

"Point," she says with a nod, and we continue down the sidewalk.

"Tuscaloosa?" asks Sarah's voice over the growing din of the crowd.

"Huh?"

"How did you know we have a field office in Tuscaloosa?"

"I didn't," I answer with a smile. "I just assumed that a barely out of high school redneck street cop wouldn't either." I glance back at her for just a split second, just long enough to catch a hint of a smirk on her face and the playful glint in those brown eyes. If only we weren't partners...

The street we're on intersects a larger, two-way street up ahead, but we can't even see it for the mass of people that writhe like some sort of energetic amoeba. Many just stand and watch, but others shout and scream. They're all white, and they shake their fists in the air or hold large, homemade signs for all to read. The words on the signs and that come from their mouths are full of prejudice and hatred. We weave through the crowd's periphery until the press of people becomes thicker, denser. It's loud, and I squint slightly as if that will offset the angry voices that assault our ears. We have to push our way past people now, and most say nothing in response as there's already so many bodies pushing or bumping into each other already. We get an occasional glare, but no one stops us.

After a few minutes of painstaking progress, it becomes apparent to me that we won't be able to go any further forward; there are hundreds of people all crammed together closer than is physically possible, and the way is simply impassible. I'm not a huge guy, but at six foot I'm tall enough that if I push up on my toes and crane my neck this way and that, I can kind of see what's going on. Sure enough, it looks like something that I remember seeing in history books. I see rows of African Americans marching calmly, solemnly through the street ahead. Some carry signs or banners, but they make no sound. They certainly do not say, much less shout anything back to the people that are held back only by lines of police officers. Based on the faces of the cops, I'm sure that some of them actually hold the same sentiments as the mob they restrain, but they're professionals doing their jobs, at least for now.

Something or someone big suddenly rams into my back, but it's not just the mass that stuns me. There it is again – the sudden and painful shock that seems to block my vision with purple stars. I'm knocked off balance, and as I collide hard into the burly man in front of me, I'm wondering what *they* changed. Something has to be different. The man turns around, and though it may be my half-dazed state, I swear the guy is as big as a silverback gorilla and just as ugly. He takes my shirt and tie in one gargantuan hand and uses it to set me back on my feet.

"Hey, watch it!" he shouts over the crowd, and I watch his eyes cut to my right. "What, you tryin' to be brave for this nigger-bitch?"

I'm still reeling a little, kind of a shock, a fog over the brain that happens immediately after *they* change things. I'm so dazed that I certainly don't even see the shot coming. His huge right fist connects with my jaw with the force of a Mack truck, and I go down to the pavement. I taste blood. I think I spit out molars as I try to push myself off the asphalt. Red and black clouds my vision, and the sound of rushing water fills my ears. They slowly clear, and I sit up just in time to see someone cracking a glass bottle over the head of a pretty, middle aged black woman as someone else bashes her knees with a two by four. People are screaming at her, at us. She was standing right next to me, and I know that I should know her. She seems so familiar.

Where's Sarah?

The visage of a forty-something African American woman in a nice church dress and hat melts away like wax to the street where it disappears, and in its place, Sarah lays there on the street, unconscious and bleeding from a nasty looking head wound. There's glass in her hair. The people continue to stand around us in a circle and shout slurs and curses. They don't see what I see. Before I know it, my Glock is in my hand, and I wave it around at the crowd aggressively. The people back away, yelling at me, and I'm yelling back at them, though I don't even know what I'm saying. It's just self-preservation at this point. A form pushes its way past people, and the young cop from earlier appears in the circle.

He doesn't even look around before he speaks, "You done made trouble. This is what I meant when I said I ain't wanna see no trouble made. Now put the gun down, mister."

I just look at him for a second. I hear what he says, but his words seem completely incomprehensible to me, and I'm not doing what he wants. It's not going to happen. A booming metallic *pop pop pop* fills the air as I bury three forty caliber rounds into the cop's chest. Red mist puffs out from his shirt, and I know one round managed to make its way through his body to hit someone behind him. I should feel bad about that, but I don't have time for it. They're probably all dead anyway. Everyone around us runs away, screaming in terror. Even if they didn't see the shots fired, they heard them, and they know everyone else is running and screaming too. People are no less panicky than antelope when it comes down to it.

Something huge and heavy lands on me from behind, forcing me to the asphalt with crushing weight. It's probably the guy who socked me. The cop's body seems to fall forward in slow motion to the ground, actually draping itself over the prone form of my partner. His head bangs on the asphalt, and his eyes are wide open staring at me from only a few feet away. I think he's dead already, but then he winks at me.

"This won't change anything," he whispers, bloody foam spitting from his mouth, and then the skin of his face and clothes on his body melt away like wax, leaving behind something dark that my mind will not let me see.

Made in the USA
Middletown, DE
28 July 2024